Praise for *The Empty Room*

'Regret is only one kind of torment in a world generous with pain', writes Sadia Abbas. In her debut novel, regret and pain appear in light, luminous hues as the story of a new nation, struggling to retain its democratic resolve, is enmeshed with the story of a rocky marriage. The courage, wit and capacity for love displayed by the characters are sure to linger long after the last chapter has been read.

– Annie Zaidi, author of *Gulab* and *Love Stories #1–14*

A novel about many compelling subjects—friendship, marriage, art, and politics among them—*The Empty Room* brilliantly portrays the challenges of a young woman adapting to a problematic marriage and living in a newly formed country, itself full of tension. Lifelong best friends Tahira and Andaleep, are passionate women committed to exploring and understanding the strands of their lives that draw them close and come between them. The depiction of their intellectual development and how it informs their choices, is very real, and inspiring. Other relationships in the book are equally well drawn. I was holding my breath in many scenes; there is a great deal at stake for every character in this novel. I particularly loved reading about Tahira's fraught relationship to her talent and painting. Sadia Abbas is a welcome voice in fiction. I know I'll return to this novel again and again.

– Alice Elliott Dark, author of *Think of England* and *In the Gloaming*

A gripping and wonderfully observed account of domestic life and its many perils in Pakistan's early decades. The portrait of a marriage set in the minefield of an extended family, this novel offers us an extraordinarily nuanced view of a woman's life.

– Faisal Devji, author of *The Impossible Indian: Gandhi and the Temptation of Violence*

The personal and the political come together in this tale of a nation and a young, newly-married woman, as they push against horizons, stretch boundaries and make painful self discoveries.

– Rakhshanda Jalil, writer and translator

The Empty Room, writer, scholar and critic Sadia Abbas's evocative, illuminating debut novel, unveils a vivid portrait of a woman painter and activist creating a life in 1970s Karachi. Exploring the private and public, the personal and political, Abbas's poetic and psychologically probing story reveals not just her profound grasp of a key moment in Pakistani history, but an artist's capacity to create a world.

– John Keene, author of *Counternarratives*

the EMPTY ROOM

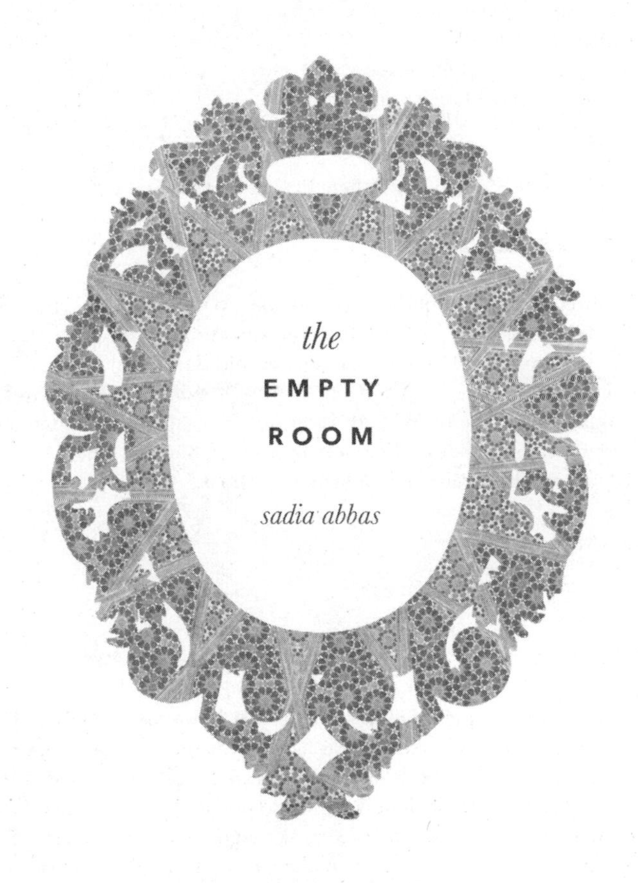

the

EMPTY ROOM

sadia abbas

ZUBAAN
128 B Shahpur Jat, 1st floor
NEW DELHI 110 049
Email: contact@zubaanbooks.com
Website: www.zubaanbooks.com

First published by Zubaan Publishers Pvt. Ltd 2018

The author and the publishers would like to thank Faber and Faber Limited for permission to reproduce the quotation by Seamus Heaney; Rogers, Coleridge & White Literary Agency and A. S. Byatt for permission to reproduce the quote by A.S.Byatt; Curtis Brown & Co for permission to reproduce the quote by William Empson; the estate of Ismat Chughtai for permission to reproduce the quote by Ismat Chughtai, which has been translated from the Urdu original by Sadia Abbas.

10 9 8 7 6 5 4 3 2 1

ISBN 978 93 85932 26 7

Zubaan is an independent feminist publishing house based in New Delhi with a strong academic and general list. It was set up as an imprint of India's first feminist publishing house, Kali for Women, and carries forward Kali's tradition of publishing world quality books to high editorial and production standards. *Zubaan* means tongue, voice, language, speech in Hindustani. Zubaan publishes in the areas of the humanities, social sciences, as well as in fiction, general non-fiction, and books for children and young adults under its Young Zubaan imprint.

Typeset by in Baskerville 11/13 by Jojy Philip, New Delhi 110 015
Printed and bound at Replika Press Pvt. Ltd.

The women of my mother's generation of whom so much was asked

and

RA, with love

She sat silent and unmoving, like a masterpiece painted with an incomparable brush by nature's most skilled artist.

– Ismat Chughtai, *Amar Bel*

All those desiderata of the feminine mystique, the lover, the house, the nursery, the kitchen were "indeed a goal of grief for which the wisest run."

– A.S. Byatt, "Preface," *The Shadow of the Sun*

Feign then what's by a decent tact believed
And act that state is only so conceived,
And build an edifice of form
For house where phantoms may keep warm

– William Empson, "This Last Pain"

You confused evasion and artistic tact

– Seamus Heaney, *Station Island*

BOOK *one*

1

The terse knock on the door the morning after the wedding allowed Tahira to open her eyes. She had been lying very still, worrying that her eyelids might flicker and betray her waking state to Shehzad, who lay next to her, unmoving, perhaps because he too was trying to feign sleep. After a perfunctory pause—in which she grabbed the gharara by the side of her bed and rushed to the bathroom, freed from the paralysis that had kept her under the sheets, pretending to be asleep, and in which Shehzad pulled on his trousers in a quick and complicated manouevre—all four of his sisters, Shaista, Asma, Farah and Nazneen, entered the bedroom and sat themselves on and around the bed to talk with their brother.

In the bathroom, Tahira avoided the mirror, more shy than usual of her body, and put on the heavily worked shalwar kameez her sisters had left on a hanger on the door the night before. She came out into the dressing room and lingered, trying to distinguish words in the murmur of voices in the bedroom. She put on the necklace, earrings and bangles her sisters had laid out, folded the gharara and examined her face with embarrassed, careful attention, wincing at the brightness of the lipstick she had been told by her mother she must wear the first few days—yes, even in the glare of daylight Miriam had insisted. She gave her dupatta a final tug and turned, pausing at the little raised threshold to square her shoulders, and re-entered the room. Shaista, her oldest sister-in-law, looked at her, wincing just a little. "Bring us some tea. We want to talk to our brother. Alone."

"I don't know where the kitchen is."

"You'll find it. It's across from the stairs."

Shehzad said nothing.

Tahira left the room. She tried to remember how she had arrived in the bedroom the night before, exhausted, nervous, certain she was about to faint. After the wedding, they had been brought home to the drawing room, where close members of the extended family had watched, chuckling and salacious, as Shehzad and she were made to share kheer from the same bowl, feeding each other excruciating, hesitant spoonfuls. She remembered being escorted upstairs—heavy, trailing endless yards of crimson silk, anonymous hands under her elbows, straightening her folding back. Her sisters-in-law had arranged her on the flower-strewn bed, poking and worrying, spread her gharara around her feet, adjusted the dupatta around her head for chastely tantalizing erotic effect, giggling her anticipation for her. Her own sisters, Seema and Nilofer, had watched silently, put her things away, prepared her clothes for the next day and left.

She looked around, trying to recognize her surroundings, and saw the staircase to her right, with a thick, curved, gleaming wooden banister. A patterned inlay of pink and slate-grey granite shone random and scattered through the translucent marble of the stairs. The steps were incongruous, artificially grand in the not very large house. At the bottom was a lounge, which led to the kitchen. A man was chopping onions. He looked up, brushing away a tear. Tahira tried not to notice his startled expression.

"I need to make tea."

"I'll do it, Dulhan bibi."

She wondered who had told him to call her that, watching carefully as he made the tea and laid the tray. She refused his offer to take it up for her and went back up, holding the tray like a child given a new responsibility. She did not notice her father-in-law sitting, hidden from sight, beneath the underbelly of the stairs, which swelled and hung like a monstrous cement pregnancy.

There was a long pause after she knocked on the door, in which she had time to lift the tray back up from the floor and balance it carefully, willing the sugarpot to stop its slide. Nazneen, the youngest, opened the door, just enough, so Tahira knew she was not to look inside, and took the tray. "Wait outside until we're done."

She heard the lock click, firm and exclusive, as it turned. The sofa, covered with green velveteen, unhappily positioned on a brown carpet in the small, square upstairs lounge was soft and she fought the temptation to fall back into it, sitting upright on the edge of the cushion. Her trunks were resting against the wall next to her. Across the carpet, the television she had brought as part of her dowry stared at her as she waited with startled patience to be let back into her bedroom.

She stared back at the television, wondering if she should go down for tea. If she went down and said she was hungry they would think her brazen. They might see everything in her face. She was not sure if hunger was seemly under the circumstances. Then, she wondered what the circumstances were. She brushed away the question and waited.

After an hour, the cook came up. She pretended again not to notice his visible surprise to see her sitting by herself in the lounge.

"Dulhan Bibi, your brother is here to take you home."

She wondered what she would say if they asked if she had been treated well the night before. She supposed she could tell them that she bore no bruises, that he wasn't impotent.

She knocked at the bedroom door for her evening clothes. Shaista opened it, "Wait outside. We're not done yet."

So she went down to the drawing room. Waseem stood up as Tahira entered. The smile quickly receded from his eyes and settled on his lips. Tahira took in the gangly, curly haired, angular, intense form of the brother who adored her in a long slow stare, relieved by his familiarity, surprised that he could be familiar. He said nothing and sat down, continuing to chat with her mother-in-law.

"I must see what the cook is doing. One has to be vigilant. It's not easy to run a house." Shireen looked at Tahira, who was busy trying to figure out what to tell her brother, waiting for her to understand *she* could never learn such skill. Tahira realized that Shireen was looking at her with expectation and was baffled; she tried to look acquiescent, assuming that that might cover everything and succeeded only in looking blank. Shireen walked off; the girl was stubborn and shameless. It was not an auspicious start for her son. She would have to watch her carefully.

After they had waited for another hour—Waseem bursting with suppressed questions and worry, Tahira adding extra sugar to her tea to stave off the hunger—Shehzad's sisters came into the drawing room, looking at her as if they were not seen. Shaista greeted Waseem coolly, "*Assalaam alaikuum.*"

The younger three said nothing. Shaista gestured to Tahira, "You can go into the room now."

She went up to the room wondering when she would finally get some food. Shehzad was in the bathroom. He came out, a towel around his midriff, thick white lather on his face, holding a mahogony brush with a fat bunch of fine bristles. It reminded her of one of her expensive paintbrushes. She looked down and paused, not knowing what to call him, and then said, "My brother is waiting downstairs. I'm expected to go home."

"Very well."

"Will you come later?"

"Yes."

She had met him once before and they had not spoken. She wondered if he was always this taciturn. She gathered her things, trying to quiet their rustle and left the room.

In the car, Waseem asked, "What was all that about? Are they the wicked in-laws already? You look terrible—what happened?"

"Nothing. I'm tired. Don't tell Amma and Abba anything."

"But…"

"Don't, Waseem. Please. Promise you won't. Not yet."

"Okay."

When they got home, their mother ushered Tahira into the drawing room, as if the occasion demanded its own new propriety. Tahira waited to see if Waseem would say anything—not sure if she were relieved that he did not.

She sat down quietly, unsure what to do next. She opened her mouth to speak and then thought she did not know how to speak or of what. So she stopped and tried to smile. She felt the smile settle and hoped that she looked happy in her celebratory garb. Her mother and sisters fussed, her father smiled. She could see his shy pride in his newly married daughter, his pleasure at having discharged a duty.

"Can I get you something?" he asked.

She was shocked, half getting up—"No, no"—and then stopped herself. Let him, she thought, why shouldn't he? "I'll have some kalakand."

She saw Waseem staring at her as she ate the sweet, angry at the worried question in his eyes. Did he not understand it would be unseemly with hands still hennaed, closely, intricately, formally patterned and soles still burgundy brown with a hint of orange waiting to burst through, to raise the question of being locked outside for two hours early in the morning? It appeared unseemlier still when she felt the indigo silk with its delicate tracery of gold draped liquidly around her body, the chiffon dupatta spread across her shoulders. She tugged at one of its corners, twisted it into a tight little knot and looked away.

The sweat gathered under the obligatory glass bangles as they slithered and clinked on her flesh. She pulled them apart, separating the gold ones in between, and then dissatisfied by their asymmetry pushed them back together. Her parents' celebration swirled around her. She felt their happiness that she would be well cared for, for Shehzad was successful and up and coming, and wanted to mirror their pleasure. Her smile had faded. She thought about smiling again and then remembered, relieved, that she was not expected to be too visibly happy. She stared at her bangles. The day passed.

In the evening, Shehzad came to pick her up in time for dinner with his family. Intizar went out to the gate with Waseem and Seema to invite him in, greeting him with the formality and deference due a son-in-law. Shehzad did not get out of the car, and stayed behind the wheel, perfunctory, determined to discourage them from assuming too great an intimacy. If not taught the proper distance and respect, they might become an interfering presence in his life. He would not let that happen! His sisters should have known he needed no warning, but he was a good brother, so of course he had tried to reassure them.

He was curt. "No. Just send Tahira out."

"Of course, beta. Of course." He turned to Seema, "Can you call her, please?"

Intizar tried again: "Are you sure you won't come in. Have a cup of tea, at least?"

Shehzad remained seated in the car. "No." And then, after a pause, feeling he had been less than polite, even though he knew he was entitled to dignified, opaque distance, "Thank you."

Intizar bit his lip. "Of course. Of course. I hope your parents are well. Please give them my regards. You must come over for dinner." He looked around to see if Tahira had appeared.

Shehzad drummed his fingers on the wheel.

Waseem watched his father's anxious, scattered servility and clenched his fists behind his back.

Tahira came out, accompanied by Seema, Nilofer and Mariam. Mariam stood at Intizar's side, bending towards Shehzad's window. "Beta, do come in. I've made gaajar ka halva. Remember you told me you loved it?"

"No. I have to go. Tahira are you coming?"

She got into the car. Mariam and Intizar held their smiles as Shehzad drove Tahira away. She leaned into the seat as the car made their humiliation invisible.

After dinner, Tahira went to her new bedroom. Strewn with dying rose petals, stiffening as they relinquished their last bit of moisture, it smelled like the infrequently attended shrine of a minor saint. On her way, she stumbled and stopped and saw her suitcases open in the lounge, contents spread on the floor. Shehzad was in front of her. He turned around to see what had made her stop, saw her shocked face and turned his own away. Tahira saw quickly that two of the most elaborately worked saris were missing. She wondered if she should say something and didn't know how.

At dinner that night, the family had talked amongst themselves, mostly excluding her until Shaista came in and tilted her face up with a finger delicately poised under her chin, made a half-hearted cooing noise. She looked down at Tahira's arms and frowned. "You have to wear more bangles. You have to look like a dulhan. What will people think?"

She was to glitter more.

Tahira nodded silently, unable to understand why she who could normally talk was simply unable to do so. Her face felt heavy and inert, as if moving her lips would require an effort akin to lifting one's body out of sludge. So she sat, her face growing heavier, languor creeping into her bones, spreading through her limbs.

Shehzad's touch on her the night before had been quick, silent, pleasurable but brief. She was unprepared for the pleasure that followed the initial sharp pain, unprepared also for its brevity, but perhaps least prepared for the impossibility of speech with the act lying between them in the instant transition from strangers to husband and wife. They seemed to have had no conversation. She wondered how this could be possible—if she had, in her exhaustion, simply forgotten something that had been said, something important. Then she wondered whether there would ever be any familiarity, for after that entirely silent night, broken only by the slither of heavy crimson silk in the dark, talk seemed impossible. The rustle had sounded crimson to her. Crimson turned black in the midnight blue dark, lit only with the finest sliver of a moonbeam entering the room through a slit in the curtain. Even that light had felt too bright as she had lain there in the unfamiliar dark and waited, guilt-ridden over her unfathomable pleasure, and never more alone than when she heard a little snore. Half an hour later, surprisingly, she had slept too.

The memory of the previous night danced, elusive and irritating, at the edge of her thoughts. She wanted to talk about it, give it solidity, *know* that it had happened, but did not know how. She could only look forward to that night to make the previous one seem real. And she was shamed by the anticipation. After dinner, they went up to the bedroom and on the way encountered the suitcases again, open in the lounge. She stopped and decided to organize the scattered piles, see what else had been taken. Shehzad turned around. "Leave it till morning."

When they arrived at the bedroom door, she rushed into the bathroom to wash her face and change into the nightie her mother had told her to wear. She bumped into Shehzad who was waiting outside the bathroom, mumbled a barely audible, "Sorry," and tried not to rush to the bed. She lay very straight, pulling up the sheet to her chin and wondered whether she should close her eyes. The prospect of watching him walk to the bed or trying not to look with her eyes open was nerve-wracking. She closed her eyes and heard him shut the bathroom door, and then the click of the light switch. She half opened her eyes as she felt him near the bed, looking out of the corner of one as she lay very still, trying to make out his silhouette in the dark to see how far he was and what he would do next. She closed them quickly as she felt him climb in. He reached for her, silent as the night before, and she realized it was a pattern and, as was proper, there would be no talk framing these nocturnal activities. She wondered, as he pushed up her nightie, by what strange fiat older women could speak in the presence of their husbands, how they could overcome the unspeakability of their nightly activities and yet keep the required daily distance? Would they ever talk? What would happen if she said something now? He parted her legs, and began to push inside. She clenched her teeth, anticipating pain like the night before, but as he entered there was no pain, only a slow, growing pleasure as he continued to thrust. She felt like crying out and decided not to. He thrust one final time suppressing a grunt, withdrew and went to the bathroom to wash. She tried to stay awake so she could wash away the slowly congealing trickle inside her thigh and do her ablutions, but she was asleep by the time he came out.

The next morning the ritual was repeated. Shehzad's sisters entered, demanded tea and banished her. She made brief contact with the cook. "I'm sorry, I don't know your name. I need some tea for Shaista Bibi and her sisters."

"I'm Khair Ali. We are out of tea. The extra boxes are in there." He pointed to the pantry, which had a lock on it. "Begum Sahiba has the key."

She asked her mother-in-law, "May I have a box of tea?"

"Why?"

"Because they want me to make some. And Khair Ali says we have run out."

Shireen relinquished the fat, jangling bunch of keys with visible reluctance, watched her as she found the tea leaves and then held out her hand. She showed Tahira where the tray, tea cosies and crockery were kept. Tahira set the tray, carefully. Elegantly, making the most of the pink napkins with pale blue embroidery and the matching pink tea cosy, as she had been taught, knocked on the door and handed it to Nazneen, who took it without a word, but with a triumphant smile, the door open just an insulting slit.

Tahira went back to the lounge and started sorting through her dowry and her new possessions. She had been told she could not take old and tattered things into her new life. "They'll inspect them and try to assess their value," a distant cousin had said and her mother had concurred. The cousin had continued with prurient foreboding, "You'll be condemned for the cheapness of your possessions. You are meant to be all new, not used and worn." Tahira had made her sisters slide some of her favourite old clothes in between the new ones. She collected the clothes, the fancier ones now out of their thin cotton wrappings edged with gold which her sisters had stitched with painstaking festivity. The relatively everyday ones were still precisely folded in polythene. She placed them back in the suitcases and realized that there were five saris missing, not two, as were four shalwar kameezes. She tidied, shocked, wondering why she was shocked. After all, she knew—who didn't?—that such things happened.

Shehzad came out of the room with his sisters. They walked over to the television and carpets she had brought as part of her dowry.

Shaista turned to Shehzad. "This is second-hand. So is the carpet."

Tahira spoke up, "It is not."

Farah, the one older than Nazneen, glared. "It is."

Shehzad did not say a word.

His mother came upstairs. "We'll send them back," she said.

To her shame, Tahira felt two fat tears roll down her face.

Shehzad stared at her grimly.

Tahira wiped them away, took a deep breath and said, "Please don't send them back." She wanted to say it would hurt her parents unbearably. "Please don't," she said again, more softly, and then realized that the faces looking at her were empty of expression, would not be moved by this display, would, in fact, despise her more.

Shehzad was angry. Were not all his sisters perfectly generous, his mother the angelic all that a mother could be? After all, heaven resided beneath her feet. Tahira's tears were revolting. He retreated like a general who has lost enough men to withdraw honourably from battle into his revulsion, which freed him, for the moment, from having to confront his own sisters or his mother, who would remind him of his colossal debt to her. And he would crumble, he knew, be reduced to tears himself by its iredeemable greatness. "Stop crying," he snapped and turned to go. "I hate tears."

Tahira stood silent in the middle of the room. She wanted to leave but did not know how. She felt dimly that leaving would be a defeat, but then that she was already defeated, and did not understand her own struggle, did not recognize in it the possibility of defiance. When they left, she walked slowly to the bathroom and cried, with the tap running, so she would not be heard.

Waseem did not come to pick her up that day. But her things were sent back to her family's house with Shaista's husband, always, she would learn, an eager conscript for such tasks. That afternoon she went to the parlour to have her hair done for the Valima dinner—the public display that all was well—and then dressed with the help of her sisters-in-law, who fussed and grumbled at the difficulty of working with such, Nazneen paused, searching for the right word, such *inadequate* material. She was meant to be glorious, bedecked with the wealth and distinction of the family, but, *alas*—the word seemed to be sighed by all together as they pushed more pins into her dupatta—one could only work with what one had.

Sitting on the podium, she wondered if each glimmer of a jewel, every glitter of metallic thread caught in the light would convince people who had come to gawk and prod that all was well. She saw her parents walking up to her, guests at her new family's reception. They looked stunned, but even at a distance she could see the politeness in their gestures and smiles as they mingled decorously, stopped every few steps by their guests. She watched as they took refuge in the stiltedness of custom, displaying the habitual propriety of a society always on display. *Even to itself*, she thought savagely. Then worried that her anger might be visible, she bent her head, willing the ghoonghat to cover more of her face, wondering if the abundance of colour and glitter around her was part of the attempt to stave off the bleakness they all felt but did not know how to name. Then she wondered if it were just an attempt to hide the rage.

Mariam came onto the stage. "Shehzad beta, you look very dashing. This is a lovely occasion."

Shehzad smiled. "Thank you."

Intizar nodded vigorously. "Yes, yes. A lovely occasion."

"Yes, my sisters and parents did a wonderful job," he said, lying. He had arranged and paid for it himself.

Mariam angled her daughter's face, searching it for signs of pain. She saw the anger, masked quickly by blankness in her daughter's eyes, and flinched, but let it pass without remark. Shehzad was sitting next to Tahira on the stage and comment was impossible. In any case, there were hundreds of guests milling around, their eyes intermittently on the stage, which Shehzad could leave but Tahira, weighted by gold and heavily embroidered sand-coloured silk, could not.

Shehzad's sisters had done a thorough job. She was held in place from top to toe, the dupatta over her head kept in place by innumerable pins digging into her scalp through hair brushed back and up to hold up the heavy fabric and keep it from slipping off. In order to hold everything in place she herself was not to move. Looking at a photograph later, she would think: if she had moved, the entire arrangement might have come undone. She would have become more than the luxuriant drape of silk and the intricate architecture of gold. The long black line moulding her eyes was like the formal symmetry of the Chughtai painting her dearest friend, Andaleep, had sent as a wedding present, liquid with yearning. The finely achieved balance of covered head, tika, perfect in the middle of the forehead, impossibly long eyes and pierced nose had suspended her face, even and still, in exquisite balance. Staring at that photograph she realized she had been transfixed by the dreadful and, she supposed, gorgeous harmony of almond eye and solitary, unremarked, entirely proper tear.

The next morning, Waseem came to pick her up again but she did not know how to tell him, or her parents, what was happening. It seemed silly to say she didn't understand what was happening. She felt she had not spoken for so long she had forgotten how. She had certainly not spoken the previous night after the Valima. When they had arrived home—she tried not to let the word jolt her—Shehzad's mother and sisters had been jubilant at the success of the evening.

"Did you see Shamim Baji's face? She looked so jealous."

"I told Parveen Auntie and Munni Phuppo and Afshaan Naani that the dowry was huge."

"I think it's the best Valima dinner thrown in the family for years. Don't you think Shehzad?"

Shehzad had said little, had looked tired. He turned to Tahira, who was listening silently to the conversation, thinking about her mother's expression as she had searched her eyes, of her father's awkward hug. Her sisters had been strained, not knowing how to convey their horror to Tahira, who was twenty-one to the twins' sixteen. They had wanted to show their support, which had taken the form of Seema clutching her hand tightly, Nilofer adjusting her teeka, offering to get her food, and feeding her spoonfuls since Tahira could not move. Waseem had simply stood around with his friend Safdar offering, occasionally and ineffectually, to help. They had made polite and very decorous conversation with Shehzad who had responded kindly, been chatty. They had all been surprised. Tahira was particularly surprised but relieved that he had made an effort at civility with Waseem, but did not know how he could act as if the past two days had not occurred. Later, much later, she would realize that he was capable of remorse, even of sorrow. And even later that such remorse meant little.

Shehzad turned to Tahira, as she sat thinking, wanting to phone home but too shy to move, telling herself that she had to learn she couldn't go running to her mother every time something was wrong. She was married. This was her home.

"You look tired," he said. "You should go to sleep."

She looked at him, surprised and shy. "Yes." And then, gathering courage, "You look tired too."

He smiled, "I am."

His mother had intercepted that look. "Shehzad I want to talk to you about something important." She motioned Tahira to go on ahead.

Tahira went to the bedroom, falling instantly asleep. She awoke the following morning, surprised that she had been so deeply asleep she had not heard Shehzad come in.

Shehzad put his lathered face round the bathroom door. "Tell your parents that the clothes sent for my sisters were insulting. Take them back with you when you go today."

Tahira stared at him, wondering if she had imagined their moment of tenderness the night before.

On the way to her parents' home, Waseem said, with an optimism he didn't feel, "Maybe it'll get better now." She nodded her head heavily, feeling the now familiar languor creeping into her body. She felt her neck relax; the effort to keep it from flopping back was monumental. Her eyes were heavy. She felt a sudden urge to sleep, to lie down and let her body sink into a bed. She wanted to be inert, not be expected to talk or move, remove herself from a situation she was not equipped to handle. What was she say to her parents? What would they say to her? Perhaps, she thought hopefully, they would ask her to come home again, to tell her that all would be well. She could come home, not be expected to negotiate for tea leaves, for the right to stay in her bedroom. She thought fleetingly of her nightly activities with Shehzad, and was ashamed that she thought of them at all.

They pulled up. The long driveway was flanked by beds flush with red ixoras, thick, white, fragrant mogra, twisted frangipani trees and cactus plants. The house was long, new, affluent. Shehzad and his parents had been impressed, when they came to view her for the first time. Not wanting to go inside, she fidgeted with the strap of her sandal, adjusted her dupatta. Waseem waited, watching but silent. Finally, when she could delay no more, they went inside.

Her parents were sitting in the drawing room. It was decorated with African wood carvings, murano glass ashtrays and vases and a large red, gold and blue Kermani carpet. A reproduction of a painting of a horse drawing a cart trotting into garishly autumnal, impossibly orange woods hung on the teak-panelled wall behind them. Waseem lingered at the door. Mariam said they wanted to talk with Tahira alone. Tahira stared at the woods, orange-brown with paint thickly laid on, brushstrokes straining to be distinctive, but succeeding only in being like thousands of other paintings trying to be distinctive, flattened by reproduction. She had refused to let Mariam put up one of hers in its stead. Now she wondered why her mother had wanted one of hers when she could put up such an ugly vision. Then she realized that looking at the painting showed her parents too much of her face and looked down, staring, instead, at her feet, mesmerised now by the henna on her toes. She remembered that her hands too were hennaed and stared at them, twisting her rings, attempting to push them deeper into her flesh with each twist. Her mother, realizing that Tahira would not speak, motioned her husband to leave.

"You have to tell me what's been happening," she said as soon as they were alone.

Tahira said nothing. Her mother asked again, "What is happening? What are they doing? What have they said to you? Don't just sit there. Tell me. What is it? What have they done?" Finally, reluctant, minimal, Tahira told her about the scene in the lounge, about being locked out of the bedroom. "They lock themselves in the room alone with Shehzad. They said the dowry was inadequate."

Mariam called Intizar in. "They are not treating her well. It could be worse, though." She paused, as if determined to outwit the pain, and then said, "It could be much worse." Tahira saw that she understood more than she was saying.

Her father turned to Tahira, helpless, hands splayed and pleading. "What can we do? If we say anything, it'll ruin the family's name. Who will marry your sisters? What will become of you?"

Tahira felt the heaviness come back, realizing that she would have to go back to Shehzad's house.

"They said the carpets and television were old," she said, wanting to hurt them. "They said we were low people."

Her father stopped as she had meant him to. She hated him at that moment, hated her mother for not being more emphatic in her indignation. She saw that they wanted Tahira to rescue them from the decision, save them from having to show that they wanted Tahira to go back, so that they would be freed of the necessity of trying to come up with a solution they all knew didn't exist.

Tahira said, "I'm alright. I don't want a separation." She saw that the fact that she had uttered the word, even in denial, that she might have *considered* a separation, shocked them. She wanted them to ignore her offer, to recognize her bravery but free her of her duty, interrupt her and say: don't be silly. Of course you don't have to go back. Nothing matters as much as you do. Then perhaps she could assert her desire to go back, to do the right thing. But they did not give her the opportunity to make that added gesture, which would have been made possible by the comfort afforded by more emphatic lies.

She went back to Shehzad's house that day, worried now about her parents, whose helplessness she felt more than her own. They had seemed so diminished. Their helplessness intensified her own, added to her heaviness, made her incapable of thinking about how to act, what to do in order to create some room for movement in her new home. She hated them too, for being diminished, for teaching her now, of all times, that they too could be so easily reduced by others. The anger was followed rapidly by remorse and guilt. She wanted to cry at their helplessness—furious at its demand that she forget her own.

She told Shehzad, "My parents said they'll send new clothes."

"Good. Make sure they're respectable and worthy of my family. I will brook no insults to them. You're only accepted in this house as long as my family is happy with you. Make sure they stay happy. And my father said you did not greet him yesterday morning. Show them respect—or else…"

"When?" Tahira asked, startled.

"Are you questioning my father? It should be enough that we said so."

Tahira felt the familiar, *ridiculous* tears welling up. She clenched her hands at her side, willing herself not to cry, like a little girl determined to prove that she was grown up, she thought contemptuously, that she could handle anything her older playmates thought fit to throw her way.

She whispered, "Yes. I understand"—not at all sure she did.

"Women think they can wrench their husbands away from their families. That will not work in this one. I love my parents and sisters. I'm a good son and brother and no one will come between us."

Tahira was suddenly, fiercely happy. She had always been determined never to become such a woman; if she could show that she was not at all manipulative in that way, that she found such behaviour abhorrent, they could clear up what she could see had been a profound and unnecessary misunderstanding. If that were what he was afraid of, she could allay his fears!

She leapt in, reassuring, vehement. "Of course not. I would never try to come between you and your family." She was certain everything would be alright now. "I think it's wrong to do that. I want you to know how wrong I think that kind of behaviour is. I want to be a good, loving daughter-in-law…." She paused and then said, shyly, "and a good wife."

Shehzad smiled tersely."Don't worry. You won't be given the opportunity not to be. By the way, I'm not easily fooled. I intend to remain a dutiful son and a loving brother, no matter what you do. Don't be late for dinner," he said and left.

As he went downstairs, Shehzad was puzzled by his own abruptness. He was quick to disapprove of husbands who treated their wives with disrespect. Had he not, after all, often criticized his own cousin for being cruel and insulting to his wife? And although he could never be rude to his own father, he did not like it when his father treated his mother with his habitual contempt. But this was different, he concluded, he wasn't being disrespectful to Tahira; he was simply doing his familial and religious duty. She would realize this one day. He felt a slight twinge of guilt, and then heard his mother's voice, insistent, "Beta, they have so much money and see with what indifference they have treated your sisters"—then, showing her strongest hand, knowing Nazneen was his favourite—"the clothes they sent for Nazneen were cheap. Would they have done this if they were sincere in their desire to be good in-laws?"

Shehzad, who had felt himself softening towards Tahira, was glad his mother had spoken in time. Now he thought, he would train her to be a good wife, proud of his kindness. He would make her a gift of *Heavenly Ornaments*. His wife would be active, literate, but her virtue would rely on his guidance. He would teach her to behave with a propriety that was pure in intention as well as behaviour. Yes. He would purify her in thought as well as deed. On that rested the comfort of his family, the long-term preservation of his virtue, her own salvation.

The encounter had transformed for him into an exemplum of his gently scourging guidance—he was going to save her. She had looked hurt, but that was necessary. She did not know what he was doing for her. Once she had learned to be a good woman—in thought as well as deed—she would be grateful to him.

Yes. That was it! He understood now why he had softened towards her but also why he had hardened again. She couldn't help it, poor thing, but she was being protected until she could. He would help her. By the time he reached the dining table, he knew that his attitude towards Tahira was prompted by a deep and boundless charity, generous indeed to the point of profligacy. He beamed, skirting the edge of rapture.

His mother was worried: that girl's wiles were beginning to work on him.

Upstairs, Tahira examined herself in the mirror, framed in baroque, ornately carved sheesham wood, her parents had given her as part of the dowry. She had thought it was ugly but her mother had said that the simple designs she preferred would be understood as evidence of her family's meanness. She looked at herself closely, wincing a little—could shame and hurt be seen in the angle of one's face, the tilt of one's body, the very gestures of one's hands? Surely, they must. She adjusted the pallu of her honey-coloured silk sari, worked with gold, cobalt and turquoise thread shimmering when she moved. Its sheen, warm and iridescent, seemed designed to mask the cold, hard fact of her shame. She applied more antimony, reciting a poem by Ghalib like a prayer. And then, dreading being sent back to dress up more, she added bangles in a precise configuration, counting, sacerdotal and exact: one gold, a dozen honey, six cobalt, two gold, six cobalt, a dozen honey, and one more gold—and then again on the other hand. The glass ones caught the light, refracting it on the wall. I am layering myself with light and colour, so that all eyes will be deflected by my blinding incandescence, becoming, she thought bitterly, my own most elaborately worked canvas.

The poems she loved so often celebrated the beauty of silence and suffering, the power of apocalypse granted to soldered lips, the vitality of blood becoming alive only when shed as tears. She thought now that she had been the worst kind of dabbler, naïve, playing at life, thinking she understood what they meant. Even now, she acted as if she knew what suffering was when she ought to use them to school herself in patience, perhaps even in living. That's what she would do, she resolved with sudden decision. She stood a little straighter and murmured a list:

I will be brave.

I will understand the triviality of my pain.

I will remember the modesty of my suffering and the much greater grief of true tragedy.

She smoothed her sari and went down to dinner.

2

The dhobi arrived just as Shehzad left for work without saying goodbye. He hadn't spoken all morning. Tahira had wondered what had caused this particular silence but did not know how to break it, surprised that she could dread his silence as much as she dreaded his conversation. She had risked an ineffectual goodbye at his retreating back, nonetheless, conscious of the smug smile Shireen was pretending to suppress, probably, Tahira was learning, to intensify it's effect. "I'll get the dirty clothes," Tahira said to no one in particular and rushed upstairs, glad to have a chance to hide her hurt. She collected the clothes from the basket and carried them downstairs in an ungainly armload, pulling up a sheet as it caught on the bannister. She put the clothes on the floor, next to Shireen's piles, saying, "I have already written them down in the book you gave me."

"Make sure you check the clean ones against the list, too."

"Oh, I left the book upstairs."

Shireen sighed and shook her head, ostentatious in her despair. "Bring it down, then."

Tahira ran up and tripped a little at the top of the stairs, glad Nazneen and Farah had already left for university. She found the book and took it back down "I have it."

"Wait. I have to do ours first. You are not the only one who lives here, you know."

Tahira sat down on the sofa next to Shireen, careful not to look comfortable. The dhobi shifted on the floor, separating two piles and then looked up to smile sympathetically at Shireen.

"Pay attention, how will you learn if you sit there like a lost princess?"

No rescue from this witch, Tahira thought, and sat up straighter, trying not to giggle. She opened the book and counted the vests, underwear, shalwars, kameezes, sheets, and towels and then looked at Shireen.

"What are you waiting for? Go put them away."

Tahira jumped up and took the folded bundle, "Yes, of course," grateful that the task required her to be alone in the room.

Silks and brocades could not given to the dhobi and the clothes belonged mostly to Shehzad. She sorted them, casual trousers, shirts, shalwars, kurtas, tracing the raised threads on a kurta she had embroidered and that had been sent to him on a tray of gifts for the whole family the week before the wedding. She reached for his vests and underwear, wincing at the intrusion, and placed them in the drawer as Shireen had instructed her to do two days ago.

After the clothes had been put away, she began to reorganize the jewellery in the carved cupboard that had been part of her dowry, wondering whether Shireen would take all of this jewellery from her as well. She had told her the day before that she had put away the clothes she had taken from her suitcases and two pairs of her gold earrings for Farah's and Nazneen's dowries, including a pair had been displayed as part of the groom's family's offerings to the bride.

The jewels caught the morning light, winking and glittering in their intricate filgrees. She traced the patterns recalling the night of the encounter that had led to her resolve to be brave. He had turned to her with more—silent—passion than he had yet shown, taking more time, seeming pleased by his sexual stamina, even more by his sexual largesse. She was not sure how she knew this but she realized, surprised, that she did.

She was unsure if this was his way of mitigating his earlier harshness or intensifying it. She had felt the glisten of sweat on his body as his flesh slid upon hers, slippery, silent, demanding that she relinquish her mind's control over her own still but confusingly responsive body. She had nothing with which she could compare this alien intimacy, but loving him was her duty. Perhaps trying would it make it possible. Perhaps his wanting to touch her despite his mother and father and sisters, meant that he would come to love her after all.

The following day, he had summoned her away from his mother, who was quizzing her on her family's way of cooking bhindi, tut-tutting with exaggerated horror at the lack of refinement evinced by their addition of tomatoes. She hoped, with deep feigned concern, that Tahira would learn more civilized ways soon. Tahira said nothing. He told her to come upstairs, stern and self-important. She followed him, fearful, conscious of Shireen's intrusive prurience, of Nazneen and Farah—back from university—observing his demeanour with gleeful complicitous spite. They tried to follow him upstairs. He said, "Later."

"But Bhai," Nazneen was smooth as an oil-spill, "we've missed you all day. We've so looked forward to sitting with you."

"Not now. It's something important and private." He smiled to soften his rejection. "I'll be down soon."

Shireen had started to follow immediately. She stopped and went into the kitchen.

Tahira's fear grew as she followed him. In their bedroom, he had motioned her to sit on the bed, placing himself in an armchair by the window. He cleared his throat and then paused, for maximal oratorical and, he told himself, moral effect. The education of another human being, the very salvation of many, including himself, depended upon what he would do next. He cleared his throat again.

Tahira could feel her heart beating very loudly, like the heroine of a bad Urdu film, she thought, trying to calm herself. She racked her brain, trying to fathom what she could have done, feeling the silence stretch and shrink, rise and fall, its own ghostly accordion—audibly punctuated, she was certain, by her own very loud heartbeat. Perhaps he would send her back.

"Your parents," he began, and then paused to clear his throat for the third time. Tahira waited. "Your parents," he began again with conscious and, he concluded, fitting gravity, "have been deficient in your upbringing. We must overcome this shortcoming. I will teach you your duties but not deny your conjugal rights, which are, my religious duty as well."

Tahira felt the already familiar tears begin to gather in her eyes. She bit the inside of her mouth, clenching the hand that lay on the blue velvet and lace bedspread. The lace caught on her rings. Shehzad reached for his briefcase, opening it with ostentatious ceremony; the occasion had to reflect his magnanimity of spirit. The back of the textured black patent leather case blocked her vision. He shut the briefcase with an officious snap and handed her a square package, wrapped in green paper with a tessellated pattern of mauve and yellow triangles.

"May I open it?" Her smile was sweet with relief and gratitude. He nodded his head, solemn and stern, wincing a little at her smile. She unwrapped the present with her habitual meticulousness and felt rather than saw him nod his head approvingly. It was a book. She saw the title and tried to mask her incredulous disappointment. At that moment, Shireen knocked and, without waiting for a response, entered the room. Tahira jumped up, grateful for the distraction. She hurried to take the tray, setting the present aside with what she hoped would not be recognized as relieved and indecorous haste.

Shehzad snapped, "Not now, Ammi jaan." Shireen slid a quick, surreptitious glance at the bed, saw the wrapping paper and looked down, struggling to hide her annoyance. She left the room apologizing profusely, "I'm sorry I disturbed you beta, I didn't mean to intrude; I only came upstairs because you looked *so* tired. And I know how much you like your tea as soon as you come back from work." She smiled blandly at Tahira. Her words hung in the air, portents of greater, more tragic disappointments to come.

"I'm so sorry. I didn't know. I would have brought up the tea," Tahira said.

Shehzad interrupted, "We are in the middle of an important conversation, Ammi jaan. Not now."

Shireen left, scowling with fury and humilation.

"May I pour you some tea?"

He nodded. She handed him the cup, holding it with tense and careful grace.

"I gave you the book because I am concerned about your character. A wife must conduct herself with decorum and propriety at all times. She must be the ornament of her family. She must uphold by example the very highest ideals of virtue. Indeed, she must," he paused, aware that he was about to make a dangerous (but necessary) concession, "even be the source of her *husband's* virtue. His conduct is a moral reflection of her goodness. She must at all times make it possible."

He continued to speak, embroidering the importance of fulfilling a husband's expectations. Orotund about the horrors that could befall a wife who was not always on guard against failures of decorum and propriety, grace and virtue. He described with eloquent, shuddering horror, frightening even himself, what happened to men who had thoughtless wives who could not divine their husband's desires from the angle of his eyebrow, the curl of his lip, the blankness of his eyes. Such husbands were unfortunate, he proclaimed, investing the word with the thunderous power of destiny—the judgment of fate that exposed profound, culpable, hell-deserving evil. Such misfortune was a taint that drenched the bearer, and all that she touched, with shame. He saw his own life and career lost, destroyed through no moral failing of his own. He spoke of what could become of her in such circumstances, of the way the world would witness her condition with public mockery, derision, the most humiliating contempt.

When Tahira tried to speak, to reassure or just agree, he spoke louder and faster until she subsided. He ignored a knock on the door and continued—about the future of their children, her salvation, the entire family's fate on the Day of Judgment.

Hell lay gaping and exposed at her feet—laughter overheard by a neighbour, walking too fast, neglected children, a husband insulted by less than immaculate crockery, by not being waited for at the dinner table, all merged into a vision so apocalyptic Tahira began to see Shehzad and their children, as yet imaginary, engulfed in the fires of hell, reproaching her as their flesh blackened and crisped and smoked in eternal torment.

But slowly, without quite knowing how, even as Shehzad rose and fell, in the grip of his own vivid eloquence, she found she couldn't concentrate. Her mind wandered. She was glad that the obligatory downward cast of her eyes allowed her to veil the slow creep of a numbing boredom. She stared at his shoes, which glistened, immaculate and polished, the crease of his trousers like the edge of his most prized razors, the carpet on the floor, black and patterned with dull and dirty blue flowers, which she would remember later and learn to be distantly related to William Morris's patterns, themselves based on South Asian designs. She must get rid of it, she thought, it only added to the gaudy and oppressive gloom of the room. And then she was surprised by the boldness of the thought. She realized that she was hungry and hoped they would be called to dinner soon. Perhaps Shireen would summon her to help prepare it.

It did not occur to Shehzad that he had lost his audience, or that he could.

Over the next few days, a pattern had emerged. During the day she was taught the laws of the kitchen and the pantry, the quirks of family recipes, ways to deal with servants and the dhobi. She was expected at all times to dress ornately, lavish with jewels and her most elaborate, vivid and plush clothing. Shireen missed few opportunities to deride and school, torment and asphyxiate. "You think my son will succumb to your wiles? Well he won't!" Tahira's bafflement seemed to make her sharper, even more severe. "You think you can play the innocent? Well, some of us weren't born yesterday," she said in time to her daughters' nodding chorus. She mocked Tahira's family and her education. She sent her back to her room to dress up more, to add bangles, or earrings, or to change the colour of her clothes: indigo—too close to black and inauspicious; yellow—cheap and garish (it hurt her eyes, didn't it Tahira's?), pale beige—even richly embroidered with gold and flattering to warm, softly brown skin—inadequately festive. Nazneen and Farah watched, adding to their mother's little humiliations.

Nazneen seemed particularly determined to ensure that Tahira know her place. She commented on Tahira's clothes (*sooo* cheap), her sisters' manners (they really were unbecomingly modern—who would marry them, especially after they saw how accursed Shehzad's life was?), her parents' lack of true refinement (new money what could one expect?). Farah contributed by supporting Nazneen with meaningfully exchanged looks, little giggles at her jibes, sighs sharing with Nazneen and Shireen her sympathy for Shehzad, for the pathos of his colossal, huge, tragic misfortune. Their sighs were long, wistful, ostentatious like fake, ineffectual ghosts haunting a B-movie, Tahira thought savagely, when she was able to think savagely, in those days, which was not often.

After his two-hour lecture, Shehzad had reverted to his earlier taciturn self. Saying little to Tahira but watching her, she could feel, to see how much she had absorbed from his instruction. She did not know how to persuade him that she was willing to be the most dutiful of wives. She hoped he would come to see the propriety of her intentions in her daily behaviour. She acquiesced to Shireen's demands. She pretended not to notice her sisters-in-law at their most spiteful. She greeted her father-in-law with conscious politeness and frequency. She tried also to find time to read *Heavenly Ornaments*, which she had heard about but never read, and which was long and boring and particularly difficult to concentrate on when she was unhappy and bemused and lost.

If she were in her room for more than twenty minutes, Shireen would send someone to fetch her or come looking for her herself. Seeing her with a book would prompt a comment about those who imagined that other people had the time to do their work as well as complete their own burdensome, exhausting, trying tasks. Flustered, Tahira would rush to help, realizing that there wasn't terribly much to be done, that the cook was efficient and hard-working and managed the kitchen perfectly without Tahira or Shireen for guidance.

Three days after giving her the present, Shehzad had asked, "Have you been reading the book I gave you?"

"I've been trying."

"What do you mean?" She felt him bristle.

"It's hard to…" she began, but then interrupted herself, "I'm a slow reader."

"Well. Try to read faster. We will talk about it."

At dinner, Shireen, insinuating, smiled, "Tahira seems to like reading very much. I think household chores are a burden for her."

"I have told her to read. It is my desire."

Shireen subsided, annoyed. After dinner, Shehzad turned to Tahira, "Come with me." He ignored Nazneen's little start and waved at her her to sit down. At the top of the stairs, he said, "I'll read it with you." And, then, as if Tahira had not understood the the magnitude of the offer, "I will sacrifice my time for you. Let's begin now." He flicked through, looking for an appropriate section. "Did you notice how progressive are the writer's views? He believes in the moral ability of women; he thinks they have the capacity to equal men in their virtue."

He looked at her sharply, seeming to sense a lack of assent, "Do you see that?"

"Yes."

He looked at her again, more carefully, as if examining her words for sincerity. He began to read to her a section from the rights of husbands.

"'*The prophet has said that had he ordered women to bow to anyone other than God, it would have been to their husbands. If a man orders his wife to take rocks from one mountain onto another, and then to take the rocks from the second mountain and transfer them to the first she should do so.*' What do you think that means?"

"That it is a woman's duty to obey her husband at all times." She paused and then said, "No matter how unreasonable the request." And then she wondered why she had spoken again.

"No," he shouted. "It is not your place to judge the reason of your husband's demands. Make sure you read all of this."

"But I only meant that that's what the *author* is suggesting."

"Are you contradicting me?" he shouted again.

"No. I only..." she tried to explain herself.

"That's enough," he said, and slapped her. Tahira, who had begun to think she was inured to surprise, was stunned. Her father was a mild-mannered man. She had never seen this kind aggression at home. Shehzad left the room, "Make sure you read the book properly."

She had sat, cradling the book, fat tears falling as she flicked through it, blurring the swaying lines of the Urdu script. She was furious with herself for being weak-willed, for not being able to master herself, for being too foolish to be able to communicate that, despite everything, even now, she intended to live the life of a virtuous, obedient wife, that indeed she believed in the rightness, the justice, the *truth* of such a life. But how, she asked herself, could she say this if he wouldn't listen? She did not know, but felt it must be her failure that he would not. Perhaps if she tried harder...

Some days, Shehzad would barely utter a sentence, minimal and only about the most pressing of necessities, others he would quiz and lecture and yell. Tahira spoke only when questioned, paring her answers down to the most uncontroversial readings she could contrive. And contrive she did, exercising all her imagination and intelligence, she felt, in trying to come up with short dutiful answers that would allow her to compress as much of her most decorous and proper ideas of behaviour into snippets short enough to quickly slide into the imperceptible crevices of his speech, so that he would *know* her, and how he had misunderstood her intentions. She had learned to assess her answers, turn and examine them quickly before they were uttered, to avert a confrontation that would postpone further the day of their ultimate understanding.

But, she thought now, stacking the blue and maroon velvet

jewellery boxes at the back of the shelf, if such constant self-examination prevented crises of the most violent kind (at least, he had not hit her again), its larger intention seemed to remain dispiritingly unrealized. A skeptical inflection, an undesired interpretation could elicit anger that would leave her tearful and trembling. She tried not to contradict him at all times, but it seemed impossible to anticipate the rage. The merest intimation of bewilderment only made things worse. Rage would be followed by elaborate, punitive silences. She was not sure what to do at such times, so she tried apologizing, taking the blame upon herself. This worked, sometimes. It also brought upon her even longer discussions of conjugal duty, about her vulnerability to corruption—because of her education, her family, her attitude, her (female) nature.

She placed the jewellery boxes behind her clothes and locked the door to the cupboard—as if a lock were any protection against Shireen and her daughters, she thought bitterly. She sat on the stool in front of the dressing table, and took a deep breath to prepare herself—although all preparation seemed futile, she thought, rolling a lipstick on the glass topped table.

She wanted to crawl into a corner and sleep, unwatched, unconscious, blissful. She knew she feared yearning even more than she feared her despair and wished she were capable of a *true*, complete desolation, so she would be able to give up—if only she knew how.

She sat a little straighter: she couldn't let Shireen and Nazneen see her despair. She grinned a small, weak grin; it was some comfort, after all, that her apparent good cheer seemed to madden Shireen and Nazneen.

She thought of her brother and slumped a little, angry that the mirror threw the movement back at her. She knew Waseem was angry and worried because she said nothing about how Shehzad was treating her. She could see that he knew she was hiding a lot but had decided to try and distract her with talk of politics and poetry and painting. She tried to respond with valiant, determined interest, pretending that what the general and the former foreign minister were doing was interesting or appalling or frightening, that she was moved by Faiz Ahmad Faiz's new collection of verse, that she wanted to read the new book Waseem had bought for her about Van Gogh and Gauguin from Thomas and Thomas, her favourite bookstore, where the owner had asked where she was, his sweet, eager, intelligent, young customer. She knew they saw that she had drifted, that she was paying little attention to what was said to her and to what she herself said in response. Even thinking about the effort was exhausting. What more did they want from her? She slumped a little more.

She knew Waseem, Seema and Nilofer had banded together. They insisted that she play carrom and cards, made bad jokes at which they laughed too heartily. Seema and Nilofer ran around, rushing to oil her hair, asking her to design their clothes, embroidering a kurta for her, asking her for help—which they didn't need—with their homework, telling her that their art teacher had mentioned her in class, as an exemplary, talented, *serious* student.

She played with them and shrieked her outrage when they cheated, let Nilofer and Seema oil and brush and henna her hair, which shone lustrous and thick with the attention, matched their overstated, bluff heartiness with her own, pretending not to notice how they looked away from her eyes or the hush that layered and pervaded their words and actions, which hung like dirty fog around them, even as they smiled, and yelled and cheated so that they would be caught and she would react.

Fragments from these conversations, memories of the angle of Waseem's head, the passion of his political analysis, the bright Persian blue airiness of the curtains in the room, the chill beaded condensation on a glass of frothy sugar cane juice, stone-green like the torn flesh of an olive, drifted in an out of her consciousness as she walked around the new house, occasionally bracing, more often adding to her humiliation. Surprising, she often thought, as she did now, that they could penetrate the sear blackness of her misery.

She knew that her silence about what went on in her new home was only partly prompted by her determination to be brave in a way that exhibited fortitude without fuss and display, without bids for intrusive and shaming public sympathy. She wanted to protect her parents, but she also wanted—the thought shocked her—to punish them. Since Shehzad had slapped her, she had felt her disgrace more intensely than before, and she was afraid that no matter what she said, people—here her family and society became one, blended into a great, judging, terrifying mass—would think that she had deserved it. Even her family which thought itself so different would think that she had done something to deserve it, for did she not think so herself? How could she blame that book, which only said what she had always known and heard and believed? She stared at the mirror; it seemed to have become her most trusted companion, she thought, seeing the little ironic grimace reflected in it. She took a deep breath and decided to go down before she was summoned.

A few days later, Tahira went to see what her mother-in-law wanted her to do. "May I help?" Shireen looked at Tahira, assessing her state, trying to decide whether she needed another reminder of her place in the scheme of things. She saw no assertion in Tahira's eyes or body, still draped in the festive irony of garnet silk, but decided in favour of another lesson. Just to make sure.

"Why aren't you wearing bigger earrings? Didn't your family give you anything decent? We should have known how cheap they were. We should have married into a respectable family, not such miserly low people."

Tahira wondered whether Shireen ever got bored with the sameness of her jibes. She heard her father asking her who would marry her sisters and wondered if the rest of her life would be like this. She went upstairs again to change her earrings, to wear ones that made her head ache with their weight.

When she came downstairs again, her mother-in-law told her that a woman had called for her.

"Who was it?"

"I don't know. I'm not a maid. I told her to call back later."

Tahira began to prepare dinner; the cook had been given an extra holiday. Shireen experimented with modulations of silent contempt as she watched.

At dinner, Shehzad said to his mother, "I have to go to London on a business trip. Tahira will go with me."

"There's no need for her to go." His mother was flat. "Do you think we can't look after her?"

"She has to. It's a business trip with a fair amount of entertaining. It's expected."

Shireen was livid. It did not show. "Of course, if that is the case, she must go." The phone rang. Tahira jumped up.

"Sit down," her mother-in-law said. "I'll get it."

She was audible from the other room, "No, she can't come to the phone. Is this the time to call a respectable person's house?"

Shehzad got up and went into the next room. "Who is it?"

"You need not concern yourself with this," his mother responded, but then recognizing his annoyance said, "Some friend of Tahira's."

Shehzad took the receiver from his mother and called to Tahira, who came running. She took the phone.

"I called your mother. She sounded devastated. What's happened?"

"Andaleep! You're calling from Beirut!" Tahira started crying.

Shehzad went into the dining room, visibly repelled.

"Oh no. Don't cry. What have they done to you?"

"I don't know. When are you coming to visit?"

"Oh, I wish I could. But not yet. You haven't written to me for three months and I knew you would be busy; but I wanted to know how you were, so I called. What have they done?"

"I don't know. But I cry a lot. Silly of me, no?" Tahira tried to sound amused and deprecating. Instead, she thought, she sounded trite, artificial, pathetic.

"You don't have to pretend with me. I thought you would be enjoying your new adult freedom."

"Yes. You said that in your letter, before I was married."

"Oh. I wish I were there. What an absurd, terrible time to be away."

"It's okay. You wouldn't be able to do much even if you were here."

"Perhaps. But I could at least try to be a comfort to you. Tell me more."

"I can't. We were in the middle of dinner and there are people around."

"Then write to me. Are you painting?"

"No."

"You must."

"I'll try."

Andaleep was Tahira's dearest friend. They had become neighbours when her father, a civil servant, had been transferred to Karachi. She had peered over the boundary wall and decided she liked the earnest girl painting in the corner of the garden, rendering the rockery plants with an almost fretful precision, brow furrowed with anguish at not being able to capture the savagery of the cactus, which was doubling its lankiness to make two spires that would offer large, white and pale yellow flowers, petals spiky and ferocious, determined it seemed to defy the fact that they lasted only a night when they bloomed.

Andaleep hoisted herself over the wall. "We have to be friends. What's your name? I'm Andaleep. I paint too," she looked over Tahira's shoulder, "although, not like that. I wish I did. My father has a collection of Japanese woodcuts and some Chughtai and Tagore paintings. Your drawing reminds me of those."

Tahira had looked up annoyed at this interruption, prepared to be frigidly angry. But the face grinning at her was so winning in its intrusion, she had instead fallen for Andaleep. "Paint with me."

Andaleep swung herself back over the wall. "I'll be back in a moment. Want some imli?"

"My mother says that girls who eat too many sour things stay short and have big breasts."

"So does mine. Want some anyway?"

"Yes."

Andaleep catapulted back over the wall, brandishing the tamarind and then attempted to disentangle her white georgette dupatta, which was sticking on the roughness of the wall on one end and had caught on the thorns of a cactus on the other. She looked as if she were about to be strangled.

Tahira finally decided to help her. "There is a gate you know." Tahira took the tamarind offering.

"Yes. But then I would be on the street, and that is not respectable."

"So, what are you doing in Karachi?"

"I'm from Karachi actually, although we have lived in Lahore, Quetta and Peshawar. My father works for the government and he has been transferred back. I'm going to go to school here."

"Where?"

"St. Sebastian's Convent."

"I go there. I'm on the matric side."

"I'll be on the other side."

"Then we can't be friends."

"Alright, but can I draw with you?"

"If you must," Tahira laughed.

Andaleep began to sketch the same cactus with quick strokes, which made up in reckless boldness what they lacked in accuracy. Tahira decided not to comment. Andaleep could feel her determined silence and was determined to break it. Her strokes became more ferocious. Tahira responded by being even more fussily precise. They continued in this silent argument for a while. Finally Andaleep surrendered, "Okay. You win. I'm exhausted."

Tahira looked at her, completely innocent. "I don't know what you mean. Win at what?"

Andaleep told her later that she realized that Tahira's confusion was only partially feigned. She was puzzled and fascinated. "Invite me in for tea."

"Would you like to come in for tea?"

"Yes. Please."

They walked into the kitchen. "Amma. This is Andaleep. She's moved in next door."

Mariam was welcoming, in part because one could never have enough connections with the Civil Service. After all, the bureaucracy ruled the nation along with the military, and who could deny that businessmen like her husband needed the benefaction of the bureaucrats, who knew this and bestowed their favour with an inscrutable caprice equal to the cruellest of the poets' elusive beloveds.

"Beta, I've just made samosas and gulab jamuns. You must have some."

"I would love some. Thank you, auntie."

Tahira was impressed. Andaleep had managed to observe none of the customary, excruciating conventions—the importance of which her mother repeatedly drilled into Tahira and her siblings—and she had still been winning and seemed polite.

That was the beginning of a friendship that had become central to their adolescence. She loved the Mughal and Persian miniatures Andaleep's father collected; their intoxicated lilt of letters, the intricate jewels of frozen activity, and had been enthralled by his collection of Chughtai and Tagore paintings. Munnawar Uncle went on delegations and to conferences abroad and brought back stacks of books on art, which Andaleep and Tahira read together. Tahira had learned how to think about paintings in language through those books. She had pored over the pages and studied the ones on the walls, memorising the paintings, and copying them for practice.

She thought of some of those books now: The inflamed bristle of Van Gogh in Provence, the gentle sometimes still blues of Renoir's umbrellas, the tranquil pallor of Paris in the rain, the fierce, ruddy cheeks of his young girls—so very odd and exotic in Karachi. Monet's façades of Rouen Cathedral, of haystacks on fire with the setting sun, of gardens gaudy in a way that could almost be made to match the colour around her, but which were immeasurably different from the spiky, angry, unwashed vegetation of a city so chronically short of water that even the plants seemed to forget their need for it. There was Matisse with brilliant reds that echoed the Pakistani and central Asian obsession with the colour, and blues that would make Morocco seem like home when she finally went there. The memory of their foreignness, transporting her elsewhere for a moment, was calming.

Together they had read poetry and novels, discussing them with passion and hunger and curiosity, blending the poetry of love and sacrifice into their own visions and aspirations. How immeasurably young and idealistic they had been, she thought, moved by the wistful yearning and regret and intoxicated denials of Urdu poetry and fascinated by sacrifice and the virtue of silence and loss and the terrible and beautiful abstraction of Ghalib who could turn the memory of being into a fleeting, elusive desire, slipping out of one's reach, always on the verge of dissolution. In English, they read T.S. Eliot and strove not to strive and wished to surrender themselves to duty and love and extinction. They read Keats and longed for music and lavish, sensuous, luxuriant beauty and talked hungrily about negative capability.

After *Lady Chatterley's Lover* circulated in brown wrappings among their parents, they read it secretly and giggled. They compared Ghalib and Shakespeare and read Elizabeth Bowen alongside Hyder and Manto and Chughtai—laughing about their own social world and yet in love with its ethos of sacrifice and virtue, which they had invested with moral glamour and beauty and resonance.

Andaleep had installed herself in Tahira's family. She had one, much older, brother who was studying in England, and indulgent but busy parents. She said she loved the loud and constant bustle of the Hassan family. There were cousins and aunts and relatives streaming in and out of the house, always children to look after, young people to play with, things to do. When Tahira and Andaleep tired of the activity, they went over to Andaleep's house, where they could read in peace. They would paint side-by-side, Andaleep sighing with theatrical envy at Tahira's perfection. Tahira wondered now if it could really have been such a wonderful period of reading and discovery and friendship, why her mother had not prepared her for how fleeting, how *unreal* it would become.

When they turned nineteen, Munnawar Uncle had been transferred to Lebanon. They wrote regularly to each other, long effusions about what was going on, which book they had read, what they were painting. Then Tahira had written that she was to be married—the groom well-placed, sauve, persuasive. "Amma," Tahira wrote, "is impressed and determined. I think he looks frightening, but that might just be my fear of leaving home."

Throughout dinner, after Andaleep's phone call, Tahira tried to keep the tears from falling. She concentrated on her food with desperate composure. The look of revulsion on Shehzad's face was unbearable. Even more, she hated herself for caring. She made little cones with the roti, filled with a precisely measured mix of daal, meat, chutney and achaar. She added a little mound of green chillies to each mouthful so the heat would make her flinch and burn her body into forgetting her humiliation. She stared at the plate, feeling as if looking up would undo her completely. She tried not to think, concentrating more fiercely upon the food, arranging the lurid yellow of the daal against the burnished glow of the perfectly browned, almost auburn, curry, the stony olive of the pickled mangos, the turmeric dyed translucency of the oils from the achaar and curry. Her attempt felt like a pathetic parody of her painting. She wanted to smash the arrangement, to crack the plate with the force of her erasure. The violence of her desire surprised her. She opted, instead, to stir some roti into the mix. The jerky suppression of the movement rattled the plate loudly, echoing in the room.

"Tahira bhabhi, will you paint soon?" Nazneen asked, arch. She hoped that Tahira would not be allowed to do so. Tahira was learning to fear her instinctive, random malice. Startled out of her unhappiness, she looked up, struggling to formulate an answer.

Shehzad snapped, "Of course, she will." Puzzled, Tahira noticed Nazneen's astonishment. She had begun to pout; her brother never spoke to her like this. Having repudiated one emotional female, Shehzad was not inclined to be responsive to another, even if she was his favourite sister. Nazneen held the injured look, which began to waver from the effort of being maintained in the absence of a responsive audience. Shireen was furious. She wished that Nazneen understood Shehzad better, forgetting for a moment that she herself did not understand him these days. He was still irritated by Shireen's interference in the phone call. Nazneen had spoken too soon.

Shehzad had been impressed by Tahira's paintings. They had been brought out by Waseem, so Shehzad could see them, at the first viewing.

Before Tahira had been brought into the drawing room, Mariam had said, "My daughter is a wonderful painter. We will not marry her into a family that will not let her paint. That is our only condition."

Eager to impress and delighted by the wealth in the house, Shehzad's mother agreed. "Of course. We are educated. We are not backward people. Of course, she will paint."

Shehzad had found the paintings and the house impressive. But he did not let his approval show. It would give too much away. When Tahira was brought out, he quickly, surreptitiously, saw that she was beautiful. He felt even less inclined to show that he was impressed by the paintings.

Tahira looked at Shehzad, curious about this unexpected support. She gathered courage: "When can I begin?"

"Whenever you want."

Shireen intervened, unable to be tactical in her rage: "Well, you won't be able to any time soon. We have social obligations. Tomorrow is out of the question. I have to take you to visit Afshaan Naani."

"What about the day after?"

"Then we have to visit Munni Phuppo." They went through a few more relatives before she finally said, "Maybe next month."

"You can begin when we get back from London. We have to go in two weeks." Shehzad interrupted his mother.

"What?" Shireen was furious and astonished. She had hoped the trip was far enough away to give her time to devise some means of keeping Tahira in Karachi.

"How long will we be there?" Tahira asked.

"Almost three weeks."

Tahira forgot the shy paralysis of her misery. "Can we go to museums when we're in London? I've always yearned to do that."

"I'll be busy during the days, but you can."

"She doesn't need to go," Shireen intervened, trying again.

"She will," Shehzad was flat.

Shireen bit her lip, now furious with herself. She would have to be more careful.

Nazneen said, "Can I come too?" She smiled a slightly wavering smile as if willing him to remember she was his favourite sister.

Softened by his own indulgence, he said, "Some other time."

"But I want to come with you now. Why are you taking *her*?"

"Because it's an official trip."

"Yes. But you can take me, too."

"Not this time." Shehzad was still smiling.

Shireen intervened before Shehzad was irritated again. "Of course not. I need you here."

Nazneen looked livid, and then quickly changed her expression to one of sweet resignation.

Tahira was worried by the look Nazneen flashed at her. "It would be nice if Nazneen came along."

Shehzad beamed at her, pleased by her generosity. "I'm afraid she can't."

This time, Nazneen's look was even more rancorous. "I don't need you to plead my case."

Shehzad scowled. "Be polite to your bhabhi."

"Can you make the tea, Dulhan? I love the taste of it when you make it." Shireen smiled sweetly at Tahira, who—confused by the politeness of the request and grateful to be allowed to escape—fled the table. When Tahira brought back the tea, Shireen told her that Shehzad had gone to bed. Uncertain about what to do, she asked, "Should I go too?"

"No. You have to help me clean up."

By the time Tahira went up to her room, an hour later, Shehzad was asleep. She lay down next to him, thinking about the events of the day. She could feel the heat of his body next to hers. Unable to sleep, she wondered if this could really be her eighth week here. What would she do? She tried not to think about her parents. She had always been close to them, their oldest, indulged daughter. She wondered if other daughters would have felt so betrayed, if other women would have been equally defeated in her place. She thought about Shireen and Nazneen, puzzled by Shehzad's championing of her painting. Perhaps, she thought hopefully, it would be okay after all.

Shehzad turned on his side and flung out his arm which lay, heavy as a corpse, upon her chest.

While she had supervised Tahira as she put away the food under her mother-in-law's supervision, Shireen had spoken to Nazneen.

"Beta, of course your brother would rather take you to London with him, but he has professional duties."

Nazneen, preternaturally attuned to opportunities for malice, said, "He wouldn't take her otherwise, would he?"

"Of course not."

Pacified, Nazneen had gone off to bed, leaving Shireen and Tahira alone in the kitchen.

Tahira shuddered as she remembered the look on Nazneen's face—such venom frightened her. She thought of her parents in her—now only theirs, she corrected herself—home. She thought of Shehzad, at the wedding, brute and, she supposed, handsome. She thought of him at her parents' house the first time she had seen him, polite and inscrutable; at the dining table, presiding and powerful; with her family, exerting his charm; on the morning before the Valima, curt and cold; in their lessons, quizzing and shouting—always, everywhere remote. Unreachable, even now, with his arm across her body. She wondered if she would ever dare wake him, to talk or touch. Each seemed equally impossible. She lay very still as she willed herself to fall asleep and cross off one more night from all of those to come.

3

As soon as the car left Shehzad's house, Tahira rolled down her window, breathing deeply of the breeze. She was slowly, unknowingly, training herself to forget his presence. For a few moments, the day before, she had even succeeded. At night, it helped that he seemed not to know she was there, even when he touched her.

She loved the drive from his house to hers. Federal B. Area was not so far from North Nazimabad, but as you drove down wide avenues and turned in and out of narrow lanes you could glimpse the hills, little offshoots of the Kirthar range that separated Karachi from Baluchistan. The sight of the hills, the width of the avenues, the memory of walking to Haidery with her siblings and Andaleep, aroused a deep and familiar comfort. As a child, looking at those hills, she would think that if she only made up her mind she could scale them, and then she would walk from one province to another. And then up through Kabul to Samkarkand and Bokhara to follow the trail of the Mughal Kings. It was a strange and powerful thought. She was never sure why it moved her so, or why it came to her now.

Next to her, Shehzad drove the car with every appearance of indifference and nonchalance. He would never have admitted that he was increasingly baffled and unnerved by her. He told himself that she was responding to her education. She was polite just as he had desired, but he had not known how elusive a reserve such politeness would create. She seemed to hedge and retreat and disappear, as if he were frightening! He, who was only concerned for her well-being, for her preservation and safety. Must not her fear and distance be signs of her insincerity? Revealing what had seemed to him, in his innocence, an artless eagerness to be instead a disturbing capacity to feign—timely evidence of her dangerous, ensnaring dishonesty.

He felt her next to him, neat as a perfectly folded napkin. Precise and absorbed and away. He felt she was breathing in her imminent, desperately desired freedom from him. He could see her profile out of the corner of his eye, the sweep of her eyelashes, the softness of her cheek, which he had never touched. He had woken a few nights ago and had wanted to touch the down on her cheek, had wished to see if it felt the way it looked, but had not known how. It had seemed too intimate a revelation.

They pulled up at the gate of her parents' house. The vine framing it was covered with small jasmine blossoms, scattered like distant stars. It was cool enough this early in the morning for the scent to carry. The gate itself was stark, large, inset with a little door, modern, its lines spare, like the house itself. Tahira wondered if she would ever be able to approach it without a wrenching sense that it was hers. Was this what exile felt like?

"I'll pick you up tomorrow after work. Make sure you make preparations for Europe. You'll need some warm clothes and comfortable shoes to walk in." Tahira couldn't identify the edge in his voice, not knowing that he resented her distance.

"I don't have any money."

Wanting to punish her, he said, "Ask your parents for some."

"Will you have dinner here?"

"No." He pressed on the horn.

Latif, a small wiry man, a fringe of grey hair around a shiny pate that seemed permanently covered with little beads of sweat, appeared in the little door. "Should I open the gate?"

Shehzad shook his head.

"Goodbye," said Tahira.

He drove away without replying.

"Tahira Bibi, are you alright?" Latif asked. He had known her since infancy, watched her as a precise little child, earnest, always drawing and reading, careful, polite—not at all like that dreadful mother of hers, who always *wanted* something, wanted more of everything. Basheeran and he had stayed because they had no children of their own and they had come to love Tahira and Waseem, and then the twins, when they were born. But Tahira remained Basheeran's favourite, he knew. They had taken excited part in the preparations for her wedding. He had even danced at the Mehndi, pulled by Waseem and Seema into the dancing circle.

"Of course," she said, thinking: I must get better at lying.

He looked skeptical but said nothing.

"How are you and Basheeran?"

He did not say that Basheeran was, like everyone else in the house, praying to be shown a way out of "the calamity" as her marriage had been dubbed by Tahira's siblings. They all felt dimly that this was inauspicious, but weren't quite sure if one could be inauspicious after the event, which made things complicated. For if this were the event, what was the rest of her life going to be? Latif found it all terribly confusing, so he just shook his head. Telling himself—as he had for weeks—that this was the way things were did not seem convincing to him or, more vociferously, to his wife and the children in the house.

Tahira stopped to pick some jasmine. She stared at the crown-of-thorns euphorbia next to the jasmine vine. The flowers, spherical and red, were scattered amongst the menacing thorns, like carefully crafted buttons of blood on branches that jutted out like cylindrical swords. Perhaps this will be my life, she thought, even the flowers will be bloody. She tried to berate herself for being melodramatic, but then was defiant, if she were to be subjected to the petty tyrannizings of her mother-in-law, the casual malice of Shehzad's sisters, Shehzad's own alternations of indifference and contempt, made witness to her parents' weakness, she was, she decided with grim amusement, entitled to melodrama.

She went in through the kitchen door, reaching for a large, pale green, half-ripened guava, growing sturdy and dense, on the tree next to the kitchen. She asked Basheeran to cut it up and serve it with salt and red pepper. Basheeran looked at her carefully, searching her face. Tahira swung it violently away from her gaze and called out with, what she decided was heroic, bonhomie, wishing she could suppress the anger in her voice, "Where *is* everyone? I'm home!"

Waseem, Seema and Nilofer all ran into the kitchen, talking at the same time.

"Did you hear what President Yahya Khan has done now?"

"Do you want tea?"

"You look so beautiful in that sari!"

"Do you realize the cricket series is about to begin?"

Tahira was aware of their eyes searching her, to look for hurt or pain or change. "One at a time," she said, forcing herself to laugh. A few weeks ago they had been a happy family at noisy play. Now they were a family noisily playing at noisy play.

She was glad her mother did not seem to be around. She was not sure she could bear to see her just yet. She did not want to be reminded of her parents' defeat, her own entrapment. She herded her brother and sisters into the large sunlit breezy verandah, with an old swinging *takht*, piled high with cushions and bolsters with covers embroidered by Nilofer, Seema and Tahira. There were pots of cactus and money plant vines strewn around the space. On one of the walls, hung two still lifes of a clay pot, ripe, coppery ber and large, green guavas, in the style of Cezanne, made by Tahira as homework for an art class. She remembered she had chosen the ber and pots for their colour and the guavas because she felt their density matched the mass, the sheer architectural presence of Cezanne's fruit. Her mother had had them framed. In the bright familiarity of the verandah, her new home seemed like an improbable fairytale, set in a drear and cold land, seven seas away and populated with mythic witches and unimaginable dangers—and as real.

She decided to savour the moment, to pretend that Shehzad did not exist, that the past few weeks had not occurred, that that this was truly home. Seema returned with a cup of tea and her guava, followed by Latif pushing a trolley laden with samosas, pakoras and halva. Tahira took a samosa and the guava, and then jumped up suddenly to go to her room, trying to keep her word to Andaleep and to herself—she would make preparations to paint.

Her old room was still covered with drawings and paintings. Many of her clothes and shoes still occupied the cupboard, and the single bed was covered with a pale gold silk quilt she had had made herself. On one side of the room was a meticulous arrangement of colours, pencils, charcoal, paper and a collection of objects which had made their way into her work: some clay pots, a stainless-steel glass, a large sea shell from the beach at Clifton, pearly-white with pale bronze and mustard striations and the faintest sheen of pink. There were stones with rose and aquamarine and cerulean hues and an occasional iridescent shimmer. There were drinking glasses, translucent salmon-pink with a threadlike gold band and a repeating pattern of horizontal turquoise-coloured diamonds around the rim—a gift to the family from an uncle who lived in the States. There were sandals with gold tassels and black and russet embroidery. Tahira looked at these and wondered: if her life were to be told in objects what witness would these bear? Were they gaudy and tasteless, did they betray a lamentable lack of consistency and austerity, could the artist be one with so undisciplined, so promiscuous an eye for colour?

Next to these was a cane shelf creaking with books on Persian and Mughal miniatures, Monet, Van Gogh and Picasso and Braque, on The Impressionists and the Pre-Raphaelites. There were books of poetry by Ghalib and Faiz and Zehra Nigah, and collections of stories and novels by Chughtai and Manto and Quratulain Hyder. Tahira looked at the ones she and Andaleep had read together and ones that were new and marked the years of her absence. She would have to send Andaleep a copy of the collection of poems by Fehmida Riaz: she would like it. She ran her hand caressingly over the spines, closing her eyes and taking a long, deep breath as if to feel and smell and swallow those long afternoons that seemed so irremediably lost.

Waseem, who had followed her, watched, feeling the loss she had expressed through the longing in her fingers, through the emphatic and protective nostalgia of eyes shut fiercely tight against the present. She opened her eyes and turned to the table on which rested a stack of drawings, keeping the easel that stood in the corner of the room for last. She looked through them, as if trying to remember herself in them, as if, she thought, they could help her. The drawings and paintings were diverse, characteristically meticulous, evidence of a varied and controlled talent. There were still lifes in charcoal and watercolours and oil–powerful, sometimes muscular, at other times sensitive and loving figures, tracing the vertebrae at the base of a neck, a fluid, minimally suggested, vulnerable nape, the angle of a head observed with care and suggested with gracile, elusive lines. Tahira felt an unutterable distance from them.

Occasionally, there was a face drawn with a startling, fussy perspicuity. In a portrait of Mariam, Tahira had captured a slight, vain willfulness and arrogance, which she had not known she had depicted, alongside her mother's almost overbearing lovingness and generous competence.

She walked to the easel, she had moved into the bedroom when she had left for Shehzad's house, wanting all her things to be in one place, and lifted the cloth. There was nothing on it. She had wanted to make something that expressed how she had felt leading up to the wedding, but it wouldn't come so it waited. Now she wasn't sure what the proper expression for imminent catastrophe was. She turned to one of the canvases stacked against the wall, their faces turned to it. There were two half-completed portraits of Shehzad. He looked forbidding, frightening and unreadable—the lack of invitation in his eyes almost an expression of contempt. There were three fabular landscapes, which looked enigmatic and alien and dangerous. Missing from them all was any excitement. She thought she had felt some, but had not known how to express it, but she couldn't be sure anymore.

She tried to imagine working in Shehzad's house, and shuddered at the thought of Nazneen poking through her things, watching her as she painted, crawling serpent-like into the crevices of her being, coiling herself around her greatest and purest passion, tainting it with her prurience and malice and boundless emotional greed.

Waseem spoke from the door, startling her. "Why won't you tell me what's going on?"

"Because there's nothing to tell."

"You know that's not true."

"But it is. It has to be."

"What does that mean?"

"Just that. It has to be."

"It does not."

"What would you know? You're a man."

"I know that this is wrong. That you don't have to take it. That you can't let them win."

"They already have. They had before it began."

"That's just silly defeatist talk. If you won't fight, how will things change?"

"Things don't change. Only fools and revolutionaries think they do." Tahira hated the bitterness of her jibe, but persisted, "Why can't you be realistic?"

Waseem was hurt. "Not you too?'

"I'm sorry." I mustn't punish him for caring too much, she thought. Or for the failure of others to care at all.

Waseem turned to the paintings. "Will you start painting soon?"

"He said I could."

"Generous of him. Will you?"

"We have to go to London soon, but he said I could when we got back. I thought I wanted to, but I'm not sure any more. It's hard to imagine working in that house."

"Work here, then."

"This is not my house anymore."

"Yes it damn well is. Tell him that the light is better here, that it's easier."

"I suppose I could."

Mariam entered the room. "It's time for lunch," she said, surreptitiously checking Tahira's face. Mariam was exhausted. She could see that Tahira was retreating from her. She had visited Intizar's sister, who had been intrusive, prim and officious, like an irrelevant hen that had suddenly discovered it could lay eggs again. She had almost seemed happy that this was happening. Mariam herself did not know what to do. Intizar seemed broken and spent; her first-born child was in pain; Waseem looked at them with anger and reproach, and Seema and Nilofer with bewilderment and fear. She feared for Tahira, and looking at her made Mariam's body ache with unshed tears. But what lay ahead for the family if she were divorced would be so much worse. In any case, this is the way things were, had always been.

"Amma, what are we going to do about Tahira?"

Tahira held her breath, longing for a surprise.

"What *can* we do, beta? This is the way things are."

"But they don't have to be," Waseem said hotly. "We make them so."

"And then what?" Mariam asked flatly. "Then what? Beta, you were always unrealistic. Do you see how our society treats divorced women? What about Seema and Nilofer?"

She left the room. "I have to arrange lunch."

Tahira smiled sarcastically at Waseem. "You were saying?"

"*She* might not be able to imagine a way out. But we can. We can't let ourselves be defined by their horizons."

"This *is* the horizon—it's sitting upon us, pressing us into the ground, and we try to imagine it further away and more generous and open than it is. Let's have lunch. I'm hungry."

That night, she finally sat down to write to Andaleep.

My dearest Andaleep,

It was unbearably lovely to hear your voice. I can't believe we have not spoken for two years. Letters are no substitute. I am sorry for being a child. It was hearing your voice that did it—so sweet and familiar and so far away. I'm not sure what to tell you about my new life. My husband barely talks to me. He says I'm from a low family, that my parents are cheap. He ignores me for hours, sometimes a day or two, but then he talks and talks and talks, about my duties as a wife, a woman, a religious person. His parents and sisters said my dowry was inadequate, that my parents had given me old things. They returned them.

The effort of writing exhausted her. She stared at the paper as the ink dried, darkening as it lost its sheen, aging in an instant, dessicated and yet ready to smudge and run at the sheerest, most circumspect touch of a tear drop. The ink ran as she searched for words for the emptiness, the sense that she had no future. Andaleep had teased her about her new, married adult freedom. Tahira wanted to write that this was a strange adulthood that tied you up and made you so helpless, giving you only the power to hide your tears. She didn't have the words to explain about time anticipated only with dread, about body and talk constrained, about the weird and final sense that *this was it*. How to describe the contempt that shamed her more in the telling?

Even more, she felt she could not speak about her parents.

She read the letter again. It seemed bald and infantile and self-indulgent. She noticed with contempt that she hadn't expressed any interest in Andaleep and tore it up.

4

Tahira had, with incredulous fascination, been reading a passage, which described in meticulous detail the proper way to clean after a shit, when Shehzad came home from work and walked into the bedroom.

She leapt up and greeted him—not by name. She still did not know what to call him. He seemed content with that. "I'm so sorry. I didn't hear you arrive."

He smiled. "It's good; you were absorbed in the book."

"Yes. It's fascinating. Such detail. He talks about whether gond and achwani should be distributed after a child's a birth, or whether a barber should be sent with a news of the birth to a bride's home. He must have spent months studying the household arts. Such dedication. Listen to this…."

Shehzad's smile grew wider. He said with gentle condescension, "Later. Would you like to go for Chinese food tonight?"

Tahira was startled, relieved he had not noticed the irony that had crept, unbidden, into her words. She would have to be more careful. "I love Chinese food. There's a good restaurant on Tariq Road: Kowloon Palace."

"Yes. I like that one."

It was not just the sight of Tahira reading the book he had prescribed that prompted Shehzad's reward. An old girlfriend had called at work that day and the call had mitigated somewhat the unnerving effects of Tahira's distance. Charm, he recalled, had worked beautifully with Aneela Khan, the memory of whose voluptuous offerings made him long for something a little different than what he had so far found in his marriage. Truth be told, marriage had proved too staid; and he was bored with its paltry yield. He had always been successful with women, how galling that his own wife could appear indifferent to him. It was convenient that she had been reading the book—it showed that she was making an effort and his invitation seemed like a reward. There would be no loss of face. The instruction could resume later.

Nazneen appeared, insinuating, like molasses melting slowly on a flame, at the door. "Bhai. How was your day? I missed you. You look so handsome in that suit."

Tahira's heart plummeted. She could feel it, settling between her toes, every time she heard Nazneen's voice, or saw her exquisite little face. She had smooth, clear skin (white as a colonial Memsahib's, Shireen would say), perfectly formed rose-coloured lips, the long, straight nose that ran in the family and with which they were all so tediously pleased. ("It shows our proud Persian ancestry—like our fair skin. Doesn't it Amma?" Then Nazneen would look sympathetically at Tahira. "It must be hard to be so dark. Poor Bhabhi.") Tahira wondered if Shehzad would ever realize what a poisonous little snake she was, or whether she would continue to creep into their lives, arriving with perfect, destructive felicity at every moment where there seemed a possibility of peace, perhaps even (infinitesimal, no doubt) progress.

"How was your day?" Shehzad asked Nazneen, loosening his tie as he walked to the bathroom.

"It was alright. University wasn't very interesting. I saw some lovely cloth. But," she sighed a long, wistful sigh, "I had no money."

"I'll give you some. In fact, you can go with your Bhabhi tomorrow; she'll buy you whatever you want," Shehzad said, indulgent, beaming.

Tahira was amazed at how she played him, transparent as the sari of an actress singing in the rain. She remembered an act from the last time she had seen the man with the monkey who performed for the children in their neighbourhood, and had a sudden vision of Nazneen leading Shehzad on a leash, shaking a little drum, ordering: "English gentleman. English gentleman," and Shehzad straightening up, folding his hands behind his back, strutting with careful, simian dignity in a red velvet waistcoat and khaki shorts. A giggle rose to her lips. She bit them. Nazneen and Shehzad turned to look at her. She converted the stifled giggle into a paroxysm of emphysematic coughing.

"Are you alright?" Shehzad asked with some concern. Nazneen looked furious.

"Just an itch,"she spluttered. "When should we get ready to go?" As soon as the question left her mouth she realized she had committed a colossal blunder.

Nazneen looked at Shehzad, alert. "Where are you going?"

"For dinner."

"Alone?" she purred.

"Do you want to come as well?" Shehzad asked, hoping she would say no.

"I would love to. Oh, I'm delighted. I was so bored today. I'll go and tell Farah to get ready."

Nazneen stood by the door of the front passenger seat. Her body was twisted, part of it facing Shehzad over the car, one shoulder angled toward the back. Tahira wondered how she could split it so perfectly into two completely different attitudes. The side facing Shehzad was ingratiating, sweet with the adoring devotion of an admiring daughter towards a lofty but indulgent father. The shoulder pointed at Tahira was stiff with contempt, a belligerent provocation to combat.

Tahira slid quietly into the back seat.

Shireen watched them drive away, glad the girls were going with them. In his older age, her husband had become relatively easy to control, almost docile. But Shireen could remember the days when he had had a cruel, ungovernable temper. He would gamble every moment he was at home, screaming if he and his friends were interrupted. If asked for money, he would hit her, raising his hand with careful, preparatory malice—and then the systematic, thumping blows. She tried not to ask him for money until it was absolutely necessary, until the pantry was empty and there was no food in the house, and the children were beginning to go hungry. She remembered days when she thought they would have to remove the girls from school because there was no money for school uniforms, and because they could not afford food.

She had, finally, after thirty-six years of marriage, begun to relax.

Her husband had subsided and could even be made useful. The way he had, so obligingly, noticed, when she had gently pointed out to him that Tahira had not greeted him had made her shiver with a vindicated satisfaction that had been far too long in the coming. It was convenient that he had always been as attuned to disrespect as a mad man to the voices in his head.

Even better, her son was earning a substantial amount of money, most of which he dutifully presented to her at the beginning of each month. She had told him often that he was the father of the family, that it was his duty to pay for the dowries of his sisters, that they were his *responsibility*. He was, she said, her beautiful, handsome son. He had to be careful, she had told him: modern girls were grasping and greedy. All they wanted was to tear husbands away from their families. She had been preparing Shehzad for years. She hoped he would not forget her lessons.

Tariq Road was bright with lights and people. The city surged and moved through the road and the shops around it. For a moment Tahira almost forgot everything; she tuned out Nazneen's incessant drip of slow, infected honey, Farah's desperate, embarrassing assent, Shehzad's indulgence—condescending and spoiling in simultaneous broad strokes.

She lowered her window, and the evening breeze, that improbable Karachi benediction, cooled the gules of sweat that had gathered like tiny crystal beads on her upper lip and that had formed a little string where her hair met her forehead. She could feel them evaporating, little pinpricks of coolness, on her damp, warm skin.

Fabric, of every colour and madly conceived pattern, draped walls and ceilings, spilled out on to pavements. It hung from hooks pierced into awnings, folded into little amputated people—cloth for shirts folded and hanging above the shalwar-piece, with dupattas draped chastely around the necks of hangers. Naked light bulbs, incendiary and hazardous and almost too bright to behold, suspended behind bright patterns of traditional weaves—marigold and green, turquoise and indigo, amethyst and burgundy—jumped out, twisting depth and pressuring perspective. Men and women passed under the fabric, heads brushing against it, stepped over it on pavements, negotiated it—the way they did the beggars with twisted limbs and ingratiating quavers in their voices, expert at ignoring the inconvenient spill that would wrap them in it, thrashing and imprisoned, as they fell.

Bolsters of the most outrageous prints, grand slashes of crimson and turquoise on yellow backgrounds, purple swirls and emerald triangles on orange surfaces, colours hideous and beautiful, for every taste were stacked in neat rows against the walls. Every few yards, flanking the pavement were small plastic and glass counters, glittering with earrings and bangles and necklaces.

The scurry of people, the noise of burst silencers, the headlights—which drivers seemed to think it was a point of honour not to dim—created a kaleidoscopic frenzy of colour and movement and sound. The light—of cars, of illegal bulbs—was like burning streaks, as if a god with a flaming torch were repeatedly slashing a frenetic, jagged impasto across the deep, embered burnish of the night.

She thought: *Street At Night, Karachi, 1969*, and wondered how she could render it.

Shehzad turned into a lane and pulled up in front of a house. Kowloon Palace was emblazoned on a sign, curved in a large semi-circle above the gate. Underneath this, fitting the concavity of the sign, were Chinese characters. The doors were a bright, lacquered red, on each side were stone lanterns, like tall houses. Pointing upwards, nestled between large, waxy dark-green plants, were rotating green lights that shot an eldritch, wavering glow onto the doors and the people who walked through them.

They walked into the restaurant and sat across from a large aquarium. Tahira stared at a bright, orange fish blowing air through pouting fleshy lips. Nazneen said, desperate to prevent Shehzad from talking to Tahira. "I'll order, Bhai. I know what you like don't I?"

"Ask your Bhabhi what she would like."

Nazneen's face fell. Tahira thought: can she really be nineteen? "Let Nazneen order. I'm sure she'll do a wonderful job." Nazneen's face fell further, never one to forgive a grace.

Farah spoke, hoping to gain her brother's attention. "I think Bhabhi likes chillies. I think we should order dry beef with chillies."

Tahira looked at her, startled by such attention. "I'd love that. How did you know?" Shehzad smiled approvingly. Nazneen was furious. Farah was pleased. It was not often she got more attention than Nazneen. It was difficult, sometimes, being the dark one.

After the food had been ordered and everyone had begun to eat, Nazneen said, "Bhai, I forgot to tell you; something interesting did happen today. I saw Tahira Bhabhi's brother leaving a rally with Safdar Naqvi, the famous campus leftist." She turned to Tahira, "I never realized your brother was so close to Safdar." She knew her brother thought the socialists were ungodly and evil.

Tahira said, "I thought everyone on campus knew that Waseem and Safdar are very close friends. They are always together."

"He shouldn't waste his time," Shehzad said.

"I admire my brother, admire his principles," Tahira said, unable to control herself. Then she waited, terrified, for what would happen next.

Nazneen smiled.

Shehzad decided not to create a scene in public. Nazneen began to speak. "Bhai…"

"Not now, Nazneen," he snapped.

They finished their meal in silence. Tahira stared at a fish, with skin pink and smooth as meticulously flayed flesh, drained of blood. Nazneen concentrated on her food, hungry and triumphant. Farah wondered why Nazneen couldn't have waited until they got home, now there was no hope of stopping for kulfi. Shehzad thought: that brother of hers better not be a bad influence. What does she see in him anyway?

A month before her wedding Tahira had promised Waseem she would visit campus with him.

She knew he loved the bus ride from North Nazimabad to the university. The surroundings were not beautiful, but the dusty miles across which the bus rolled made him feel as if he were in some more dramatic desert. He said it always surprised him how quickly his relatively green corner of the city could give way to the engulfing sand.

They had greeted the driver, who smiled broadly at them and told Waseem not to work too hard, as he did to everyone who got on the bus. Inayat Khan was a squat, mahogany-coloured man with pock-marks, a broad nose and dancing, eager eyes. He was currently part of the most exciting drama on the bus. Every day a dark, curvy young woman, with an aquiline nose pierced with a large keel and a cautious but wide smile would board at one of the Gulshan stops. Her name seemed to be unknown to Inayat, although Waseem knew her as Fatima Chaudhry, a Master's student in Chemistry. And every morning, before Fatima's bus stop, Inayat would begin to sing under his breath, like a happy, recently-fed parakeet. He would pull up at the bus stop with elaborate slowness, as if signalling to Fatima that his bus were her chariot to command. Fatima appeared to know this, and as she boarded, she would slide a surreptitious, searching glance at him—as if to check that he was still the same as the day before—before she lowered her eyes and walked quickly to her seat. Every day, Waseem saw their heads struggle not to turn and look at each other—Inayat as he tried to ensure that he showed no disrespect and Fatima because she did not want to appear immodest. Their struggle and relative success at restraining necks from turning and eyes from lifting seemed superhuman, Waseem said.

He had dubbed the daily ritual the 'The Romance of the Eyes.' It came, he said to Tahira who liked the idea, out of the culture's deepest fantasies and archetypes of love, longing, and the power of the eyes to subvert the necessary silence of the tongue. He had been reading Jung and Northrop Frye and Freud and thinking about how to understand the ghazal as a form shaped by culture and archetype and primal sublimated urge. He thought this romance provided a crucial clue to the essence of the ghazal. He had decided that Fatima and Inayat were a fascinating and touching case of cultural codes and primal urges caught in a complex dance of accommodation. The other regulars on the bus might not have shared his very particular response to the daily encounter, but they were supporting the romance. There were exceptions. At the front, a couple of rather fashionable girls, from whom could be heard horrified mutterings about the violation of divisions of class filtered through horror at the looseness of Fatima and the lewdness of Inayat and, at the back, a number of the religious campus police, who disapproved of mixed buses because they enabled precisely this kind of obscenity they said. Both groups were usually ignored by most on the bus.

Waseem had looked out of the window and seen a slender, beautiful light-skinned woman with a soft, round face. She wore a sari the colour of ripe lemons. A mangal sutra glittered black and gold around her neck, dark against the sari's pomegranate-red border. She walked fast, carrying a broom in her left hand, and pulling a little boy with her right. The child danced two steps forward and then one back, slowing their progress. She tugged with affectionate exasperation at the boy, who tugged back, transported at being able to draw her into the dancing recalcitrance of his game. Waseem pointed her out to Tahira, enchanted by the lift in her step and the occasional glimpse of a fat, richly filigreed silver anklet. She wondered now if she had imagined the piercing, wistful pleasure it had all given her.

The bus had pulled up on campus, which was electric with excitement; as if the students, had—through exposed and newly sensitized nerve-endings—communicated their knowledge that something was about to change, to the air itself, it seemed, which appeared to glimmer and tremble with hope and expectation. Perhaps martial law would finally end and perhaps they would have a chance at a different workable political system. He felt, he had said, that he dared not be more hopeful than that, but sometimes found he was anyway. The students and even some of the teachers seemed like insects at the end of winter, or a colony of mosquitoes after the rain. The imminence was new and fresh and exhilarating, Waseem had said, but he felt fear as well.

They walked into the field where Safdar was to speak at a rally. He was standing by the podium looking impatiently at his watch and longingly at the book in his hand. Waseem went up to him, amused by the restless play of thought on his face, and cleared his throat.

Safdar laughed. "Yes. I am impatient. Always."

"Good luck," said Tahira.

"It's good to see you, Tahira. I hope you approve of the speech."

She grinned. "I'm sure you'll mesmerize them, especially the girls."

He winced.

That Safdar had become something of a campus phenomenon was at least in part due to biological accident. He had deep green eyes—heritage, perhaps, of some ancient plunder—skin the colour of lightly brewed, milkless tea, and a startling, sudden, unbridled smile. Men and women alike wanted to earn that smile and this added to his charm and confidence. But his beauty was not, Tahira knew, the only reason for the powerful effect he had on people.

The son of a short-story writer, who worked as a clerk in a government office, and a poetess, his assurance was artless, eager, sometimes even tender, and a world apart from that of his peers. His parents had met at Aligarh University before Partition and had fallen deeply and dangerously in love. She was not a Shia, and her family was far wealthier than his. They had defied their families and married. He had given up his hopes for further education and an intellectual career, because of the necessity of supporting a family. They were still friends and lovers, and had brought up their only child on little money but with an abundance of conversation, and in the company of books and poets. People predicted a great political career for him. He wanted to be a teacher and to write. His intellectual hunger, curiosity and passion had drawn Waseem to him when they had met at school. They remained close, made closer by a deep, shared revulsion at injustice. They were a familiar sight on campus—always together, talking, arguing, reading, and now canvassing to rally people for the former Foreign Minister's party and working with party activists to build and connect grassroots support. Tahira had always teased them, but loved to watch them together, intense and passionate and absorbed—unaware of how similar she and Andaleep seemed.

Safdar began to speak.

"These are exciting and promising times. Our history has been chequered by betrayals of promise and by innumerable usurpations. Our power, our rights, our dignity have been wrested from us. But if we do not demand them, if we do not fight for them, if we do not assert our being, we will get nothing. We have waited for the promise of this country to realize itself for far too long. Too long have we let the military run this country.

"There is too much injustice in this land. There is unconscionable, intolerable poverty in this land. Too much is taken from decent, struggling people every day. It is our duty and our right to ensure that they receive what they, and we, deserve. For we do not deserve to stand tall in a land where some throw away more in an evening than most will eat in a year.

"We have some hope," he paused, "but we must be careful. This is a land that has been subject too long to medieval, torturing, cruel feudalism. Our habits of barbarism run deep. We must rid ourselves of these and stay committed to our principles. We must repeat the party's slogan 'Food, Clothing and Shelter.' But we must also demand truth, justice, and dignity. Remember what Iqbal wrote: 'Raise your selfhood so high that before every destiny God himself asks his creature, *Tell me what is your will?*' Let us get rid of the military, let us keep the party honest and let us make the nation just. They are ours."

They watched the crowd as Safdar spoke. Some heckled at the back, but were ignored. Most listened, rapt, compelled by the measured and passionate modulation of his voice. Heady and textured, deep and intimate and warm. When he ended, one of the religious party members at the back cried out, "How dare you end with those lines?" And somebody turned around and screamed, "You live in a land based on Iqbal's dream. Will you turn on him too?"

Safdar left the podium and came down to join them. People rushed up to congratulate and hug him. He tried ineffectually to hide his embarrassment.

He came up to them. Waseem said, "I'm surprised. I thought you were even more equivocal about the Party leader than me."

Safdar smiled. "I know I seemed so convinced up there. But I'm more ambivalent than it seemed. He *is* a feudal. But... most of those associated with the Party do seem moved and energized by its potential, and military rule does have to end. And we are a people of habit it seems; so he's popular. So I tell myself that maybe he'll defeat ancestry and patrimony and live by his promises. Deluded or hopeful—I'm not sure which. Depends largely on the day."

"But he's so close to the military."

"How else do you survive in this country?" Safdar asked bitterly.

"Let's hope you aren't betrayed," Tahira said, watching them both closely.

"Perhaps we won't be if we don't expect too much. But I'm not sure I can keep arguing against myself." Safdar had smiled a small, rueful smile, and they had walked back to the bus-stop.

Tahira had just finished praying when, two days later, Shehzad said, "Haven't your family been wanting to have us over for dinner? Tell them we will come immediately after we get back from England." Tahira was shocked. There had been little said between them since the dinner at the Chinese restaurant. But Shehzad had not yelled, quizzed or shouted either. He had seemed preoccupied, thoughtful even. Occasionally, she had even seen him observing her, as if she were a peculiar, exotic exhibit at Gandhi Gardens. Maybe he thinks I'm like that creature, who's half-woman half-cat, she thought with hysterical imagination. She remembered seeing it when she was a child, clambering up on to a bench and looking through iron bars with Waseem. She hadn't been able to look for very long at all, and had rushed off the bench so quickly she had grazed her knee. "What happened?" her mother had asked, cleaning and plastering her cut.

"Nothing. I just didn't want to look at her." She had been terrified: by the makeup—she remembered pistachio-green eyeshadow, shocking pink lipstick and emphatic rouge gashes on cheeks with the barest hint of pale green stubble—by the head with the back-combed bouffant hairdo, disproportionately large against the folded leonine body. It looked as if a heavily made-up fully-grown man-woman had been cut, twisted and poured into the hindquarters of a lion's cub. Then the creature had spoken, husky and sensual with menace. "Pity me, little girl. For I was once like you, free in the wild." And Tahira had turned and run, forgetting that she was not on the ground. Its malicious laughter had echoed frighteningly in her ears for days. She wondered why she remembered this. Perhaps, she thought, I'm going mad. And then: that might not be so bad.

Her parents were delighted. They had not been able to persuade Shehzad to come over for dinner alone yet. There had been one, excruciating dinner with his whole family. His father had complained about the food—the biryani particularly, he said audibly, was made from low quality rice. This was not true. Intizar was a generous, hospitable man, for whom was it a point of some considerable honour to buy the supplies for his family's frequent dinners himself. Mariam was an excellent cook and Latif cooked food that was famous throughout the neighbourhood. Shehzad had been opaque and distant, like a king controlling his subjects with snubbing, enigmatic silence. Shireen had clucked with dismay and sympathy, taken her husband's biryani onto her own plate, eaten it with virtuous, visible reluctance and dished out different food for him. Intizar had watched, mortified. Tahira had watched his mortification. Asma was back with her husband in Sargodha. She had finally left a week after the wedding. The remaining three sisters had been polite, indistinguishable, at their drawing-room best—as if they were competing to see how boring they could be. Shaista's husband had walked around, looking at the things in the drawing room, as if putting price tags on each vase and carving and ash-tray. Waseem had whispered to Seema. "Do you think we should just give everything to him? Tell him we can buy more."

Seema had noticed that Nazneen was upset she had received no attention from Waseem. "She doesn't like being ignored," she said afterwards. Waseem chuckled. "Perhaps I should flirt with her. She'll be nicer to Tahira then. I'm happy to prostitute myself for my sister. After all, she's in bondage for us."

"Absolutely."

"That's enough Waseem. Your sisters are here."

"Sorry. Yes. My sisters… But being fragile isn't going to help is it? Not if this is what they have to look forward to. Perhaps we should prepare them better. Then they won't be like Tahira, shell-shocked and bleached, when reality hits."

He was furious that his parents were so delighted about Shehzad's acceptance of the invitation, and said to Tahira, unable to help it, regretting each syllable as it was uttered, wishing Tahira weren't there to hear it, knowing he wanted her to. "We now have to be grateful that that man will agree to eat at our house? How honoured we are."

"Shut up, Waseem," said Mariam.

Tahira looked stricken. "I'm sorry," she whispered. "I don't want him to treat Amma and Abba this way."

Waseem said, "No. I'm sorry. It's not your fault."

Tahira said, "Perhaps it is."

5

Andaleep crept into the verandah behind Latif, ducking, weaving and hamming invisibility. She bent her leg, sweeping off an imaginary, plumed hat. "*Malka*, your *kaneez* presents herself." Tahira scrambled off the swing, sending cushions flying. "Fool! Ladies-in-waiting don't sweep off their hats, heroes in Georgette Heyer novels do." She flung herself at Andaleep, catapulted into an innocent past. "What are you doing in Karachi? When did you get here? How long will you stay?" They sat down, hands entwined.

"One thing at time and all will be explained. I'm in Karachi because I begged, pleaded, nagged and cajoled until my parents bought me a ticket out of exhaustion." She did not say that they had agreed very quickly when she told them that things were not going well with Tahira. "I arrived last night and am here for ten days. I wanted to see you, to find out what was happening, to be of use, instead of worrying helplessly in Beirut."

Tahira had thought that she wanted to tell Andaleep everything, that—although she had been unable to write to her—it would be easier to tell her in person. But now she didn't know what to say, where to begin. She tried to think of an example that would justify some of the horror she felt at an existence whose remorseless reach made the future seem bleak and ceaseless as a mirageless desert. But words seemed paltry and hopelessly, absurdly inadequate. She thought of the slap; the shame of it still choked her. To say that it had happened was impossible, even to Andaleep. Perhaps especially to Andaleep, who looked undefeated and outrageous in a mad marigold kurta, parrot-green cotton bell-bottoms and unpainted wooden beads. Her own gold-laden, silk-bedecked body felt ridiculous and ostentatious and *old*.

Andaleep held her hand. The exhaustion in Tahira's eyes, the defeated angle of her neck, the slump of her shoulders sat uneasily with her memory of her fussily precise, graceful and proud friend. She wanted to do something, say anything to dispel the look on Tahira's face. "What were you painting before you got married? I'm sure you haven't had a chance to start painting again."

"Ah yes. Painting. Waseem brings it up again and again, like a talisman at a dying man's bedside." Hurt by the savagery of Tahira's tone, Andaleep turned to the still lifes on the wall, and then dropped her gaze, realizing what she was doing.

Tahira drew a deep breath and tried again. "I'm so sorry. I don't mean to be hurtful—sometimes I don't know where to begin. My mother-in-law nags. My sisters-in-law are bitchy. They complained about the dowry. They returned the clothes. I'm not sure my husband..." She clutched Andaleep's hand more tightly and fell silent. They sat there for an hour, saying nothing, Tahira's head on Andaleep's shoulder. The swing swayed gently.

Waseem arrived at the door.

Andaleep lit up, only partly with relief. She had always liked his closeness to Tahira, keenly aware of the absence of her own much older and far-away brother.

"How are you? You're going to have to fill me in on the political situation."

Waseem grinned, taking in Andaleep's clothes. "You look like the lovechild of a ripe lemon and a moulting parrot."

"You don't need to put up a brave front any more. You are skinnier than ever. You can stop pining and start eating again now that I'm back."

"I'll start right away. I've been sent with summons for lunch."

She wondered when she could talk with him alone to ask about Shehzad and how the family was handling it.

The table was heavy with food, with glowing amber glasses, and the iridescent sheen of the Japanese bone-china dinner set. The plates were ringed with a densely woven pattern, fine black lines threading themselves through each other, in and out and around an occasional, thick gold one, sinuous and deft as an embroidress' needle. The tablecloth was creamy white with fine beige appliqué and pale salmon shadow-work. On the dark lacquered dining cabinet, large Afghani lamps stood upright, the chilled red of watermelon on which crystals of ice have formed, leaves etched in angular relief in the fluted glass. Frosted quartz in the shape of diamonds hung from the rosette that connected the flutes to the stem. A Bokhara rug, crimson as thickened blood, lay under the table.

"Mariam Aunty, I've missed the food in this house so much; Intizar Uncle, the rice is perfect." Andaleep forced a conversation, pushing through the resentment and constraint that lay thick as the opulence around her. Waseem would not look at his parents, and seemed to try not to look at Tahira either—failing miserably. Seema and Nilofer shot quick, worried glances at their sister and then at each other, self-sufficient and separate even in their concern.

Intizar said, "It's good to see you, Andaleep beta. You are all grown up now. Both you and Tahira."

He almost knocked his glass over, clumsy with sudden

evasion, then resumed with a feeble, pleading chuckle. "Yes. You are all grown up. I feel old. *Twenty-one*!"

Waseem slumped deep into his chair with embarrassment and pain.

Mariam spoke, watchful and tight. "It's good to see you my dear. Intizar is right... How long will you be in Karachi?" The diagonal edge of Mariam's sari, on which little embroidered elephants marched, quivered—sending the elephants sliding with the slippery silk—as she seemed to hold her breath, waiting for Andaleep's answer.

She wants her to leave Karachi, Tahira looked up with sudden insight. She thinks she will persuade me to leave Shehzad. She realized as Andaleep's eyes shot indignant little sparks that Andaleep knew this. She looked across at Waseem, who seemed to know it too. His disgust seemed to be growing as he twirled his glass in his hand, ostentatiously holding it at angles where it would catch light from the chandelier, each twirl a new modulation in a slow swell of contempt.

Later, Andaleep telephoned Waseem. "I remember the house with a constant stream of visitors, doors swinging always open. Now it seems...." she trailed off. Even Waseem, generally indifferent to proprieties, might take offence.

"Don't worry. I know. We don't like visitors very much these days. I think of the house as an Egyptian tomb, an ostentatious pyramid with a deep swaddled silence at its heart." He noticed Mariam hovering nearby, trying to hear what he was saying, and raised his voice. "I asked Amma how many treasures we could bury with ourselves."

"What's Shehzad like?"

"It's hard to tell. He treats us all with a sort of barely checked, enigmatic contempt, as if he's exercising tremendous self-control. I think he might treat Tahira that way too. We haven't seen them together much, but she won't tell me anything." He could not keep the hurt from creeping into his voice. "I know brothers and sisters are meant to observe a tactful reserve on anything relating to marriage. But Tahira and I always had a different, special closeness. I wasn't like those hectoring, morally superior bastards who bully their sisters. There were plenty of invitations to be that way. All I feel from her is a tense, suppressed antagonism. How could this happen to us? We were friends." It was a baffled and raw cry.

"She was tense with me as well. She's in pain. She doesn't mean it."

"I know. I know. I try not to feel betrayed. But…" He began again, "Do you remember Safdar?"

"Yes. Of course. The dishy one. Tahira and I once had a competition about how to describe his eyes. I won. I said they were like rain-washed jade."

"I'll let him know. I spoke to his mother. We could persuade Tahira to talk to her."

"We can try. But I'm not sure it would work. Besides we were all brought up to not talk about these things."

"That's what Apa (everyone, including Safdar, calls Safdar's mother, Apa) said. But she said I should bring Tahira along anyway."

"Okay. I'll work on it tomorrow."

The next day Tahira said, "I can show you what I was doing before the wedding. Come. My room is still as it used to be." Perhaps the only thing that still is, she thought to herself.

Andaleep noticed anew Tahira's range and technique, her ability to enter chameleon-like into different representational modes and attitudes, unsure whether this was an advantage or not. She busied herself with one of the landscapes, a disturbing composition of mysterious viridiscent forest and shimmering stone, and said, "You know Safdar's mother? I've always wanted to meet her. She sounds so fascinating. Will you come with me? I'll feel self-conscious otherwise."

"You are *never* self-conscious. Are you and Waseem up to something?"

Andaleep struck a pose of theatrically injured innocence, "Of course not. Look at Me—Virtue and so Maligned!"

"You are a terrible liar. You always were. I asked at home." She couldn't call Shehzad by his name. It became harder by the day. "He's busy, but my mother-in-law said you could come for tea. It was easy once I told her who your father was. You can meet the Wicked Witch and her monstrous daughters. If you're lucky you'll actually see the outline of my father-in-law as he lurks in the shadows."

"Of course. But will you come with me?"

"Yes. Yes. Alright."

Nazneen and Shaista placed themselves on either side of Andaleep. Farah wheeled in the trolley, each of the three tiers had white runners embroidered with large shaded pink roses and green leaves that tapered from sage to olive, on these sat the family's very best porcelain tea-set, Japanese by way of Peshawar, courtesy of Central Asian smugglers, laden with cakes and biscuits and tea. The trolley and everyone around it was elaborately dressed. Bronze and henna-green, ultramarine, maroon and ochre… Silk and georgette and glass nylon. Everyone was heavy with embroidery and gold, except Andaleep whose thick cotton kameez was a strange, mottled beige printed with brilliant, bursting scarlet poppies, with deep black-brown centres, furry as caterpillars. This was worn over a white shalwar, and a crinkled muslin dupatta in a willfully clashing shade of crimson. A chunky lapis lazuli ring set in tarnished silver flashed on her finger. Tahira had enjoyed Shireen's shock.

Shireen leaned over the coffee table, stretched over the cut-glass vase in the centre, ignoring the points of the vase that pushed up into her quite ample chest, and said, intimate and familiar, as if she knew them, "Beta, how are your parents?"

"Very well, thank you. They send their best," Andaleep lied.

Nazneen pressed into the conversation. "Is Beirut very exciting? I hear it's called the Paris of the East."

"It is." Andaleep smiled widely at Nazneen and decided to see how long Nazneen could be made to hold hers. She widened her own smile ever so slightly. Nazneen widened her own in an effort to sustain it. Andaleep continued. So did Nazneen. Andaleep reached for Nazneen's hand and squeezed it tightly, "Tahira is so lucky to have a sister-in-law like you." She waved her other hand in a grand flourish that swept the room and culminated at her heart, "A family like all of you." She produced a great gust of a sigh, "Not everyone is so lucky." She squeezed Nazneen's hand one more time. Nazneen's smile wavered. Well on her way now, Andaleep continued, "Such taste." She gestured at the pale pink walls, the black velvet wall-hanging, Shaista's daughter's yellow net frock. "Lucky indeed."

Andaleep released Nazneen's hand with a regretful exhalation that wasn't quite a sigh, and took an ostentatiously dainty sip from her cup, little finger extended and erect. She turned it deliberately into a slurp and looked embarrassedly around, shooting glances of roguish penitence at them all. They smiled back with sympathy and understanding, delighted to be drawn into the circle of intimate mischief. Farah even produced one herself. Shireen glared at her.

Shaista spoke, not to be excluded, "I believe your parents and my in-laws are from the same city in U.P."

"How wonderful!" Andaleep clapped her hands.

Tahira finally succeeded in catching her eye and tried to glare at her as unobtrusively as possible, producing a cross-eyed grimace instead.

Andaleep ignored her and turned to Shaista's daughter. "What a sweet little girl you are. What class are you in? I bet you do very well."

"I came second in class two. I'm in class three now. I'll come first this time." Amina beamed at Andaleep, who beamed back. She saw Tahira turning a slow oxygenless blue in the corner they had selected for her. Maybe they think she'll disappear if they can shove her out of sight, Andaleep thought.

Shaista said, "You must come over for dinner before you leave."

Andaleep oozed regret. "I wish I could but the evenings are so busy. My father is here too, you see."

Shaista's eyes glittered with greed. "Can't you bring him as well?"

"I would love to. I'm so sorry. But he has so many family commitments. I'm sure you'll understand."

"After all, we are family too." Shaista decided to include Tahira in the conversation, "Tahira must be like his own daughter."

Tahira enjoyed the effort of that sentence and its simultaneously poisoning and galvanizing effect upon the others.

Shireen said, "Yes. Yes. Tahira—such a good daughter-in-law." The words rolled out, little pellets of bile around which she moved her mouth with the delicacy of a bomb squad afraid of detonation.

Farah spoke, as always the least adept, "Does he really think of Tahira Bhabhi as his daughter? Oh my."

"Absolutely. He has always said he would adopt her if he could."

Nazneen crumbled cake with her fork.

Amina decided it was time for some more attention. She tugged at the edge of Andaleep's kameez. "I know the names of the capitals of all the countries."

"Australia?"

"Canberra."

"Albania?"

"Tirana."

After they had been through Poland, Czechoslovakia, France, Spain, Brazil, Uruguay and Finland, Andaleep said, "I would love to continue this game but I must go to the bathroom. Tahira, will you take me to yours? I'm so sorry to have to do this. But I'm going to have to leave right after that."

In her bedroom, Tahira hissed, "What do you think you're doing? What if they realize you were mocking them."

"They won't. Surely you know by now that they are too arrogant to imagine that anyone ever could. Anyway you're laughing aren't you? I would watch out for Nazneen though. That one is dangerous."

"I know."

Andaleep ran her hand over the baroque carvings on the bed and the mirror, "I don't need to know how much of this furniture you chose, do I? Are these monsters or fantastic flowers? *Oho*. What's this?" She picked up the copy of *Heavenly Ornaments*. "Why do you have this? It's dreadful. I didn't realize anyone still read it. My mother used to do parodies of my grandmother's copy for my father. Ah… the section on how to live with a husband." She read in portentous, doom-laden tones: "'*There was a respectable woman in Lucknow who had a wicked husband, who spent all his time with prostitutes and wouldn't come home at all. The prostitutes would want different kinds of food everyday and this lady never complained, she simply sent over whatever food her husband demanded for them. Never even breathed a complaint. Everyone praised her and then there is the separate reward she will get in the afterlife. And the day God instructed him he abandoned his wicked ways and became his wife's slave!*'"

"He bought it for me—as a gift."

"Oh."

Andaleep arched her back, rubbed her cheek on the pale gold satin of the quilt made from one of Mariam's old saris in Tahira's old room and rolled on to her stomach. "Let's have the sketches." Tahira brought them to the bed and stretched out next to her. Andaleep began to flick through them. She came upon one of Shehzad, enigmatic and uninviting.

She had finally met him. They had taken her out for dinner at Chandni Lounge at Hotel Intercontinental. It had one of the better views of a city that was still developing. Karachi winked and glittered, beautiful and vital in the night in a way that it could not be during the day. It was too large, too unevenly developed, too new and brash. She had missed its anarchic pulse, had wished she were back for good.

She had not liked Shehzad. He had been gracious, but consciously so. In fact, he was too conscious of far too much, she had decided—of his superiority to Tahira, of his grace as a host, of the women in the room. She did not know if Tahira had noticed. She wouldn't ask.

Tahira had told her that Nazneen had wanted to come along. Shehzad had said it would be inappropriate. There would be trouble later. She had called Andaleep… as had Shaista, trying to establish a separate friendship. A lack of response would be held against Tahira, so Andaleep had tried to be politely chatty, even as they insinuated, in their different ways, that Tahira was a disappointment. Now she stared at the drawing. "*This* is what you thought of him before you married him. Why didn't you say anything to Uncle and Aunty?"

"I didn't think I could. You know my mother. And she had already decided. Nothing can get in her way when she's like that. Anyway, I thought everyone felt that way. I thought it was what happened when you married someone. I thought that's how you were supposed to feel."

"I know I'm guilty too. I didn't understand what you were saying in your letters. I thought it was the usual fear people talk about. What do you want to do?"

"What is there to be done? I have to live with this. You know that. We all do."

"But we don't. This is wrong."

"You know that wrong or not, there's little to be done. What about Seema and Nilofer? Who'll marry them? And, even if I do do something, then what? You know how divorced women are treated."

Andaleep fell silent, accepting despite herself the justice of the worries about Seema and Nilofer, and because she herself did not know what would happen next. She knew in a similar situation her own response would be more equivocal, much less emphatic. It was so much easier to be indignant on Tahira's behalf. The anger was purer, less compromised by guilt and fear and necessity. She tried to whip it up, "But there *has* to be something we can do."

"Does there?" Tahira asked bitterly. "Isn't this what we wanted—to be good and silent and suffering? Perhaps I still do. We prided ourselves on our desire to be tested, to show that we were made of stronger, sacrificial mettle. Here it is—the test. And look at me: I cry like a spoilt and blubbering child.

"There is no way out of this, as well you know. Maybe he'll change with time. I just have to try harder." She rolled off the bed, tearing the drawing that had become trapped under her elbow, and paced up and down the room for a while. Then she pulled an anthology of writings on art from the shelf. "Do you remember the day we found the entry by Kierkegaard, on art and poetry? He said there were two kinds of sorrow, reflective and immediate. He said reflective sorrow was the result of deception and could not be represented in art but immediate sorrow could, and immediate sorrow was closer to the pain of an unrequited love or a love denied because of death. He said unhappy love was the deepest sorrow for a woman. We were so excited by these varieties of grief, by the highest unhappiness for a woman as if we had a wonderful, richly paying monopoly. Remember what he said about the Veronica cloth?"

She found the passage and read it aloud, her voice sharp with tears and rage and savage irony. "*Immediate sorrow is the immediate imprint and expression of the sorrow's impression, which just like the picture Veronica preserved on her linen cloth, is perfectly congruous, and sorrow's sacred lettering is stamped on the exterior, beautiful and clear and legible to all.*"

"We didn't know what a Veronica cloth was so we found out."

Andaleep continued sadly, "And we thought it must be so grand to be able to take the imprint of suffering like that cloth. We thought we could do it better—we would be the suffering and the cloth."

"I thought that if ever the need arose, and if I had a reflective sorrow, if I couldn't represent it, I'd turn myself into the silence that buried it deep, where '*the exterior is calm and grief lies like a well-guarded prisoner in an underground prison.*'"

"Yes, we did say that and a thousand other things, but we were adolescents with overwrought imaginations. This isn't the test of an artistic theory: it's your *life*. You cannot let them win," Andaleep said, hoping that saying it again would make it more believable, that the concerns about Seema and Nilofer would resolve themselves through some world-creating miracle of speech.

"You sound like Waseem: he says the same thing. Has it occurred to you they already have? They had before it was begun. Besides whose to say they are not right. Tell me: were we deceived?"

—

Safdar's house looked cluttered and small in the pinched lane in PIB colony, behind Central Jail. The gate was a tiny entry into a narrow house. The paint of the light grey gate and the pale pistachio ice-cream-green façade was peeling in places. The only intimation of things to come was the straggling and cramped but defiant laburnum tree planted outside the wall and the *ishq pechan* vine—also known, Safdar would inform anyone who could be made to listen, as Rangoon creeper and, of course, Rumphius's *Quisqualis Indica*—trained around the gate. Long clusters of headily fragrant red, pink, and white flowers hung from it. As soon as one stepped over the threshold the world changed. The small distance from gate to front door was covered with pots of mother-in-law's tongue, crown of thorns, ferns, jasmine and trumpet vines. Although most of the area leading to the door was concrete, beds had been wrenched from the unpromising site so that there were vines planted in the ground, as well as in pots, along with a guava and an ornamental pomegranate tree. Clutter and constriction had been transformed into protective, green extravagance.

Entering the house one walked immediately into a narrow lounge that ran almost its entire length, and into which opened the kitchen and two small bedrooms. Parallel to the lounge was an area open to the sky but enclosed by the walls of the house. In the centre of this small courtyard was a little fountain that had been installed by Akbar Naqvi for his wife.

The story of the fountain had become a family legend repeated in concert. "He presented it to me, eyes jumping and twinkling," Mumtaz would recount the oft-repeated tale, "with the excitement of a child bursting with a difficult and delicious secret, saying, 'my beloved Mumtaz, I can't give you your very own Taj Mahal, but I'm hoping this will be taken in the same spirit.'"

"And *she* said," Akbar would break in, "'you want me to think your fountain my tomb?'"

Akbar would pause, so his audience could assimilate fully the wit of the riposte, and then continue with a delight that seemed endlessly renewed, "And this proves that providence has truly rewarded me, for where else would such wit be combined with such devotion as she has shown, by giving up everything, and never complaining that we are poor and I cannot give her everything to which she was accustomed in her father's house."

The courtyard was less opulent than the entrance, but there were many lovingly tended plants in it. Dispersed among the plants and around the fountain were pots, matkis and jugs of Multani pottery in blue, turmeric and brown, fat, curvy and sensual, like contented and comfortable cats. Against one wall, was a takht, heaped with bolsters. In another corner was a white oleander bush in a large clay pot, by which sat an intricately carved, antique desk. They all wrote on it, and sometimes Safdar would do his homework there. His room was upstairs, small and covered with books and newspapers.

Waseem and Andaleep walked into the courtyard, Waseem soothed and happy as he always was in Safdar's house. Both were hoping that Safdar's mother would be able to help them with Tahira's plight. Mumtaz sat against the bolsters, chewing paan and rereading *Aag ka Darya.* Ghalib's *Diwan* and a collection of *marsiyas* by Anis lay open, spines stiff in the air, around her on the takht. A little tape-recorder wafted the tinny delights of '*Pyaar kiya to darna kya*' into the air.

Mumtaz was a regal looking woman. She had thin careful lips, with a slight sensual curve in her lower lip and a long, oval face. A solitary clear stone glinted on a straight and proud nose. Her hair, which was sprinkled with grey, and which she refused to blacken, was parted in the middle with military precision and pulled back into a neat bun, held habitually in place with a pencil. She was wearing a pale blue cotton gharara, a pristine, starched white muslin chikan kurta and a muslin dupatta edged with white and pale blue lace, as if she had decided to commemorate the ceremony of UP in her new refugee world. She looked up as Waseem and Andaleep came up to her, and smiled a bright smile that exuded dignity and delight.

They had come with Tahira the day before. The visit had been difficult. Tahira had observed the proprieties but been mostly silent. The others had launched into a conversation about politics and literature, stymied by her blankness and unwilling to show they were a little bored by it. Waseem brought up U.S. support for Sukarno and their own military, wishing their usual interests were not so forced and desperate in Tahira's presence. All life and pain and protest became fake and seemed part of an over-acted play whenever she was around.

While agreeing vigorously about the disaster of what America was doing in the world, Andaleep had suddenly noticed the copy of *Women in Love* on the desk in the courtyard. "Oh no! Not Lawrence…"

Safdar bridled. "I like Lawrence."

"Oh come on. All that metaphysics of sex."

"But women are so powerful—if it is metaphysical."

Andaleep sighed, enjoying herself. "Either way, as objects of unattainable desire or routes to something else, we are only vessels for your dreams but you don't notice and, worse, expect us to be grateful. Maybe we don't notice either. More fools us.

As if we can't imagine anything other than abandonment or erotic idealization. The Lawrentian glories of consummation are no better than some sort of Platonic invisibility."

Safdar was determined not to look impressed. Waseem smiled to himself.

Mumtaz caught a look of envy on Tahira's face. "Do you like Lawrence or does my son have to deal with some seriously united opposition?" She seemed pleased at the thought.

Tahira resented the kindness. "I haven't read him."

Andaleep looked up, wondering why she had lied.

"Pity." Mumtaz grinned at her son. "Safdar needs more argument."

Later Tahira was furious with Waseem and Andaleep. "I'm not a dying pet to be taken around in desperate hope that someone will be able to cure me. I don't want to be pitied and poked and helped. I want to be left alone. There's nothing anyone can do. Do you understand? Nothing."

Mumtaz said to them, "I've always liked Tahira. She seems thoughtful. And such talent."

Waseem said, "Don't you think she ought to leave him?"

"Perhaps. But I can also see why she won't. It's not easy. We're not a forgiving people."

"It's such a cliché. Sometimes that's what annoys me the most."

"Maybe that's what we excel at, finding ever more inventive ways to live our own worst clichés."

Andaleep spoke, "But you broke with family and tradition and sect."

"Yes. And my brothers made sure that I wasn't allowed to see my mother when she was dying. She was the only one who ever met Akbar, and she liked him too."

Safdar interrupted, worried that there was something new and irreparable in his mother's separateness. "Do you regret it?"

"Of course not. But regret is only one kind of torment in a world generous with pain, if with nothing else. I wonder if they looked after her, what it was like after I left, whether my brother's wives cared for her at all. Her letters were cheerful, but they seemed too brave, as if she weren't telling me something. And towards the end I'm not certain she was receiving mine."

She laughed. "Don't look so destroyed. I wanted to leave that house and I wouldn't exchange a day with your father for acceptance there. But you are old enough to know that even mothers have histories that are not always shared, no? I was lucky: your father is a rare and gentle husband. Imagine what my choice would have looked like if he were a different sort of man. What looks brave to *some* now would have looked foolish to *all* then."

She turned to Waseem. "Tahira is fortunate she has a brother like you. But she has to want to do this. And," she hesitated, "your parents have to help—maybe even decide for her."

6

Tahira stood at the window of her hotel room in London, clutching the sill with excitement. She had not expected the light to be so subtle. The buildings shone in the evening. Old Georgian white slid into a soft golden glow, as if lit by the edges of a candle's flame. She tried to imagine them in the seared dust of Karachi.

She heard Shehzad tip the bellboy and walk over to where she stood. A scene came to her of a man and a woman at a window—sharing the world. The woman was leaning against the man's shoulder, which was tender with love. She tried to place the memory and realized it was from a romance novel whose name and every other detail she had forgotten. Perhaps she had imagined it. She wondered what would happen if she let her head slip without announcement or ceremony onto his shoulder. Would it yield with invitation or stiffen with rejection? She wished she dared find out.

She said without turning, "It's so beautiful. Thank you for bringing me. I've never been abroad." She thought she felt him smile.

He wondered what she had been thinking and said, "What would you like to do?"

"Could we go for a walk?"

They walked past a window-display, a precisely contrived antique Asian pastiche, Rosewood Chinese desk inlaid with mother of pearl, Irani ceramics of a bright translucent turquoise, and two Mughal miniatures: of a man in a courtly dress strolling in a garden, the other a woman squeezing her hair after a bath, one woman drying her feet, another preparing her clothes. As they paused to look at the miniatures, Shehzad said, "I wonder if any Pakistani ever comes to England without feeling a strange recognition, and resentment at that recognition."

Tahira looked at him in surprise. "I was wondering that myself. I looked at the guidebook Waseem gave me when I left," she felt him stiffen and continued, "and all the names seem so familiar: King's Cross, Pimlico, Hyde Park. I had an uncle who spoke at Speaker's Corner once. He said it made him feel good to be able to tell the colonial masters what he thought of them. And now, walking here, it's so strange to feel as if I should have seen this before and to know that I haven't. I wonder if the English even know how that feels. If they feel anything like it when they come to India or Pakistan." She thought that was her longest speech to him yet.

"I want to ask my British colleagues that sometimes. But I never have."

"Why not?"

"I don't know. Maybe I should. Or perhaps," he grinned at her, "you can?"

She was startled by the mischief in his smile. Before she had a chance to reply, he went on, "What will you do when I'm at work tomorrow?"

"I think I would like to go to the museums."

"We'll talk to the concierge when we get back; and we'll figure out how to get there. I'll show you how to get to the underground, and how to use it in the morning."

She was surprised and grateful and hoped her surprise

wouldn't show. A woman walked by wearing a black and white mini-skirt, white gloves and a pillbox hat, with pert, assertive nipples pushing through a stretchy black shirt. Tahira stared.

Dinner was quiet. They sat at a table near the window, watching people walk by, jetlagged and formal, and alone at dinner for the first time since their wedding. It had been three months, Tahira thought. Three month—yet, she wasn't sure what to say. She searched for the right question, trying not to push the fish around her plate, consciously loosening her grip on the fork. The smell of garlic and a herb she did not recognize mingled with the scent of his aftershave. His watch glinted gold among the curling black hairs on his wrist, nestled like an egg in a hospitable nest. His hands were large, powerful, the hair on the knuckles thick and springy. For a man fastidious about his appearance, as she had learned him to be, the frayed nails were a touching sign of humanity.

Outside, the extended twilight of the temperate zone acquired deeper layers of a liquid, glinting blue. Inside the restaurant, the bulb behind her, Tahira sat in shadow, silhouetted against the light, a delicate shape with invisible eyes.

Shehzad tried not to stare at her too obviously. Marriage perplexed him. It was meant to be easier than this. She was his wife after all, why could he think of nothing to say? It was true he could not say to her many of the things he could have to his girlfriends, but every one knew that wives were different, more worthy of conversational respect. He began to feel resentful. Why wouldn't she say something? Wasn't it her duty to make things smoother for him, to relax him at he the end of the day, to know his desires before he knew them himself?

The silence stretched. At the other end of the restaurant a woman with solemn grey eyes reached across the table to touch the hand of her companion, curled around the stem of a glass in which wine swirled and winked like garnets in the lamplight; at the table next to theirs, a man raised his hand to touch the bronze curls of the young man across from him, and withdrew it quickly, nervy and muffled. He placed it on the table where it twitched like a self-conscious smile. A waiter came over to Shehzad and Tahira's table, wondered at the silence that lay thick and solid between them and asked them if they would like some dessert. Tahira looked questioningly at Shehzad. Shehzad nodded. The waiter left.

Suddenly Tahira asked, brave with resolve, "Do you like movies?"

It was the right question. He was pleased. "I do. A lot."

She was delighted. "Me too. Indian or English?"

"Both. I'll watch anything with Madhubala, Dilip Kumar or Marilyn Monroe in it."

"What a combination!"

"What about you?

"I do think Madhubala is beautiful. I'll tell you who I think is really beautiful too. Did you see Gina Lollobrigida in *Come September*?" She decided not to strain the fragile web of conversation with the revelation that she had had a crush on Rock Hudson for months afterwards.

They talked through dessert ("English desserts," Shehzad said, "are not to be missed"), animated and pleased. Names flew through the air like uncaged birds: Meena Kumari and Doris Day; Spencer Tracy and Raj Kumar; *Pillow Talk*, *Adam's Rib*, *Mughal-e-Azam* and *Sahib Bibi aur Ghulam*. They left the restaurant lightheaded with exhaustion and relief. The waiter watched them go and wondered what had happened.

The next morning, preparing to leave the hotel room, Tahira pulled a wad of traveller's cheques from her purse and said, "Do you think these will be enough?"

Startled, he asked, "Where did you get that?"

"You told me to ask my parents for money." She did not say that her parents had seemed hurt by her hesitant request, that she had wondered if the flustered speed with which her father had rushed to his large antique, teak cupboard, had been an attempt to assuage his guilt or buy her compliance. He had stood in front of the cupboard with its multiple locks to which only he had keys, in which he kept money, gold guineas, and, unfathomably, always six months supply of soap—Surf for clothes, Lux for humans—and asked, fumbling the locks, eager to be of use, "How much do you need? Just tell me."

"As much as you think appropriate."

Intizar had offered the money with urgent, pressing hands and she had taken it with a composed, formal thank you which, whether or not it had been intended to disconcert her parents, had elicited further discomfort. She had been glad.

Her mother had said, "Oh beta, you don't need to thank us." And then hurried on when Tahira had looked studiously, politely blank, "We are your parents, after all."

"Of course, of course." Intizar had rushed in.

Now Shehzad said, "You won't need that. Here's some for you. And I can give you more later." He handed her a thicker stack. "I'll show you how to use them on the way to the Tube."

"They taught me at the bank in Karachi."

"Oh."

As they left the hotel Shehzad asked, "Will you be alright on your own?"

"I think so. I'll be careful to only go to one or two places today, and I'll be back at the hotel before you are."

"Aren't you a little intimidated?"

"A little, but also excited." She smiled. "Very excited. I can't wait to go to the museums."

"I'm impressed."

She looked at him, startled "Why?"

"Because you've never done this before, because it's a foreign country, and you don't seem flustered at all."

"Thank you." She wondered what he would say if she told him that London—in all its dazzling new immensity—seemed less threatening than the path from their bedroom to the kitchen. She had learned to look carefully around the curve of the stairs, search the corners of rooms, peer into shadows to ensure that her father-in-law was not hidden from sight, waiting to be offended, that Nazneen and Farah weren't giggling in prurient consort, that Shireen wasn't lurking behind a door with a carefully honed barb.

He helped her buy the ticket and then left to go to his meetings.

She walked from Leicester Square Station to the National Gallery. The area was already cluttered with tourists. A young man, bearded, in an Indian-style brick kurta, jeans and green beads handed her a pamphlet against the Vietnam war, "Peace, Sister." Further along a tall pale woman in a white robe, red stubble on her head eyed her sari greedily and tried to sell her a copy of the *Gita* and a packet of incense. She shook her head, and then decided to say, "Sorry. Incense reminds me of funerals."

She counted the mini-skirts, which she had only seen on screen or in the pages of occasional fashion magazines before. She remembered reading somewhere that London was the centre of fashion and decided to count the number of pillbox hats, bouffant hairdos and short dresses she saw on the trip, suddenly gleeful when she saw a woman walk by in a short sleeveless dress that looked like a Mondrian painting, unaware that her own grey and blue sari was attracting surreptitious English curiosity. It was novel and invigoratingly calm to walk in a city, engaged in such purposeless observation, unaccompanied, unfettered, blissfully anonymous.

She wondered what had happened to Shehzad. He seemed to have forgotten about the book; and his temper seemed more even, less prone to sudden, frightening outbursts, which made her body shake with fear and shock. They came with so little warning. Whatever it was, she thought, perhaps it would last. Perhaps, finally, things would get better.

She arrived at the National Gallery and stood outside looking at it for a while, awed by its size. Inside, the bounty was giddying. As she walked through room after room filled with paintings, whose names she had only seen in books, of many of which she had never heard, her excitement grew. She had expected to be delighted by the Impressionists, by the uncompromising, incendiary sunbursts of Van Gogh's sunflowers. She had no way of knowing about the effect that the older paintings would have.

Late in the day, she came upon Botticelli's *Mars and Venus*, and stopped, stricken by the lambent light, by the lucidity of tempera, by the honesty of bodily abandon. Mars exposed, his foot touching Venus's body, Venus's hand, easy, upon his foot. She wondered if she imagined the tranquil distance on Venus's face. How could she stare so boldly ahead, without fear of discovery, of being known to have seen? She looked again. She didn't think Venus's hand was touching Mars's foot at all. She read the description. Venus symbol, and person, of love conquering war. She stared at Venus's hand, at her grave, remote composure. Was this how love conquered? Looking at Venus, she wondered if Botticelli had known that Venus had conquered Mars by conquering herself. How else to explain her reticent serenity?

She realized she was late and ran, almost tripping over her sari, bumping into a fat, red-faced man with open pores in his nose, who muttered, "Watch where you're going, Paki bitch," clutching her bag, so the sketchpad and newly acquired book would not fall out. She arrived panting and terrified in the train and sat down next to woman with a thin beak of a nose, reading *The Shadow of a Sun* and hoped she would remember to buy it. She liked the title. The ride which had seemed full of possibility and the imminence of discovery in the morning seemed interminable and then too fast, as if she were being hurtled towards catastrophe. To calm herself she tried to make a list of the paintings she had loved the most and thought of the tranquil absorption and exquisite colour of the *Reading Magdalen*, of the chaste serenity of the Virgin in Sassoferato's painting, hidden and protected by veil and shadow. She tried to summon their serenity and Venus's composure to her aid. She mumbled a prayer under her breath, clasping and unclasping her hands, then looked up right into the scrutiny of an African couple. The woman's russet and saffron headdress and shift were defiantly undimmed in the lurid glare of the train's interior. The broadness of her smile was radiant and loud against the scared hush of the English. The man had sympathetic, small rheumy eyes. As the train hurtled and lurched, their hips slid back and forth in unison like glasses on a table in a ship on stormy seas. Both examined her with anxious friendliness.

"Are you alright?" asked the woman.

"Thank you. Yes. Just hoping I won't be late."

"Something important."

"Yes. Very."

"First time in London?"

"How did you know?"

"I did not. It is ours."

The train stopped. Tahira almost tumbled face forward into the woman's broad, flat lap. She steadied herself against a pole, said in an apologetic, disappearing rush, "Sorry I have to go," and half-ran, half-stumbled her way out of the train, scraping her shoulder against the door.

The hotel room was empty. She looked in the bathroom. There was no one there. She was terrified. Perhaps he had left in fury. She called the reception to see if there were any messages. The receptionist's voice was nasal, with an unplaceable accent, professional with impersonal sympathy, "Mr. Ehsan said he would be working late tonight. You should get dinner on your own."

Tahira hung up, relieved, and felt a fool.

She stared at green wallpaper and the subdued gold light of the lamps and realized that she was starving. The thought of going out brought on a sudden embarrassed inhibition at being in a restaurant alone in the evening so she decided to call room service instead. An evening in the hotel room, remembering the day, would be nice.

She began to read the book she had bought in the Museum bookshop earlier in the day, needing to take a break from the sheer number and intensity of the paintings. She learned that Bottticelli lived during a period known as the Italian Quattrocento, that he had always been devout, that he had been influenced by Savonarola, the puritanical preacher who had been the scourge of the Medici. The food arrived, elaborately dressed on a plate under a stainless-steel dome, which the waiter removed with a flourish to reveal chicken sandwiches with a garnish of parsley and carrot shavings. She accepted the intrusion with preoccupied good manners, restrained the impulse to ask the waiter whether the sandwiches could live up to his gesture, tipped him and returned to the book as soon as he left.

She skipped ahead to the part about Savonarola's take-over of the city of Florence and read that Botticelli had participated in the 'Bonfire of the Vanities,' that he had burned his own paintings in an act of renunciation so grand that she shuddered. She realized vaguely that the sandwiches were boring, but continued eating, stoic, absorbed. She imagined *Mars and Venus* burning, flames licking the feet of Mars, crawling like blossoming, burning serpents out of some fairytale pit up towards Venus's face, consuming her composure, until it no longer mattered, until it was no longer even a memory. Had he edged closer to the fire, feeling the heat as the flames grew higher and hotter, until sweat crept all over him? Had he hesitated before he consigned his paintings to the flames, walked delicately around the edges of the zealous, devouring fire, imagined the terror of immolation? Or had he flung them in without pause, without imagining? Did it take tremendous courage to do what he had done or was it just an act of cowardice? She thought it must take discipline and commitment and strength. And then wished he hadn't had it.

She fell asleep with the book open on her face.

The next morning, she awoke to find the book on the floor next to the bed, her sari crumpled all around her, and Shehzad emerging fully dressed from the bathroom. The handkerchief, poking erect and immaculate from his suit pocket, mocked her disarray.

"Oh. I'm sorry," she said. "You should have woken me up."

"It's fine. I have to leave soon and there was no point in waking you. Did you enjoy yourself?" he asked, reaching for the briefcase.

"Oh, it was wonderful. I've never seen anything like it. Will you come with me?"

"No. I have to work late today and tomorrow as well. So you should do what you want. On Saturday we'll go see my cousin, Faraz, in a place called High Wycombe."

"Oh."

"What did you do for dinner yesterday?"

"I called room service. I was too embarrassed to go out."

"You should. No reason not to enjoy the city just because I'm busy."

"Will we have a chance to go shopping together? We'll

have to get presents for your sisters and parents. I'm not sure what would be appropriate."

"Yes. Don't worry we will shop together. And we'll have dinner with my colleagues before we leave. But the next few days have become unexpectedly busy." He gestured to the book and to the sketches she had done in the museum. "But it looks as if you'll be fine."

She wondered why he seemed so determinedly cheery, why he wouldn't meet her eyes.

Over the next few days, she visited more galleries and took a guided tour of the city. At the Victoria and Albert Museum she seethed, muttering to herself in the sections of Indian and Muslim art, "These are ours. I wouldn't need to be here to look at these if they hadn't ripped us off."

She found herself returning to National Gallery to look again at the *The Reading Magdalen*, *The Virgin Praying* and *Mars and Venus* to see if she had imagined their surprise, to look carefully and long at Botticelli's *Mystic Nativity*. The composition was odd and entrancing. The Virgin was kneeling with her head bent over the Baby Jesus. Angels sat above them on the roof of their shelter and, even higher, danced, circling in the air. Except for the Virgin and the Baby, the figures were frenzied, in restless motion. She did not like it. She did like the way the ultimate focus of the painting, despite its different areas of activity, remained the infant Christ and the Virgin. But the motion and fussy frenzy of the painting made the lambency and composed reticence of *Mars and Venus* seem even more remarkable.

She sketched them all, over and over again, and decided she preferred the deep glow of Flemish oils to the bright clarity of Botticelli's tempera.

They were lonely, liberating, exhilarating days. She sat alone in the evenings at restaurants and experimented with food, French and Italian, with elaborate sauces and slithery spaghetti. She was approached by men and was unsure how to handle herself: she stiffened and looked down until they left. And when it worked, what had begun as necessity was cultivated as art. She did not know how tempting and elusive she seemed, delicate and graceful and distant. To sit in a restaurant alone, without company or scrutiny was new. But then so was every thing else, she thought.

They took the train to High Wycombe from Marylebone station. They had not spent this much time together since their first day in London. "So. I've been busy working, but how have you been? What have you done?"

"A lot. I feel bad though. You are working and I'm just having a good time. Doing things I've always wanted to do."

"Don't worry. I told you, no reason for you not to have a good time. Go ahead, tell me what you have been doing. I saw some of the sketches last night when I came back from work. They're very good."

"Thank you. I've been to the museums a lot as you can tell. I took the guided tour as you suggested. I went to Foyle's, the bookstore, because I had heard so much about it. It was spectacular. Books from floor to ceiling, for several floors. It was hard to buy books, though. They have a very complicated system. Besides," she laughed nervously, "I wasn't sure if I should spend too much money."

He frowned. "I gave you enough. You can't have spent it already."

"I haven't. I just wasn't sure I should."

"Do."

She was sorry to have brought it up. "How has your work been?" She tried to shift the focus of the conversation.

"Fine. I want to be silent now."

She wondered what she had done. The train sped past tiny backyards, behind tiny houses of dirty reddish brick, each of which seemed to have a regulation-issue apple tree—she wondered if it were a national prerequisite—and large, improbable roses. She thought of the effort Intizar expended on his one hybrid rose and thought she must take some cuttings for him. Shehzad shifted in his seat, and snored, his mouth open, a bit of saliva had gathered in the corner. She looked away, repelled and maliciously gratified. The houses gave way to fields, which were a gentle pale green she had never seen before, as if ground emerald had been mixed with topaz. On the edges of the fields were small yellow flowers, and sometimes red. She had taken a train from Karachi to Islamabad once and the fields had seemed equally exotic and fascinating; she had delighted in their freshness as only a truly urban child could. She thought guiltily that these were prettier.

The train pulled up at the station. She touched Shehzad's shoulder gently. "I think we're here."

He jumped up, irritated. "Why didn't you say so earlier?"

"I didn't know."

Shehzad's cousin-in-law was waiting outside the station, stout and earnest and welcoming, "Bhabhi! How lovely to meet you. Shehzad Bhai, it's been too long. My wife and children are at home. Farida wanted to come but she had to cook lunch."

"Oh, she didn't have to do that."

"Of course she did. And we know how desperate you must be for Pakistani cooking by now."

"It is true. I've been craving daal and rice for a week now," Tahira said.

"Oh no, her biryani and qorma will be wasted," Faraz chuckled.

"Oh no, no, no. I didn't mean to be rude."

The men laughed, hearty and comfortably artificial. She realized it had not taken long to forget how difficult and boring conversation could be. The drive was thankfully short.

They arrived at the house and Faraz called out to his wife, "Begum, come and see who I've brought home." Farida came out running, pretty and plump, dimples and smiles, with a long braid and a smudge of flour on her temple.

"Shehzad Bhai," she squealed, "Bhabhi is so beautiful. You must have done many good deeds to deserve this."

Shehzad accepted the compliment as if all the credit were his own. Farida put her arm through Tahira's and squealed closer to Tahira's ear this time, "Naazo. Usman. Come down and meet Shehzad Mamu and his lovely new bride." Tahira tried not to flinch. After all, Farida was the first member of Shehzad's family to be friendly to her.

The children came into the little hallway, which seemed smaller because of the ochre wallpaper, to meet them. The boy was older, tall, the beginnings of acne sprinkled across his face. The girl was small, with an intent pointy face. Both were bespectacled, earnest, a little otherworldly. They greeted Shehzad and Tahira in solemn unison, "Assalam alaikum Shehzad Mamu, Tahira Maami."

Faraz led them into the living room. The walls were covered with burgundy wallpaper. There were a couple of intricately filigreed brass lamps tall as Usman in the corner. Small round tables, inlaid with brass and ivory were scattered around the room. A large framed black velvet wall-hanging, like the one in Shehzad's living room, dominated one wall. The Arabic calligraphy glinted brassily against the iridescent black of the velvet. The room looked as if the decorator had raided a Pakistan Handicrafts store.

Faraz noticed Tahira looking around and said, "Yes. Yes. It's all Farida's magic. She is so talented."

"I can see that." Tahira hoped her expressionlessness would be interpreted as shyness.

Farida spoke, elaborate with modesty, "Oh. It's nothing. I can teach you how to do it. It's easy once you know how."

"I'm sure it's not. You must be very talented. Do all English interiors have wallpaper?" Tahira made a bet with herself that Farida would giggle.

"Yes. Isn't it lovely? I've always thought we should start using it in Pakistan. After all why should the English be the only ones to have this wonderful thing?" she giggled, happy to take credit for English taste.

"Very." Tahira tried not to shudder.

Shehzad was bored. "Farida. Won't you ask us to sit down? And how about something to drink?" Tahira bit back a giggle. It's infectious, she thought. Maybe I'll simper soon as well. Then we can pretend we're in a film. She can be Nisho and I'll be Shamim Ara.

"*Arre.* How bad I am. Of course, please sit. Would you like some tea? Or juice?"

"Tea would be lovely." Shehzad said.

"Tahira Bhabhi?"

"I'll have tea as well. But I'll help you make it." Tahira jumped up.

At lunch, Naazo exhaled a deep, yearning sigh at Tahira. "Tahira Bhabhi, you are so lucky to live in Pakistan, surrounded by Muslims, by your own people."

Tahira felt her eyebrows shoot up her forehead. She wasn't used to children who talked like this, or grown-ups.

"I had never really thought about it." She thought of Waseem and how he would respond to this statement. How appalled he would be.

"But," Naazo persisted, "it must be so different. The people must be so pure."

"Pure?"

"It's a clean culture. That's what my parents always say."

"It is," Farida intervened, worried that Tahira would

confuse her children, especially after she had worked so hard on them.

Faraz spoke, "It's hard raising children in this culture, Bhabhi. There are so many obscenities. You must have seen them. Drink, skirts, dating."

He continued, "You know our Naazo is a poet. She has a book of poems. Beta, get a copy for Bhabhi."

"I'll be back in a minute." She ran out of the room—Tahira realized she hadn't thought her capable of running—and bounded back with a sheaf of handmade paper, elegantly bound with green ribbon. The poems were in English, but the title page had the names of God in slightly amateurish Arabic calligraphy all over. In the centre, in an English calligraphic script was the title *I'll walk to Medina Alone*. Underneath it: Naazish Saleem (12 years old).

"Come here beta," Shehzad was at his most expansive. He handed her five pounds. "Such children should be rewarded." He stroked her head. "Well done."

Tahira decided to take her cue from him, "*Mashallah*, beta. How impressive. Well done."

Something mauve ringed with angry purple and a creamy white centre slowly began to take over her vision, and she realized she had let her eyes fall out of focus on one of Usmaan's pimples. She looked away quickly.

Farida, Faraz and Usman beamed with pride. Naazo glowed with rapture. Shehzad sat pleased and generous. Tahira hoped the day would end soon. Then she wondered why she was being so mean. Farida was quite nice. And anyway she loved *naats*, especially the one about the green minarets of Medina. What's wrong with me that I can no longer be kind to people? How intolerant I've become.

"So Tahira Bhabhi, what have you been doing in London? You and Shehzad Bhai must have done a lot of sightseeing together?" Faraz said.

"Unfortunately not. I've had to work late most days so Tahira has had to be on her own. It's been hard on her I'm sure. But she's been having a good time at the museums. Tahira is a talented artist, you see."

Farida squealed coy outrage. "Shehzad Bhai! What sort of a newly-wed are you? You should have let us know. We would have brought Bhabhi here and looked after her as well as we could."

Faraz broke in. "Indeed she would lack for nothing. In fact, we could do it now. She can stay here starting tonight."

Tahira's heart plummeted. "Thank you. That's very kind. But I haven't brought any clothes with me."

"No problem. You can wear mine. We'll be like sisters."

Shehzad decided to take pity on Tahira. "I'm afraid, that's not possible. I should be free soon, and then we will do things together. Tomorrow we'll go shopping for my family. And in any case, I promised Tahira that she could spend most of her time in the art galleries, studying for her own work."

"My Farida is quite talented too. And she doesn't need to go to the galleries." Faraz scuttled over to a shelf where there was a small painting and brought it over. "See." He showed it to them. Tahira recognized it as an imitation of Chughtai. It was competent, but there was something slightly odd about it. She walked closer, peering, puzzled.

Shehzad was beginning to get irritated. Even he could see it wasn't stunning, and that it was an imitation. "Well. Different people have different ways of doing things."

Tahira smiled at Farida, "It's very lovely. I love Chughtai, too. I used to practice copying his work—a friend's family has quite a few."

"Oh. You are lucky." Farida sighed. "The only problem is that sometimes he becomes a little—you know…"

"I'm sorry. I don't understand."

"He's not always," she paused and lowered her eyes and said, almost whispering "not always decent."

Tahira was completely mystified.

"Ufff." Farida began to sound exasperated. "It's just that when I traced the outline for this from a print I had, I changed certain… certain features."

Suddenly Tahira understood. The woman's clothing was no longer diaphanous and Farida had blanked out the nipples. She bit her tongue to prevent herself from laughing. She would have to write to Andaleep as soon as she got back to the hotel.

Shehzad's colleague, Jeremy Williams, was a pale, portly man, with a broad, flat face, "So, Mrs. Ehsan," he began, once they had been seated for dinner and placed their orders. Jeremy had recommended the fish, Shehzad the steak. She loved fish, especially trout, but decided to get steak. "What's surprised you most about England?"

She tallied the surprises of the past two weeks: the intricate shock of Gothic architecture—although rather like Frere Hall she supposed. The plush, gentle green of English grass. Shehzad's relatives, raising quaint, frightening, devout otherworldly children, the likes of whom she had never encountered in Pakistan. The ubiquitous wallpaper. She had never seen any before. Complex weaves of vines and clusters of purple grapes on ochre walls in Faraz and Farida's small living room. Urns the colour of—what she had learned was—Cotswold stone on textured tea-green wallpaper in the hotel room, cream roses on a dark pink base in the tea-rooms. New visions to put to names. Botticelli. Some new names. Sassoferato. Rogier Van Der Weyden. The Flemish Primitives and their astonishing combination of jewelled colours and latent violence. Italian Quattrocento. Fra Filippo Lippi. Jan and Hubert Van Eyck. The fact that she hadn't really thought about colonial theft and museums before.

She looked around. There was more wallpaper, indigo with silver stripes, starting at chest-level of the taller, seated customers. "The wallpaper," she said.

Shehzad burst out laughing. After a startled pause, Jeremy smiled as well, still evidently discomfited. Tahira was glad. He was too confident. And she didn't like the admiration, or the sympathy, in his eyes.

Shehzad spoke, "I had never really thought about it. You are right."

"Yes. We don't have any. The rooms here are often so small it's surprising that they use so much."

Jeremy said, clearly fighting his irritation, "Surely there must be other things?"

"Of course," she smiled politely, "but you asked me what had surprised me the *most*."

Shehzad intervened, thoroughly amused, "What else?"

She rattled off a list, self-conscious as a child asked to entertain adults before dinner. "Gothic architecture, the colour of English grass, the Flemish primitives."

Shehzad was pleased with the answer. Jeremy was even more surprised.

"Tahira is a talented painter. She has been spending a lot of time at the museums. She's done several drawings. When I come home from work each evening, the pile seems to have doubled."

"Right."

Shehzad was impressed with the number of sketches she had done, and by how good they were. It had been gratifying to watch Faraz praising Farida and to realize that Tahira's talents were so much greater, the real thing. It was satisfying to have a talented wife. It made one feel talented oneself.

The watch he had bought her the day before, wanting to reward her, glinted on her wrist, making it seem even more fragile. How easily bone can snap, he thought, surprised at himself.

Yet he had been frustrated by the trip. It felt as if there were a conspiracy to prevent him from acting on his intention to overcome Tahira's distance. In Karachi, his sisters and mother were present everywhere. Strange how spending time with one's own wife could make one feel like such a delinquent. Not that he didn't love them. And of course it was his duty to be with them, but sometimes it seemed that they were always there. As if they waited around corners to make sure that they could not be alone. He banished the thought; it was unworthy, disloyal. And then the work in London had been unexpectedly time-consuming. He was pleased that they had been able to shop together. He had specially enjoyed showing her Harrods, although her reaction had not been as enthusiastic as he had hoped. Still… as long as she wasn't ungrateful. He was particularly pleased by the way she had always chosen expensive gifts for his family. She had not tried to prevent him from spending money upon them.

Tahira saw him looking at her watch. It was his first gift to her since the book. They had been shopping for gifts in a large department store, under orders to acquire expensive watches for Farah and Nazneen's dowries. They chose two gold ones for the girls. The displays glinted and winked under the massive chandeliers and suddenly Tahira spotted it. It was silver, with a thin strap, like a delicate austere bangle. She pointed. "That one's so pretty and unusual."

"Would you like it?"

"Oh no." She was embarrassed. She had not meant to hint that she wanted it. Besides she didn't enjoy shopping. It required decision and choice. And she hated waste. He motioned the saleswoman to show it and then clasped it around her wrist.

Tahira was even more embarrassed. "I really didn't mean it you know," she said.

"I was going to buy you a present anyway. You just made it easier."

"Really?"

"Yes. I have hardly spent any time with you. And you haven't complained. I think you should be rewarded."

"Thank you."

He paid for all three watches, asked for the other two to be giftwrapped and said, "I am now going to take you to do one of my favourite things."

"What's that?"

"You'll see."

Getting into a London cab in a sari was an art Tahira was certain she would never perfect. How was one to hitch one's sari to a modest height, so that too much leg did not show? And even if one could get in, how was one to turn gracefully so one could back into the seat without falling? She tripped and laughed, shy and absurdly happy when Shehzad steadied her elbow with a proprietary hand and helped her in.

The surprise was clotted cream and jam on scones. "This is your favorite thing to do in London?"

The cream smeared itself over his lip and he grinned sheepishly. 'Yes. I don't know if you've noticed but I have a sweet tooth. And I love cream. Remember the cook always skims cream of the milk for me, and I have it on toast in the morning."

Maybe she had thought, exultant and happy, things will finally be alright.

There hadn't been enough time, he realized, surprised at how relaxed the time they had spent alone had been, angry that even then her reserve wavered so little.

7

The pink tea-cosy lay athwart the top tier of a trolley bearing the wreckage of an elaborate tea: two samosas, one with an edge broken off, the congealing residue of yoghurt streaked with tamarind and date chutney on a precarious stack of dirty plates, crumbled sand-coloured remnants of freshly baked salty-sweet biscuits with caraway seeds from the neighbourhood bakery, a few pakoras, a third of a fruitcake. Crows circled and screeched overhead. Shehzad's family, bursting with suppressed expectation, sat in the garden around the trolley, framed by the bougainvillea which covered the boundary wall, thick and untamed as a jungle vine.

Shaista's husband pushed his square, dark-rimmed glasses further up his nose. Behind the thick lenses his eyes were quite attractive, now avid and puckered with greed. "Go ahead," he said to his daughter, officious in a sparkling pink net frock. "Ask your uncle what he bought for you in London."

Amina leapt into Shehzad's lap and twined her arms around his neck, coy, accomplished, and eight. "Mamu. Did you bring me lots of presents? You love me the most don't you?"

Tahira felt the release of tension in the circle. It had been asked.

She turned to Shehzad. “Should I get them?”

He nodded.

Nazneen asked, “Should I go too?” And then with an elaborate little laugh, “I wouldn’t want Bhabhi to give something you bought for us to her sisters by mistake.” The softly underlined “you” was artistic.

Tahira held her breath, waiting to see how he would respond, said a little prayer to herself, promising to say an extra namaz if he didn’t let her down.

“No,” he said. “I want you to sit here and tell me all about what you did while I was gone. I missed you. How can you bear to leave my side for a few, paltry presents?”

Nazneen forced an affectionate, teased laugh and sat back down, shooting poison into the grass.

Tahira knew that this little victory would be paid for later; probably in blood, she thought to herself, giggling nervously as she gathered the parcels. They slipped and slid out of her grasp. She walked cautiously down the stairs, peering around the tower in her arms, and placed it on the grass in front of Shehzad, where it tumbled untidily into an abundant diagonal heap. “There’s more,” she said quickly, “I’ll be right back.”

The parcels began to be unwrapped, paper accumulated in impatient shredded piles. Shirts were unfolded, striped and solid, sky blue and bright, laundry white, frocks vivid with yellow primroses and scarlet strawberries and aquamarine butterflies held against Amina, a doll—woolly copper ringlets, cotton flesh, arched, startled button eyes—embraced. A navy wool blazer for Shaista’s husband. A tea-set. Lipsticks. Sweating bottles of chilly perfume. Two exhausted days of shopping.

Shehzad’s father held up a shirt to fastidious scrutiny. “In my day the English knew how to make shirts,” he said. Shehzad smiled, expansive, big with his ability to give. Tahira felt the glisten of greed that hung like fug in an over-worked kitchen, watched their impatient hungry hands and Shehzad presiding, and wondered how he could be so blind. Shireen carefully folded two sweaters, primly placed the new tea-set and a bottle of perfume atop them and set them aside. "Did you get the watches for the girls' dowries?" Shehzad motioned Tahira to hand them to his mother. Nazneen and Farah crowded around as she opened the boxes. Tahira still standing close-by saw the look of delight on Nazneen's face, the golden sheen reflected on it. Then Nazneen turned and said a restrained thank you to her brother, as if waging a heroic battle with disappointment.

"Not what you wanted?" he asked.

"Oh no, no. It is. It's just that I was hoping for something more unusual. I thought you would know that. But," she smiled gravely, "this is very nice." She walked over to sit by his side on the grass next to his chair. Her hand holding his, the barest hint of hurt in the delicate determination of the chin angled his way with sisterly devotion.

"Next time," he said, still smiling.

Amina wriggled out of her mother's grasp, doll tucked firmly under one arm, and scrambled into Shehzad's lap again. "Mamu, don't you love your sisters, any more?"

"Of course I do. What a silly question."

"They say you don't. They say Tahira Maami is taking you away from them." She tucked the doll's head under her chin, and nestled hers on his shoulder. "But I say you must love us, you bought us such nice things."

The next morning Tahira unpacked properly. She pulled out Shehzad's trousers and began putting them away, trying to fold them with military precision, the way he liked, creases meticulously aligned, the legs falling sharp and thin over the hangers. She made a pile of the shirts that had to go to the laundry, a separate one for those that would go to the dhobi. The work acquired a soothing rhythm, a limp white shirt stale with sweat for the laundry pile, unraveling yards of cobalt georgette for the dhobi, a small pile of bras and panties to wash later and tuck out of sight to dry, another male shirt for the laundry pile.

She began to extract the presents she had brought for her own family, the books she had bought for herself, pausing to lock the room. Soon the suitcases were empty. Her family's presents sat in a heap in the centre of the bed: colognes, make-up, the bras her mother had requested for Seema's and Nilofer's dowries, books for Waseem—George Orwell's *Homage to Catalonia*, Marx's translated and unabridged *The German Ideology*, and an illustrated copy of *Songs of Innocence and Experience*. He had asked for the first two; the choice of books at the local bookstores was whimsical, subject to the arbitrary determinations of customs officials and buyers. Overwhelmed by the plenitude of Foyle's, she had felt there was a peculiar luxury in the ad hoc surprises of Karachi's bookstores. She smiled—but she had overcome her panic—and placed her own stack on the table by the window. The collection of poems had been her choice.

She looked around the room; it was beginning to become hers. She straightened the edge of the bedspread, repositioned the make-up on the chest of drawers. The mirror reflected lipsticks and a bottle of talcum powder with an incandescent blonde standing between blowsy, pink chrysanthemum-like flowers, a couple of bottles of cologne, Shehzad's hairbrush and comb, her own silver-backed set. Above these extended her body, still slender and narrow, her face as it was before she was married. She wondered how this was possible and moved closer to the mirror and looked into her eyes. They weren't the same she thought, and then:

perhaps eyes only show you what you already know. She ran her hand fleetingly over her belly and wondered when it would begin to show, how it would swell and curve. Shireen had begun to hint—heavy with the resentment of a misled shopper—that there was something wrong with her for not having conceived already, but she would not tell anyone just yet. It felt good, strong, to know something Shireen and Nazneen did not. Not just them, that no one knew but herself; it was the kind of anonymity you chose yourself, not the kind they thrust upon you when they told you to become what they wanted.

Things seemed different with Shehzad now. The flight back had been silent, but it had been a different kind of silence, not tense at all, blue like the cloudless sky in the evening. Still and cool. He had become quiet after Amina had said he must still love them. That had been a different kind, like the jagged edge of hot grey metal, but it seemed to have passed. Anyway, she was determined not to worry. She sang her favourite Farida Khanum song under her breath, *meiney pairon mein payal to baandhi nahin*, and beat her foot against the floor as if she could hear the happy bells of its phantom anklet. She flicked her wrist, as if picking jasmine from the air and turned a tight graceful circle. Perhaps it was time to start a work routine after all.

Waseem came to pick her up. As he opened the door for her, he watched her face as he was not yet aware had become a habit. She shook her head, trying to shrug off his eyes.

In the car he said, "I envy you the trip," trying to mean it.

She decided to pretend he did. "Shehzad was kind," she said and watched him stiffen and then relax and smile a bleak, fake smile.

"I'm glad."

"Please," she said, pleading, "I need you to understand. Please."

"You don't need to ask like that." She stared at his pale yellowy brown knuckles, transparent as a baby lizard's belly as he gripped the gear stick. "Never."

The car jerked and bucked over a speed bump. He swerved to avoid an open manhole. It had rained the evening before and little puddles had accumulated in ruts and bumps in the side streets. The car ran through several of these, sending spurts of muddy water into the air in dirty inverted raindrops. On one of the main roads a canal was brimming with water, sewage collected in scattered floating clusters, plastic bags, shredded papers, bunches of cotton stained with blood. If it rained again, the puddles would turn to rivers. Funny, she thought, the city was perennially short of water yet they couldn't manage two annual days of rain.

Once they passed the canal, she poked her head out of the window and smelled the air. The rain had cleansed it and the earth smelled as if the water had released some imprisoned magical essence. The long, curling algae-green of the mango leaves, the ubiquitous bougainvillea, the laburnum and gulmohar trees were suddenly spotless, like freshly bathed children, scrubbed and sparkling and warmly fragrant.

She turned to Waseem. "Let's walk in the lawn, let's ask Latif to make kachoris and let's have tea on the verandah."

"At once?" he laughed.

"At once!"

In the garden, the grass crunched damply under their feet. The clouds were an azure-infused slate with luminous white edges. Light filtered through in improbably straight shafts and fell in broad diagonal stripes across a row of shrubs here, revealing the gold in the emerald there, deepening a filigreed square of leaves to cobalt grey-green lit with molten silvery tips.

She picked a leaf to see how it would look on its own. "I miss Andaleep."

"Me too. She made you laugh. I was almost jealous."

"Don't be silly." She flicked his arm, glad that he was going to accept things, to accept her.

"I think Safdar misses her too. I think he's in love with her."

"Because she made fun of him for reading D.H. Lawrence? What did she say? 'The women are still only gateways to something else in Lawrence but you don't notice and expect us to be grateful'." Tahira tried to remember her words. "Where does she come up with this stuff?"

"I don't think women do that very often to him."

"Do what? Laugh at him or challenge him?"

"Either. He's made me read *Women in Love* and *The Sun* because he feels he has to answer her."

"Oh no."

"His mother liked her too. She said she was innocent and laughed aloud. Said it took courage to laugh like that."

"It does." They saw Intizar standing at the edge of the garden, uncertain of his welcome.

"Come walk with us," she called gaily, "it's lovely."

He walked over, grateful, still unsure. Tahira thought: I should be kind to him. He's my father. And he means well. He's a simple man, easily pleased, easily flustered. She smiled at him, kind, loving. "We asked Latif for kachoris and tea. Sit with us."

He knelt to pick a weed from one of the beds. "Let's walk to Haidery; we'll get jalebis to have with the tea." They walked in companionable silence to the market, negotiating puddles and mud. She said to her father, "I think silence has colours. What do you think the colour of this one is?"

He said, self-conscious with the poetic effort, "The colour of your skin when you were first born. Soft and unblemished and perfect." She put her arm through his and hummed. He stroked her arm and smiled a suddenly comfortable, easy smile. Waseem whistled and kicked a stone into a puddle, spattering mud all around. A sparrow flew into the air.

They reached the market. The jalebis spun in sizzling oil, little bubbles formed rushing spirals around the intricate whorls. The man making them was wearing a stained yellowing vest, chocolate skin glistening with sweat as he stirred and watched the oil. She wanted to draw him, to see the muscles take shape in her hand. To paint the transparent sheen of the oil in the huge black vat, the sizzling deep orange of the sweet as it cooked, the ripple of muscle and sinew, the knowledge of bone under living skin. They bought a pound and walked back, Tahira and Intizar nibbling at the crispness of the hot syrup-bleeding sweet.

When they reached the verandah, Waseem rifled through a pile of records, a dog, a gramophone and the label *His Master's Voice* on the sleeves. He placed a Mehdi Hassan record on the player, walked over and took a jalebi from the brown paper bag and lay back on the swing. It had begun to drizzle. The soft patter mingled with the sound of the tabla.

"It's good to be back," Tahira said suddenly. "I had thought that I felt some recognition when I first got to London, just because I knew the names and some of the history. But I think you have to share a present just as much as a past for true recognition."

Latif brought tea. Tahira poured it, prepared a cup with extra sugar and milk for her father. She gave it an extra proprietorial stir and handed it to him. The singer's voice teased the audience and the tabla with the refrain *Ghazab kiya tere waadey pe eitbaar kiya*. The tabla withheld resolution, weaved in and out of the singer's embrace. As if sound could dance, Tahira thought and then: but if one didn't believe in any promise, how would one live? She handed Waseem and

Intizar their presents, poured cups of the cardamom-infused tea already brewed with milk she and Waseem had requested and sat back, letting the music drift over them.

Waseem ran his hand over the book fingered the frontispiece of the *Songs of Innocence*. "Maybe innocence is the state of thinking things can only get better."

"And experience?" Tahira cradled her cup and inhaled the cardamom-milk steam.

"The realization that life would be unbearable if we didn't," said Intizar.

Waseem and Tahira turned to him. He never talked liked this. He smiled a quiet, half-apologetic smile, "Sometimes… sometimes…"

They smiled at him with tenderness and the sudden knowledge that his evasions must have a cost of which neither of them knew anything.

She thought about the stories he had told, in rare moments of garrulity, of growing up in Benares with a widowed mother and no money for books, or for the dowries of his sisters, or much else. How they had moved to live with their mother's older brother in Aligarh. She had gathered, more from the pauses in these conversations than from anything he said, that it had been difficult to be the recipient of his uncle's charity, that his aunt had made his mother feel the burden of every grain consumed, the pain of every new expense. How he had yearned to go to college and how, miraculously, his uncle had sent him after his aunt's premature death.

He had built his business up after that. There were little leaked snippets of treks all over U.P., of nights spent in railway station waiting rooms, the myriad unrepeatable humiliations of building a business in a society that thought serving colonial administrators was better than being a shopkeeper. Slowly he had made money, paid for his sisters' dowries. Then, his uncle had suggested he marry his daughter. Intizar had refused a dowry. Sometimes Tahira thought Mariam had still not forgiven her father for being pulled out of college and married to him. Nonetheless, they seemed to get along.

—~—

"So," Shehzad took the cigarette Waseem offered and allowed it to be lit, "I hear you're a socialist. He leant back in his sofa and took a deep drag, the tip glowed a bright inflamed orange in an ashy grey circle.

Waseem walked back to his place next to Mariam and attempted to resist the provocation. He said neutrally, trying not to be too flat, "Yes, I am."

The dinner had been difficult, Tahira thought, but not as tense as her family seemed to have expected. She had spent the morning helping her mother make arrangements. The preparations had been intense. She had participated with a kind of gay giddiness (He prefers biryani with green chillies, and no fresh coriander leaves on anything, sawiyyan but no almonds, lots of pistachios though. Make sure there are plenty of ashtrays around, and coca-cola). Her mother had agreed eagerly. Latif and Basheeran had fussed, hovering around her. Even Seema and Nilofer had presented themselves in the kitchen to help. Waseem had made an effort only partly visible to herself, who had attentively been searching for evidence, to join the family's enthusiasm, its burial of fear in frenetic preparation. Their eager compliance had thrilled—and hurt.

At home she had dressed for dinner, with a care and pleasure she realized was increasingly rare. Funny how being made to do a thing one enjoyed could taint the pleasure of doing it. Perhaps the trick is to find a way to protect the pleasure, to strengthen it with thought and practice. She applied the garnet-brown lipstick with sensuous precision, combed her hair, which fell thick and straight to her hips, brown-black with a faint auburn hint, and rolled it into a French twist. She had pinned a string of Arabian jasmine around it, tweaked the pallu of her henna-and-brick Benarsi sari and turned to face Shehzad with an implicit flourish, whose happy triumphant offering she quickly realized he simply hadn't noticed. He had emerged from the bathroom in grey gabardine trousers and a grey, blue and mauve batik shirt wild with a pattern of entwined, abstracted dragons and tropical leaves anthropomorphic with menace. The sleeves were short and made his arms and big, knuckly hands seem curiously exposed and—the thought pulled her up short—loveable.

He had seemed tense when she got home. She had attributed it to the dinner and hoped that the tension would dissipate in the presence of her family's evident sincerity, its palpable eagerness to please, to include and accommodate, to *agree*, she thought with emphatic optimism. Yes, to agree.

They left the house in silence, walking past Shireen, Farah, Nazneen and Shehzad's father, seated in front of the televison Tahira's family had sent as a replacement for the one they had given in the dowry. Shireen and Nazneen said limp goodbyes. Farah had been more energetic. Shehzad's father did not look around from the grey and white flickers on the screen. Tahira looked to Shehzad for some cue about how to leave, and unable to read his quiet *khuda-hafiz*, had walked over to Shireen, offering her head for her blessing. Shireen had run her hand over her with an ill-sounding, "Long may you live."

In the car, Tahira prayed, "Please God. Let it go well."

And for the most part it had been alright. Her sisters had been charmingly deferential, neatly dressed in similar shalwar-kameezes, lemon yellow for Seema, pale mauve for Nilofer, thin skeins of emerald and red embroidery winding around the necklines and hems and sleeves, plain georgette dupattas wrapped with tidy formality around their necks. They had asked polite questions about his trip to London, about his sisters. Seema had run to get him a glass of water, presenting it to him with an eager, befriending grace that masked, Tahira suddenly realized, a deep anger.

Intizar had talked hesistantly, but tried to be expansive about how he had gone to Bunder Road especially to get rabri for Shehzad, for he had heard what a sweet tooth Shehzad had, and which he shared himself. Shehzad had made an effort. Tahira wondered if her father had thought so. He was so shy. It hurt to see him so eager to please, almost servile. But, she thought, he doesn't need to be. Shehzad is making an effort. He's enjoying the food, even if he isn't saying much.

Intizar had talked about his work in the factory, and gradually Shehzad had begun to talk about the ever-expanding market for polymers. How it was the future, how his company would continue to revolutionize fabric, terylene and crimplene were only the beginning… Intizar had hastened to agree. Waseem had been polite, asking engaged, intelligently curious questions that convinced even Tahira of his interest in Shehzad's work, of his respect for him. Dinner had become less difficult.

Mariam, resplendent in an exquisitely draped plain slate silk sari, hair pulled back in a tight formal bun had presided, asking poised questions about his mother, paying his sisters elaborate compliments, on their propriety, their dress, their (Mariam insisted) abundant, evident affection for him.

But Tahira had worried nonetheless; Shehzad was stiff with Waseem, he approached his questions with a predatory bristle she recognized, as if searching for signs of disrespect. She had continued to hope that there would be no trouble, and so far it had been alright. Now she held her breath. Shehzad continued, "Isn't all that childish? As if the world can be changed. Human nature is just too corrupt."

Waseem tried not to wince at the cliché. He said, conciliatory, obviously restrained, "Perhaps that's a good reason to change it, to take human nature out of the equation, to make society change so that we're not at each others' mercy. So that we don't need to protect ourselves from each other."

Shehzad did not like the hidden patience in Waseem's tone. He tapped the tip of his cigarette against the lip of a turquoise Murano glass ashtray. "Yes, well, how will you get there? You need people to cooperate and they won't."

Waseem said nothing. Mariam tried to change the subject. "Beta, how is Asma? We didn't really see her after the wedding."

"She had to go back to her husband and children in Sargodha," he said curtly.

"We would have loved to have met him as well. What does he do again? I think your mother mentioned it but I seem to have forgotten. I'm so sorry."

"He's in the Air Force. You can meet him the next time they're in Karachi."

He turned back to Waseem. "Socialists are, *inaaoozubillah*, atheists. They'll be punished for that."

Waseem stubbed his cigarette out violently. Shehhzad opened his mouth to continue. Tahira spoke with obvious panic, "Would you like some more tea? I can get some."

Shehzad was furious at the interruption. He spoke over her. "The Left didn't want a separate nation. They're traitors. The Americans are right to crush the Communists."

Waseem couldn't stay silent any longer. "Most people didn't want a separate nation. The religious parties opposed it too. Or have you forgotten that? And how does selling the nation to America help you?" He had spoken with an inadvertent deliberate restraint, itself a provocation.

Tahira spoke again, reckless with desperation and guilt at the effort Waseem was making to control himself: "Please. Let's talk about something else. Something pleasant."

Shehzad smashed his fist on the table. "Shut up!" he screamed. "How dare you interrupt? Bitch! I picked you up from the gutter. You don't know how to behave. I was tricked into marrying you. Shut up."

Waseem began to stand up, fists clenched. Intizar stared in shock. Seema began to shake. Mariam gripped Waseem's hand and pulled him down. Tahira felt the all too ready tears gather in her eyes and prayed, "Please don't let them spill. Please." Nilofer used one hand to caress Tahira's arm with urgent quieting strokes and clutched Seema's hand with the other.

Shehzad continued, still screaming, each word emitted with hissing venom, "You deceived me into marrying her. You humiliated me with a second-hand television, with an inadequate dowry. I could have done better. I had options. I was ensnared."

Tahira's tears spilled over. I had almost forgotten this sensation, she thought, feeling her body become formless and heavy as spilled viscous liquid. She wanted to put her head on Nilofer's shoulder and sleep.

Waseem finally threw off his mother's hand. "You don't have to go."

Tahira waited for an interminable second for her parents to say something. The room was suddenly still and expectant. They said nothing. She said, "Yes I do," and got up to leave.

Waseem stared at his parents in disbelief. They scurried behind Tahira and Shehzad to the car. Mariam said, "Beta, don't mind Waseem. He's a hothead."

"Yes, please don't." Intizar rushed to open the gate.

Shehzad got into the car and leaned over, grim and impatient, to unlock the door for Tahira. She got in. Shehzad released the clutch with a violent jerk. The car bucked and accelerated in reverse. They pulled out of the driveway with a screech.

Tahira looked away from her parents as they receded into the house and thought: this is a curiously empty thing to think right now. But if this weren't happening, I would think it weren't possible.

The next day, after finishing his Isha prayers, and while Tahira was still praying in their bedroom, Shehzad went into his mother's bedroom to resume the conversation they had begun while Tahira was at her parents' house, preparing for the dinner. Nazneen and Farah were already waiting in the room. Afzaal sat in the corner, eating chikoos which he cut into thick chunks with rapid, impatient strokes, and which he then, with incongruous discipline, placed on the mound that was accumulating in the centre of the plate sitting on the laminated white formica surface of a folding table. He did not offer the fruit to anyone in the room.

The others grouped around Shireen's bed, at the other end of the room. Nazneen settled herself on the arm of Shehzad's chair, twirling her downward pointed shoe in little half circles. Farah wished she had the courage to make her brother recognize her presence with such poise and assurance. Shireen picked up where they had left off, wondering what had happened at dinner they night before. Tahira had been puffy-eyed all day and Shehzad seemed in a terrible temper. But as long as he was amenable… "You know, beta—we had such high hopes when we found Tahira for you. We thought it was a respectable family, and she was an educated girl so she wouldn't play games. But she's been a great disappointment." She paused to assess his expression. He seemed to be in an accepting mood, despite whatever it was that was bothering him. "Because…," she subtly shifted emphasis, injected a greater note of pity, "because she appears so indifferent to your needs."

Nazneen got up and stood behind him, kneading his shoulders, comforting, sympathetic. Each squeeze, every rub a reassuring reminder of loyalty. "You know Bhai, when I spoke to her friend Andaleep, (when she called I picked up the phone)," she inserted quickly, "she seemed to suggest that Tahira Bhabhi had spoken to her about you, said bad things."

Farah chimed in, worried she might be forgotten. "How disloyal. After all you've done for her."

"She stays in her room as if despises us, goes too often to her parents' house," Shireen continued as if Farah hadn't spoken. She wished Farah didn't have such an irritating voice, high with the desperation to be noticed. She had been this way since she was a baby.

"A new studio would cost a lot, but we could build an extension behind the kitchen," he said irritably.

"No. No. You didn't understand what I meant. It's *how* she goes. As if we were just nobodies, as if *your* house isn't good enough."

Shehzad closed his eyes and rubbed his temples. Nazneen began to speak again. Shireen looked up at her and put a swift finger to her lips. He didn't say anything for a while. Nazneen took his hands and placed them gently on the arms of his chair. She began to rub his temples and forehead. He sighed.

Afzaal skewered a piece of chikoo from the now quite impressive mound and asked from his corner, "Why is everyone so quiet? What's wrong?"

"It's Tahira Bhabhi," Farah said. "She's not all what Shehzad Bhai and Ammi had hoped for. Poor Bhai."

"Hmm. I thought she was very polite to me yesterday."

"You don't remember. You've forgotten how she walked past you twice day before yesterday, as if you weren't there. I can tell you, I had stiff words with her about that," Shireen improvised.

"Oh, of course." He lost interest in the conversation as the bronze mound beckoned and gleamed.

Shehzad frowned. "You shouldn't have had to. Thank you, Nazneen this is very comforting."

His head ached as he thought about what they said. It was hard to forget the annoyance, the embarrassment of watching Tahira's solicitude for that appalling brother of hers. During dinner she had seemed almost grateful to him when he spoke to Shehzad, when he showed an only proper interest in him, in his—her husband's!—work.

Aloud, he said, "Did you say yesterday that you preferred Tahira's watch to the one I bought for you?"

"Yes. It's so much more to my taste. So simple and beautiful. I thought Tahira Bhabhi would have known that. I told her before she left."

Farah wished she could make things up with such smooth assurance.

"Alright," he said, his eyes still closed. He got up with sudden resolution: "Alright" and left the room.

"But Bhai don't you want me to continue rubbing your head?" Nazneen called. Concern in the voice trailing after him, the beginnings of a satisfied smile on the exquisite bow of the mouth turned to her mother and sister.

Farah said what her mother and sister were thinking. "Now we'll have fun."

Shezad walked upstairs to his bedroom. Tahira was sitting by the window, a book open in her lap. Bruised mauve shadows lay under eyes puffy with crying. Shehzad grimaced with distaste. "Have you finished reading the book? My mother says you spend a lot of time in your room, so you must have had time to complete it."

She wondered what he was up to now. "You told me not to worry until we got back from London. And we have only been back for five days. But I have begun to read it again."

"Oh."

He thought of the night before, trying to retrieve his anger. Her little encouraging delighted smiles at her brother, the way she had squeezed his shoulder on her way to the kitchen, as if providing moral support in a situation of great distress. He had been forced into losing his temper, into seeming unreasonable and ill-mannered. If one couldn't expect loyalty from one's wife, how bleak and threatening the world would become. The anger returned: "That watch I bought for you in London. I would like you to give that to Nazneen. She likes it more than the one we bought for her. I think she feels I don't care about her enough. My mother thinks she's quite depressed."

The shocked expression on her face embarrassed him as tears could not. But it was done now. "I'm sure you won't mind. I'll get you a different one."

She took it off, tracing the band with absent fingers. "Let me get you the box it came in." She walked into the dressing room and pulled the top drawer of the bureau open gently, as if afraid of her own strength, placed the watch on the raised grey arc, centred the face carefully and handed the box to Shehzad. Then she turned away from the growing embarrassment on his face and walked into the bedroom to prepare for bed.

Waseem went into his parents' bedroom as they sat discussing Tahira. He had been unable to do much since the night of the dinner. It had been a week and they hadn't seen Tahira. He had wanted to call but his mother had told him that it would only make things worse for her. She thought Shehzad's anger was at least in part caused by jealousy. It was wiser for Waseem to lie low for a while. He had made Seema call instead, and then taken the phone from her, had expected Tahira to be cautious and subdued but was still sickened when she had begun to offer a pained, guilty apology. She had rung off quickly. That had been four days ago. He had to rely on his mother and sisters for news that she was alright. He laughed a hollow, sardonic laugh and slumped into the armchair. "So what are we going to do?" he asked listlessly, more out of habit than expectation.

He was, he reflected, becoming increasingly inured to contradiction. The family had tended to congregate in the large bedroom when not on the verandah. That had changed after Tahira's marriage. Now all he wanted to do when he was home was be in this room. But being in their presence enraged him even more.

His mother stood up to pull the curtains with a decisive swish. "We are going to ask her to leave him."

His head jerked out of its slump with shock. "Really? What happened?"

"We just thought it was for the best. Before it's too late."

"What do you mean?"

"Well… You know…"

"What does it matter if she's pregnant?"

"Don't be silly."

"I think she should leave him whether or not she's pregnant."

"We'll see." Mariam ended the conversation.

The next day Mariam went with Waseem to pick up Tahira. She seemed to have lost weight in the past week. Always slender, now she looked skeletal. Shadows lay under her eyes like decomposing moths. Waseem looked at his mother to see how she would react. She seemed not to have noticed. Then he saw that she gave her an uncharacteristically tight hug.

Mariam gave Shireen the presents she had brought for her, Afzaal and the girls. "Just in case," she had said grimly to Waseem when he had asked why. She said, "I wanted to come and pay my respects myself. I haven't seen you for so long. Please do come to our house for dinner soon. Please do.

"I hope you don't mind if we borrow Tahira for the afternoon. Of course, she's yours now. But you're too kind to deny us, I know."

Shireen grimaced, retreating from the juggernaut of Mariam's politeness. "Of course. Of course. When do we ever stop her from going to your house? It has nothing to do with us. She is," she said with a barely perceptible toss of her head, "her own mistress."

In the car, Tahira tilted her head absently out of the window after an initial polite inquiry into their health that made Waseem want to slam into the livid red mountains and winding archetypal river painted on the back of the bus in front. At home Mariam ushered Tahira into the bedroom. Waseem followed and inserted himself inside the door before Mariam could bolt it. "I'm staying for this."

Tahira sat down on one of the two armchairs facing the bed. Waseem placed himself on the bed behind Mariam. Intizar stood at the window, fiddling with a tassle on the curtain.

Mariam began to speak. "Beta, your father and I have been talking. We want you to know that we think you should leave Shehzad. It broke our hearts to see the way he spoke to you."

"Do you both think this?" She wanted them to go on. She had waited long enough to hear it.

"Yes." Intizar gripped the cord tightly. "We do."

"It's too late."

"Do you mean…?"

"Yes."

Waseem grabbed the blanket and bunched a handful into a tight, crumpled ball. “Do it. We’ll look after you and the child. I’ll look after you.”

She wondered if the charity of a brother was better than that of a husband. “What if he wants the child. What if it’s a girl? Who’ll marry her if her parents are divorced?”

BOOK
two

8

A few days after the first birthday of their son, Shireen announced to Tahira and Shehzad that it was time to consider the proposals that had been arriving for Nazneen. Shehzad was relieved. The nation roiled in shame. The generals were humbled. The leader of the party that had won the majority in what was once the West Wing of a slowly shrinking nation had been invited back to take the reigns by an army normally all too reluctant to concede power to anyone other than its own Sandhurst-buffed command. The defeat in the East was shocking and disillusioning and the pleasure of goading Waseem about the left's support for a '"democratic"' leader who was going to take over as Chief Martial Law Administrator could not make up for the pain and the shame and the uncertainty. Even if one didn't believe—and he most emphatically did not!—that the religious parties had colluded in the '"atrocities"' the foreign press insisted had occurred in the East. He needed a distraction.

He had another reason for being pleased. Something else was troubling him, something he was reluctant to name and hoped he would not be required to. He tried not to think of it too often. Since he was a boy, his mother had told him how necessary he was to the family. She had, with a complicity quite delicious to a ten-year-old boy (albeit when his father wasn't around), called him "little father." While his father was out gambling and philandering with his corrupt friends, he had sat with his mother and promised her he would look after them all. He would do what his father had failed to do. He would provide. His mother had told him that he was wonderful, that she was lucky, so what if his father was a gambler and a violent man. He, her son, she said with back-stiffening pride, would make up for this. He had snuggled against her, wriggling with pleasure and importance in his ten-year-old body, and felt adult and sophisticated and strong.

And he had tried over the years to live up to his role, as protector, guide and provider. He had done it, he knew, with patience and sensitivity, without undermining his father, without encouraging his sisters to disrespect, without showing any himself. He had put himself through college, even set aside money for his mother when he had none himself. He remembered days of being without food, of eating a handful of chanas to get by while he was at university and working, always working, thinking if he had only ten more rupees he could give them to his mother so his sisters and his mother would never be shamed, so they could behave like the respectable people, the *Shurfa*, they were.

He remembered vividly the numerous small economies—a meal skipped here, books borrowed from friends under elaborate, increasingly threadbare pretexts, and, after the initial crippling embarrassment, the growing camaraderie with Hasnain Baba, the cobbler, who had known his family back when they were in Bulandshahr in India. His mother had always said that the lower orders should never be allowed to see one's weaknesses; they were simply waiting to prey upon ones vulnerabilities. He had had dreams of crow-faced hordes swooping to pick eyes, pecking at heads, stealing the little gold hoops right off his sisters' bleeding ears for days after Shireen had first said this to him. But he had been, and remained, a good son, and he had not questioned his mother. His shame at the hole in his shoe, at the need for patches and elaborate repair work, had been gradually overlain by that odd camaraderie. The cobbler had joked and laughed and pretended that the shoes were not too beaten and still treated him like a Sahib. And he had responded with complicit laughter laced with an unacknowledgeable gratitude.

At university he had had many rich friends, had envied them their father's cars, their knowledge of futures assured by quietly made phone calls, the carefully placed word, the even more carefully placed uncle. He had struggled and overcome fear and a poverty all the more crushing because it could not be named, and he had become well-connected and popular and finally landed a wonderful job.

His mother had prayed with gratitude, had had food distributed at the local mosque with the money he had given her. The first thing he had done was pray. The second: tell his mother he would open bank accounts for his sisters' dowries. And then when he had received his first salary how proudly he had come to his mother and placed the entire amount in his mother's hand. How she had placed her hand on his head and said, "How proud I am today of my little father. Prouder than any mother has ever been." He had bowed his head under the weight of that hand, would willingly have put it under her foot, and felt that he had finally earned his mother's faith.

That had been almost fourteen years ago. He still gave his mother most of his money and now that Tahira was teaching Urdu at a nearby school she handed her entire salary to his mother each month as well. Even after he had married Tahira, he had remained loyal to his family, had not let her compromise, in any way adulterate, his loyalty. He had insisted that she accept his priorities without protest or even question. And she had seemed to do so.

He had loved his sisters. He remembered evenings when Nazneen and Shaista were studying. He had peeled pomegranates, squeezed oranges and taken trays to them when they were studying for their exams. He had wanted them to concentrate on their education in a way he had never had the luxury to do. He enjoyed their pleasure far more than his new-found affluence, which he had never ceased to find surprising.

But recently he had to admit he had found it difficult to mask his confusion at their attitude towards his son. He hoped Tahira hadn't noticed. Sometimes he was certain he could see pity in her eyes.

He loved Amina and his nephews in Sargodha and he had expected to love his son. But even prepared for love as he was, he had been felled from the very first instant he saw Armaan, tiny, his scrunched and wrinkled red raisin of a face, the sudden definition of a mouth open to bawl his hunger, hands feebly splayed in intentionless miniscule perfection. He had held him, arm properly angled under the neck, steadying his head, snug in the crease of his elbow, and loved the boy.

His mother had shown some enthusiasm but it seemed sometimes that it was strained. His sisters, especially Nazneen… he could hardly bear to think about it.

Aloud he said, "We will do whatever you want. Tahira will assist you. And I will give as much money as I can. Just let me know what you need."

Armaan wriggled in Tahira's arms, protesting against the hard swell of her stomach, reaching for his father. Shehzad took him, still delighted that his son wanted to be held by him, that he recognized him. He clutched him tight and buried his face in his hair. He smelled of shampoo, the milk skin of infancy, of Tahira.

"Isn't he beautiful, my son?" he asked his mother, wondering why he was asking, what it was he wanted to know.

"Of course. He takes after you—such fair, lovely skin."

Shehzad persisted, "It must be particularly nice to have your first pota." He handed Armaan to her, reluctant to relinquish him, fearful of what he would see but unable to stop himself, wondering what fatal urge made him do so in front of Tahira.

Shireen took Armaan and settled him gingerly into her lap. She made a number of listless stroking movements, bringing her hand slowly down in a loose arc that began at the top of his head and settled in her lap by his side, but which missed his body by a few inches. Armaan turned a toothless dribbling half-grin up at her, quizzical and inviting.

She smiled a quick rubber-band smile at him, "Yes. He looks just like you at that age."

Armaan flailed and feinted, gurgling with an ecstatic lack of discrimination.

Shehzad attempted possessive pleasure as he watched his mother, a little disturbed, a little puzzled at his disturbance. Armaan began to cry; Tahira attempted to lumber to her feet with more speed than she could manage. Shehzad rushed to get him, rough with the race. Armaan cried louder. Seized with remorse, Shehzad began to rock him back and forth on his shoulder. He paced up and down the room—restless with guilt—patted the small of his back, made indiscernible comforting sounds. Armaan's body was rigid with infant fury against his own. Soon it relaxed, his face settled into Shehzad's shoulder; the enraged sobs turned into small hiccupping whimpers.

Nazneen came into the room. She paused upon seeing Shehzad with Armaan, as Tahira sat fat and exhausted in the corner: "Bhai, let me take Armaan. You must be so tired after a long day's work. Why don't you sit and rest?"

Shehzad handed Armaan to her, glad she wanted to hold his son.

Nazneen began to pace, coming to a rest in front of Tahira and then turning back. Armaan gurgled at the sight of his mother, buried his face in Nazneen's white georgette kurta and a fat gobbet of drool slid onto her shoulder. She rubbed it with surreptitious disgust.

Shehzad said, "We think it's time to consider the matter of your marriage. You should let your Bhabhi know if there are particular things you want in your dowry." Nazneen stopped abruptly. Armaan began to cry. She patted his back roughly and began to pace again. Tahira began to rise to her feet. Shehzad motioned her to sit and said to Nazneen, "Here give him to me. I'll take him."

Shehzad had noticed the stumble. It showed a very proper modesty. He was glad to know his sisters were living up to their upbringing, to the family's reputation.

Tahira sat in the converted storeroom next to their bedroom that now functioned as Armaan's room, with a stack of dictation she had given her Class Two students that morning. She had placed a little desk for herself by the window. By the door was a table for changing nappies. On the wall behind the cot that was never used at night, since Armaan slept in their room in a second crib, her sisters had painted a large banyan tree with long hanging roots. Magical little people, fairies and elves, sat in the hollows, climbed the branches, swung from the roots. The tree bore three different kinds of fruit: at the bottom, apricots; then, pomegranates, and finally—"Of course," Seema had said—mangoes. The top of the tree skimmed glowing white clouds that turned into a large mass of land. The tree was Seema's idea, homage to her beloved *The Faraway Tree*. The walls were a bright apricot yellow. Shireen had said it was a waste of time and money. Farah had seemed to want to join in but had stayed away, out of loyalty to Nazneen. Shehzad seemed to have been pleased that her sisters were involved with the preparations for the baby. And now that she was working, she could use the room for work in the evenings.

She balanced Armaan on her knee while she marked the spelling test, wincing at the inept graphite squiggles, amazed that a script that had produced some of the finest calligraphic art in the world could be reduced to this. Armaan pulled at the edge of the notebook she was marking, almost tearing the carefully taped brown covering. "Don't Armaan. Some poor mother spent hours covering this little girl's books. I'll have to do it for you some day as well. Be good."

She pushed it away with the hand that held her pen before it tore further and held him a bit more tightly with the other. "Just let me finish this, beta. Please."

He reached with more determination for the book. She put it aside and pulled a rueful face at him. He gurgled and blew a series of spit bubbles at her. "Thhoo. You're disgusting," she said and wiped his mouth and pulled him close. It was difficult to fit him around her stomach. She pushed all the books further aside and sat him on the desk. He flailed and blew another happy raspberry at her. She touched his face, his huge eyes the beginnings of the Ehsaan family nose, the mouth that seemed permanently wet.

She thought about Nazneen's stumble when Shehzad had mentioned marriage. Was it modesty or was something else going on? She wondered if Shehzad had noticed. She was worried about him. He seemed preoccupied these days. She had hoped he hadn't noticed his family's attitude towards Armaan. She had been surprised by their lack of interest in him. Sometimes they seemed to resent him. Amina had said to her, "You don't know anything. Mamu still loves me more. He'll never love anyone as much as he loves me." She wondered what would happen if Amina said this to Shehzad.

Perhaps Shehzad had noticed something already; there had been a strange question in his eyes when he had handed Armaan to Shireen earlier in the day. Armaan smiled back at her, as she chuckled at the memory of Shireen's expression. She leaned over to kiss him in a complicated manoeuvre that involved tilting him forward and extending her neck so her stomach wouldn't push too far into the table, and breathed his milk and powder smell. The smell of uncorrupted flesh, she thought, when all can happen and possibility hasn't been extinguished by reality. When flesh and hope are one.

The lights went out. She groaned. It served her right for weaving portentous, metaphysical webs around a spitting, dribbling baby. Now what was she to do? The walk to the door with Armaan and her stomach would be difficult enough without the toys that had not yet been cleared from the floor. She called to Shehzad, "O, listen." She had, a month after Armaan's birth finally tried to call Shehzad by his name, thinking she was a mother now, but he had shaken his head and puckered into a look of pained disgust. So he remained permanently suspended in the vocative. In uncomprehending company it required ingenuity sometimes, but she had discovered a buried talent for inflecting pronouns.

"I can't see anything and I'm afraid for Armaan." Shehzad appeared at the door, the candle in his hand guttering as he moved. It cast long flickering shadows on the banyan tree; the hanging roots seemed to sway, swinging the fairy people.

"Here. Take the candle. I'll take him from you. We can sit on the terrace for a while." She followed, ungainly and heavy, feeling as she often did these days like a seal on stilts. Afzaal and Shireen were already there. She settled into a chair next to her father-in-law, knowing it would please him. It would annoy Shireen, but then most things did.

Tahira had concluded that what had begun as indifference to his family had allowed him to settle into a happily unconscious irrelevance. The rest of the family took him seriously only as long as they were remembering his past failures, which were worked into the varieties of grievance in the family, Shireen's, Shehzad's, Shaista's. Her father-in-law seemed to be playing his part by becoming a hollowed version of his younger self, quick to anger, equally quick to settle, easier with every day to appease and manipulate. Farah was the best source for most of the information. Some Tahira had gleaned for herself.

The lights were out for as far as the eye could see. The sky was a purple-blue, with the strange lack of depth of a watercolour wash. The trees were precisely articulated dense black shapes against the different hues of night. She sat back in the chair and drifted.

In the room she shared with Farah, Nazneen brushed her hair with rough strokes. The brush caught on a large bird's nest of a knot. She began to disentangle it and then broke it off with an angry tug, which brought tears to her eyes, drowning the ones already there.

Farah walked into the room. "What's the matter? Why are you crying?"

"I'm not crying. It's very tangled. I haven't oiled it all week."

"Are you sure? You don't look very happy. I'll oil it if you want."

"Not now. I have work to do." She braided her hair quickly into a thick short braid. As she walked over to her desk the lights went out and fan whirred slowly to a halt. Farah groaned, groping for a candle. "Let's go out. It'll be stifling soon."

"You go. I'm tired. I think I'll lie down."

Farah found the matches. She lit the candle, and walked out grumbling. "You aren't any fun these days. I don't know what's the matter with you." She bumped into the edge of the door, gave it a little kick, trying to balance the stainless-steel lid, from an old Nido tin, on which the candle was stuck with one hand while cupping the flame with the other. It cast large spectral shadows on the walls and doors, lighting her chin, which was round and dimpled and curiously out of proportion with the thin nose and narrow face, from below.

Nazneen crossed her arms on her notebook and made a bony pillow for herself. She closed her eyes and the features of a boy from her Chemistry class swung into view, framed by test tubes and pipettes and the flames from Bunsen burners. She had checked to see if he looked at other girls the way he looked at her, and learned that the regard of his beautiful intent brown eyes was reserved for her. Recently he had slipped a note in her copybook asking her if he could send his parents to her house. It was a respectful note, she had been glad to see. It didn't take liberties. She was pleased he knew she wasn't that kind of girl. She didn't know if she dared tell her mother or brother. She did like it when he looked at her, though. As if eyes could touch like the gentle ripples of water at the edge of an evening lake.

The electricity came on. Tahira and Shehzad walked back to their bedroom, shutting their eyes against the suddenly painful light. In the bedroom, Shehzad placed Armaan in the cot, covered him with the blanket. He changed into a pair of striped pyjamas and lay down next to her. He said, "It's a big responsibility, the wedding of a sister. We must do it well."

She shifted, trying to make herself comfortable without bumping into him. "Of course."

"It's hard to find good, caring husbands for girls. It can be a difficult life."

You could be married for two years, Tahira reflected, and not know whether the head on the pillow next to yours had a sense of irony or not. She shifted again, reaching as gingerly as she could manage to plump the pillow.

"Do you have to move so much? It's shaking the bed."

"Sorry. It is difficult. But I'm sure you'll do as much as you can."

He turned on his side, reassured.

Tahira lay still, trying not to move. From the corner of her eye she could see the slats in Armaan's cot, black againt the blue dark. Outside a car passed by, lighting the window. She felt rather than heard her son shift. He let out a little mew of sound. Shehzad began to snore. She wished she could turn onto her side and tried to sleep.

Tahira waited in the staff room for Nazneen and Farah to pick her up. They were to go shopping for Nazneen's dowry. Through the netting in the open widow she could see dozens of girls running in blue-grey uniforms, little frocks with white trim and, for the older girls white shalwars, regulation white socks and polished black shoes. They blurred and merged in purposeless manic circles, which swelled and shrank and swelled again, moving with the frenzied energy of a collective prison-break. One attempted to climb up the ancient tamarind tree in the centre of the yard, trying to pick the ridged, raw fruit. Another stood below, urging her on. She thought vaguely about intervening, glad when one of the English teachers made the protesting girl—"But it's home time Miss. Please, Miss."—come down.

Just outside the gate was a man selling corn, which he turned on hot coals, fanning them with frazzled attention as he sorted through the loud urgency of the girls clustered around his cart. He sold them the blackened cobs dipped in a special, fiercely hot tamarind chutney, the real attraction. He withdrew the cobs, dripping with the impossibly sour brown sauce, dotted with little visible flecks of red chili powder and without wiping them placed the cobs back in their pale, green stiffening skins. The chutney collected underneath, coalescing into tiny globular puddles. Tahira liked the little man, whom she, like the girls, called Bari Baba. Dark and compact with steel stubble that poked like little chopped needles out of flesh the colour of his coals as they flared, orange and burgundy pan-stained teeth and small, graying eyes, he reminded her of her Naana, who had died when she was thirteen.

She recalled her horror when she had learned he had been ordered here by Mahvish Butt, the Maths teacher. The school was relatively new and had a small student population. He had worked outside a larger one not too far away. Mrs. Butt who had winced pityingly at Tahira's English accent, and dismissed her as irrelevant as Urdu teachers usually were, until she had seen her reading a book on European painting, had told her the story: She had driven by Bari Baba's cart and tried the corn. It really was very fine, especially the fiery chutney. She had told him to come and to stand outside their school. He had protested, saying there wasn't enough custom there. She had reported herself as saying: "Do you know who I am? I'm Colonel Butt's wife. I can have you picked up and beaten." She had produced a gratified chuckle at Tahira's look of shocked horror, mistaking it for stunned admiration and said with conscious modesty, "It was nothing. It was easy." Tahira had thought it must indeed make things easy to have such moral freedom. After that, she had barely been able to stop at his cart, but she had forced herself to chat to him. He had a widowed daughter, he said, and a grandson. His hopes were pinned on him. "My life is over, Bibi. Now I live for them." She slipped him money for his grandson's books every now and then, and gave him clothes for his daughter, a shalwar-kameez for him at Eid. She told Waseem. He said, "We need a revolution, instead we trim a little here, even less there, give it away and make ourselves feel better about ourselves." He had given her some money for Bari Baba, nonetheless.

She saw the driver at the gate and got up gingerly, bumping the edge of the table with her stomach anyway. Two months to go and then a day of tearing pains, of heaving effort and another beautiful silken baby, flailing and unfurling. They tore your body and left you with love settling invisibly inside, tight as the coils of inescapable destiny. The simile lied as they so often did. It wasn't as if destiny had been escapable before. It felt heavier now, she argued with herself, and then smiled as she looked down at the jutting prow of her stomach. She imagined the baby suspended in amniotic fluid, which sloshed and ebbed as she moved. She thought: Some ships carry seas within them. If one has to be entangled by destiny, and who said there was ever any other choice, perhaps this isn't so bad. And then: Or perhaps it is.

She followed Muazzam Khan, smart in a company uniform, carrying her bag, and a stack of notebooks to be marked, smiled a quick, apologetic goodbye at Bari Baba and got into the front seat of the car. She turned to greet Nazneen and Farah. "*Assalam alaikum*. What should we do about lunch? Should we stop somewhere first, or go for chaat after the silk shop? We can go to the jeweller's after that."

"Oh. Let's go for chaat." Farah was delighted.

"Nazneen?"

"Whatever you want."

"Okay." Sunglasses were a mercy, rendering all smiles equally sincere. She turned around, relieved that sitting in the front seat made conversation impossible in her current condition.

The drive was long. She was glad she had had a Fanta and samosas and sandwiches at break, still astonished at how much she could eat. In Saddar, the traffic was a cluttered cacophony. The indiscriminate irritation of horns, the invariably burst silencers of rickshaws and scooters tore the air. Next to their own car, a Vespa scooter weaved quickly through the glacial inch of the traffic. A woman rode pillion, clutching a little girl in a white uniform stale from the day, her pigtails bobbing with each jolt. Tahira smiled at the girl, who smiled widely back, revealing two missing front teeth. Above her head, her mother's dupatta was a dusky amethyst nylon fluttering dangerously in the wind. Tahira decided to smile at her too, glad at the possibility of human recognition, however temporary, fragile or imagined. The scooter moved on.

They pulled up at the silk shop. Tahira climbed up the stairs, clutching Farah's elbow to steady herself. Nazneen followed, quiet and, to all appearances, unconnected. The owner sat on a raised dais, his great barrel of a paunch cradled in his lap, a lush moustache covering his upper lip. Emerald and ruby, ultramarine and turquoise silk, plain and intricately woven, formed a tightly folded wall behind him. He recognized Tahira, asked after her mother, ordered Cokes, ignoring their protestations, for all of them. An adolescent boy with spidery fuzz above his mouth stood ready to pull out the fabric that spread like spilled ink onto the bright white sheet covering the dais.

Tahira, under instruction to get Nazneen whatever she wanted, spoke when Nazneen just sat there saying nothing. "Which ones would you like to see?" Nazneen pointed indifferently to a jade *tanchoi* and a magenta and gold sari, which opened to reveal entwined paisleys almost half her height, waving and possessed, like the rocks in a Persian miniature.

Tahira braced herself, and finally asked softly, "Is something wrong? You don't seem very happy."

"It's nothing," Nazneen brushed the question angrily aside.

Farah said, too loudly, "I don't know what's wrong with her. *I'd* be excited if I were in her place."

"Sshh," Nazneen and Tahira hissed in unison.

The shopkeeper smiled vague, embarrassed distaste at them. His assistant hoped his eager efficiency would be noticed by the beautiful fair girl with the lovely lips. They bought five saris, turquoise, pink, the jade *tanchoi*, the magenta *benarsi*, a two-tone grey-mauve with the thick raised gold embroidery of *karchob*.

They drove a little distance and got out at the entrance to the narrow lane that held the chaat shop. Farah paused to look at some bangles, shrugging irritably when Nazneen snapped, "Don't dawdle!"

Tahira smiled apologetically. "I need to eat something."

Farah said, "Sorry. I'll hurry, but I *really* don't know what's come over her."

At the entrance of the shop, a mound of cubed potatoes, boiled chickpeas decorated with coriander leaves, green chillies and thinly sliced wilting tomatoes sat in front of the man handing out the newly filled plates to the waiters, dipping the dirty returns in a bucket behind him. Flies buzzed and settled on the garnish. Tahira, Nazneen and Farah walked to a bench covered with torn ragazine against the back wall. The stiffened torn edges bit into Tahira's flesh.

After they had ordered, Tahira tried to tease Nazneen, uncertain as usual about why she was trying. Perhaps, she had thought sometimes, humans aren't capable of being in such proximity with people without caring about them. The thought always foundered on the argument that Nazneen and Shireen refuted the hypothesis, exposed its deluded innocence. Then she felt a fool.

She said, "It's okay, you don't have to be shy. What do you think of the doctor with the fat mother and the mole on his cheek?"

Nazneen shuddered.

"I think the engineer who travels to Europe is exciting. Think of how much she'll get to travel, Tahira Bhabhi."

"What does it matter? I'll do what they want me to." Nazneen stared defiantly at them both.

"But you must be excited. How abnormal you are Nazneen." Farah took an experimental bite of the chaat the waiter had just handed them, and then spooned some more masala into the mix of chickpeas, yoghurt and tamarind chutney.

Nazneen turned to Tahira. "Anyway what does it have to do with you? Just because you're shopping with me, doesn't mean you're anything but an outsider. So why don't you mind your own business, and stick to what you can do."

~

Tahira, Shireen and Shehzad catalogued the proposals:

Ahmar Sheikh: college teacher. Respectable family. Roots in Lucknow. Tall, quite fair. "No." Shehzad and Shireen agreed. Respectable family, but no prospects. "Pity," Shireen said, "the children would be beautiful and fair."

Fareed Qazi: doctor. Good practice. Large family from Bareilly. Six sisters. Very good prospects. Mole on the right cheek was a bit large, Shehzad thought. "Too many sisters," Shireen said. "Her life will be hell."

Bareilly had a famous madhouse, Tahira remembered but did not say, startled to be so included in the process of selection—"It's your Bhabhi's role," Shehzad had instructed Nazneen gravely. "Otherwise the boys' families will think we are not respectable people. It must be done with propriety." She was only glad that Nazneen would be gone and unable to exact some protracted, duly artistic revenge for her involvement.

Tariq Saleem: Merchant Navy. Small family. Mother-in-law dead. One sister, living abroad. Good future.

Unfortunately, from the Punjab. "Sad," Shireen said. "She would have ruled in that house."

Qamar Usman: Engineer. Very respectable family from Aligarh. Two sisters. Not much money yet, but excellent prospects. A bit short. Would probably become round when he was older.

Shireen and Shehzad agreed. "He sounds like the most promising candidate. I liked his mother and sisters. Very dignified and they seemed as if they would treat her well. Perhaps we should ask Nazneen what she thinks," Shehzad said. Tahira wondered if she should say she suspected there was someone else.

Shireen shook her head, irritated, puzzled. "Why?"

"I want to make sure she is happy."

"Very well."

Tahira was sent to call Nazneen from her room where she was studying. "Can I come too?" Farah asked.

"Sorry. I think it's married people only. Don't look at me like that. I don't make the decisions here."

It took longer than normal to walk to and from Nazneen's room and the drawing room where they were having the conversation. Shireen said, "*Uff.* We've been waiting for so long."

Shehzad motioned Nazneen gravely to a seat, "We have made a decision. We wanted to ask what you thought. Whether you have any objections."

Shireen shook her head as if to ensure everyone knew *her* objection to these new-fangled notions. She hoped Nazneen would not be silly enough to admit that there was anyone else. It wasn't as if Shireen would let anything happen in that direction, whatever it was. She wasn't dead yet.

Nazneen shook her head.

Tahira thought fast, and decided it had nothing to do with her.

9

Tahira folded a scarlet blouse and a heavily worked crimson-and-gold dupatta and handed it to Farah. She was helping her pack the clothes and jewellery Nazneen would need at the beauty parlour, so that her hair and make-up could be worked into and around her jewels and the dupatta. She carefully disentangled the supports for Nazneen's earrings and placed them in a box with a kundan satlara and plain gold choker. "Be sure to count everything. Nazneen might be too tense to remember and once the dupatta has been pinned in place, she won't really be able to move freely. Your brother will pick you up, and you can come home and dress yourself. I would come too, but I'm sure Nazneen would rather be alone with you. In my state, it's just as well. If Qamar's parents hadn't been in such a hurry, we wouldn't have agreed to have the wedding so soon." She felt a sudden rush of warm water down her thigh. "Oh. I think it's coming. Call someone."

Farah ran to her mother, who was setting out her sari shoes and jewellery to match. "How inconvenient. Couldn't she have waited two days? I suppose the driver can take her before he takes you to the parlour. I'll call her mother."

"Shouldn't someone go with her?"

"She'll manage. Women give birth in the fields after all, without doctors or all this modern drama."

"I didn't know you knew people who had had babies in fields." Farah paused, arrested at the possibility, "Who?"

"Tcch. Just go and tell her. It's good that Armaan is already at her mother's house."

"Maybe I can go with her and you can take Nazneen to the parlour."

"Don't be ridiculous. Now go and tell her and the driver what to do." Farah joined Tahira, who was already at the door, clutching the edge for support.

"Can you get my bag from upstairs please? I don't think I can go up."

Farah ran up to get the bag and then helped Tahira into the car. "We'll call your mother right away."

Tahira tried to wind the window down a little, sliding in her seat as Muazzam Khan turned the corner at the end of their street. The seat-covers, which had just returned from the laundry, were searing white horizontal streaks. She felt the stickiness of the shalwar clinging damply to her thigh. Muazzam Khan looked anxiously in the rear-view mirror to check she was alright. "We'll be there soon, Bibi. I'm driving as fast as I can."

They pulled up at the hospital. Muazzam rushed out of the car and grabbed an orderly. The orderly called for a nurse. Tahira gasped, "It might be coming soon," as a wave of pain was followed by a contraction. She thought she would fall, and wondered what would happen if her legs just gave. She tried experimentally to let go and found she couldn't. The nurse commandeered a stretcher and another orderly. They manouevred Tahira onto it. The nurse clicked by her side, coming in and out of focus, pert in her white uniform and then a streaky blur. The stretcher complicated the contractions, which pulled and tore, even as she was rolled ahead. She thought with eerie lucidity about the different arcs of movement, her body caught in their eye, and clenched her fists, biting on her lip, and felt the sudden taste of iron on her tongue. They rolled her onto the bed. Another nurse joined the first, ushering the orderlies out as she entered. A doctor came in. Brown faces and eyes bobbed and weaved, alternating with burning golden-black flashes, as she closed eyes resentful at their intrusive persistence. A brisk voice said, "Come, come, ma'am, you can do better than that. Now *push*!" reminding her of an old schoolteacher she had hated, a sudden focus for her growing rage. Hot white surges of pain were followed by an ironic moment of relief and then a wrenching pressure and another unbelievably hot white surge. She thought she might faint and couldn't, so she screamed instead, furious with herself for having expended the extra effort.

After an hour in which disbelief, rage and pain alternated, she gave a final push and felt a little plop and the slithery rush of afterbirth. She heard a wet slap and a shocked wail. She thought, I can sleep now and I can have my body back. Then with more certainty: Yes it'll be nice to have my body back. The doctor brought the purple-red body, thick, black, springing hair defying the damp and placed it on her own, suddenly empty and separate. The body unfurled and tightened. Tahira remembered seeing a sea anemone, curling and uncurling in slow aqueous motion. She placed her lips on her baby daughter's damp forehead and thought: perhaps it is worth it after all and then: are love and resentment to be forever mingled?

Shehzad rolled over and lay back, panting, staring with unseeing eyes at the ceiling. Outside, the noise of the traffic was at a mid-afternoon ebb, but still loud. The ceiling fan spun, muted somehow by the cool dark of the room. His heart returned to its normal pace.

At his side Aneela, still under the sheet, inched to the edge of the bed, and sat up. She pulled a large towel off the chair next to the bed and wrapped herself in it, still sitting. "I have to leave."

"So soon?" He wondered why he asked. He had to leave himself. Nazneen's wedding was that evening and he had to be at the scene early to make sure things were going smoothly.

"Sorry. Yes."

"Anyway. You have to go to get back, don't you?"

"Yes." But her haste did seem unseemly.

She walked into the bathroom, swaying with the awareness of being watched, the towel suddenly tighter around her body. It was odd, he thought, the way she covered herself after they had finished, with a sudden access of modesty, happy to stand naked before him when she first arrived. The coyness seemed to come later as if no longer an impediment to other urgencies. He heard the toilet flush. She came out, dressed only in a blouse and petticoat, full breasts, wide hips, finely arched eyebrows and a full, long mouth. She leaned over to pick up her sari, a sharp deep line between the flesh curving out of the v-shaped neck of the blouse. Shehzad imagined the weight of her breasts, tumbling like loosened hair into his hands, nipples stiffening between his fingers. She stood up and began to drape her sari. He wondered what it would have been like to have married her.

She looked up, brow still furrowed with concentration from measuring the width of the falls on the sari, and said as if she knew what he was thinking. "Same time in three days?"

"Yes."

"By the way, when is your wife due?"

"Any day now."

"Hmm." She flicked the sari over her shoulder, smoothing

it over her chest, walked over to where he lay, ruffled the tight, abundant curls on his chest, and left.

Shehzad lingered, brooding, his arms folded under his head. He remembered the first time he had seen her, four years ago. He had been having dinner with some English colleagues at the hotel. She had been with a group of friends, men and women mixed. He had seen a friend of his from university days among them. He had gone over to greet him, aware of her startling unguarded interest. The next day, his friend had called to ask if Shehzad would be interested in calling her. Her name was Aneela Khan, the daughter of the prominent diplomat, Mohsin Akhtar Khan.

A meeting had been arranged. She had arrived late, wearing a white shalwar kameez. Diamonds glittering at her ears, a long gold chain around her neck, poised and unafraid. She had responded to flirtation with frank flirtatious interest. The next time she had invited him to meet at the house of one of her friends. She had a key, she had said, and her friend would be out during the day.

Later, he had been to her house and met her family, introduced as a friend, of whom there might be, he had thought, far too many around. He had not enjoyed meeting the family, was certain he had detected a wince when he had declined her father's offer of a drink. He had hoped she didn't drink. She hadn't that day, but sometimes he wondered. He remembered the disconcerting array of sepia and more recent black and white photographs in the drawing-room. Generations of Khans sat in rows in schools with the leaders of India and Pakistan, at events with colonial viceroys and nawabs and rajas, stood behind world-famous figures as pacts were signed and accords confirmed, laughed at dinner with Jinnah and Liaqat Ali Khan and General-presidents. He had become uncomfortably aware of his own English, competent but with a more pronounced accent, and lacking the generations of assurance and poise conferred by that sepia display. He had, with gratified malice, later identified the way Aneela's father spoke as mutant Pakistani-Oxbridge—"what, what" in brown face, the absurdity of the English upper classes worn like an ill-fitting cast-off!

He had thought fleetingly about the potential embarrassment of a meeting between their families, relieved that that was impossible anyway—of course, you didn't marry women who had already yielded to you. He thought now that she had never even seemed to hint at marriage and wondered what that meant.

They had continued until a friend of his father had suggested Tahira as a prospect. His mother had proceeded with the arrangements. Tahira's family was rich, part of the displaced Indian Muslim Ashraf, but it wasn't part of the older moneyed Oxbridge-educated set. He had felt confident in the presence of its newer money—and it wasn't as if they lacked respectability. After all, they were part of the old Urdu-speaking gentry from U.P.

He had been good to Tahira, he thought. He had stopped seeing Aneela when he married. She had called a few months after their wedding and they had flirted but nothing more. Then Tahira had become pregnant. He shuddered with distaste at the memory of hearing her retch in the bathroom, the sound making him ill himself, of the growing intrusion of her body, its graceless immensity. He had called Aneela and arranged a meeting. He had considered breaking it off again after Armaan was born, but had reconsidered. After all, it would not have been right to be so cruel to Aneela. He could not do that!

He stood up and stretched, reached his arms towards the ceiling and massaged his armpits, releasing the tension. He climbed into the tub and took a quick warm, unsatisfying shower, hopped out and pummeled himself with the towel.

He put on his brown safari suit, pulled a small comb out of his pocket and combed his hair carefully. It was beginning to gray at the temples. He stared at the face in the mirror: long frond-like lashes fringed, heavy lidded, large, dark brown eyes, a nose stiff and proud as any Ehsan's, finely curved nostrils, a broad face and thin sculpted lips, gave the Waheed Murad-like strand falling across his face a loving flick and put the comb back in his pocket. He walked to the door, turned a rapid eye around to check that he hadn't left anything behind, smiled at the rumpled sheets, left the room and walked down the stairs. In the lobby, he slipped an envelope with the key to the clerk in the lobby, meeting his complicitous grin with a blank stare that shrivelled it like a salted slug, and walked to the car.

He drove to the wedding-hall, pulling up in front of the ethereal trellises of the white gate, Gulistan Shaadi Hall emblazoned in waving red Urdu letters above. The shamiana, where the food was to be served, extended out and to the right of the hall in a precise L, bright with a pattern of emerald and scarlet clubs on a thick saffron cloth, stretched erect on the poles, providing taut walls, a livid ceiling. Inside the hall, chairs were arrayed in neat rows. On the raised dais, a dark green sofa was flanked by two chairs on either side. A glass coffee table stood in front. Behind the sofa the decorative backdrop—a screen of steel-wire and coloured paper bunched and moulded into a tight weave, conveying a very distant suggestion of a garden of flowers—rustled and crunched as men, adjusting chairs and placing tables, scraped against it.

Shehzad had been there in the morning and made sure the preparations were in place. He walked to the section where dinner would be served. Behind the wall of the shamiana, the deghs were already bubbling on large wood fire, the woodsmoke mingled with the smell of onions and roasted spices, dissipating their heaviness. He sniffed the air appreciatively, greeted the head cook, and walked back under the tent to make sure there were enough plates on the tables.

He saw Shaista arrive with her husband, who wandered off to taste the food.

"It seems under control. Can you think of anything else that needs doing?"

"I'll look around and make sure."

"Thanks. I haven't been home all day."

"But I was here an hour ago and you weren't."

"I had to do some errands for work. How's Nazneen?"

"She's fine but Tahira's pains seem to have begun. She was taken to the hospital."

"Oh. I better go then."

"I'm sure she'll be fine. Armaan wasn't a difficult delivery."

"True. I have to go home to get ready anyway, though."

Waseem sat in his room, working on a draft of a piece he was planning to submit to a local newspaper on the dangers of any left collusion with the military.

We have already seen the effect upon the morale of the left of the Chinese backing for the last military government. Now the nation has been reduced to one wounded wing of a bird that once had the potential to soar to great heights. That is still possible, but only if we are canny and if we admit that our current leader is not an innocent and unwitting beneficiary of a military adventure. He has been instrumental in the loss of the East Wing, but many on our side act as if he is an innocent bystander, picked up by accident for deserved glory.

The nation remains in shock, and we should, of course, be glad that the military is out of power, but we have learned to be too grateful for only the smallest of mercies. The kind of shock we exhibit at accounts of what has happened in the East Wing is the result of a disbelief that comes from the shaking of our deepest delusions, but we must use the clarity of this moment. We must learn to overcome servile gratitude for only the smallest of mercies and find the courage to demand more.

There was a loud, hard knock on the door. Seema flew in, barely waiting for his "come in." "Tahira Apa is at the hospital. There's no one with her. Shireen Auntie said she tried to call more than hour ago and couldn't get through. But no one was on the phone. Anyway, Amma says you need to take her to the hospital right away—it's the driver's holiday.

"Of course." He ran around the room, looking for something, he wasn't sure what.

"What are you doing?"

"Looking for my sandals."

Seema saw them poking out from under the bed. "Here take them. Hurry."

He grinned sheepishly at her, sliding his feet under the overlapping swatches of worn black leather.

Mariam was already waiting at the car, clutching and unclutching the handle, as if expecting to find the door unlocked at the next try. Waseem took her hand, squeezing it hard to calm her, unlocked the door and held it open. "Hold on. I'm going to drive very fast."

At the hospital, Tahira was asleep but they were shown into her room. The baby was brought to them. Mariam took her granddaughter. Waseem reached instinctively to place his finger in his niece's hand. Both bent down to kiss her, bumping their heads against each other. She started to cry. "Can I hold her?"

Mariam handed him the baby. She stretched and yawned as he cradled her, and he wondered how such fragile innocence could be born of so much injustice. He thought about what a good father Shehzad was, and wondered why he was not as comforted by the thought as he had hoped. The baby began to cry as if sensing the sudden tension. He handed her to his mother.

"I'm going to have to go to the wedding."

"Why?"

"Shireen will raise hell if I don't."

"I'll stay with Tahira."

"No. I think you should put in an appearance at the wedding. Why don't you go and get Seema, and I'll stay here till she comes. I can come back after the wedding."

"How I hate those people."

At the wedding, Mariam walked up to Shehzad, "Congratulations on your new daughter. What will you call her?

"My mother suggested Saira. Will you be spending the night at the hospital?"

"Yes."

"Will you tell her I'll come to see her tomorrow. Today was too busy." He had intended to stop by before the wedding, but his mother had insisted she needed his attention on a number of, she had said, *pressing* matters. He wished he could confide to someone that he had realized she had made up their urgency.

"Of course. She'll understand you have many responsibilities today."

"I do."

On the dais, Nazneen's dupatta was lifted to cover both Nazneen and Qamar. Nazneen's new mother-in-law pressed their heads down while Shireen held a mirror under the veil—their first official glimpse of each other of themselves together in the mirror. The symbolism made the women cry. Waseem and Nilofer stood just below one corner of the dais, waiting to ascend to have their photographs taken. Armaan leaned across from Waseem's arms to tug at the shining cascade of pearls and gold spilling from Nilofer's ear. "Don't, Maani. It's already heavier than you are."

"Why are you wearing it?"

"I don't know. We're of an age to begin to make an impression, Amma says."

Waseem turned to the ceremony on the stage, "Please have the sense to rebel before they do this to you."

She grinned at him. "Don't you think it's quite erotic?"

"Not you too?" He rocked Armaan mechanically, trying to still his restless reaching.

"No. But you get so annoyed, it's even more fun. Wonder if you can call it erotic shock." She gestured at the newly minted couple.

"Shock—certainly." He grimaced. "And then the long slow attrition. I wonder, though, if the shock ever *truly* dissipates."

Nazneen saw her face reflected next to her husband's and began to cry. The mothers exchanged happy knowing glances.

"All modest girls cry at the prospect of leaving home. We are lucky, indeed, to have such a daughter-in-law." Qamar's mother tucked Nazneen's dupatta back in place.

Shireen said, "Look after my daughter. I've brought her up with great, indulged care."

Nazneen tried not to think of what lay ahead, wondering if she should have spoken about that other boy, if it would have made a difference. Now she would never know.

The next day, Shehzad called Aneela from the office. "Tahira's in hospital, so I'm free this evening."

"Okay."

"It's a girl."

"Congratulations."

After work he went to see Armaan, who had stayed at Tahira's parents the night before. It was embarrassing to be so dependent on her family for such things. But his mother and sisters were preoccupied with Nazneen, so what else was there to be done?

Armaan was fitful and irritable. He hadn't seen either of his parents for two days. He screamed and pummeled as if angry at Shehzad, refusing to settle in his arms. Shehzad handed him back to Seema with an apologetic smile. "I'm sorry to have to leave so soon. I haven't seen Tahira or the new baby yet. Thank you for looking after him."

"Of course."

Armaan screamed, body curved and resistant as an overstrung bow. Seema gripped him tightly with both arms, making soothing noises to calm him into relaxing the electrified arc. As Shehzad was pulling out of the driveway, he strained towards it as if trying to fly to the car. Seema turned around and took him inside.

At the hospital, Mariam was sitting with Tahira as she held her daughter. She left as Shehzad entered.

He held out his arms for the miniscule parcel, swaddled in a pink flannel sheet with tiny yellow daisies. "How are you?"

"I'm well and you?"

"Alright."

"How was the wedding?"

"It went well. Nazneen was a graceful bride." He stared intently at his daughter. "Ammi Jaan says we should call her Saira."

"Okay."

Saira opened her eyes, and appeared to look straight up at her father. "She's looking at me. Isn't she beautiful?"

He pulled the swaddled bundle closer into his flesh, feeling it's warm miniature imprint through the cloth. She was darker than he remembered Armaan being, and had large, very bright, eyes. He traced the tiny triangle of her chin with a reverent finger and thought about how to describe the feel of her skin.

"You know what her skin feels like?"

"What?"

"Like the very soft film that forms on hot melted wax as it starts to cool. Do you know what I'm talking about?"

"I think so."

He moved his hand around Saira's head and found the soft indentation on her scalp, and was suddenly very afraid for her devastating vulnerability. He closed his eyes at the sudden rush of fear, then swallowed and opened them. He bent his head to kiss her and stood up, handing her to Tahira. "I think I'm in love."

Tahira took her and smiled a pale, tired smile.

"I'm afraid I have to go."

"So soon?"

"I have to take a client out for dinner." He bent his head to kiss his daughter's head one last time, breathed a lingering breath of her skin and left, hoping he wouldn't be too late.

He walked out into the evening air, stepping aside as a stretcher was rolled in, followed by a doctor crying urgent instructions to some one behind Shehzad. At the edge of the stairs a woman and young girl sat side by side, saying their rosaries. He hoped whoever they were praying for would be alright. He walked to the car and wondered why Tahira had looked so wistful. Perhaps he should have brought flowers, or at least something from the sweetshop. He would try to remember tomorrow.

~

The next morning Waseem paused at the door to Tahira's hospital room. The night before, after returning from a rally with trade union workers, he had gone to Hill Park for kebabs and drinks with Safdar. They had been trying to decide whether Safdar should stay with the Party, or join one further to the left. Waseem had already decided that he wanted nothing to do with it. The events leading up to the war had confirmed his ambivalence; the leader's refusal to hold discussions with the party that had won the most votes in the East, simply because of what no one was bothering to hide was a racial objection, had seemed obscene to him, and he had said as much, at great length. Expediency had never been his greatest skill. Perhaps his family were right to think of him as a hothead.

Last night Safdar had told him that rumours were already swirling thickly, about the CMLA's autocratic tendencies, a desire to centralize authority not just in the capital but in himself, already the first whiffs of the all too familiar stench of an uncontrollable urge for power. Safdar had sighed, laughed and leaned his head deeper into the backrest, "I don't know whether to stay with the Party. It does have the popular support to be effective and important, crucial changes could be made. On the other hand, I feel I should join a Party that reflects my convictions better. I suppose even the dilemma is a luxury, after years of military rule."

"The "democratically" elected leader refused to accept the results of the democratic election, colluded in a war that lost us part of the country, and accepted the post of Chief Martial Law Administrator. What do you mean: *after* years of military rule?

That's when Safdar had seen them. "Isn't that your brother-in-law?" Then he had added quickly. "No. It's someone else."

Waseem swiveled to look out of Safdar's window. A streetlight, a searing burst curving from a rigid shaft, dropped light in a nightclub circle on a car not too far away. The woman in it was a laughing, sensual profile. Waseem didn't think he had ever seen Shehzad laugh like that, relaxed, delighted.

Now he swore under his breath, prepared a face and knocked on the door.

"Come in."

He entered to see her feeding Saira from a tiny bottle.

"How's my favourite sister and my favourite niece? How come you're alone?"

He waved the flowers at her, a little too heartily, he realized.

"Can you put these in the vase? There's an extra one in the cabinet. Amma had to go home and bathe. She said she would be back soon, and I think the girls are at college. Look at her. I don't think she sleeps and see how greedy she is."

Saira uncurled a tractionless fist against the increasingly transparent plastic, paused to draw breath, gulped and started pulling at the teat again. Waseem watched Tahira as she looked down at her daughter—she seemed tired and strangely wistful—and realized he couldn't tell her. He wondered how he had ever thought he could.

10

Three months after Saira's birth, Tahira sat down at her desk with guilty disbelief. She couldn't quite understand how she had managed not to write to Andaleep for more than seven months, but time seemed to have acquired a strange elasticity. Some moments stretched interminable as an insomniac's night, others merged into a rapid clutter of soiled nappies, screaming children, bottles endlessly emptied, refilled, heated, emptied again.

My dear Andaleep,

I'm so sorry I haven't written for so long. It's no excuse to say this but I will anyway, the children keep me so busy and I haven't stopped working, except for a month after Saira's birth. It is a luxury to be able to leave Saira and Armaan at Amma and Abba's every day.

People are surprised that my mother-in-law hasn't forbidden it, but I give her my salary every month, which means she doesn't complain. I think she doesn't like the children going there so much, but she likes the money and the alternative would be to have the children in the house, even with Basheeran. So she puts up with it. I do enjoy watching her struggle sometimes.

You've kept a remarkable silence on the subject of my painting. You must be bursting with the effort!

She paused, absently rolling a stray lock of hair around her index finger, until the corkscrewed curl tugged her scalp.

I haven't given up. At least, I don't think I have. As you know, the first few months of each of my pregnancies were absolutely wretched. I had to stop and then I wouldn't even draw because I was so unhappy. I certainly couldn't paint. I'm sure it makes no sense, especially since my parents built an expanded studio suite for me on the top floor of the house. Perhaps I was just compounding my unhappiness. But I did try to make things a little better by getting the job, thinking it would make me think less about things. I remember how pleased you wrote you were. Waseem was too. His silence on the subject has been even more remarkable than yours.

After Armaan was born I was busy and distracted and then the second pregnancy… Can one ever really explain these things? I'm not sure I can. Time is precious and daunting and…

She stopped again. The explanations seemed indulgent, amorphous. Her reasons—elaborate pretexts for avoiding the truth: that she would never paint again. She had even thought once—absurdly, she realized—that perhaps she needed to be happy to paint. But what kind of a reason was that? She wondered why suddenly she felt compelled to explain.

But I've promised myself

The resolve firmed with the drying ink.

that I will begin again soon, definitely before Saira is a year old. Sooner I hope, but I'm trying not to be so ambitious that I end up disappointed. I think I have an idea for a series.

Tell me how you are. I worry about you. There's a reticence in your letters I can't describe. What is it? Or am I being fanciful?

I must stop writing now. Armaan and Saira are asleep at the same time for once. It doesn't happen often, believe me. One of them will be up any minute.

I miss you more than I can say. I'm glad you'll be back soon. I wish it weren't just for a visit.

Your loving friend,
Tahira

She folded the grey-blue puzzle of the aerogramme, turning the trapezoid flaps and portruding strips into a neat rectangular envelope, wrote Andaleep's address and put it aside, grateful that its enforced brevity cast a respectable veil of necessity on letters that had steadily shrunk since her marriage.

She walked to Saira's crib. She was beginning to awaken. Tahira reached under her to see if her nappy needed changing. It did. She walked to the next room to get a clean one and new sheet to cover the plastic on which she lay, savouring the last moments of silence. Back in the bedroom, she wiped Saira and folded the thick, white triangle around her, securing the pin by pushing it into the receptive, red smile of a bright, plastic clown's head.

In the cot adjacent to Saira's, Armaan began to stir. He had been fretful of late. Her mother attributed it to Saira's birth. She had said it was only to be expected now that Tahira's attention was more divided. Tahira tried to compensate to the best of what, despite Basheeran's help, felt like ever more sapped abilities. She reached to pick him up, to embrace and soothe. He seemed hot. She knelt to open the top drawer of her bedside table, looking for the thermometer, trying to reassure him with the tightness of her grip, nuzzling his hair with the side of her face. She rummaged in the drawer, pushing aside a postcard of a Lebanese beach, a ballpoint pen encrusted with a rubbery leaked wrinkle of royal-blue ink, a skin-coloured prayer book with a gold tassel for a bookmark and lilting Arabic letters surrounded by salmon and turquoise leaves suspended in a broad horizontal gold trellis, then remembered that she had loaned the thermometer to Shireen a few weeks ago when Afzaal had the flu. She straightened and went to get Saira from her cot. "Hush Armaan. It'll be okay. Let's go and see what's wrong." Saira began to cry. She rocked her gently, walking to the stairs. Halfway down, the staircase swerved into the sliced cross section of a gyre, the stairs narrowed at one end like the base of a tightly fanned hand of cards. With two children, the descent required concentrated slowness. She walked carefully down the wide end.

In the lounge at the bottom, Nazneen and Qamar were having tea with Shireen, Afzaal and Farah. Qamar stood up to help as she reached the last few stairs.

"It's okay. She'll manage." Shireen waved him down.

"It's no problem." He attempted to take Armaan from Tahira. Armaan turned away, shrieking his protest, burrowing into her collarbone in an attempt to reenter her body.

"I'm sorry. I think he's not well. Do you mind taking her instead?" She handed Saira over. Qamar took her gingerly, less certain about what to do with an infant her size.

Tahira turned to her mother-in-law. "Do you remember the thermometer I loaned you? May I have it? I want to check Armaan's temperature."

"What thermometer?"

Tahira wondered why every conversation had to turn into a tedious ritual of recalcitrance and supplication. Her son wasn't well. She was not, she decided with sudden, irritated assurance, in the mood to propitiate. In the event, she didn't have to. Farah said, "I remember. It was when Abba Jan had a fever."

"I'm sure I returned it."

"But I saw it on your dresser. I'll get it."

"Thank you," Tahira smiled gratefully at her.

She sat down next to Nazneen, wondering why she looked so listless. Beautiful, in a pale lemon, silk suit, clusters of seed pearls glinting on her ears, but listless. Tahira liked Qamar. He was polite and helpful, and seemed to mean well, accommodating and kind to Nazneen. She wondered why Nazneen didn't appreciate his adoration, why she didn't realize how precious it was, how rare.

In the months since Saira's birth and Nazneen's wedding, they had seen fair bit of Qamar. He had been invited to dinner a number of times, but would sometimes accompany Nazneen without invitation, seeming to expect no ceremony, visibly uncomfortable at any attempt to honour his status as a son-in-law. Tahira tried not to compare his disarming ease with Shehzad's punitive choreographies of withdrawal and reticence and rage.

Farah handed her the thermometer. "I washed it for you." She inserted the thin mercury filled tube under Armaan's arm, pinioning it against his body, which wriggled and slid like an eel eluding capture. "Let me help." Farah waved a hypnotic spoon above his eyes. Saffron flecks of laddoo flew about, one settled on Armaan's nose.

Qamar handed Saira to Shireen. "Do you mind? I'll be back in a second." Shireen extended reluctant arms beneath an eager smile. Saira stopped crying. "See? She knows how much you love her," he smiled at his mother-in-law—who smiled thinly back—and escaped into the bathroom.

Tahira withdrew the thermometer and squinted, trying to locate the mercury thread through layers of glass, white paint and microscopic numbers. "It says 101. What should I do?"

"Just give him some medicine, he'll be fine. Anyway, placing the thermometer under the arm doesn't give an accurate reading."

Qamar came out of the bathroom. "Armaan has a fever," Farah announced to him.

"Oh no! We could take him to the doctor I know. Shehzad Bhai has the car."

Nazneen had had enough. "I think your mother said we had to visit someone at five. Look: it's 4:15. I'll have to go home and change."

He cast a worshipful eye at her face. "You don't need to do anything."

Shireen intervened. "He's fine. It's not too high. I know these things."

He turned regretfully to Tahira who was looking for a means of escape so she could call home and ask Mariam what to do. "I'm so sorry."

"Please. Don't worry. I hope you won't mind if I don't see you out," she waved a helpless, apologetic arm in Armaan's direction.

Everyone left to see them off. Shireen began to hand Saira back, retracting her arms as she caught a glimpse of Qamar's quickly veiled surprise.

Tahira dialled her parents' number, telling herself such panic was only to be expected from a young, new mother. She stared as the thick white numbers seemed to rise up from the bulbous black curves of the phone. Finally, Waseem answered.

"Armaan's not well, and there's no car, and I don't know what to do."

"I'll be right there. I'll bring Amma. She'll know what to do."

Later that evening, Tahira sat cross-legged on the bed, rocking Armaan gently on the folded triangle of her leg. He had fallen into a restless sleep, interrupted with little whimpers that woke him up, after vomiting twice. She watched over him with panicked love. Earlier in the day she had looked on as the doctor placed a stethoscope against his skin, pulled his lower lids to peer into his eyes, inserted a black sharply tapered nozzle into the dark whorl of his ear. Armaan had cried louder with every intrusion; Tahira had tried not to resent each violation as much as her son.

The doctor had said that he wasn't absolutely sure what it was yet but the mild yellowy hue of his eyes suggested some sort of jaundice. He had written a prescription and instructions for a blood test, to check for hepatitis. They had driven Mariam and Saira home, where they decided Saira would stay until the risk of infection had passed, and then taken Armaan for the blood test. Tahira flinched at the memory. She had watched with intent masochism as the steel pierced his flesh, gagging as the crimson rush surged up the syringe.

Now she looked up from his face as Shehzad walked into the room. Shehzad took in the scene, her absent expression, Saira's empty cot, Armaan's restive sleep and walked over to the bed, controlling his fear, "What's wrong? Why didn't you call me?"

"I'm sorry. I didn't know what to do. I asked your mother but she said I shouldn't call you; you would be busy. The doctor thinks it's jaundice. I have to take him back tomorrow. He had a blood test. They're waiting to see if he has hepatitis."

"You should have called me. Next time there's an emergency, do. How did you get Armaan to the doctor's?"

"Waseem took me."

He sat down, loosened his tie and held his head. "Tell him how grateful I am." Seeming to mean it.

She looked at him, surprised. He asked, "So what do we do now?"

"We wait and we give him plenty of liquids."

The next day Shehzad took her to the doctor himself. Armaan's fever was high. His forehead burned a hectic, flushed red and he had retained little of what he had eaten. On the way they picked up the report from the laboratory. The doctor glanced gravely at the report, said it was hepatitis A. If the fever didn't abate by evening they were to take him to the hospital.

Shehzad drove them home, the most apologetic she had ever seen him when he told her that he had to return to work. In the car there had been a strangely fortifying new camaraderie, a pact of mutually checked panic. Shireen and Afzaal were in the lounge, reading different sections of *Jang*, when she entered carrying a winded, grizzling Armaan.

Shireen asked, "What did the doctor say?"

"It's hepatitis. He says if he's still retaining nothing by the end of the day, we should admit him to the hospital."

"Is the expense really necessary? I'm sure he'll be fine at home. Hospitals are expensive." Shireen folded the newspaper and placed it on the table, along with her glasses. Tahira paused and stared at her mother-in-law's face, a naked war between contempt and fury taking place on her own. "Do you care about anything other than money? I do earn you know, and my parents will help if necessary. Your son doesn't have to contribute a rupee if he doesn't want to."

She turned and walked up the stairs, gripping the wooden banister to contain her rage. The wood felt smooth and full in her hand. A splinter, a graze, any roughness would have concentrated her rage she thought, and gripped the wrought iron grille beneath to steady herself. It bit satisfyingly deep into her hand. An exhausted ache had been gradually spreading across her back since breakfast. She stretched slightly from side to side and straightened to relieve the pressure. Armaan shifted on her shoulder. She thought: now there'll be trouble and realized for the first time in longer than she remembered that she didn't care.

Late that afternoon, Tahira called Shehzad. It was time to take Armaan to the hospital she said. He was admitted immediately. Tahira, watched, tears dripping off her chin, as the doctor inserted the needle attached to a drip into his arm. He lay supine and inert, too tired even to grizzle at this latest invasion. Unable to bear the sight, Shehzad paced just outside the open door. He was dehydrated, the doctor said, but he would be okay. Shehzad hoped the echoing hollowness of his assurance was a result of social ineptitude, not some more evasive hopelessness. They sat by his side—Tahira with the prayerbook she had hastily shoved into her purse before she left, Shehzad with the rosary she extracted from it and handed to him—and waited.

The next day Waseem walked to the hospital gate from the bus stop, a few yards, away. He was half an hour early for the official visiting hours. But clusters of people were already present outside the gates, in the little strip of garden, in the lobby. Tiffin carriers with food for patients, and the one official attendant each was allowed, were rushed into rooms, given to families waiting outside for the attendants to come out with news. Outside the hospital, a row of laburnum trees sentinelled the wall. Underneath these, the vendors inched and shifted throughout the day, searching for what shade they could find: a man sold corn, another crushed ice, successively doused in sweet, lurid, dark green, maroon, brown syrups, a third a varied assortment of chaats and cold drinks.

Waseem paused to buy himself a gola ganda: he loved the cold intemperate taste of colours nowhere to be found in nature, and which, he often said, only, a madly defiant artifice could have conceived. His sisters teased him, saying he liked the idea more than the fact of the ices. He bit into the subsiding pyramid, wincing as the sugary cold hit his teeth and shot up behind his eye. He was not looking forward to seeing Shehzad. They had, he supposed settled into a truce of sorts, but he couldn't bring himself to like the man. He had never overcome the sense that an explosion was imminent. It made conversation unbearable, hobbled, tense, immeasurably more difficult because Shehzad wanted to be engaged. He seemed to take it personally if Waseem avoided conversation on politics or religion. After that catastrophic first fight, Waseem had experimented with a number of strategies. At first his mother had suggested he avoid Tahira for a while which, he remembered with a sudden surge of bile, hadn't been difficult. She had seemed eager enough on her own. For a while his anger at Shehzad had been surpassed by his anger and deep hurt at Tahira. Perhaps it still was. But what most people didn't realize, he told himself, was that all hurts became stale. Perhaps enforced proximity, or maybe simply the fact that his sister would be treated worse if he weren't civil—or ingratiating—ensured that they ceased to be relevant.

Shehzad had seemed to want to see him, had taken them all out for dinner. There had been no apology. Waseem was still convinced that Shehzad detested him, which made his desire to talk all the more puzzling. At that first dinner, Shehzad had not brought up politics either. But since then there had been arguments. Initially Waseem had said nothing, and then had realized with increasing bewilderment that his silence would be understood as deliberate insolence. So he had engaged, polite, distant as if he didn't hate every word of it, and then realized that even more was desired. He wondered if Tahira realized that she had become the gun held to his head in these conversations. Now the knowledge of that woman in the car made him even less eager to see Shehzad. Why couldn't he just go see his nephew?

He braced himself and entered the gates, crossed the lobby, walked past a Rorschasch blot gallery of paan stains, spotting a predictable butterfly, a crab, a fallen foreshortened giant, and turned the corner to see Shehzad gripping the railing that looked out upon the front of the hospital. Behind him the door to Armaan's room was open. He could see his mother's silhouette, head covered and bent in prayer.

He had tried all day not to think about Armaan. The family was quietly devastated. He was the oldest grandchild, adored by everyone, had quickly become Mariam's particular favourite. She had been at the hospital all day. Intizar had visited once already, as had Nilofer and Seema, taking turns so someone would remain with Saira. They would be coming again soon.

His pace quickened with fear. Shehzad turned to look at him.

"Is everything alright?"

"So the doctor says."

Waseem gripped Shehzad's shoulder and said, "He'll be alright. Don't you worry. He'll be fine."

Shehzad smiled gratefully at him. "Thank you for taking him to the doctor yesterday. It was very kind."

"How can you even mention it? Do you mind if I go inside and see Armaan?"

"Of course not."

Waseem entered. Tahira was hunched over the bed at Armaan's side. He looked thinner, limp. He opened his eyes as Waseem greeted his grandmother and flashed a smile flickering with a tired glint of mischief. Waseem realized he had never seen him awake with no tension or struggle in his body. He walked over and drew an affectionate circle on his stomach.

There was a knock at the door. "I hope we're not interrupting." Nazneen transformed the courtesy into an accusation.

"Of course not. Please come in." Mariam stood up hurriedly, clearing newspapaers, bags, some of Armaan's toys off the extra chair.

Waseem walked to the door, "I'll wait outside."

Nazneen laughed softly, "I didn't mean to drive Bhabhi's family out."

Shehzad and Qamar were just behind her, smiling, indulgent. Waseem wondered if blindness were a form of stupidity or a brilliant evolutionary tactic. He smiled and left the room, murmuring politenesses indiscernible to himself.

Tahira looked up from Armaan's side and pointed mutely to the rosary in her hand.

Nazneen turned to her brother. "If Bhabhi had an extra one, I could pray too."

Shehzad handed her his own, smile widening with gratitude.

Outside the room, Waseem and Mariam stood by the railing and tried not to exchange revealing glances.

A keening wail suddenly shredded the air. A middle-aged woman stood at once side of the entrance, hitting and clutching her head with both hands, crying, "Save my son. Someone save my son. He's dying. Please someone save him." Next to her a grey-haired man with despairing eyes stood with his hands at his side, watching the woman. People walked by, some staring openly, others trying discreetly to avert their eyes. A man, clothes as faded as theirs, went up to her. "What is it, Bibi?"

They didn't have money, the woman said, for the medicines, for the operation. More people gathered around as they heard the story, shaking their heads in a communion of helplessness.

Mariam shivered. "Maybe we should do something for Armaan's sake. I feel so guilty."

Waseem bit his lip. "I'll go and see."

Shehzad sat at Armaan's side reading him a story about ducks, a dog and a lake. The book had vivid primary coloured pictures with long-lashed animals that looked like ungainly humans. Armaan didn't understand much but he liked the sound of the words and their vague connection with the pictures in the book. He was almost completely well, and would be discharged in a day. Tahira had finally gone to her parents' to see Saira and take a proper shower and a nap. Shehzad tried to suppress his growing jealousy at the supportive presence of Tahira's family. Shireen, Nazneen, Farah and Afzaal had visited at prescribed times. Shaista had pled the fear of infection to her own daughter. He knew he couldn't speak about it to Tahira. Her concern for him, and she showed it in little ways he sometimes noticed, embarrassed him. What right did she have to pity him? Why did she ask with such concern whether he was tired, if he was alright, if he had eaten at home? As Armaan's condition improved she had urged him to go home and rest. Sometimes, he thought, she was exploiting the situation, hoping to create a rift between him and his family by performing an extravagant concern. Of course, Shireen couldn't come as often as he would have liked, she had to look after his father, and Farah was just an unmarried girl. Nazneen had new obligations at her in-laws… The list wearied him. The impulse to make it even more so.

Tahira arrived, carrying food for him, including his favourite—special samosas filled with daal and an abundance of green chillies and little dashes of mint her mother had made. He heard himself snapping at her about the unnecessary waste of time and food and saw her wounded face. She had no business looking betrayed, he thought, and snapped more and tried not to think about his family. Before he was married he had never had to make excuses for them, never doubted their affection for him, their absolute committed loyalty.

He hadn't been able to see Aneela while Armaan was ill. Perhaps it was time to call her. He would do it from work the next day.

~

Two days after Tahira and Shehzad brought Armaan home from the hospital, Nazneen and Shaista visited in the late afternoon. After Tahira had gone upstairs to change Saira's nappy, Shaista turned to Shireen, "I think we should tell Shehzad now."

"Tell me what?"

"Come into my room," Shireen said. "We'll have more privacy, that way. Farah bring me another cup of tea." She walked to her room followed by Nazneen, Shehzad, Shaista and Amina. Afzaal lay on his bed, propped by a heap of pillows, reading the latest copy of *Urdu Digest.* A technicolour woman, like a miniaturized version of an actress from a film billboard, full scarlet lips and waving eyes, stared seductively from the cover. The children arranged themselves around Shireen's bed.

Shehzad thought of Tahira's parents' room when they had gone to pick up Saira after Armaan had been released from the hospital. Saira had lain moated by pillows in the centre of her grandparents' bed, while Intizar and Seema entertained her with a silver rattle and a swimming pool, blue and yellow plastic butterfly that opened and shut its wings. She seemed happy. Intizar had stopped shaking the rattle when Tahira and Shehzad walked in. Shehzad had noticed the sudden cautious veil that dropped over his father-in-law's face—almost like fear—with irritation (as if he were frightening!) and a crushing sense of exclusion. Seema had stood up, smoothing her kameez self-consciously. He had envied Tahira the certainty of her family's affection for her children. He wondered if Saira and Armaan would ever be as welcome in this room.

Above the beds was a picture of a valley in Kaghan. The mountains were angular, stiff, sharp ridges extending downwards from snow-capped peaks, softening and spreading upon reaching the valley. The floor of which was wide and flat, scattered with gravelly pewter sand and level with a deep, pale blue lake.

"Shehzad," his mother said sharply. "You're not listening."

"Bhai doesn't listen much since he got married," Nazneen smiled her reproach.

Amina, curled up next to her mother, looked as if she were about to cry.

Shaista watched Shehzad and her mother, uncertain whether she should speak. Farah entered with her mother's cup of tea and looked around. "Why is everyone so tense? Bhai, you look so angry. You should be happy, Armaan is better."

Shehzad ignored her, speaking to Nazneen instead, "How can you say that? How can you of all people say that?"

"What do you mean?"

Shireen interrupted, "Beta, we are very upset. You don't seem to realize what's going on. Men are simple—they don't understand these things." She paused to take a sip of tea, closing her eyes as if battling the desire to abandon the unpleasant but necessary task ahead. She took a second fortifying sip.

"What things?"

"You know... the way Tahira and her family have been behaving."

Afzaal who had been immersed in his magazine, looked up suddenly and said, "What have they done? I hope they've been behaving well. You really should keep them in line, Shehzad." He settled back against the pillow.

Shehzad looked down, trying not to lose his temper. "How have they been behaving?" he asked with conscious control.

"Well... you don't know this. I didn't want to say anything before Armaan recovered, but Tahira was very rude to me the day you took him to the hospital."

"I know. She told me."

"She did?" Shireen was genuinely astonished.

"Yes. What else?"

"I don't know what to say, if you aren't outraged by that. Whoever said you should raise your sons and then just hand them over to their wives was wise indeed."

"What else?" He demanded.

Amina sat straight up to watch what would happen next, shifting her mother's suddenly rigid body.

Nazneen spoke. "I really don't think you should speak to Amma like this."

"I want to know what else."

"Very well." Shireen continued. "They made us feel unwelcome at the hospital. They took over—as if Armaan weren't our grandson as well."

"Enough!" Shehzad shouted. "Do you take me for a complete fool? Do you think I don't know what has been going on since Armaan's birth? You have no love for my children. You have never had any interest in them. Do you realize how humiliating it has been for me: watching Tahira's family support her, take care of our children?"

"They're doing it for the display."

"No. They're not. I can *see* how much they care. And I've been pretending to myself since Armaan's birth that this isn't the case. You know, in the hospital his grandmother offered to pay for the treatment of a young man whose family couldn't afford to. I pretended—*lied*—that you had given some money too, but she wouldn't take it. There I was, reduced to pathetic lies, because I was ashamed of my family's indifference, ashamed and fearful to think that you might have been manipulating me all these years. Her parents and siblings were constantly present, and the ones who weren't at the hospital were home looking after Saira. You people seemed to grudge every moment you spent there—and it was only nine days."

Nazneen shifted irritably and began to speak. Shehzad rounded on her. "And you. You, my favourite sister, what have you done, but been involved in the crudest family politics? I never expected this from you, of all people." He got up and left, slamming the door furiously behind him. In the room his sisters and parents exchanged stunned looks. Amina began to cry.

"That woman," his mother said, "has finally turned him against us."

11

When Tahira finally tried seriously to begin painting again, she found her chief obstacle was not Shehzad or Shireen or Nazneen, but memory. She had no idea what to do or why she was there. The brushes—soft, thick, fine—the paints—cobalt and ochre and vermilion and thick bright white—the easel were disconnected, insuperably separate. What they had to do with each other, or she with them was unfathomable. She tried touching the brushes, walking closer to the canvas of an older unfinished painting she had put up, away from the easel in the middle of the room towards the charcoal and chalk and glinting steely tubes of oil paint on a shelf against the wall. The tubes lay inert as bodies without souls, waiting for some igniting spark. She supposed she ought to provide it but had no idea how—or even why. The stained apron, the smell of the turpentine, the soiled rags were not just distant from her, they marked, she realized, the insurmountable distance between epochs.

She had expected some difficulty but nothing quite like this, none of this engulfing sense of loss in a room that seemed suddenly too large. The windows, which had been washed and cleaned for the occasion, let in a startling clear light that was just soft enough to permit shadows and reveal the shapes hidden within things. She noticed the thought and the observation with which it came wrapped, but still didn't know what to do.

She walked into the next room to collect some objects; perhaps arranging them for a still life would kindle something. Basheeran sat with Saira in her lap, a chuckling Armaan crawling around her, entertaining both the children with an array of toys and tales of life in her village. She picked up a deep cobalt vase, a large, unglazed, clay plate and wooden stand, and a pewter bowl with elaborate delicate embossed patterns, outlined in brass, surrounding repeating scenes of men in turbans and women veiled with seductive decorum. Armaan crawled up to her as she collected the things, trying to follow her into the next room. She put the objects on the table and knelt to scoop him up and kiss him, holding him aloft, shrieking with glee, legs wriggling in the air.

"What am I going to do, Maani?" she whispered and put him down and walked back into the studio.

She replaced the canvas on the easel and arranged the vase, bowl and plate on a silky cream cloth. The objects stared at her, still and refractory, echoing the sullen blankness of the canvas. She sat in a chair by the window staring at the arrangement, got up and moved the bowl so that it bit more into the vase, which stood in front of the left hand third of the plate. She heard her children and wished she could join them. The thought surprised her. She had wanted for so long to be able to do this. She had even resented her own children, she thought with a prickling of guilt, as if her inability to paint were their fault.

She sat still, staring at the objects, for an hour, until Basheeran came in to ask if she would like a cup of tea. Tahira turned away from the canvas, smiling gratefully at the interruption, "I would love some. I think I'll go and make some with Latif; you stay with the children."

She walked downstairs to the kitchen, passing Seema and Nilofer's open door. Nilofer sat with her books, studying. Seema lay on her side, reading *Frederica*, curled like a snail. Tahira paused at the door. "Aren't you meant to be studying?"

Seema groaned. "Not you too. Waseem and Amma are enough. I will study; don't worry. Just let me finish this—there are only twenty pages left."

"Isn't that my copy?" Tahira peered at it. "Actually, I wouldn't mind reading it myself."

"I thought you were painting."

"Yes. But it's not happening. Maybe it never will."

Nilofer looked up, concerned. "What do you mean?"

"Just that maybe I've forgotten how."

"I'm sure that's not true." Seema sat up. "You better not let Waseem Bhai hear you say that. He'll nag incessantly."

"I know," Tahira laughed. "But maybe that's what I need—or something… I'm going to get some tea. Do either of you want something?"

"I'd love an ice-cream soda." Nilofer said.

Seema said, "How you drink that stuff, I don't know. You'll turn a bright, bright green and glow in the dark like some phosphorescent undersea creature."

"It helps me concentrate. I just stare at the glass and enter a different state."

"The whole family is mad. Obsessed with colour." Seema turned to Tahira. "What did the in-laws say about the return to the painting?"

"Shehzad's mother made some remark about my wasting time and neglecting the children. I don't know why. Then I said I could always leave the job. And that was that. It usually works. She likes the paycheck too much." She turned around. "I need my tea."

She arrived in the kitchen to see Latif taking the kettle off the stove. "I need strong tea." She reached into the refrigerator, looking for anything to prolong the trip.

"What is it, Bibi? What would you like? I can make anything you want."

"It's nothing. Don't worry. Just some strong tea, with a clove."

She found an apricot on the second shelf in the fridge, a rose-blush on the small pale yellow fruit. "I'll just wait here for the tea." She leaned back against the cabinet, wondering how long she could stay in the kitchen, stalling. Latif handed her her cup and Seema's drink on a tray. She went back upstairs.

People spoke, she thought, of the expulsion from Eden as an access of knowledge; but she wondered if they ever thought about how Adam had known where to sleep, how to light a fire and forage when the earth was suddenly transformed into a bewildering tangle of predators and jungle, if they realized that you could learn about good and evil and forget the most elementary habits of existence. She remembered a couplet from Ghalib: "We have been listening through the ages of the expulsion of Adam from Eden/ But it was with a great loss of self that we left the street where you lived." But even he had not named memory as the divider, as the marker of loss and the obstacle to peace in the new world.

She walked into Seema and Nilofer's room, placed the livid green glass on Nilofer's desk, picked up the tray and went back into the studio, somehow startled afresh by the emptiness of the canvas, the reproachful stillness of the arrangement. She wondered whether she had expected the canvas to fill up in her absence. She placed her cup and saucer next to the tubes of paint and thought about squeezing some paint onto the palette. She picked up the cup, took a lingering contemplative sip, placed the cup down again. The pattern of small sky-blue roses and pale green leaves on the ivory china was conventional, a safe, pretty contrast to the dim swirl of remembered ambition in the room. Suddenly the thought of having to do something, anything, with whatever came out of those tubes terrified her. She picked up her cup and walked back to the chair by the window, and stared at the easel like a connoisseur deep in tranquilized thought.

Almost half an hour later—a half hour in which the warm concavity of the cup had been a mechanical, calming recourse—she heard Saira crying, a loud wailing fury that set off Armaan. Soon they were both crying like qawwals intoxicated by their own music. Tahira stood up and went into the next room. She had neglected her children enough for one day. She looked at her watch. It was four-thirty—almost time to go home anyway. She walked gratefully into the room and took Saira from Basheeran, "Hush. I'm back."

It took fifteen minutes of walking, pacing, rocking, a little singing to calm Saira. After that, she walked downstairs, pausing briefly to say goodbye to her mother and went to the car. She gave Saira to Basheeran, who got in the front. Muazzam Khan would drop her back before dinner. Armaan sat in the back in Tahira's lap, pointing to the fluttering bright purple and magenta plastic flaps on the back of a rickshaw, trying to jump out of the car at the sight of the young boys playing cricket in one of the lanes. She cuddled and humoured mechanically, and then with a growing present pleasure, glad that she didn't have to think about what to do in the studio until the next day.

"How was your first day back in the studio?" Shehzad asked, heading over to kiss Saira as she clutched the railings of her cot, trying to climb out. Then he walked over to Tahira and took Armaan and tossed him in to the air. Both the children squealed. Armaan with pleasure, Saira with rage at being abandoned. Shehzad chuckled and took them both in his arms. "You are still my little doll, don't worry."

"Difficult. I felt as if I must have imagined I could once paint."

"It's been a long time. It'll come back. You just have to keep trying."

"Thank you. Your support means a lot to me. I *am* going to keep trying." He had been very pleasant lately. She didn't know what was causing it, but hoped whatever it was would continue.

"Good. Let's go out for dinner."

"What about the children?"

"We'll take Armaan. Saira can stay with Ammi Jan."

Tahira looked at him quizzically. "Are you sure?" She paused and then said, very tentatively, "She might not like that."

"She'll be fine. She's the one who doesn't want to hire a full-time maid, because of the expense. She'll manage," he said grimly, not saying how embarrassed he was to have to rely on Tahira's family for Basheeran's help. He had tried to give them money but they wouldn't take it, which chafed even more.

At the restaurant, the food arrived quickly: small, wilted looking batches of twelve kababs and saffron semolina halva in stainless steel plates, with large golden parathas. The room in which they ate was long, lit like an institutional eating hall, with no decoration or concession to comfort. Long doors spilled the hall into the grassless sand, on which sat a haphazard parking of cars. Cats came and went, weaving their way under the tables, searching for benevolent scraps. All the attention was concentrated on the food, which was cheap and delicious.

Armaan reached down towards a scabby, scrounging cat. Tahira pulled him back.

"You know. I worked as a waiter at a place rather like this once."

"Really?" She stared at him.

"Yes. I had been hungry for days. And I was too proud to tell anyone. So I got a job as a waiter. It meant I ate better for a while."

She wondered if she should ask why his parents hadn't known anyway. She decided to go ahead. "Did you ever tell your parents?"

"Not yet," he laughed bitterly.

"What's the matter? Has something…?" she stopped.

"No. Nothing," he said. "I'd like a nice sweet paan, lots of copra. Let's go to PIDC."

"I'd like that."

The air changed as they got closer to the little shop at the bottom of the tall commercial building, which wasn't very far from the harbour, smelling of salt and sea and lorries of fish. As they waited for their paan to arrive, sweet and filled with cerise copra for Shehzad, plain with a slight, sharp, sweet, musky infusion for Tahira, she saw a woman in the car next to theirs looking at her intently. She was curvy, elegant in white. Tahira could see the swell of the white kameez, the sheer drape of a white georgette dupatta. "There's a woman in the next car, staring at us. But I've never met her before. The man with her looks familiar, though."

Shehzad turned to look. For a fleeting moment Tahira saw a shocking familiarity in his eyes. He looked away quickly. "I don't know who she is. Probably has nothing better to do than stare. Here, have your paan."

The next day after work, Tahira went to her parents' house again. At lunch, Mariam sat feeding Armaan, who was sitting on her knee. She brought up Seema's and Nilofer's future.

"I don't see the problem," Tahira said. "Nilofer wants a degree in international relations. Seema wants to be a doctor."

"There's no problem. I'm just worried that Seema's not taking her work seriously enough."

"Why does it matter?" Waseem asked bitterly. "If she does, she might not take other, infinitely important, things seriously enough."

Mariam sighed. "It is important. One should have a backup. Anyway, who'll marry a girl without a good education? And it is our U.P. way. After all, we are not villagers or tribals. I have bad news. Latif says he's getting older. He says he longs for his village, that his mother is old. One gets so dependent on these people. You do so much for them and then…"

"Oh no. What will I do about the children without Basheeran?"

"Hire another one of *those people*," Waseem suggested. "There are plenty of *them* around. Better still, build a cage, like one of those private prisons the feudals have, and then you don't have to worry about betrayal—or ingratitude."

"I have to go to my studio," Tahira said, hoping to avert a confrontation.

Waseem subsided, looking delighted, but said nothing.

In the studio, Tahira sat on the stool in front of the easel and stared at the arrangement she had set up the day before. It seemed impossibly ambitious. What she needed she thought grimly was a colouring book, by-numbers. She jumped up and paced, desperate for distraction. Andaleep's last letter lay on the table. She hadn't responded because she hadn't liked the mock-fairytale parody of Deputy Nazir Ahmad's *The Mirror of Brides*, Andaleep had sent with it.

Andaleep had covered many of the essentials of the story of the two brothers married to two sisters. Akbari, the elder one a slothful, selfish bride, the younger, Asghari, a model of enterprising virtue, able to handle everything, to instantly understand the needs of everyone around her without anything needing to be said, self-denying, manipulative. Asghari arrived, proceeded to win over her mother-in-law, her sister-in-law and even her husband's father, who gave her the honorary title of "Brother," because of her masculine competence, especially since it came so well wrapped in feminine wisdom. She arranged a match between her sister-in-law and a much richer family by calling in a favour and insisting (a lot) and turned the family's fortunes around by making them wealthy.

Andaleep had even managed to hint at the story's hostility towards servants, its insistence that women from respectable families should not be allowed to spend too much time in the company of those of low birth, but did she have to be quite so unsubtle about it? Besides, what else were women to do but survive as best they could? She had compared the father-in-law's approval of Asghari to the plot of some film called *Devi*, directed by Satyajit Ray she said, thrown in all sorts of bizarre asides including one about Bluebeard, as if trying to cram every kind of detail about injustice towards women, added a digression about Deputy Sahib's fascination with English women and the hypocrisy of colonial administrators who approved of *The Mirror of Brides*, and then gone on to write what seemed like a list of English writers. Something about a year of readings in English literature for those in doubt about how women were treated in England. She read the list: *Samuel Richardson, Elizabeth Gaskell (especially Ruth), Charlotte Bronte (especially The Professor), although that takes us into the sadistic-masochistic territory of* Heavenly Ornaments. *More recent works like Virginia Woolf (of course), Elizabeth Bowen (Ireland really), Doris Lessing, Margaret Drabble and Angela Carter are also recommended.*

She knew Andaleep was trying to rouse her to some sort of rebellion, trying to amuse too, she supposed. It seemed no less hysterical and graceless for that. But what was the point of saying she resented the attempt? She would have to craft a careful, tactful letter. She grimaced. The distraction had worked in a way. For now, it seemed easier to try to overcome the emptiness of the canvas.

She walked to the wall, turning the canvases leaning against it around. She looked through them, trying to be dispassionate. They were good—the thought was surprising—precise, meticulous, but diffuse in conception. She remembered Mrs. Karamat, one of her art teachers, who had once said to her, that she lacked a disciplined imagination, that she was too affected by her moods, finding things suddenly, dramatically unappealing that she had loved before. "And the problem, my dear," she had said, with stern premonitory sympathy, "is that the precision and control of your technique can give the *illusion* of discipline. It is misleading, and I'm afraid that it will mislead you." Tahira had concentrated on the wrinkled wobble of flesh dangling inappropriately from Mrs. Karamat's famously sleeveless arms. But now, she thought, maybe she had been right after all. She picked out the half-finished portrait of Shehzad. He had been nice recently, hadn't snapped or yelled for more than a month. The portrait seemed inaccurate, its enigmatic unfriendliness itself strange and distant. She turned it around again, feeling guilty at its refusal to see him with sympathy.

As she flicked through more canvases, she realized, and wondered if she had known this before, that she loved the glow of oil paints, could see now the attempt to harness their possibility in the portrait, in a still life of a bowl of incendiary marigold and rose garlands, in a fabular composition of a verdant green forest and sculpted shimmering stone, the colour of polished flesh. She stared, squatting, until her arches twinged, and walked back to the canvas. But nothing seemed to have changed.

~

Over the next few days, Tahira continued to go to the studio, each day as difficult as the last. She was surprised to have discovered an earlier stubbornness, which she thought had disappeared since her marriage. So, although the room seemed a sullen cavern, she returned, unable to start, determined to stay.

One evening, after dinner, Shireen asked Tahira, "So, Dulhan, how has the painting been proceeding?"

Tahira said, hoping Shehzad wouldn't contradict her, "It's going well." She slid a quick sideways glance at Shehzad. He said nothing and showed no contrary expression.

"Good. Perhaps, we will be graced with one of these creations. After all, I would like to know what it feels like to have a talented daughter-in-law too."

Tahira picked up a grain of rice that had fallen to the side of her plate. "Of course." She stared at the yellow turmeric stained rice and potatoes, the mint leaves in the milky diluted yoghurt of the raita, the floating, fresh coriander garnish, sinking under the film of oil on the curry and wondered what she would do now.

That night she dreamt she had arrived in a castle, an elaborate assemblage, complete with turrets, spires, and a drawbridge. A moat glinted with wide rippling gunmetal arcs of water above which unrecognizable reptiles, half-crocodile, half-snake, raised iridescent scaly heads in indeterminate shades of grey and green. She rode in on a lustrous auburn horse and was swept off by a handsome enigmatic man, dressed like a Mughal prince in an ivory silk sherwani, intricate arabesques in gold and black and russet embroidered on the thin high collar, the sleeves and the hem. In his turban was set a miniature fan, like a peacock's tail, with emeralds and rubies and sapphires.

He swept her into a room covered with thousands of tiny tiles in turquoise and cobalt and indigo, as elaborately decorated as a Safavid mosque. The bed was bare, hung with layers of transparent fabric. He placed her on the bed and they had tense, silent, fully dressed sex. This is when her dream-self thought there might be something wrong.

The prince rolled off the bed and gestured towards the door at which stood a woman she understood to be the housekeeper. Small, hunchbacked with a large crooked nose, which extended down like a stalactite and ended at the beginning of her lower lip, flaring just below the end in a gleaming droplet of snot. Her eyes were small polished agates.

Although no one spoke, she understood that she would be a happy bride as long as she did not enter a particular room, the key to which jangled on the bunch bouncing against the housekeeper's starched white cotton sari, hanging from the filigreed hook inserted between the petticoat and her flesh. As long as she stayed out of this room she understood she would be able to paint "to her heart's content." Although no one spoke, the phrase struck her dream-self as richly, farcically comical. She laughed loudly, head thrown back, in the dream and the prince slapped her and went away to tend his lands. The housekeeper who had been watching through the keyhole walked in, transformed into a beautiful woman in a sari of white chantilly lace, a low-cut blouse with great indolent caramel breasts and hair that fell to her waist in blue black waves. Bunched and pushed up by her blouse, the flesh that rose above mocked Tahira with every step she took towards her.

Tahira turned and ran into the bedroom and saw a thousand tiny selves in the little blue tiles that had suddenly turned into mirrors relentlessly refracting a thousand panting girls that refracted and multiplied and multiplied again in perfect miniature detail.

She locked herself into the room and suddenly an easel appeared, complete with the apparatus of painting. She began to grind stones, lapis lazuli and malachite, to make pigment. She arranged brushes in different configurations, fan, filbert, round, angular, hog hair, sable, badger, squirrel, chanting their names. She ran around the easel, dancing with the palette in her hand and sang and it began to rain in the room and her sari became wet and the pigment and the palette and housekeeper's mascara ran. She stopped and wondered where the housekeeper had come from and realized that she hadn't shut the woman out; she had locked them both in. She shut her eyes and the woman disappeared and her dreaming self was very, very pleased. But she still could not paint.

A day went by, and then two, and three and the housekeeper turned back into a shrivelled old hag and then into the beautiful curvy woman and back into the hag, and the tiles turned into mirrors and the mirrors into cruel, scrutinizing eyes with frilly eyelashes, but she could not paint.

On the fourth day, she decided to search for the forbidden room. Every room she passed through was covered in tiny tiles, thousands, maybe more, in different shades of the same colour: she passed through a room with plum and amethyst and mauve tiles, with chartreuse and emerald and sea-green, scarlet and crimson and garnet, gunmetal and slate and coal black. Not a person did she see and not a window.

The rooms had archways that turned into doors, bronze, gilt, gold, silver, copper, that clanged tightly shut behind her, making return from the centre more and more impossible.

She arrived at the hidden room and stood at the door, heart thudding, raised her hand to knock timidly at the door. It fell to her side and she turned away and sat down next to it, buried her face in her knees and cried tears fat with self-contempt.

The electricity was off again. The family sat on the terrace with the children. Farah was playing with Armaan; Shehzad walked the length of the terrace with Saira. Tahira tried to understand why Afzaal and Shehzad seemed to engage in even less than their usual stilted politenesses. It had been like that since Armaan's illness. Attempts to extract information from Farah had failed. She seemed nervous, changing the subject with characteristic clumsiness but unmistakable finality.

"Dulhan," Shireen spoke. "You still haven't lost the weight you put on when Saira was born. It has been more than six months. Maybe you shouldn't be eating that halva your mother sent. It's too oily, anyway. The carrots are overcooked and the colour is all wrong. What a strange way to make gaajar ka halva!"

Tahira wondered what would happen if she just settled back into her chair, closed her eyes and fell asleep. She said nothing. Shireen continued softly when Shehzad was at the other end. Tahira could not see her face but thought she heard the irritation beneath the sweetness. "You know, you don't seem quite content these days; and we haven't seen any paintings. There was such fanfare when we first saw you. Maybe you should give up. It might be better that way, for you—and for the children, of course."

Shehzad reached them. "What might be better for the children?"

"Nothing. I was just suggesting to Tahira that she should rest more."

The next day, Tahira marched into the studio, Shireen's words ringing in her ears. It had been bad enough to be goaded by her on the terrace, but then the electricity hadn't returned till four in the morning, so she had lain sleepless and bathed in sweat for hours and, when she had finally fallen asleep, she had had that awful dream again. This time the housekeeper, in her hag incarnation, had acquired Shireen's features and had repeated the words she had spoken on the terrace. She wanted a painting, did she? Tahira thought, well, she would get one.

"Basheeran. Can you bring Armaan and Saira in here, please?"

Basheeran brought them in.

"Can you hold Armaan in your lap so that he's facing me."

"Like this?"

"Yes. Turn his head to the right a little. It's alright, Maani. Shush."

She began to draw. Still too angry to notice how easily the strokes took his form. Soon the round of his face, his gleeful eyes, the squirming body that had regained the fat he had lost when he had been ill, covered the paper. She made several quick sketches, each more assured than the last. Armaan running, laughing, pointing at the easel, Saira running around him, getting in the way. Finally she looked up, glowing with the effort and absorption of the work. "I don't need him here anymore, Basheeran. Thank you."

"It's good to see you look so happy, Bibi. Your face shines when you are working, did you know?"

"Does it?" She began to draw on the canvas. Perhaps, she thought with fleeting, pleasant malice, she ought to paint a portrait of Armaan in her lap, like a Raphael Madonna and Child. She squeezed some paint and added oil to it, dipped a brush into the thick pigment. It felt good. She began to lay the base, painting quickly with meticulous strokes, which made the activity seem slower, more deliberate and consciously aware than it was.

Basheeran appeared at the door. “Bibi. It’s quarter to five. It’s time to go.”

It took ten days of work to complete the painting. Ten days, in which, Tahira remembered the sheer sensuous pleasure of wielding brush and mixing oil and pigment, the curious absorbing joy of watching a slow accumulation of colours, of discovering the purple in the brown, the blue in the garden’s green, of the culling of curve and sharp, hard edge from a quiet cumulation of strokes, of the growing, heady discomfort of the fumes from the paints and the oil, of the impatience of waiting for a layer to dry and the joy of starting again.

When it was complete, she stepped back from it and looked. She had painted the garden with the house behind it. On the left was the driveway, on the right, the boundary wall. The garden was in the foreground, taking up most of the painting. The house, its windows, the right boundary wall were sharp, clear shapes in shades of grey and beige. The left wall was covered with a tangled bougainvillea vine, covered with deep purple flowers. The morning light was delicate and cool. The grass sparkled with dew. In the centre of the garden was Armaan, plump and curving, examining a disintegrating clump of earth and grass. It showed, Tahira thought, a chaste lack of ambition. But it existed.

A week later, she said to Shehzad, “I brought my first painting home. I thought we might give it to Ammi together.”

“That’s a nice idea. Where is it?”

She showed it to him. He noticed the sturdy living spill of Armaan’s body, the gleam of intent curiosity in his eyes. “It’s good. Congratulations. Let’s take it to Ammi.”

Tahira wondered if she were imagining the ironic satisfaction in his voice.

“They went downstairs together. Shireen was in her bedroom, combing her hair as she spoke to Afzaal. Shehzad knocked at the open door. “Tahira has a present for you.”

"Oh?"

Tahira pulled the canvas from behind her back and handed it to Shireen. Afzaal leaned over Shireen's shoulder as she looked at it. Tahira said, as sweetly as Nazneen she hoped, "I was certain you would love a portrait of your first pota for your room."

BOOK
three

12

Waseem marched between Safdar and Gul Khan, their trade unionist friend, in the second row of the demonstration. Behind them, heads stretched into the distance, a dark bobbing mass, scoured here and there into a colourless shimmer by the sun. The smell of asphalt, the occasional whirl of sand, the slightly rank musk of surging bodies rose in a heavy fug above the crowd.

The marchers in the row ahead came to a halt. Gul swore under his breath. Police and Rangers had formed a flat arc, which seemed to be inching slowly towards them. Waseem was accustomed to the belligerent contempt of the authorities but these men looked more sinister. He saw machine guns and, behind the arc, armoured cars.

Gul turned around. "Don't do anything. Keep calm. We must keep calm," he urged, as each successive row pushed to a halt against the next. Waseem and Safdar and a number of others repeated Gul's words, but the marchers were angry. Even if peaceable so far, they all knew how quickly it could turn.

"Why are they here?" Gul muttered. "We were told the government was on our side." Waseem felt the widening ripples of a different kind of anger. A cry was carried forward over the heads of the crowds, handed ahead by each successive row like a body at a packed funeral procession.

Nahin lenge hum yeh rusvai
Khun paseene ki kamaai
Khun paseene ki kamaai

"The earnings of our blood and sweat, blood and sweat." The refrain took over. Marchers behind pushed forward until it was impossible for Waseem to stand still. He stumbled and murmured an apology to the man ahead.

They began to move; the illusory shield of the long white banner they carried fluttering ineffectually. The police and Rangers facing them raised their guns, rigid shafts pointed at the marchers. The man ahead of Safdar halted. "Stop," he cried urgently. "Stop those behind. The police have guns trained on us." From somewhere deep in the crowd a voice called out, "They've already sucked our blood dry. What else can they take from us?" "Yes," another voice shouted. "What else can they do?" The rows at the back resumed their marching. The pressure was beginning to build again, when in the left hand corner in one of the front rows—later no one was quite sure which one—a few men broke formation and a scuffle broke out. Guns began to spew bullets. Waseem felt, before he heard, people fall, saw blood gush, firm full spurts and fine sprays like the spume at a beach spattering faces and clothes.

A sudden wave of blood blocked his vision. He wondered vaguely if he were going to die. He wiped his eyes, smudging some blood deeper into them. He looked to his left and realized Gul had fallen. Safdar was crouched next to him, calling out, "Make space! Make space! There's a man down here." Staccato bursts of gunfire continued to tear the air. He felt a man fall against his back, and reeled forward, hovering over Safdar and Gul for a moment. Then, he was never quite sure how, he steadied himself, reaching behind with a twisted arm. As suddenly as the weight had fallen on his back, it was removed. He turned his head quickly to see what had happened and saw a wounded man, blood spreading across the portion of his shalwar under the knee, being led away, his arm around another man's shoulder. He knelt down. There was blood all over Gul's face; his eyes stared straight into Waseem's, a little surprised, faintly angry. A hole rimmed with darkening red pulp gaped at his right temple.

Waseem reached a hopeful hand to look for a pulse. Safdar spoke softly. "It's no use."

Waseem decided he couldn't have heard him. The noise of men shouting, of frantic fleeing feet, of falling bodies was too loud. He must have imagined his quiet finality. He reached his hand, feeling for the vein in Gul's neck. He noticed the black thread and small taawiz folded in beaten silver at the base of his neck. Gul had laughed about it once, said his wife had made him wear it. The thread was sticky; the talisman looked as if someone had spit paan juice all over it. Nothing throbbed. He pressed harder, pretending Gul's eyes had just flickered with irritation. He saw a drop fall onto Gul's face, surprised it wasn't red, noticed the lines around his eyes, the week's worth of exhausted stubble, the little puddle of blood, which had collected in the cleft of his chin, furious when Safdar stilled his hand.

He looked up. The police were making arrests. Some of the injured men lay on the ground, surrounded by small groupings of people. Every now and then, one of these clusters was broken up by an arrest. Two policemen came closer to them. Waseem hunched over the body. "I'm going to take him home to his family."

Safdar moved closer towards Gul and looked down, trying to make himself invisible. "Of course. We both will."

They heard the noise of wood and metal battering flesh, of resistant shoes and bodies being dragged on asphalt, of defiant yells and waited, trying to be unobtrusive in their huddle.

Soon Safdar said, "Come." They dragged the body to the side of the road, laid it under a neem tree, and scanned the crowd. Safdar shaded his eyes with one hand, with the other he held Waseem's arm as if to prevent them both from trembling. The police were driving away. The mayhem continued.

"You stay here," Safdar said. "I'm going to go and see what they want done."

"I'll come with you." Waseem heard the return of steadiness to his voice.

"No. We need someone to stay with Gul. Somebody might move the body."

Safdar walked into the swirl of people and found a cluster of organizers discussing what to do next. People had gathered around, looking for direction, more for reassurance. It was decided the few vans and cars that had been used to transport the demonstrators early in the morning would take the injured to the hospital. There were not enough to take the dead to their homes; helping the survivors live was a priority.

"Gul Khan has died. So how many dead does that make?" Safdar asked.

One of the union leaders, an older man with thinning white hair, said, "Three, so far."

"And injured?"

"We don't know. Dozens."

"I'll try to find a taxi."

He walked back to Waseem who stared at Safdar's feet as they crossed streaks and patches of blood where bodies had fallen and been dragged. The brown Peshawari sandals advanced closer to Gul's body. Waseem felt as if he were watching a grave about to be robbed. He stifled the urge to push Safdar away, reaching instead for the dried carcass of a leaf. He had been trying not to look at Gul. Now he forced himself, "We need to find a taxi to take him home. There are no vans free."

"I can go to get one." The blood was beginning to dry; a weave of thin cracking lines, like the leaf's fibrous skeleton, crisscrossed Gul's face.

"No. You stay there. You seem in no state to manage."

"Please."

"Okay. I'll stay here."

The sun beat down. The heat from the asphalt radiated into Waseem's feet through and around the sandals. He could smell other people's blood and sweat mingling with his own. After walking for half a mile he saw, a little further down where the road intersected with another major one, the black and egg yolk-yellow streaks of taxis among the buses and rickshaws. He quickened his pace. A taxi drove by, the driver shaking his head in disbelief when Waseem tried to flag it. After two more attempts, one finally stopped.

Waseem took in the driver's finely embroidered white cap, his longish graying beard streaked with fading henna and said, "Haji Sahib, I have a friend. He's dead, lying about three quarters of a mile down. My friend and I need to take his body home. Will you take us?"

"Yes, of course. Get in. Are you sure you don't want to go to the hospital? You look like you need to."

"I'm fine." Waseem got into the front seat. They drove to where Safdar sat with Gul's body. Waseeem got out of the car. "You get in front. I'll sit in the back with him."

They tried to make the body sit. It flopped to one side. The prospect of it sliding around the backseat, without the respectful stiffening of life, seemed obscene to Waseem. "Let's try to lay him down," he said.

"Beta, how will you sit?" the driver asked.

"Besides," Safdar said, "he won't fit."

"I'll take his head in my lap."

The driver nodded his approval. Waseem got in. The driver and Safdar manoeuvred Gul into the back seat, pushing his head towards Waseem. After ten minutes of complicated effort, Gul's head was manoeuvred almost as far up as Waseem's shoulder, his upper torso leaning against Waseem's trunk.

The ride was long. Safdar answered the driver's kindly questions. Waseem lay his head back, a little soothed by the old man's concern, trying not to think about his difficult cargo and what lay ahead. He remembered meeting Gul that morning. He had been furious at the lockouts, the intimidation by the thugs the factory bosses had hired, but he had also been excited that the government had said it would support the workers. Gul had thumped his chest with a great curled fist and said, "I felt my heart expand when I heard that."

Waseem supposed he ought to try to be glad that Gul had felt such exhilaration on his last day alive. The taxi jerked and bounced as they came to Gul's lane. The dirt road was gravelly and pitted with little craters. Gul's head bounced against his chest. He held him closer.

Safdar turned around, concerned. "Are you alright?"

"Yes. It's okay, we're almost there."

"He has a twelve-year-old son, Jahangir, and an eighteen-year-old daughter, Safiya, right? Do you remember who else lives with him?"

The present tense was comforting, "No one. I think his father died last year. There might be brothers somewhere in the Gulf. His wife already takes in some embroidery."

They pulled up outside the lane, which was too narrow for the car. A few children were playing an improvised, constricted game of cricket by its entrance. They ran up to the taxi. One cried out, "Look! It's Gul Chacha. He looks hurt." Waseem saw a small boy at the edge of the cluster, trying to push his way through. "Safdar, that little boy trying to break through to the window is Gul's son. You better get out and try to stop him from seeing Gul like this. We'll have to carry the body from here."

"I'll go to the house and ask for a sheet."

Safdar opened the door and went up to the small, serious boy. "Jahangir Beta, will you take me to your mother?"

The boy looked down, kicking some gravel. "What's wrong with my father?"

"He's hurt. Come help me get your mother, so we can get him home."

They walked away.

Little runnels of sweat slid down Waseem's face and landed on Gul. "Haji Sahib, can you open the doors?"

The driver got out, opened the doors and asked the children to stand at some distance. They moved back, but pelted questions.

"What's happened?"

"Why is that man holding Gul Chacha like that?"

"Why isn't he moving?"

"He's dead. I know he is"

The driver said, "Hush. Let his family come."

Safdar returned with Gul's wife and children. His wife suddenly broke into a run. His son and daughter tried to follow. Safdar grabbed the son and reached for the daughter, and then stopped. He looked helplessly at an older woman who had followed them. "She shouldn't see him like that."

The woman reached for Safiya, who swung away, sliding out of her plump, mothering grasp and walked up behind her mother, who had begun to scream—a scratchy, high, unbearable sound without end. She went to the other side, away from Waseem, and pulled at her father's feet. "We need to take him home. Ammi, stop screaming. Give me the sheet."

The neighbour, who had been unable to stop Gul's daughter, brushed the children pressing behind his wife aside and reached for her shoulder.

"Come Shaheen. We have to take him inside." She called to the daughter. "Safiya. Come inside. Help your mother."

"No. I'm going to help bring him in. Look at how they've treated him. Look at how uncomfortable he is." She turned to Waseem and Safdar. "Couldn't you treat him with respect? Twisting his body like this? I'm going to carry him."

Jehangir had wrapped his arms around Safdar's waist and buried his head in his chest. He tightened his arms when Safdar tried to move. The neighbour reached for him, "Come, beta. Help your mother."

Safdar came to Waseem's door. "Here I'll hold his head. You can slide out from behind, so you can help us carry him in." He beckoned to Safiya, "I'm very sorry, the car was too small; we didn't want to be disrespectful. We loved him. Let's carry him together."

13

The soil was comforting in Safdar's hands. He kneaded the clump he had worked loose into a tight ball and then crumbled it into smaller pieces, working his fingers in and around the roots of the large oleander, which had outgrown its pot. A flower fell to his side, shaken loose by the movement.

In the months since Gul's death he had taken to spending several hours a day tending to the plants in the courtyard and in the tiny garden at the entrance to the house. Many had been repotted, new cuttings had been made, the leaves glowed waxen with the care he had lavished sometimes on each individual one, wiping the plants clean after spraying them with water. Glistening in Karachi's rainless air, they seemed incongruously tropical. "The cleanest leaves in the city," his father joked, when he did, which was not often these days.

He had made so many little pots that he had taken to giving them away to neighbours and friends and when they said they had no space to take anymore, he took them to an impromptu nursery set up on an empty plot nearby, which looked like a refugee shelter with its makeshift canvas tent pegged precariously to the ground. The owner was a friend, known to everyone as Joseph Bhaiyya. Although one night, over some Murree beer and nihari, Safdar had learned how he had come by that name. Drunk on beer and the heat of the nihari, he had started to cry.

"He loved it you know."

"Who did?"

"Joseph."

"You are Joseph."

"No, he was."

"Then who are you?"

"Sher Shah."

"Why do I call you Joseph Bhaiyya?" Safdar was sure he wasn't that drunk.

"I took his name."

"Why?

"Because they killed him thinking he was a Hindu. He wasn't circumcised. He wasn't Hindu. He just wanted to be on this side of the border. They didn't ask and they wouldn't believe him or me. They stripped me and then let me go. So I thought: you *maderchods*, here's one less Muslim cock for you, and changed my name."

"And faith?"

"What faith?"

They had never spoken of the story again. The next time Safdar went by the nursery, Joseph Bhaiyya had looked at him steadily until Safdar had said a hearty and meaningless greeting threading "Joseph Bhaiyya" through it several times and been met with an emphatic, approving grunt.

When he went over, sometimes they chatted, more often Joseph Bhaiyya tended to the plants singing bits from the latest Alamgir song while Safdar sat and read poetry on the fraying charpai by the plants. He sometimes felt he was searching the poems for a resolution to the struggle between dream and necessity. How was it that caution and skepticism had proved no inoculation against hope?

Sometimes he took along a book about gardens. In the past he had pored over these books with Joseph Bhaiyya, who was always delighted having formed an attachment to such books many years ago when his neighbour—a radi-wallah—had been showing him his day's takings and there had been what Safdar gathered was a journal of architecture and landscape in the hoard. Now the rag-and-bone man made sure to show Joseph Bhaiyya any books and magazines he had collected if they had pictures of plants in them. Once Safdar had heard this story, he had made sure to bring along a book from his mother's stack whenever he came to the nursery. She had collected many over the years; a cousin—the only relative who regularly spoke to her—brought her these from her travels with her husband, who worked for PIA. His grandmother had also managed to send some Mughal and European naturalist paintings of plants and flowers from his grandfather's collection to Mumtaz before she died. He knew that his grandfather, who had died before his parents met, had been an avid gardener and collector and inventor of stories about gardens and their gardeners in India. Safdar loved these books and pictures, and the stories his mother had repeated to him since he was a child. He had been twelve when he told his parents he wanted a piece of land so he could make a perfect garden.

These days, his visits to the nursery were different. He came for silent friendship and for breaks from reading in which he could work with the plants.

Sleep and rest seemed forever separated. Every night he dreamt of the blood on Gul's head rubbing off onto his own face. In the dream, he became the one holding his head in the back of the taxi. Gul's blood-stiffened hair grazed his chin as the taxi jerked and bounced over potholes and the unpaved lanes around Gul's home, which seemed to wind on forever. Suddenly the car radio began to play a song. Alamgir belted out, "*Dekha na tha kabhi ham ne ye samaa/Aisa nasha tere pyaar ne diya.*" His dream-self was furious: what did the intoxication of love have to do with the body in his arms? Why would anyone want to see a spectacle they hadn't witnessed before? "Turn it off," he screamed. "Turn it off." And Gul's head bounced harder against his chin as he screamed. He tried to push it away but, obeying the laws of dreams, it jerked closer to him instead.

When they finally got to Gul's neighbourhood and Safdar tried to leave the car, he couldn't. Gul's head was stuck to his chin with blood, which had puzzlingly acquired the consistency of tar. At one door, Waseem pulled on Safdar's head. At the other door, Safiya pulled at Gul's feet, screaming, "Give me my father. Give him back." She screamed it four times, each repetition more piercing and unbearable then the last, the inescapable, punishing wailing of a cat at night. He wanted to be released from the dream but it was only at the end of the fourth scream that he was able to wake up.

Each night he sat in the courtyard reading by a lantern, battling sleep, inhaling the unbearable fumes of the lantern. But sleep came and soon after that the dream. And then, the day, which, though longer than usual, filled up quickly. The care of the plants, the reading and, of course, the meetings, the political organizing continued. The political situation was absurd. Promises were being broken. The ever-mutable constitution had been amended to make the most hated minority more hated. As if the memory of Rabwah and similar events were not shameful enough. Members of the cabinet were being bullied and intimidated; students were under attack, kidnappings, murder, madness... It went on, but they hadn't given in. "And we won't!" he muttered fiercely to himself, pulling savagely at a strand of the root of the oleander plant. He angled it into the new pot and covered it with soil, smoothing it with a lingering pat and moved the plant back into the corner next to the desk. The work continued… and the battle with disillusion.

He sat down at the desk, hands still muddy. He wiped his hands on a newspaper and reached to pull out a book of seventeenth-century English poems from a pile stacked at the edge of the desk. A piece of notepaper fell out. It was one of the poems from the collection he had been working on, his *History Cycle*:

Din-e-Ilahi

The priests dispute
And tenderly tender attribute
And awe and glorious prickling fear:
Wine of love,
Rivers of wine,
Time dissolved,
Dancing blue mischief.
Beggar bowl
Or world embrace?

The king reclines,
Lazy and beautiful in silk
And brocade and emeralds and silk
Upon silk and brocade
On gold thread and silver and throne:
"Make me a religion of God.
One out of all of yours.
Multiply and divide,
Refract and shatter
Like light through a waterfall in a glade
Under a slitted sky."

Elsewhere in the palace, a prince is in love
And a dancing girl is bricked into a wall.

The poem made him more restless; he realized suddenly that he wanted to write to Andaleep. He wasn't sure why but perhaps it was her anarchic laughter he needed. Yes. That's what he'd do. He washed his hands and ripped a clean page out of his notebook and then realized he didn't know how to begin. He tried writing "Dear Andaleep;" it sounded peculiar and *wrong*. It wasn't that sort of letter he wanted to write. He began again:

The perfect garden? The perfect garden is…. and wrote steadily for an hour.

Dear Tahira,

I received a beautiful and strange piece of writing from Safdar a week ago. No letter. Not even a dear Andaleep. I'm not sure how to respond. I'm not sure what's going on with all of you. I have not received much news from you but you should read it.

I am hoping he will learn from Waseem what I am about to tell you. This is hard because I have been silent about it so long. I have been in love with a Palestinian man for a while. His name is Khaled. He is a doctor and a member of the PLO.

My parents are not happy about this. They do not think it will work. We share no culture, no way of life, my mother says. No one has married outside UP in our family for generations; it matters how you sit and how you eat, she insists. I'm not surprised. Of course, she doesn't mention Bhai, who was not allowed to marry a Punjabi girl. He did it anyway and decided to stay in London and doesn't talk to them any more. They are not happy with the estrangement, so I think if I fight, they'll accept Khaled.

He is strong and carries so many places with him. His family was driven from their village in 1956 and they settled east of the Jordan River. Sometimes the way he talks about the olive grove behind his house reminds me of the way Baba talks about his grandfather's mango orchard in India. No olive is ever as good as the ones from those trees and every tree is a reminder of another one. Then he was driven out of Jordan because of the Palestinian uprising. Did you know that a Pakistani officer helped the Jordanian government crush it? Khaled talks about his deep-set eyes and sinister eyebrows as if he were describing the devil. I am so ashamed.

I admire his commitment. I've been to meetings with him and he is always so organized and determined, despite the rage that simmers so close to the skin.

So, of course, I love him, Tahira, but he wants to stay here to continue the struggle and I want to come back home. Maybe Amma is right after all. Maybe it comes down to how we sit—it always struck me as mad that expression, uthna bethna, like a punishment at school, stand up, sit down, stand up again—or maybe its even more elemental than that and comes down to the familiarity of the smell of rotting fish and the improbable waft of night-blooming jasmine carried upon the Karachi breeze. But then who are we—the children of displaced people trying to recreate a lost land in a new country we say is ours? And yet, I have never even been to India and know no other.

And I do not want to spend my life sitting in a beautiful place, unable to see it, yearning for the different and always more perfect fig, longing for another almond and the noise of crows mingling with the azaan and the changing smell of the sea as the sun sets and we sit in the garden, missing that and some ineffable more with every bite of a fruit that will never be good enough then one waiting, or—as in Baba's case—felt to be abandoned elsewhere.

You know Baba still talks about shaving in the morning and how strange it is to do so without the monkey that used to come to his window in Bareilly. He makes me think of Kamal in Aag Ka Darya, never sure whether he was betrayed by his friends or whether he abandoned them. Now of course, he can't go back. I think that's why he becomes completely silent and distant when anyone mentions that book, pretending not to know it although I have seen him reading it. I think he is reminded of how he ceased to feel at home in his own country. Of course his own situation was different, but sometimes I think the reason he doesn't want me to marry Khaled is only that he can't bear to be in the presence of Khaled's loss or… of his anger.

I ramble. But my head is its own maze these days. How can I tell Khaled, of all people, that I love him but I miss the smell of home?

I have a decision to make.

Meanwhile, I remain yours forever,

Andaleep

Tahira leaned back in her chair and sighed. She had always imagined that when Andaleep's turn came to get married, she would be unfettered and reckless and rush headlong into whatever presented itself. She had never thought she would hesitate and worry. She was sorry that she was suffering, but liked this more cautious friend.

She had not wanted to tell Andaleep about what happened with Gul. Why write letters with so much bad news? It had seemed better not to write rather than chatter trivially about children and in-laws and cruel (she winced at the clarity of the word) husbands and disturbing political news. She couldn't bring herself to talk about Waseem's reaction to the death. She hardly saw him now. And when she did, he was restless and tense, as if he couldn't bear to be in the room for too long. There was anger in his gestures and weariness in his eyes. Tahira didn't think he would want to talk to her about Gul. She had failed him badly. He liked taking Armaan to the park. So she tried to ask him to do that whenever she could. In the absence of their older ease, there was not much else to do.

She unfolded the pages Safdar had sent, smoothing its creases. What could it be if he hadn't even addressed Andaleep? If he had intended it as a love letter was it her place to read it? But Andaleep had asked her to.

She began to read.

The perfect garden?

Green, gold, lush, abundant—where green shade nurtures and colours thought, plays upon it like sunlight through a canopy of light and breezy leaves, as you lie looking up at layered sky. The garden multiplies and refracts emerald and peridot and chartreuse and dark, waxen banana-leaf green and dances upon the mind like graceful fronds of weed under the surface of the sea. The garden must be orderly yet tempt with the imminence of disorder, seem on the beautiful verge of chaotic explosion, its bounty asking to be contained by the loving nurture of its devotee. And I am devoted to its sheltering beauty and the annihilation its shade offers. Not a Japanese garden or an ostentatious French discipline. Perhaps English country with contained tumble of flowerbeds like the voluptuous, but somehow innocent, deshabille of a recently tumbled maiden. Perhaps the tropical garden with its very own precise blend of shade and shelter and light and air, elusive and humid, contemplative with quiet sculptures of meditative buddhas and lotus and ponds that reflect his contemplation, and bursting with sudden walkways heavy with the weight of ancient growth.

Or perhaps a Mughal garden: courtyards that integrate inside and out, and water music of fountains, mosaics of inlaid marble, and canopies of carved sandstone, so you can live outside in the luminous shimmer of the subcontinental night. Flowers trained and arranged to stop you as you walk beside the tranquility of water and halt at the fragrant catch of jasmine that blooms only at night, so you cannot see what incense embalms you in its soft embrace.

Some might say a Persian one: courtyard and mosaic inlay and water laid out symmetrically in the centre, geometrically arranged corners, harmony and symmetry, pomegranate flowers and fruit and an abundant adornment of mosaic in shades of blue that have become countries, Turkish, Morroccan, Persian and an intricacy of pattern, multiplied and divided and then multiplied again motif. Out of an ancient commandment comes the exquisite patterned geometry of disciplined, intricate motif of mosaic and wood—of forms abstracted from nature and turned into mathematical harmonies; much to be preferred to putti and people, I sometimes think.

It is a colourscape: greens tranquil and hopeful with the promise of regeneration and the fullness of harvest, and cerulean, aquamarine, azure, cyan, ultamarine, indigo and royal, tranquil and serene and intoxicated, dancing blue of sky and sea that drowns. Some would say, not me, that it must have terracotta and sandstone and vermilion and crimson, worked into tile, and kilims and carpets, spread in the garden that snakes back into the house. Perhaps this red spill is memory of the oasis and desert, of the chieftain's tent and deserts kept at bay with warp and weft, of the nostalgia of nomadic kings for Central Asian plains and flowers or Arabian oases. This, too, is fitting. What's a garden without yearning and nostalgia, without the memory of what might never have been?

It must blend nature and its other, the world we create, until our violations can no longer withstand her dissolutions. It must have courtyards that open into the home and a home that spills into leaf and flower. There must be trees with fruit and green rooms that open into other ones, so the sky and the sun and earth will hold you in their sheltering, dappled, and, if you're lucky, amnesiac cradle.

Or perhaps at the heart of the garden a bower, separate from home and courtyard, like a glade in the forest, whose shade is silence—like the tropical glade: where there is no winter and more water than the earth can drink, and the green darkness of the very darkest green. Eternal and sheltering as the grave, whose day can be as still and mysterious as the night, and where plants and trees and moss grow in dense and multiple layers that evoke millennia and the prehistory of the earth rather than seasons and mortality and the delusive cruelty of April's hope. Private, alone, a place to hide, some (others) might say: to love, yet others: to die.

The perfect garden is a dream of an earlier perfection; it subdues the echo of a malevolent interdiction and grows the desire to breach it and return to that earlier place. Perhaps Promethean, this urge to snatch perfection back from the edict of the gods. The garden is revenge and envy against them, to take back what they thought they had not given, what they keep to tantalize and taunt and tease with the gift of immortality, as if immortality were a gift. Such ambiguous, ungenerous gifts they give. The garden refuses the bargain of immortality—we will take our chances, please. It is not just a reach for Eden, it is—and few will tell you this—competition for Paradise. It aims to supplant and replace and extinguish on earth the interdict and the prohibiter.

O we reach. How we reach.

All courtesy of ancient prohibitions.

The perfect garden? The perfect garden is a memory of the future.

14

Armaan clapped with delight as the ship appeared under his mother's flying fingers. Tahira continued to speak as she drew the billowing sail and the young man with a handlebar moustache and unwinding turban scrambling up its side.

So now, having escaped from the island where he had been captive for the past two months, with nothing in his pocket but the unbelievably precious egg of the Benaam Parinda, and with Basra further away then ever, the Sailor thought he could finally complete his quest for the Namumkin Janvar.

Saira stopped pulling at Basheeran's bright pink dupatta, which she had been winding around one of her fists as she sucked on the index finger of her other hand, leaned forward on Basheeran's lap and planting the wet finger, she had just pulled out of her mouth, on the sail said, "Ship."

Armaan pulled away her finger. "No, you're silly," he corrected, brow furrowed with conceptual indignation. "It's a sail. Don't make the picture wet." He turned to his mother, "But Amma, wasn't that,"—he pointed to one of the pages spread out in sequence on the table, on which the sailor chased an animal with the body of a weasel, the face of a monkey and the wings of a falcon—"an Impossible Animal?"

"Oh no," Tahira said in mock-portentous tones, "that was a Birdmonkeyweasel."

"Oh," he said curious and awed, turning back to instruct Saira. "That's not an Impossible Animal."

"What about that one?" he pointed to another page, on which the sailor wrestled an oversized creature with the body of a ripe, fleshy strawberry and the face, feet and tail of a cat.

"Oh no. That is a Strawberrycat."

"But you can't eat it."

"Well… you could, but it wouldn't be wise."

"What happens on the other island?"

"You'll have to wait till tomorrow to find out."

"Nooo," he wailed. Saira thought it was another game and made it a chorus.

"Yeess." Tahira leaned over to kiss him and then Saira. "Basheeran, can you get their things and take them downstairs? I'll come in a while."

Basheeran gathered the protesting children, putting their extra clothes, Armaan's crayons and his grey and white mechanical puppy, Saira's squeaky, yellow, plastic chick and brown koala and their sticky beakers of juice into two Marks and Spencer's bags Shehzad had brought back from his last business trip. Tahira had decided not to accompany him—because of the children she had said.

She leaned back and breathed the silence. After a few minutes of enjoying the calm, she began to organize the pages spread out on the table into a folder, leaving only the ones she had drawn today so she could add colour to them. It was hard to use paints with the children and Basheeran grouped around the table.

The story had begun when she had remembered a game she had played with Waseem when they were children. Each had to invent the most fanciful creature. Sometimes their father would be dragged into the game, asked to decide who had won.

She had hoped that Waseem might join in this storytelling, be pleased that she had remembered, but he was rarely home these days. It had been more than a year since Gul Khan's death, but sometimes it seemed to Tahira that Waseem had directed his anger at Gul's death at all those who were still alive. He avoided the family, stayed out late, and retreated into his room, door emphatically shut, when he was around. "Working," he said, when Mariam complained about his absence.

"What sort of work was it that makes no money?" she had asked Tahira. "He doesn't even do enough work at the business."

Tahira had mumbled something ineffectual. It had always been useless to argue with Mariam; even their father had never been able to counter her ambition.

Some months ago when last they had talked at any length, meeting accidentally in the kitchen—Tahira on a quest to escape from the studio, Waseem in search of some tea to revive himself—he had told her that Safdar seemed more upset than he had expected that Andaleep was in love with someone in Beirut. "I didn't realize that he cared that much for her. He hardly knows her."

Tahira had been surprised too. "Do you think it's because of Gul Khan's death?"

"No. I don't think it's that. It's possible that he's not able to hide his feelings as well as at other times, but I don't think it's only that. Women like Safdar, and he flirts but doesn't seem to notice them. This is different."

They had had a pleasant conversation when she had first told Waseem about Andaleep's letter. For a moment it had felt as if a shared past could lead to understanding in the present, that memory wasn't forever shattered by the suspicion of fancy. For how could it be possible to have shared so much and become so separate? What could one do but deride one's own imagination for infusing the past with a softening glow? That conversation had, for a moment, made her imagination seem less delusive, less desperate in its embellishing reach.

She had told him about Andaleep's letter, of how she had spoken of Khaled's longing for his village and of Munnawwar Uncle's yearning for the monkeys and mango orchards of U.P.

Waseem had chuckled. "Like Baba when he comes back with his favourite sweet, triumphant as if he's crossed the border. They are always the 'peray from Badayun' not from Lalukhet."

Tahira laughed. "But they are only available in one shop in some obscure lane which he makes sound as unreachable as an enchanted castle in a fairytale. I know he says that it's easier to get there by rickshaw, but I think he leaves the driver and car behind because he doesn't want anyone to know where it is."

"That way he can pretend they really *are* from Badayun and he's back in India."

"Do you think he would have been such a Muslim League supporter if he had known that Partition would transform him into an immigrant? I wonder, you know, even when I see Safdar's mother attempting to recreate the splendour of an imperial culture in that little courtyard. It all seems so broken, like so many shards arranged together as if archaeologists had tried to put together immeasurably precious smashed pots from some inconceivably distant era."

"It's a little heartbreaking but there's grace in the attempt."

"Why is it that grace and desperation seem so close?"

He had looked at her with sudden attention. "Do they? How?"

"It's what Andaleep seems to want to refuse. That terrible longing for ordinary things." Tahira had evaded the question.

"Yes. But I hope she makes the right decision. Whatever that is."

Wanting to continue the conversation, she had rushed on, still talking about Safdar's mother: "The squalor of that area where they live, the poverty, makes the attempt seem all the more desperate."

She had seen the distance and contempt descend like a veil over his face and not known how to pull him back. She wanted to say more, to bridge the space between them. She thought it was her fault but then that it was his as well for asking too much. Still… she had thought, maybe they could try again, not knowing that she had added to his suspicion that she had stayed with Shehzad because she feared a loss of the status and affluence the marriage gave her.

Basheeran had appeared at the door. "Shehzad Sahib is on the phone. He wants to talk to you."

She did not want to see the relief in his politeness."Go ahead. I must do some work."

"Wait for me," she had wanted to say and couldn't. Instead she said, "I must take the call."

Now she gripped the brush hard and had to pause as she filled in the colour of the sea. Her hand steadied and she began to top the waves with surf, reaching for the comfort of Armaan's description, "like the waves on the ice cream cones we have when we go to Tariq Road." She had started making the tips a little creamier and more ridged after that.

Soon the task, clearly laid out before her, took over. The rhythm was soothing and repetitive, disrupted only by the challenge of having to choose between colours. They were just illustrations for her children. The brushstrokes did not require much thought. They did not have to be grand, she told herself—which made it easier to continue—not seeing the beauty and the power of the drawings.

A little later Basheeran knocked at the door. "It's time to go, Bibi. The driver is back."

She looked up reluctantly, wondering what would happen if she refused.

The car pulled up as Faiz was answering the Radio Pakistan interviewer's question about writing in jail—*at many times things were revealed… do you know of how many colours the wild pigeon's neck is composed? Or of the changes in colour in the leaves and branches of a pipal tree from morning to*—she struggled to hear what was being said over the noise of the children, "Just a minute, Armaan, let me listen."

"But we're home, Amma."

"Yes, I know we're home." *So this is a part of one's sensation in the jailhouse—it becomes more acute. A concentration is formed in intellect, perception and emotion.*

She got out of the car. "Don't turn off the radio, yet…" lingering by the door as Armaan tugged at her hand. "One more minute Armaan." *Something akin to the responsiveness of youth returns*. She wondered what youth had to do with it.

"Okay. Let's go in." She squared her shoulders at the threshold, reaching to open the screen door. A rusted tear in the mesh caught on her *dupatta*, leaving a slight trace of copper on the blue georgette. Six years, she thought, six years… and decided not to complete the thought. She bent down and whispered to Armaan, "Make sure you greet your grandfather."

"Where?" Armaan waved around the room.

Tahira checked quickly to see the rocking chair under the stairs was empty. "Go and knock at his door. You know he'll be angry if you don't."

"Okaaay." Armaan marched to the room, back stiff with put-upon virtue. He knocked on the door, "Dada" and then—

she could see the glee spreading across his body—"Daddo," he called to his grandmother.

"Hush, you know she doesn't like that. Say Daadi, please."

"Dad*do*," he said more loudly, accenting the second syllable like the gleeful stamp of a foot.

Tahira went upstairs. There would be trouble later.

In the room, she confronted the pile of cleaned clothes on the unmade bed. Saira began to pull at the stack, rolling in the rumpled sheets.

"Take her to her room, Basheeran. I'll make the bed and take care of the clothes."

Basheeran took Saira, protesting and refusing to relinquish the sheet, sending the starched and folded clothes flying across the room. Tahira sighed and began to refold the pile, taking the clothes and linen to the appropriate drawers and shelves in the wardrobe as each group, towels glinting white with the occasional blue stripe; sheets, white with little red flowers, rough to the touch and thickened with starch, little bright frocks and shorts, was completed.

She lifted Shehzad's shalwar kameezes and took them to the drawer. As she placed them inside, she reached under the shalwar at the bottom and felt for the photograph she had placed there, pulling it out as she often did. The woman in the photograph was beautiful, jet-black hair cascading over an abundant, daring cleavage. She had found the photograph as she was emptying out the pockets of one of Shehzad's safari suits before sending it to the drycleaner more than a year ago and hidden the picture away. She remembered the woman. She had seen her years ago, in a car parked next to theirs. Now she knew why she had returned in her nightmare about being trapped in that fairy-tale castle. It still surprised her: the things one knew without knowing. She thought, as she so often had, of placing the photograph on the bureau, to see how he would defend himself, scared by the possibility that he wouldn't, and then placed it back under the shalwar.

~

Waseem came to the door and leaned against it as Tahira was completing the story for the day. *So now that Mr. Arastu had joined the sailor,* a little man with a white beard and a monocle looking over the side of the ship appeared on the page standing next to the sailor Tahira had just drawn. *The quest had become bigger. They now had other tasks. They would be looking for unusual plants as well, which Mr. Arastu would draw and collect in his Big Book of All Kinds of Knowledge.*

"Impossible plants?" Armaan asked.

"Not necessarily. Possible ones will do. You see Mr. Arastu is not just an adventurer, he's also a scholar, a scholar-*adventurer*, and he wants to know everything that is."

Waseem came over, looking down over Tahira's shoulder chuckled and joined in. "Yes. He doesn't want to close his eyes to possible things because he's too busy looking for the Impossible Animal. Because possible things can be grand too."

Tahira said, "They can, and they have to look carefully, otherwise they won't notice and then where will they be?"

Basheeran smiled at the brother and sister talking. She remembered a time when they had been like this, often. Never having had children of her own, she pretended they were hers and what happened to them hurt her and so, even though both she and Latif were tired, she postponed going back to the village, not ready to abandon Tahira who needed her so.

Armaan was impressed. "So now they have to look for the Impossible Animal *and* for Possible Things."

"Well. Plants for now but, yes, THINGS also," Tahira matched Armaan's awe. He was so serious, her son. It scared her sometimes.

Saira looked at her brother and nodded. If he was that impressed, she had to pay attention. She tugged at his sleeve. He said, "Listen to the story."

"It's over for today, my dears. Basheeran please take them away; it's time for me to complete the drawings."

"But we want to play with Waseem Mamu," Armaan said.

Saira had already run over to her uncle and was tugging at his trousers, demanding to be picked up. She squealed as Waseem tossed her in the air.

He put her down and picked up Armaan. "Hold me up high too, please Waseem Mamu."

"You're getting too big for me to lift that high little man." Waseem kissed him. "Do as your mother says and be off now. I need to talk to her." He forestalled the gathering storm. "Alone."

Tahira was delighted. She wondered what he wanted to talk about.

"Do you mind if I paint while we talk?"

"Of course not." Waseem began to leaf through the pages on the table, pulling some out of the folder. "These are wonderful." He came upon the Strawberrycat. "You came up with that one in one of our games. I was furious. I thought I was the one who liked strawberries and you had beat me to that."

"You remember."

"Of course," he frowned. "What are you going to do with these?"

"I was thinking of having them bound together. The children love them and I want them to be able to remember them. When I'm done with the colouring today, I'll write up the story."

"Why don't you publish them?

"I hadn't thought about it. Do you really think I could?"

"Tahira these are wonderful. Of course people will be interested. I'll look into it."

"Thank you. The other painting feels so… *ordinary*. Chaste still lifes and the occasional, very bland portrait. I seem to have no vision."

"It'll come," he said. Not sure anymore that it would. After all these years, there seemed no point in saying more. He tried not to be too sympathetic for fear of a sudden retreat. Every conversation seemed to require an exhausting delicacy, minute attention to the possibility of abrasion, and a constant effort to keep her from falling away. Sometimes it seemed easier not to try.

"I need a favour."

"Of course. Anything."

"You remember Gul Khan?"

"How could I forget? It was heartbreaking. We were so worried about you."

"He had a daughter—Safiya. She's a remarkable girl. Fierce. Brilliant. She was very close to her father."

"How is the family coping?"

"Struggling. That embroidery you were admiring and some extra stitching along with the money Safiya earns from her tutoring is helping. She's determined to complete medical college and they're trying to get the boy through school. They are remarkable women."

"How often do you visit?"

"Once, maybe twice, a month. One has to be careful. The neighbours would talk and that would put both Safiya and her mother in an even more difficult position. I try to take books for Safiya and textbooks for her brother—other things too. But they have to seem like gifts. I don't want to offend them. She reads a lot, quite a writer as well. Apa visits too. Safiya seems to like her. Although she is always so cautious." In any case, she wants to see the spot where her father was shot. Will you come along? I'm not sure how she'll take it and it would help. I don't think her mother wants to go."

It seemed a morbid thing to want to do, but he so rarely asked her for anything… "Of course," she said, "of course, I'll come. Poor girl."

Waseem and Tahira leaned against the Datsun, a little distance from the neem tree under which which Waseem had waited with Gul Khan's corpse. Now Safiya stood under it, staring at the ground as if she could will it to swell and split, yielding up her father's body, suddenly, miraculously, alive and firm. She began to walk into the stream of traffic to the spot Waseem had vaguely indicated her father had fallen. Waseem ran over to her, calling out, "Safiya! The traffic. Please don't. What will I say to your mother?" Safiya stopped and walked back. She said, biting out the words, "he had so many plans. So many ferocious and *believable* plans. I believed them: how could he just go?"

Tahira tried not to stare too openly. The girl—young woman, she corrected herself—was admirable. The tension in her tall, slender body as she fought the tears trailing slowly down her face was not just evidence of the battle to conquer grief, it was, she realized, part of a deeper defiance. She had seen it the car on the way there and even sitting having tea with her mother before they had driven here. She had an arresting face—narrow, almost gaunt, with large grey eyes that seemed determined to reveal nothing until you realized that she had no desire to hide her fierceness or her defiance or anything else. And yet almost without a hint of expression those eyes could make you feel utterly separate. No, Tahira realized, pulled up short by the redundancy of her pity, the word was *unnecessary*. They could make you feel *unnecessary*. Whatever need lay entwined at the base of her grief, it would not admit her, perhaps anyone. There was nothing indiscriminate about Safiya. For the first time, in what could have been years (when *had* she stopped looking?), she wondered with something approaching excitement what it would be like to paint that face.

Safiya started walking toward the car, turquoise nylon dupatta lifting in the breeze.

"Thank you. We can go now. I needed to *see*. Thank you." Muazzam Khan had been squatting behind the car, systematically probing his teeth with a toothpick. Several now lay destroyed, alongside tiny bits of meticulously excavated betel nut where he had spent the last half hour, a satisfyingly precise measure of boredom. He came round to open the door for Safiya. She looked a little surprised, as she had on the way over and then flashed him a wide smile. "You don't need to do this for me."

"It's okay."

In the car, as if sensing the question that wasn't being asked, she said, "I had to know where he had fallen so I don't forget and so I never give in, you see."

Tahira stifled a startled half-turn and saw that Safiya had noticed it. The girl leaned away and rolled the window further down, and angled her head until the rubber on the frame of the side-window bit into her cheek. She seemed to reach out as if, Tahira thought, she didn't want to be trapped with them. She turned to Tahira suddenly and said, "I'm not used to cars. I prefer rickshaws. They are more expensive than buses so I can't always afford them." Tahira said, wondering why she was arguing, "They are bumpy and tear at your eardrums and toss you like jamuns."

Waseem turned around, intervening. "I know what you mean, Safiya. They are open to the air and in sync with the madness of the city. And," he grinned sympathetically, "you don't have to deal with people."

Safiya closed her eyes and said, as if against her will, "I wanted to see where he had fallen." Then she murmured, "*Khun chalta hai tho rukta nahin sangeenon se/sar uthta hai tho dubta nahin aeenon se.*"

"What was that?" Tahira leaned towards her.

"Nothing. I just remembered some lines from Sahir."

"Which poem?"

"*Blood is still Blood.*"

"It's a powerful poem," Tahira said, trying to believe she liked it, knowing she never had.

Safiya glanced skeptically at the diamonds scattered like crushed ice on Tahira's fingers, clustered on her ears, seeming to stifle the impulse to say something rude. Instead she said, "It is. My father loved it. He would thump his chest in that way he had (we used to call him Tarzan)," she grinned suddenly, "and recite it to us."

Waseem smiled. "He used to recite it a lot and to thump his chest as if he couldn't believe his heart wasn't out there in contact with everyone."

"Yes. He told me that Ludhianvi had dedicated it to a man called Lumumba and told me the story of the assassination. I remembered that so I recited it to Haroon when Allende was assassinated."

"He was always talking about how the Europeans and the Americans would never let a revolution succeed in our part of the world. Although," the smile died, "we seem to be doing a pretty good job of helping them in that ambition." He saw Safiya scrub a tear and wished he hadn't spoken. He tried again. "'Listen' he would say, 'what powerful lines: *When the blood roars it cannot be stopped with bayonets/When the proud head rears it cannot be pressed down by laws.*'" Then he'd get all passionate and say, 'it shouldn't be comforting that bayonets cannot stop blood from flowing but it is'!"

"Yes, he said it was comforting to believe that blood could not be disappeared, that it would clot and expose the cruelty of the tyrants. Once I began to understand the poem, I told him I loved the fact that it said the unbowed head could not be pressed back down by the law, by convention, by the world. He was so proud when I said that."

A few minutes later, when the silence seemed less laden with tears, Waseem spoke again. "How is Haroon? Are his parents coming around?"

She giggled and looked as if she had been transformed into the essence of mischief, suddenly a lot younger than nineteen. "His mother is ferociously opposed. No Pathan girl is going to ruin the purity of their U.P. lineage. I don't suppose anyone can tell her they're not in India anymore. My family certainly can't. Or won't. My uncles disapprove of the way my father raised me and they would like a good Pathan boy to undo the damage. They made fun of the way Urdu-speaking people say their *qafs* to Amma, said they didn't want to have effeminate children, who spoke like that, in the family. Good thing they don't live here. Poor Amma. She pretends to be horrified but I can tell she's amused. It's her way of keeping Baba's memory alive. Anyway, she likes Haroon.

"I gave him a copy of Chughtai's story. You know the one about the Hindu boy and Muslim girl getting married and the farce that followed? Of course, I can't give it to his mother myself but I would have loved to. Maybe even turn up married and then have that crazy dance they do in the story, but we'd need a fuller cast for the opposition to have the complete drama. Maybe we could wheel in Amma and Baba's relatives. In any case, Haroon did his best. He gave it to her and said, 'She was able to imagine Hindus and Muslims in love and we can't even get past the Urdu-speaking/Pathan barrier. Chughtai was from U.P. after all.' You can imagine how his mother responded to *that*."

Waseem chuckled, "Of course! 'That girl is destroying my son!'"

She nodded, still laughing, "Although, he was pretty destroyed when I met him."

Tahira tried to chuckle, taken aback by the girl's glee. It had transformed that austere face which had seemed so piercingly mature, making her seem more like the girl she ought to be, but the frank absence of guilt and shame was still disturbing.

"Gul Khan liked him very much."

"Yes. They liked each other. It keeps me determined when the neighbours talk, and his mother is mean, and, and... But then, I remember, or," she smiled more broadly, "Haroon reminds me." She settled back into her seat, seeming surprised, Tahira thought, that she had relaxed enough to talk to them.

"You go ahead," Shehzad said to Bakhtawar Khan. "I'm enjoying the breeze and have the rest the afternoon off anyway." He leaned back and contemplated the meal. The cream of chicken soup had been a satisfyingly bland alternative to the rice and chicken qorma. Bakhtawar's shashlik had looked good too. And then, of course, the trifle—that greatest of colonial bequests—devoid now of any sherry, wobbling with jelly perched on instant custard and stale cake. And yet we all love it, he grinned at the lurid red bits of jelly stuck to the remaining plates. Jeremy had learned he liked it and, thoroughly amused, had arranged for him to have some the last time he had been in London. Such a pity he had had to decline because of the sherry.

He stared up at the coconut palms and breathed the sea air, briny and pungent and so much a part of the city.

Here at the hotel by the beach the smell was sharp and concentrated. He had always loved this place but today he was not pleased. He had seen Anjum, his latest mistress, with a junior provincial minister half an hour before Bakhtawar left. He knew she had seen him but she had carefully avoided his gaze and it had taken some effort to restrain himself so strong had been the impulse to confront her.

Bakhtawar had asked what he was looking at, and he had had to chuckle and dissimulate. "Look at that minister. These politicians seem to have all the time in the world." So humiliating to almost give himself away to a business associate. But at least now he knew why she hadn't been returning his calls. Or maybe she had become angry because he had finally told her not to call him at home. Nazneen had looked slily at Tahira and said, "Bhaiyya, somebody calls and hangs up but it never happens when you are here."

He had had to tell her to stop. Things just hadn't been the same since Aneela's marriage. She had been so wonderfully direct about these things. No drama. No games. Of course, he hadn't been upset at the ease with which she had gone off to be married. But a few tears at the parting couldn't have hurt. It had all been so cold, surgical almost and even *nice*. As if his participation were not required. It had been a couple of years and mistresses had come and some had gone and here was another one going, but *she* had been different.

It was humiliating to admit, but he missed her. Well, he had a wife and children waiting at home and he would spend the afternoon with his children. He would stop and buy some ice-cream and toys on the way. They would be delighted. Yes, that's what he would do. He stood up and stretched, just a little, a bigger stretch would be improper with so many people around.

Tahira heard Shehzad coming up the stairs and Armaan's and Saira's squeals of delight. The noise went on longer than usual; he must have bought gifts. She looked at the picture she had pulled out and put in her book. She stared at that face in its emphatic little square, which cut up the cursive lines of the script, a beautiful, savage interruption in her book. She smoothed a crease; the edge—revealing the white paper, which had taken the imprint of Aneela's face—was rough to the touch. Shehzad had stopped with the children and would be coming in soon. She put the book down and stood up, walked to the dresser, smoothed her hair and suddenly thought of Safiya and her separateness, which made her defiance seem so unshakeable. She looked at her own eyes and wondered what it would take to make them like hers, and turned with sudden decision. She pulled the photograph out of the book and held it, trembling. Her stomach fluttered as she heard Shehzad coming closer and as he opened the door, afraid that she might change her mind, she thrust the picture into his hand.

"What is this?"

She stared at him.

"What is this?" he repeated, slow and quiet.

"Why does she call here?" Tahira yelled, suddenly enraged by his pretense and his conviction that he had a right to his anger. "Does she think I'm stupid? Do you? Does she think that if she hangs up we won't know. You think I don't know how your sisters laugh behind my back every time it happens. Your mother can barely hide how delighted she is that you are humiliating me. I am the mother of your children and I'm being treated like nothing by that..." Tahira stopped, stunned that she had almost used the word in his presence.

Shehzad stared at her with growing disbelief. Was she really raising her voice at him? Aneela had never called. He needed no reminder of that today. He was even sure he had instructed Tahira in the story of the woman who had seen a picture of her husband's lover, cleaned it and put it back in its place, but such women were the stuff of legend. A man with such a wife would blessed. Such a man could do anything, instead here was this bitch raising her voice at him. At *him!*

"Am I losing my senses or have you?" His voice cracked loud as the slap through the room.

BOOK *four*

15

Tahira moved closer to the self-portrait, drawn by the restraint in the face, the chastity in the demeanour. The contained reference to the greater, more violent asymmetries of Picasso and Braque in the asymmetry of the subject's eyes added a hint of tension, showing the struggle in such restraint; even the umbers and siennas of the background and the face kept faith with that propriety. The thin, black trim at the neck, with its contrast to the grey white sweater made the possibility of a bolder, brighter colour seem like a lurid fiction—inappropriate, perennially external.

"Strange that Zubeida Agha can do some brilliantly, even violently, coloured paintings, making this one seem subdued, but its aggression is so awful because it's completely directed at herself."

Tahira jumped a little. Andaleep had crept up behind her. "I like it. It doesn't seem aggressive to me."

"Hmm. I think of it as a peculiar ode to the power of North Indian genteel femininity with the power all turned in against the women themselves, by themselves, as much as anything outside. As if, if we can perfect our own prison, we can pretend we haven't been put into one—beating anyone else to the punch."

"You always had the strangest ideas about these things." Tahira laughed a small, unfriendly laugh. "Where do you come up with them?"

Andaleep decided not to notice the tone. "Yes. I suppose I do come up with these things but I do think it's an aggressive painting."

"Thanks for bringing me here," Tahira changed the subject. "The collection is so wonderful. It always lifts my spirits." She looked at the wall of paintings: Chughtai, Jamil Naqsh, Shakir Ali, Ahmed Pervaiz whose bright, twisting, phallic forms always scared her a little, and those sketches of human figures by Sadequain… as if the word had been brought to life. So the bodies had the inflamed silhouette of calligraphic script but managed to look emphatically, unmistakably corporeal and… tortured…even when presented as a vision of triumphant man. She took a deep breath. "It's a remarkable collection. A little dizzying too. I always learn so much."

Andaleep wondered why Tahira didn't start her own. Shehzad wasn't lacking in money and the jewellery she was wearing was not cheap. She didn't say anything.

Tahira continued, "I think if I lived with such paintings, every day would bring a reproach. Such vision only seems to mock my own squandered ability."

"It's not like that. You know that. And the stories you are illustrating and composing are so wonderful. The other stuff will come."

Tahira's smile was secretive, exclusive. She said with the air of changing a subject not entirely intelligible to others: "Besides, can you imagine what my mother-in-law would say if I tried to take over any space?"

"Is there any chance of you moving out and away from those people?"

"Let's go. We have to pick up the children from school." She did not say she was not sure how she would live with

Shehzad alone, without the walls and distractions provided by his family. The longer she stayed with him, the harder it was to say anything about him without condemning herself. She had thought about it though, often.

Begum Ali, wife of a powerful civil servant and well aware of it, gloriously dressed and coordinated to the hilt as always, came into the room. "You have always liked that painting, Tahira. Ever since the first time you came with Andaleep and her mother. Such a strong face, I've always thought. So strong but not at all vulgar. Here are the clothes for your mother, Andaleep." She handed her a bundle wrapped in exquisitely fine cotton. "The embroidery took longer than usual—some crisis in the family—but it *is* perfect as always. Those *tiny*, *delicate* stitches. I'm surprised their eyes can take it."

"Thank you, auntie. She'll be thrilled. Unfortunately we have to leave."

"I know. Let me show you out. The *mogra* is laden with blooms. Please take some for your mother."

The gardener was crisscrossing the lawn—slicing the implausibly plush grass with a spindly lawnmower. It was good, Tahira thought, that government gardeners came with government water. She said, "What a beautiful lawn," looking down at Begum Ali as she gathered the thick, white flowers, heavy with scent into the little silver bowl she had brought out. Begum Ali turned her head up and smiled, serene with privilege and apparently oblivious to the tension weaving in and out between them. "Yes, we are blessed. I oversee everything that happens in the garden myself. See?" she pointed, proud of her exertions, "I just had that crate of plants sent from Bangkok. Our ambassador in Thailand arranged it."

The driver took the bundle from Andaleep, placed it in the car and came round to open the door. The Mazda pulled out of the government bungalow's driveway, Begum Ali waving and smiling, gorgeous in her royal blue, embroidered cotton sari, matching bangles and jasmine wrapped around the immaculate knot at the nape of her neck.

Andaleep took the lid of the little silver bowl and buried her nose in the blossoms, trying to think of what to say. Silence had used to be so much more comfortable between them—now it was heavy and raw, an appalling reminder that she was, after all, a creature of propriety. Talking about oneself just wasn't done, Tahira's demeanour announced, and she found herself assenting and then resenting the assent. Heavy and raw and so layered and imminent—with things that could be said, should be said and that simply receded under Tahira's disapproving reserve, sidling out backwards like the cowed subjects of a capricious king, she thought with irritation and the increasingly familiar stirrings of rebellion. She did not believe it had always been so. Or perhaps distance and absence had simply made her more sensitive to the primness and disapproval that had underlain their friendship. Then again, perhaps Tahira had changed.

She withdrew her face from the bowl as Tahira spoke, grateful to be rescued from her thoughts and from burial in the flowers, whose scent was beginning to overpower her.

"You are still coming for dinner tonight, right?" Tahira wondered why she felt the need to confirm.

Andaleep thought quickly, trying to come up with a plausible excuse and then surrendered. "Yes."

She had regularly sought Tahira's company since she had come back a few months ago, uncertain each time why she did, determined like a reluctant lover to wait longer before arranging some other meeting, determined to resist and overcome the impulse to call and visit, and instead finding that that very impulse made her call more, out of fear or guilt or both....

Tahira persisted, a little guilty now at her earlier sharpness, afraid that Andaleep might not want to come; there seemed a marked lack of enthusiasm in her confirmation. "It will be very nice. Shehzad always enjoys it when you are with us and the children love you. Armaan can't wait to show you his new glasses and Saira turns into a laughing doll around you. It's quite lovely." She kept the jealousy out of her voice; Saira was very much Shehzad's daughter she had decided, gleeful and imperious to his visible and startling delight. Now that Andaleep was back, Saira just melted every time she saw her.

She took a blossom from the bowl Andaleep had put down between them. The petals were white and firm, strangely substantial for such a small flower. She ran a finger around the edges, learning its contours and tugged at a petal. Not precisely pearly, its whiteness, she thought, more like cream. The scent was calming. She began again, "Are you going to take the job at the university?"

"I think so."

"What about…?" She stopped herself.

"… Khaled?" Andaleep smiled. "I don't know. He has a life there, an important life… and I, I can't make up my mind."

Tahira wondered if it really were because Andaleep wanted to be back here, at home. She wondered what she could say. It was strange that she had two children and Andaleep was not even married. It didn't seem right. "Can I say something that would help?" she asked, and then, "Don't you want to be married?"

Andaleep turned sideways to look at her, baffled yet again by her dearest friend. "I don't know what that means."

Tahira was startled. "Surely, it's obvious."

"No. It's not."

Now Tahira turned to stare at her, brow furrowed with irritation. "How can you not know what I mean? We were raised to be married."

"Yes, and so what does desire have to do with it? I don't remember being raised to *want* to be married. It was fate and destiny and sacrifice and inevitability and virtue and, and, and… Remember?" She sighed. "What does wanting have to do with anything?" She exhaled slowly, trying not to lose her temper completely.

"But we *wanted* it too," Tahira persisted.

"How can you want something when you don't know what wanting is, and…" knowing she was being cruel but unable to stop, she continued, "when you don't know what it is you want. Did you know what lay at the end of all that, what it was that you had wanted all that time before you got it?" She saw Tahira flinch. "I'm really sorry. I don't know when to shut up sometimes." The car pulled up at Tahira's parents' house. "I'll help you take the bags inside."

"It's okay. I can get them." She waved the driver away. "It's not that much; I can take it in. Don't leave Andaleep Bibi alone in the car." She turned to Andaleep. "I'll see you later tonight."

She walked towards the front lounge as Saira catapulted out, leaving the doors swinging violently behind her. Armaan followed, dodging the doors.

"Where were you?"

"Why didn't you take us with you?"

"What's in the bags? Can I look inside?"

Tahira laughed, happy to forget her mood. "Quiet! Let me go inside and get some water. It's hot. Do you want me to bake?"

"That would be funny," Saira giggled. "Baked mummy."

Armaan admonished her, pompous with the seniority of fifteen months. "Don't be rude to Amma."

Saira tossed her head, tugging to look inside one of her mother's bags. "Baked mummy, baked mummy with jam and cheese."

Tahira kept walking. "You might find out if there's something inside for you if you let me go inside and put the bags down. You too," she nodded at her self-important little son.

Saira surrendered her hold on the bags. "Okay, baked mummy." She looked at Armaan to see how he was responding and, apparently satisfied with what she saw, she marched ahead. "I'll hold the door open. Then you can sit down and show me."

Tahira shook her head and followed. She put her bags down and Saira began to rifle through them. Seema came into the room. "Should I get you some tea, Tahira Apa?" Then leaning down to kiss Saira, who was holding a yellow dress aloft with triumph, "Oye, brat, calm down. Should I take them away while you recover and have some tea. Shsssh…" she waved a hand at the chorus of protest.

"It's okay," Tahira said. "I haven't seen them for a few hours. Maybe a little later, when I go into the studio."

"No. I want to come and paint," Saira said.

"You know the studio is where I go to do my work. And I need silence there. We can work on the story together but then you will go with Seema Khala. No," she interrupted the protests that were coming from both children, "we will not argue about this. Besides Andaleep Khala is going to have dinner with us. Don't you want to see her? If you don't sleep in the afternoon you won't be able to do that."

"Hurrah!" Saira tried out a new word, raising her arms in the air.

"Hurrah!" Armaan joined in, not ready to surrender the word to her, raising his arms too.

Tahira looked at them and then at Seema. "'Hurrah'? I can't believe I produced them sometimes."

"I've been reading Enid Blyton to them." Seema grinned.

Tahira groaned.

She looked at Saira who was rifling through the bags looking to see what else she could find, mischievous, playful, so easy with her father.

Seema looked at Tahira, a little stern. "She's only a child."

Tahira looked up, startled, and shook her head, pretending not to know what Seema meant. Waseem had said something similar recently; they seemed to think that she was unfair to Saira, as if one could be jealous of one's own child. She reached for anger, "I know, but she is hard to control."

Armaan looked from his aunt to his mother and then turned to Saira, "You are making Amma angry."

"No. You are silly. Amma are you angry?" She crawled into her mother's lap.

"No. Of course, not." Tahira stifled a pang of guilt. She kissed her head. Armaan clambered next to her and wriggled to fit himself into her side, determined not to be excluded.

"I'll get some tea." Seema went out, glad to have intervened.

Tahira turned Saira around on her lap, looking intently at her face. Then, not wanting to upset her with the intensity of her stare, she started tidying Saira's hair and wiped an invisible smudge from her nose. She was a wiry child, with her father's large eyes and dimple. People often said she looked like her father. How could one have produced a child in whom there appeared no trace of oneself?

Saira returned the look, then, as if skeptical of the seriousness of her mother's scrutiny, started tidying her mother's hair with ostentatious solemnity. Armaan squirmed, annoyed at the exclusion.

"Armaan's turn," Tahira forced a laugh, hoping that they were too young to understand her tones.

Saira narrowed her eyes, whether to assess her mother's change of mood or in mischievous mimicry of her father, Tahira didn't know. She hoped it was mischief. Besides, she consoled herself with a question, how could a child who was just a few months over five be so astute? She ought not let her mood colour her judgment, she thought, settling into the now familiar comfort of self-admonition.

~

Having had lunch, heard a story and coaxed, cajoled, whined and flirted their grandmother into giving them some condensed milk, which both then licked off their little plates with their fingers, Saira and Armaan had finally been persuaded to fall asleep. Tahira wondered if they would be able to find anyone to truly replace Basheeran who had finally said that she and Latif were too old to work anymore and wanted to return to their village. She wondered if the children seemed more unmanageable because they were angry she had let Basheeran go. She had overheard Mariam tell Waseem she had said that and winced at his response, sardonic, dismissive: "Never having had to manage them herself—not really," he overruled Mariam's protest, "she isn't really qualified to make the judgment, is she?" Malice had always seemed impossible from Waseem, but he was angry these days. She shook her head, clearing the noise; she *could* not think about *all* the sources of his anger.

She picked up the latest volume of the collection of stories she had finally had bound and published at Waseem's urging. The children loved them. And, as she flicked through the pages, looking at the bold ink-outlined scenes and figures and solidly rendered Urdu script, the fluidity of the characters' movement, the precision of the cartoons and whimsical intelligence of the stories, even Tahira felt she was capable of accomplishment, of *completing* things. She placed it on the shelf where the children's books and games were kept and moved from the small antechamber, where she usually played and drew with the children, into the studio.

She had redecorated it a few months ago. A *takht* had been placed in an alcove, where she lay down when she wanted to rest away from the children. An armchair sat next to a two-tier end-table, which usually had a stack of books she was reading on the lower shelf. When she went in after lunch, her tea was brought in and placed on the top tier. In one corner of the large room, a long industrial table with large drawers held supplies. In front of the table was a stool on which she sometimes sat to write in her notebooks or mark exercise books. Behind this were tall bookshelves with books of philosophy and English and Urdu literature, books on painting and painters.

In the centre of the room was a large open space with an easel on which waited a half finished painting. When there was no painting in progress, she would leave a prepped canvas on the easel. It waited in a state of expectation, ready to take her imprint, reassuringly, insuperably hers, not needing to be shared. She told herself she was learning how to paint and she would practice painting still lifes and portraits. The humility of the conceit had been safe and then, almost without notice, freeing. A few weeks ago, suddenly, she had started a series that seemed to suggest a graduation of sorts.

After finishing her tea, she had assembled objects for a still life. First, a large, ripe chaunsa, a hint of saffron suffusing its yellow. She had peeled off a couple of strips of its skin, varying in thickness to reveal the different tones of the mango's flesh, sucking on the peel as she arranged it next to some dried apricots, a couple of chikoos and small green grapes that seemed to have caramelized as they edged towards rot. The fruit lay around or tumbled off a terracotta plate with the outlines of a large, abstracted black flower painted at its centre. The arrangement was beautiful, already a powerful study in colour and textures close to each other but subtle enough in their differentiation to reward her characteristically meticulous work. Her paintings had acquired a density over the years. Small, heavy, carefully cumulative strokes gave an impression of solidity and mass, deepening the hues but still luminous.

When she began to draw the arrangement, she found she did not want to. Suddenly struck by terror that the restlessness would send her back to the time she could not do anything, she had run to the garden to pick flowers which she then arranged into a carefully dishevelled cluster, mauve bougainvillea, subsiding clumps of crimson and pink rangoon creeper blooms, scarlet ixoras and put them in an indigo ceramic vase, placed on ruched and folded starched white tablecloth, a few papery bougainvillea blossoms and graceful eucalyptus leaves scattered at the base.

She went to the canvas, hoping the competing intensity of the colours would overcome her mood, but found she did not want to look at the arrangement. She began to draw out of desperation—anything, any mark, any movement was better than the paralysis of those early years—and saw that she had drawn an armchair and a table. She forced a deep breath and continued to draw, careful not to think about what was happening. A little while later, she found a room empty of people had taken shape on the canvas.

In the far left corner of the background, was an armchair next to which sat a small table on which lay an open book. In the right foreground was a tall round dining table without chairs. On it were two large plates and two glasses. All were empty. In the centre was a bowl piled with mangoes, guavas, apricots and plums. A half-eaten guava rolled incongruous and discarded next to the bowl. The painting was cut in half by a kilim woven with a repeating pattern of hexagonal forms, which she decided would be beige, deep purple and black.

In the subsequent days, Tahira had painted this in rich, densely applied oils, deep hued with the lightest sheen. The scene was powerful and throbbed with expectation as if the closed windows she had painted on the two sides could open any instant to let in an exuberant child, a friend, or, she had thought, stepping back to assess the completed painting, a thief. The guava brought a whiff of abandonment into the room, which seemed to wait for so much. Tahira had been surprised and decided to embark on a series titled 'The Empty Room.' Perhaps she could live up to her own promise after all, the thought had formed and quickly been pushed aside…

Today, close to completion, the third painting, a canvas with another empty room, waited on the easel. A single bed covered with a maroon quilt took up the left side of the painting. Above the bed was a portrait of an old woman in a grey sari, a garland of roses flung around it. A vase packed with pink, mauve, yellow, and white snapdragons, a small transistor radio, and a half drunk glass of milk sat on the bedside table. Just under was a pewter spittoon. A small settee with a coffee table faced the bed. The coffee table was stacked with magazines held down by a small, tourist's Gandharan Buddha head, next to which lay an open book and a cup of tea.

Each one of the paintings would have an open book, and each book would have some script, a signature, lines from different novels, short stories or poems visible on the open pages, she had decided after completing the first painting. In the first painting, she had written the description of Gautam sculpting the statue of the woman with the kadamba bough in *Ag ka Darya*. In the novel, the statue had survived over centuries only to end up curated and unintelligible in a museum more than two thousand years later, yet another discarded woman, surviving in the novel only as a memory of a different beauty, she thought.

Tahira found the novel's vision of time terrifying and riveting and—thinking of the stupas, statues and ruins, emblems of destroyed civilizations and mute histories, scattered throughout it—had painted a full Gandharan Buddha into her second room. Its opaque grace dominated the painting, imagined as a room in a museum designated for a solitary sculpture. The statue was placed in the centre, the focus of an artful, curatorial light, presiding, powerful and inscrutable, a reminder of the terrible persistence of endings and the necessity of human loneliness, emancipating and devastating all at once. She had loved painting the carved stone—creating the illusion of its heft and mass, seeming to defy the limit of painting, entirely contained within its two dimensions. A small book with her signature floated in the lower right hand corner.

She had decided to add a small, ornamental and fake Buddha head to the third painting, perhaps, she had thought, to remind the viewer of the indulgence in such a beautiful arrangement of muteness. It was time to complete it. She walked over to the table with the books and picked up the Ghalib *ghazal* she had written on a loose leaf of paper the day before. She had always been drawn to it, always found its first couplet disconcerting, a little dizzying, a little frightening, but she wanted to write it down, to place it in the room she was painting, staring up from the open pages, tempting the reader with its ambiguous invitation. She could never decide if Ghalib had only meant in that extraordinary, *demanding* first couplet that if there had been nothing there would still have been God—attesting to God's completeness, His lack of *need*, to the irrelevance and redundancy of the Universe, or whether he also meant, in some punning but not at all trivial way, that he would have been God himself even if there were nothing else.

Unable to believe in that slippery, wondrous ambiguity she had written the first couplet with variant meanings in parentheses once, trying to see if she had imagined it. She had found the diary in which she had written it a while ago and put it in the studio. She rifled the books and papers on the table and found the notebook:

When there was nothing there was God, had there been nothing there would have been God,

(When he (Ghalib) was nothing he was God, had he been nothing he would still have been God)

Existence took me under, but had I not existed what would it have mattered?

(Being took me under, but had I not existed what would have been or could possibly have existed.)

She had wondered, still wondered: how could one suggest something so terribly grand and yet be so unable to celebrate being itself? How could being be the cause of one's own dissolution and at the same time provide one with the capacity to compete for divinity? What did it mean to say that one had been sunk by *being*, to write: had I not existed what would have been? To negate everything in one sweeping and compact phrase? Could he really mean that being itself would have been undone if he had not existed? And then to say in those last two lines that Ghalib had died long ago but missed himself (that tremblingly passive phrase—but was missed!), and, dead, still missed the possibility of wondering at every turn what would happen if things were arranged differently, missed the ability to wonder at the possibility of different futures. What a signature that was—how perfectly had an ambition, divine in its scope, merged with self-extinction. She read the poem aloud one more time and walked over to the canvas, to begin to ink it on to the blank pages of the open book, next to the magazine and the small Buddha head on the coffee table, in careful *nastaliq* script.

نہ تھا کچھ تو خدا تھا کچھ نہ ہوتا تو خدا ہوتا

ڈبویا مجھ کو ہونے نے نہ ہوتا میں تو کیا ہوتا

ہوا جب غم سے یوں بے حس تو غم کیا سر کے کٹنے کا
نہ ہوتا گر جدا تن سے تو زانوں پر دھرا ہوتا
ہوئی مدت کہ غالب مر گیا پر یاد آتا ہے
وہ ہر ایک بات پہ کہنا کہ یوں ہوتا تو کیا ہوتا

She stepped back. The poem seemed to dominate the painting, which was vivid and sad and in a state of waiting like the other two but could not match the poem. She would have to find a more fitting frame.

She heard a clock strike somewhere in the house. It would be time get the children ready for dinner soon. It made things easier that her parents were happy to take care of them while she worked in the studio. Shireen complained about never getting to see her grandchildren, but even Shehzad no longer listened. She shook her head at the invasion of the studio by that other life. Thinking and painting and peace—being itself, she sometimes felt—had become confined to these walls.

In the studio these past few weeks, thought had been powerful and absorbing, connected with so much, and yet so amnesiac and mercifully severed from so much else. She *could* not take her thinking outside to be tainted by the prurience and need of others, to be used to explain her life or make those who loved her more comfortable. So much need and insistence and anger, so much enervating *demand*. She would not tell Andaleep and Waseem what she was doing, had not even been tempted to today, standing before that wall of paintings. It did not occur to her that she did not think of telling Shehzad.

16

Andaleep called Waseem. "I've been back for months and want to see you."

"Parrot! Thanks for those copies of *Lotus* you sent with Tahira. Safdar and I've been reading them. Of course. I'd love to see you too," he paused. "Safdar, too, you know."

"Did Tahira tell you?"

"About your man in Beirut. Yes, she did. And I told Safdar. But I'm sure he'd like to see you anyway. He's very depressed about the political situation. What happened in Beirut anyway? You're still with him, then?"

She stroked the curves of the black telephone, tracing the swelling mounds and sudden dips. "I don't know. I find I'm discovering quite a talent for evasion and postponement."

"Like your friend."

She winced. "Perhaps. But I don't think she's postponing anything. I'm not sure she thinks there could ever be an 'after'. How do you postpone when you think like that? I think you just wait for time to pass."

Waseem sighed a bitter, frustrated sigh. "We have to become philosophers of time to deal with such ordinary obscenity."

"You haven't changed."

He bristled. "Should I?"

"No: I'm glad. When fine poets need to write poems called 'Samjotha', it's clear that some of us need to remain immune to compromise. Let's go to the beach with halva-puri and kebabs. My parents still have their cottage at Sandspit. Ask Safdar along if you think it won't be too awkward."

"He'll be fine."

Andaleep clenched and then spread her toes, feeling the water dissolve the sand between them. The breeze and waves were cool against her skin. It was good to be home. She looked up at Waseem and smiled. He turned to the hut where Safdar sat on the porch, smoking a cigarette and sipping tea from a plastic cup. "Come down, lazybones."

"Later. Come up and have some tea. It's a perfect Kashmiri pink."

"He got up at the crack of dawn to brew it. Crazy man," Waseem chuckled.

They began to walk slowly to the verandah, feet sinking in the sand. "Ah mercy, mercy me/Ah things aren't what they used to be" Marvin Gaye's voice, tender, a little wistful wafted from the small taperecorder sitting on a table by Safdar's side.

"He loves that song."

Andaleep thought of the prose poem on gardens he had sent her in Beirut. "Of course, he does. I love that song, too, and Marvin Gaye's voice, so plaintive and gentle and so much latent pain."

"You should tell Safdar."

Andaleep struck at the opportunism. "Khaled introduced me to Marvin Gaye."

"Sorry. Believe me, I'm not trying to broker a marriage here."

"Really?"

"Well, it seems like you are not going back and the two of you like each other. Seems such a waste. And you have been back for months and seem fine. Doesn't he mind?"

"Of course, he minds. But he has much more important things to do," she paused and then said, "You want Safdar to be miserable? But, yes," she grimaced, "it has occurred to me. What's happened to us that we have become so insensitive?"

He nodded, a little embarrassed. "I'm sure he does... But I don't think it's insensitive. Friendship and attraction matter and I know there's both here. Anyway, see how things turn out. You'll have a clearer sense of what you want."

"Or not."

"Don't let the commitment to misery get you too."

"Okay." She knelt to pick up a shell, caressing its whorls and tracing the raised pinpricks encircling it. She liked its opalescent sheen and the salmon and sienna striations, the faint line of mauve running through the pink. She handed it to Waseem and watched him turn it over in his hands.

"Keep it."

"I'll give it to Armaan." Neither wanted to comment on Tahira's absence or their tacit agreement not to ask her along. It was impossible to think or talk in her presence, Andaleep thought; she seemed to suck everything into the vortex of her despair. But one couldn't even show that one recognized it as such, so one had to try to agree with whatever newly implacable mode of justification for her life she happened to be comfortable with on the day one was with her.

Dinner with Tahira and Shehzad had been intolerable, as it so often was. He was flirtatious with Andaleep, practiced, impersonal, ingratiating all at once ("Your independence is so attractive. There should be more women like you.") Terse and monitory with Tahira ("Can't you even oversee a dinner properly? This is the wrong dinner set. Why do I buy all these fine things when my wife is incapable of valuing them?") Confiding and disappointed to Andaleep ("If I only had a good manager, a major domo, I could do so much more with my life. It's difficult when you have to oversee everything yourself. One needs a good wife, a true *partner* you know.") Indulgent to the children, especially Saira, whom he managed to indicate—with the turn of a back on Tahira, an ostentatious incline of the head towards his daughter just as Tahira said something—was somehow unconnected to her, his without the taint of disappointment or imperfection, his without her.

It was intolerable to be caught in the eddies and swirls of that tension, to feel such helpless pity for the children having to differentiate the moment of being loved from the moment they were brandished as weapons, trying to understand when both were true in the same instance. Tahira already resented her daughter. Andaleep had caught Tahira's surreptitious looks of envy when Saira sat in her father's lap, tugging his hair and gleefully, imperiously, tweaking his nose, saw the way she looked at Andaleep when Saira showed her melting delight in Andaleep's presence.

And Tahira? Why did she put up with such needless, endless humiliation? Why did she subject all who loved her to the sullying laceration of witnessing this year in and year out? Andaleep found it exhausting, as if her own life were being slowly consumed, disappearing into some cavernous monster's maw. And then came the guilt and then the impatience and anger at the guilt.... With each encounter, she understood a little more the layers of resentment and rage and bitterness in Waseem's voice when he mentioned her.

She picked up a stone, a perfect polished slate crossed by veins of translucent white and pink. The crystals caught the light; miniscule glitters in the sun. "You know Tahira taught me to notice the colours in things. I was an aspiring and not very good painter. Tons of enthusiasm; some, not much, talent, and no patience. She taught me to look and paint a little better."

"Me too. Not painting.—I can't do that—but she did teach me to see the colours hidden in things." They hoisted themselves over the ledge onto the verandah and took the cups Safdar handed to them. The tea was fragrant; the hint of cardamom delicate and independent in the briny air.

Safdar leaned back in the chair, humming to the music and lit a cigarette. He looked beautiful as always, Andaleep thought. It was hard not to stare at those cheekbones and luminous dark skin. The slight hint of stubble added a tinge of olive. She was loath to reveal what lay beneath the apparent tranquility of the moment. There was sadness in his eyes, in the tilt of his head. She had been wondering all day if it were really that bad. He had always seemed so proud, even brash—all that insistent nonsense about Lawrence, she smiled to herself.

He looked at her quizzically. "What?"

"I'm remembering your brash assertions about Lawrence all those years ago," hoping to provoke him out of the sadness.

"I was brash, wasn't I?"

It wasn't the answer she had hoped to elicit, "Oh don't give in so easily." She paused, and then said, "Is it really that bad?"

"Yes, I suppose it is."

"Why now, why particularly so?" Waseem looked up from the copy of *Lotus* in which he had been hiding to let them talk, curious to hear what Safdar would say. Gul Khan's death still lay as a barrier to the most ordinary conversation, as if the grief were lurking beneath the taut silence they had stretched and hammered into place. A slip here, a stray word there, could make it swell and overwhelm. Even thinking about it made one reach for the most overwrought description.

"I could tell you how the PM had his own minister picked up and beaten. Some say he had the son tortured because he was angry that his father wouldn't wait for him for dinner and dared to say something about his autocratic ways. You know he's taken to inviting his ministers for dinner and then making them wait for hours. So Akhtar walked out and the PM had the Federal Security Forces go to his house and beat him and torture his son."

He looked at Andaleep as she drew in her breath sharply. Akhtar had been such a charismatic student leader and an important figure in the Party, he had even written the party manifesto. "Or I could talk about Sino-Soviet splits on the left… or, of course, Gul Khan's death… or obscene constitutional amendments… or about the minister stuck in a dungeon… or the suppression of students… or what's happening to the Baluch, about how we were aided by American supplied Irani helicopters and Irani pilots against them…. But in the end it's about the despair that comes when the language of hope and aspiration and justice that you thought was yours has been infected by the very people who claim to espouse your own principles. What's the antidote to that? What do you say then? Even thinking becomes harder because there's a split in your self. Besides, we knew how deep the PM's connections to the military were, knew about how toxic his brand of nationalism was. We thought we were being sophisticated and strategic. So what right do we have to be in despair? And I ask myself: how dare we be surprised?"

He smiled bleakly. "So silence is easier but then impossible, as this moment so generously demonstrates. It's all just waiting to disgorge itself in a crazy torrent." He smiled again, apologetically, and then as if correcting the smile, said, "Why apologize? This is the rage and the despair. At least, the rage helps."

Waseem spoke. "I'm glad you said that. I feel sometimes if I admit it, I'll betray everything, as if confusion and failure are a form of betrayal, and betrayal lurks everywhere, around every corner."

Andaleep exhaled…a long, deep sigh. The music took over as Safdar poured more tea and they sipped it slowly. A little while later Andaleep said, "I'm going to go for a walk."

"Company?" Safdar asked.

"If you like."

"I'll stay here and read."

Waseem ignored their smiles at his ploy and kept reading, ostentatious in his absorption.

"Let's run," Andaleep called as she rushed ahead.

Safdar followed. Half a mile later, she stopped and collapsed into the sand. He fell next to her. "I've missed you."

"It's been years. How could you even remember me?"

"I don't know. I've wondered that myself, but I did and so it was…" he corrected himself, "and so it *is*. Besides, I missed getting to know you, which I wanted to do…terribly."

"You know what happened, might still be happening, in Beirut. I can't offer much."

"I know."

"You deserve better."

"Probably," he said and leaned over to kiss her, bringing cardamom and smoke and sweat.

She bit his tongue gently and then kissed him with growing passion and thought: maybe this is not so bad after all.

17

Mariam came running to Waseem as he entered the house. "Seema has locked herself in her room and won't come out. When I try to speak to her through the door, she screams, this mad, unceasing howl like a wolf baying at the moon. Maybe you can talk some sense into her. Where have you been these past two days? You have to stop your political activities. You'll get yourself killed one of these days."

"Why has she locked herself in?" He ignored the question and then looked carefully at her face. "What did you do? And where is Abba?"

As if on cue, his father came into the lounge. Helpless, embattled, habitually in need of rescue. Mariam looked at him with contempt and turned to Waseem. "There he is, ineffectual as ever."

"What did *you* do?" He repeated the question, refusing to be distracted. His father's uselessness at such times, amplified over the years, was too familiar to be interesting.

She tried to look injured and innocent. "What do you mean? What could I have done? You know she's been difficult ever since Nilofer left to study in London. We should never have let her go. I don't know why your father agreed."

Intizar ignored the barb and sat down heavily, diving for the copy of *Afkaar* that lay on the table.

Waseem tried not to raise his voice, "What did you do? Oh what's the point?" He turned to go to Seema's room. "Don't follow me," he said as he walked up the stairs and knocked. Seema started screaming.

"It's not Amma, it's me. Stop that infernal noise and tell me what she's done."

The screaming stopped. "She's produced some bureaucrat's son for me to marry. I've told her I'm not going to do it. She's not content with one miserable daughter. She wants another one. Do you remember how much she liked Shehzad? I should have left to go to England with Nilofer. But I don't want to be abroad," she started crying.

"Do you really not want to marry anyone or is there someone else?"

She opened the door and let him in, peering suspiciously around to see if her mother was with him. She saw her, standing behind the corner at the entrance to the stairs. "Of course, she's listening."

Waseem sighed. "Of course, she is. Let me come in. We can talk with the door closed. You can listen at the door," he called out, "we'll just whisper."

He sat on the edge of the bed. "Tell me."

"There is a boy who likes me and who might be human. But I don't want to find out if he is. Look around. There's Shehzad, the monster, Abba, who hides in his books, and you, so driven, you hardly seem to notice anyone. Lost in your politics, immune to women, or anything romantic... why would I want to find out?"

He winced at the injustice.

"But that's not why I'm crying. I don't want to marry and certainly not someone she produces. She's been at it for weeks, first it was hints, then it was stories about his accomplishments; he's studied engineering in the States, apparently. Then she told me it would make her happy and, of course, when that didn't work, she brandished Abba's unhappiness. He seems so helpless, who would want to make him more unhappy?"

"He's not that helpless." Waseem was terse. "He's chosen to let her make us all insane because it's easier for him and he can hide. You don't have to protect him, just so he can continue to inhabit his evasive little island."

"I can't help him anyway. When I think about it, I feel like I'm going to choke. You know, I think Shehzad Bhai hits Tahira Apa. I told Amma I thought so and she cursed him and then said it's between a man and his wife. I hate them all sometimes. I think Nilofer left because she couldn't bear to be around all this, not just because she wanted to study more. We all try to escape in our different ways, don't we?"

Waseem was taken aback but also proud. Perhaps at least one sister would escape the trap.

Seema turned to him, intense and demanding, "What about you? Why don't *you* marry? Is there someone?"

He smiled a little ruefully. "No. I wonder if I'm strange sometimes. There was a girl I liked at college, but she was married. Anyway, I think all my fierceness deserts me when I am in those situations. More of my father's son then I care to admit." He tried a deflection. "Besides, can you imagine Amma as a mother-in-law?"

"True," she laughed, "she'd be awful." Then waited for him to continue.

His smile was rueful. "I do watch Safdar when he's flirting. Although, there's less of that these days. He really is in love with Andaleep."

Seema smiled. "I like Andaleep Apa. She gives one hope. It's the laughter. Women don't laugh like that, as if ones freedom lies in a loud laugh. It's gorgeous."

He was glad she had stopped sobbing. "I'm going to tell Amma to leave you alone. But we have to come up with some longer-term strategy. Not everyone is like Shehzad, or Abba, or..." he grimaced, "me. And the family has unravelled since Tahira's marriage. Things are much worse."

"Yes, but enough are...and the family might be worse, but Abba was always in hiding and Amma was always ambitious and controlling and determined to protect our place in society, whatever that means. Prowling the perimeter of the family like a cheetah, but protecting the family means sacrificing each one of us in turn. Different jungle. Different rules. So, yes, it might be worse, but you know very well it's not new."

She got up and touched a painting on the wall. It was from before Tahira's wedding, a series of graceful interwoven shapes, not wrenched out of any alphabet but sinuous as calligraphy. The shimmering reds and oranges and yellows seemed to glow in a bath of ultramarine, inviting and full of promise. "Look," she said, stabbing the painting, the tears of rage and futility about to reappear, "she used to do *this*—and now..."

Waseem bowed his head and sighed again. "I know... But you can't let her life become yours."

"*That*, Waseem Bhai, is precisely what I'm trying to avoid."

"Maani, go sit with your father," Tahira said, as she prepared dinner in the kitchen. Armaan was watching her cook. Saira, always more comfortable with her father, was in the lounge with her grandparents, nestled in his lap, tugging at his ear. He was always so indulgent with her. Tahira tried to imagine approaching his person with such unselfconsciousness, such ease and habit.

"I don't want to play with him."

"But you should: he's your father."

"Why does he hit you?"

"Shhh," she said, afraid lest someone walk in and accuse her of intrigue and conspiracy against Shehzad and the family yet again. Shireen's insinuations, coming in subtly different and yet numbing and relentlessly familiar variations—virtuoso in their own way, Tahira supposed—that she was turning the children against their father had increased over the years as the children grew older and asserted their preference for Tahira's family, their love for their mother, their right to demand things from their father. What was the point in insisting that he didn't need any help? That would just be insolent. She sighed with exhaustion.

"Forget that happened, Armaan, things happen between grown-ups. It's like you and Saira fighting. You know how you fight." She chuckled, unconvincing even to herself. "Anyway, I'm almost done and I'll join you soon."

He paused, thinking carefully in that way he was developing—in the way she found so beautiful and disconcerting. And then shook his head. "No, it's not the same. She hits me too."

She felt the all too familiar tears come and bit her lip. "Go play with your father, please."

His lip quivered little, and then he said, "Okay," and marched out as if aware he had been given a large responsibility.

She stared at the rice she was washing, watching the water change colour, a little less milky with each rinse, enjoying the firmness of the grains of fine basmati as she sifted. Just when you thought you had mastered yourself, they shattered your equilibrium, she thought, these children who see things you have learned not to notice. She filled the pot with water and placed it on the stove to boil, watching the flames leap and dance, blue and red and gold, distracting and dangerous and beautiful.

She began to assemble the ingredients for the *bhagaar* for the daal. The jar of whole red peppers was empty. She went to the large pantry to get some, enjoying the jangle of the keys in her hand, unlocked the door, and looked at the shelves with satisfaction—the spices were labelled and the shelves ordered the way she liked, whole spices on the top, ground ones lower down, bottles of squash and rosewater at the bottom. The rice and grains to the right. The onions and potatoes in wood crates, on the left. When mangoes were in season, she liked to keep them by the rice, far away from the onions and garlic and potatoes and tomatoes not just for the smell, she had realized, but to differentiate the system from the one that Shireen had had in place, as if terrible things lay ahead if the pantry were not organized just so, as if a battle over a properly applied taxonomy—she smiled at the self-importance of the term—could hide that it was really two women fighting over territory and one man. She thought she had won the battle. Shireen's jabs ("Not everything has to be arranged like a painting you know. If you did some real painting you wouldn't need to rearrange everything,") ineffectual in the end. It was only a little later that Tahira had realized Shireen was tired of the kitchen, was merely securing the terms of a much-desired retirement. Not ready to relinquish the arsenal of injury, she sighed longingly every time she came into the kitchen, every now and then asking Tahira's permission to enter the kitchen, theatrical and wounded as a deposed queen.

Farah, never certain enough to be consistent in her animosity, exulted when Tahira gradually took over the supervision of the kitchen. Tahira was indulgent with treats and requests and the cook took her more seriously. After all, Shehzad was the source of the money in the house, Farah had told her mother within Tahira's hearing—to annoy her mother or ingratiate herself with her sister-in-law, Tahira couldn't tell.

The garlic turned translucent, ready to crisp in the hot oil. She added the whole red peppers and cumin seeds. They turned in an instant and she poured the mixture onto the lentils, enjoying the sizzle as it seared the daal. The kitchen was quiet, the sounds of the cooking calming: just a woman in a kitchen, she thought. It was the cook's day off and Farah had been staying with Asma at Badaber, the military base outside Peshawar, where Asma's husband was now stationed, for the past two months. Farah loved the place, "It makes me feel like I'm in America, Bhabhi. So neat and orderly." "Yes, yes," Shehzad had approved. "Such orderly little houses, and neat lawns. What discipline!" Waseem, predictably, had muttered about CIA listening posts and collusion ("Why not just hand the whole damn country over? Why maintain the illusion of independence?") when he had heard of Tahira's visit with the family a year ago.

The rice was almost ready. She drained it. The starch collected and thickened in the sink. She placed the pot back on the stove and lowered the flame. Each grain had to be perfect and separate. On this, Intizar and Shehzad were agreed.

She began to make the roti. After she had made five, there were enough to serve dinner. She went into the lounge where Shireen stopped talking as she entered, as if fearful of an intruder. "Dinner will be ready in five minutes," she announced. "No. No, Ammi Jaan. Please don't bother," she smiled brightly at her mother-in-law, as Shireen winced and reached to rub her back, careful to make the difficulty of stretching her arm visible to everyone in the room. "I can do it and the children will help me, won't you?"

Saira leapt up. "Yes! I want to help. I'm grown up. Aren't I? I am six years old." She turned to her father, imperious, precocious, assured of his love.

"Of course." He smiled a wide, encouraging smile.

Armaan, who had been sitting as far away from his father as the room allowed, stood up. "Me too."

Once the table had been laid, carefully arranged by Tahira, as she weaved in and out of the children's noisy interference, and the children and Shireen seated, Aftaab entered the room, followed by Shehzad, who seated his father at the head of the table and then sat down at the other end himself. Shireen served Aftaab his food, arranging it on the plate the way he liked it, the daal and rice separate, the meat on one side.

Tahira came into the room, bringing a hot roti.

Armaan said, "Sit with me, Amma. I want you to feed me."

Saira, glanced slyly at her brother, "I'm a big girl. I can eat with my *own* hands. I am *not* a baby."

Shehzad stroked his son's face. "You know she has to make hot rotis for your grandparents and for me," narrowing his eyes as Armaan flinched at his touch.

"The rotis are hot. Look." Armaan touched the basket, which contained the ones Tahira had already made, disapproving of his father's lack of understanding.

"That's enough," Shehzad snapped.

Shireen looked from father to son and shook her head, "That's what happens when mothers don't teach children to respect their fathers. I always knew we would have to see this day."

Aftaab looked up from his plate, querulous at the necessity but respect was important. "Who has been disrespectful?"

Saira stared at her grandmother and shook her finger, eyes narrowed, scowling fiercely: "Don't say anything about my Amma. Abba," she tugged his sleeve urgently, "make her stop."

Tahira entered the room with another roti. "Don't be disrespectful to your grandparents."

Saira folded her arms and sat back in her chair, dramatic, rebellious, mouth pursed in fury.

Armaan glared at his plate.

"It's okay." Shehzad waved Tahira away and turned to his mother. "Don't disturb my children. I won't tolerate it."

His father began to say something.

"No. I don't want to hear anything," Shehzad interrupted before he could begin. "If you want me to live in this house, if you want me to support you, then you will have to be careful with my children."

Aftaab thumped the table and pushed his chair back. "I don't have to put up with this humiliation. Such insolence." Shireen rushed over to help him stand. He attempted to kick the door on his way out and missed, stumbling instead—querulous, diminished, furious at the futility of an old man's anger.

Shireen took him to his room and came back to the dinner table, beginning to cry. "Whoever said children are only on loan, and you raise your sons to give them to some woman from outside, didn't know what truth he spoke."

The children watched, wide-eyed, a little scared, a little triumphant. They turned in unison to see what their father would say. He continued to eat, calm, as if nothing had happened, apparently absorbed in mopping up the saalan with the last bit of roti. Armaan took a deep breath and then broke off a bit of the bread, imitating his father.

Saira turned to her grandmother, eyes narrowed into fierce little slits. "See? I told you not to say anything about my Amma."

Shehzad continued to eat as if his daughter had said nothing.

"What's wrong with Armaan?" Shehzad asked as he climbed into bed later that night. "He's been distant with me for a few weeks."

Tahira wondered why it had taken him so long to notice. She tugged the covers a little to readjust them and then, buying time, said, “What do you mean?”

“He acts as if he’s angry at me and as if he’s scared.” Tahira overcame a hint of gratified malice. It was tempting to tell him that Armaan was avoiding him because he had seen Shehzad slap her. She winced, remembering her tearful admonition to him not to tell anyone, but that had been months ago. Even she had almost forgotten about it. “I’ll see what I can do,” she said.

“Okay.” He swung to the side of the bed to wriggle out of his shalwar and then turned and leaned over to pull up her nightgown. He liked satin. She closed her eyes as he switched off the lamp with his other hand.

18

Safdar felt the room throb as he hit his palm against his chest, hand connecting with breast at the same moment as the hundred men around him. The lament shuddered through the room as hands lifted with the refrain, pulling back, and landing on a hundred chests again… and again, as the men called upon the Prophet's daughter to accept condolences for the murdered caravan of seventy-two, picking up the chant to follow the beautiful voice of the man reciting the poem, "*Zehra, Zehra pursa lo bahatar ka*." The *nauha* ended and with it the refrain. They picked up another call, chanting *Ya Husain* to a harder rhythm. Louder, more fervent. He missed the more plaintive refrain of the *nauha*. He had always found it terrifying and incomprehensibly sad, this calling upon the dead to accept condolences for the more recent dead, to absorb the pain of the more recent dead.

Out of the corner of his eye, he saw his father's hand waver a little, out of sync, and turned to him. He hadn't been well lately. Akbar shook his head at him, reassuring, and returned himself to the rhythm. Safdar recalled his earliest memory of a *majlis*: it was the first time he had seen his father cry. Terrified, he had crawled frantically into his lap, burying his face in Akbar's neck. As he had grown a little older he had begun to find the spectacle of hundreds of men beating their chest in unison thrilling, heard the exultation and defiance in their mourning and wanted to be one of them, competing with the other young boys.

Sometimes he wondered why he still came, now that he had nothing approaching faith. To keep his father company, he knew, but also because he found it powerful and strange that grown men would sit and listen to the same story they had heard so many times before, bursting into tears upon the mention of a name—Abbas, or Husain, or Zainab—or the reference to a little girl's love for her father, her fear and sleeplessness without the comfort of his embrace, or to an arrow in a parched infant's neck. He had started paying attention to the language, to the many different ways in which the same story could be told again and again, even in one gathering, beginning with the long poem, and then the oration, and then the *nauha*. He had learned language here, he sometimes thought, in these very moments of poem and speech and song, where every word could be a harbinger of lamentation, of the devotion of an entire community to a story, and a story could be told, and retold, and language seemed capable of infinite surprise, even if every story were already known.

As the gathering ended, he followed his father outside looking for their shoes amongst the jumble of other people searching, the scramble in the midst of the greetings and pleasure at having spotted friends. The transition from the pulsating grief of the *majlis* to the sudden conviviality was startling as always and then (oddly) happy, bracing, like the cold night air, after the intensity and sickly sweet mingle of sweat and the rosewater spattered into the air inside at regular intervals. Safdar flipped through the mass of black and brown leather, spotted his father's sandal and held it aloft with triumph. His father took it and waited for the other.

Once it had been retrieved, he ambled off to greet his friends. Safdar put on his own sandals and then watched as his father talked—to everyone it seemed. He wandered, as he often had, watching Akbar, jovial, concerned, eager to connect, whether such bonhomie had some cost he had managed to hide from his son all these years, whether it was as exhausting to live as it was to witness.

Akbar broke free and came up to him after collecting the paper bags, already damp with oil, two men were handing out. "Sheermal and kebab—they gave me two extra packets. Your mother loves them. We should go. I'm tired."

Safdar was worried. "You need to see the doctor."

"You worry too much. It's nothing. I'd say I'm getting old but I'm not ready to admit it. You know it's funny, the zakir reminded me of the one in India, the beautiful purity and grace of his Urdu..." He shook his head, "Strange—the things one misses."

"Don't some come from Lucknow just for Muharram?"

"Yes, but the visas are difficult to obtain and then there can be that police reporting business." He paused. "My father used to talk about Imam Husain, even when it wasn't Muharram. He said it was the fight of justice against power and that's why we had to fight the British because if seventy-two people could brave hunger and thirst and forget fear, if a little girl could brave such cruelty, we had no choice but to fight."

Safdar grimaced. "And look what we've become."

"And look what we've become." His father sighed, back in Lucknow, in a time when battles had seemed cleaner and justice a realizable dream.

"You never wanted to come though," Safdar said. "You weren't even a Muslim League supporter."

"It wasn't planned. It just happened as it did to so many. Wrong place, wrong faith and before you knew it you found yourself pushed, and you clawed and suddenly you were in one country that used to be yours but now it was one of many and none were your own." He shrugged. "And so it is… And I hear from friends there that Muslims are not treated well and the culture and Urdu are disappearing. We really turned out to be the same, I suppose, there and here…"

Just outside the gate was a cart of meticulously arranged dried fruits. A naked bulb strung up above created its own halo in the winter dark. A man wrapped in a shawl and Peshawari hat sat by it, roasting peanuts. They bought some and walked a little distance to the main road, companionable and silent, shelling the warm peanuts. Safdar hailed a rickshaw. "You know I always want to talk when I'm in these."

His father laughed. "You always did attempt the triumph of will over reality—even as a little boy."

"Why must all conversations with parents be stuck in one's past? It never really gets past toilet-training."

"Do you know how difficult that was with a willful child like you?"

Safdar groaned. "Anyway," he laughed, shouting above the engine, "it's like a cross between a bumper car at Playland and a dance floor. You get tossed around and occasionally manage to communicate as your hips move from side to side. And it's so exhilarating when you make contact."

Akbar put his hand next to his hip, willing it not to slide to the center of the seat.

Safdar grinned.

The rickshaw bucked over a pothole and came to a halt at the entrance to the lane. They climbed out and walked to the house, which was deep in the lane, pausing to pick up some garbage outside their neighbour's house. The gate was slightly ajar. "We really should keep this closed," Safdar muttered.

Waseem was in the courtyard with Mumtaz. Akbar paused at the threshold and looked at Safdar, one never knew these days how Safdar would respond to Waseem: as an unwelcome reminder of that awful day or, occasionally, as a merciful rescuer from the sadness of his memories. He wanted to tell him that he couldn't hide with his family forever or fuss about his parents' health as an excuse. He liked that girl, Andaleep. Things seemed to be better since she had come back, or so Mumtaz had explained to him. Safdar was more relaxed even around Waseem when she was with them. Mumtaz liked her. That was good. Although he wondered how her family would react when they found out. His own family might have been part of the *Ashraf* of North India once, but they had so little now. What senior member of the civil service would allow his daughter to marry into this?

Mumtaz spoke, "The protests got ugly again. Waseem, Safiya and her husband were at one earlier."

Waseem added, "Safiya and Haroon are going to be here soon. We are going to help Saad, a friend of Haroon's, submit his election papers in a few days. We also need to make other plans."

The doorbell rang, as if one cue. "No. No. I'll get it," Akbar waved Safdar toward a chair next to Waseem, eager to please and smooth and enable.

He returned with Safiya and Haroon, a tall young man, with a broad face and small, bright eyes. Safiya walked to the *takht*, bending to kiss Mumtaz before she sat next to her. Mumtaz leaned over to caress her cheek, searching, pleased, "How are you? And your mother and brother?"

Safiya chuckled. "She likes having Haroon living with us. He keeps the relatives at bay. She likes that very much. They have been tormenting her since Baba died and now we use Haroon like a shield."

Mumtaz smiled. "I wish you didn't need one, but I'm glad it's helping."

"She wants to come see you," Safiya continued. "She was

so grateful for your help with the wedding and your *presence*—both you and Akbar uncle. It made things easier and even," she paused, "happy."

"We wanted you to feel you had support and wanted your mother to know she wasn't alone." She turned to include everyone, changing the subject. "I wish I could tell you to be careful. But I don't know if being careful would make you any safer. The madness is everywhere. One can't even hide. Assuming, of course," she smiled wrily, "you… we… were capable of such retreat. I wish I could join you. This damn back."

Safdar spoke, "I'm glad we don't have to have that argument."

Akbar smiled, nostalgic, reminiscing, "Remember the days we went to demonstrations together?" He paused, grimacing. "What we thought we were fighting for…"

Mumtaz completed the thought, pride and sadness warring in her tone, "…and what we got."

Safiya looked at Haroon, wondering if they would be able to complete each other's thoughts one day. He smiled in recognition. Perhaps they would, she thought, and… Baba would have been pleased.

Safdar slapped his hands on his knees. "Okay. Let's sort out what we are going to do over the next few weeks."

19

The moon was a mother of pearl disc above the midnight sea, presiding, massive, lighting an ivory and silver path on its ridged silk. Andaleep could hear Safdar behind her, asleep and breathing steadily; she turned to look at him, sprawled and beautiful in the moonlight, which entered with the sea breeze through the open windows lining the room on three sides. She turned back to look at the sea's still glitter, imagining the broad silver path connecting to all the oceans and seas of the world, remembering the Mediterranean at night as she realized that she would not be going back to Khaled. She did not know yet if she loved Safdar or if he were simply an emblem of home—and safe. That she might be falling, might already have fallen, in love with him made her wonder at her own fickleness, fearful of her own duplicity, if it were indeed duplicity. She wondered if it were a form of courage and fierce truth to insist that it was. But it was easier, she thought, to believe in that than know that one could fall in and out of love with such ease, so quickly, that all it took was absence and another familiarity.

She heard Safdar turn and mutter, a little ripple of agitation running the length of his body and went to lie down, placing her head on his shoulder and curling toward him. He slid his arm under her body and clutched her waist, demanding in his sleep in a way that he was careful not to be when awake, pulling her in without waking. The hair on his chest was springy, a little damp with sweat. She breathed his smell, of soap and sweat and a faint whiff of *Old Spice*, looking at the moon, which was now partially covered by his chin. She could live like this; if this were not love, it seemed good enough. Perhaps living in a world where love and marriage had little to do with each other meant that love had to be perfect, bearing the weight of the expectations of all who had not been permitted to think they should or could love—and there were so many of those. And then there were those, she thought, like her own parents who would have been unhappy no matter whom they married, tucked in their perfectly coiffed and immaculately attired selves. Her parents whose public politeness and occasional warmth transformed—the minute people left—into a tense membrane of punctiliously checked hostility. That it never broke made it so much worse, sharpening the anticipation of a doom that seemed all the greater because it never came, but was always imminent. She was sure they took pleasure in the dance. Their indulgence toward her was simply part of its choreography, vying to prove to her their generosity, competitive even in that. She laughed, she sometimes thought, to escape their war and the decorum and elegance with which they fought—and hid—it. She drew closer to Safdar; how could love then be filled with such beautiful but, finally it had to be said, ordinary, *haveable* pleasure? She kissed the edge of his jaw and decided to let herself fall asleep.

She woke to find him looking down at her.

"You are lovely in the morning." His smile was slow and tender and satisfied.

She grinned, stretching slowly, unfolding like a cat. "Not as lovely as you. We had a competition to see who could describe your eyes better."

He grimaced. "Do I have to know?"

"I haven't decided. Perhaps… what's that smell?"

"I made tea."

"Gorgeous man. What else can you do?"

"Heat leftover parathas and…" he bent to kiss her slowly and then said, "…kiss?"

"And not smug at all," she smiled, pulling him back down.

A while later, after they had disentangled, he brought her tea and sat down next to her on the edge of the bed. She took it gratefully, sipping slowly as she looked out at the sea.

"How did you manage to get away for the night, alone? Aren't your parents furious?"

"They are away and I'm at home with the cook and the other servants. And I usually have the use of the car and this hut. I told the cook to tell them I was going with some friends to the beach."

"They are liberal."

"No. It's not principle. They want to pursue his career and their social lives. And they are indulgent. Otherwise they might have to be more present. It works for all of us. Besides, they don't want to lose me as they did my brother."

"What happened?"

"He wanted to marry someone he loved, she was a Punjabi and not appropriate. They objected. Her parents did too. *We* were Urdu-speaking and not appropriate." She shrugged with disdain. "They did it anyway, and live in London. They may not have wanted to be involved parents but they didn't want an estrangement either. So…" She shook her head, clearing the thoughts, and stared at the sea, conscious of the intentness of his gaze.

"I always thought you were so carefree."

"Not exactly full of care either." She turned to smile at him. "I wouldn't take Waseem and Tahira's vision at face value. They saw what they wanted, or perhaps…what they could."

He inclined his head slightly, taking the correction. "Okay. So did I?"

"Perhaps—I don't know." The mischief reentered her eyes and she waved vaguely at her body, partially covered by a thin, grey blanket, "You are certainly seeing a lot more now."

He grinned. "Not so wrong after all. You know I love you?"

She took a deep breath, but kept looking at him, "Yes."

He tried not to look hurt but couldn't mask the desire, or the expectation.

"You know it's complicated, but I will tell you when I can."

"Okay." He did not say that the tenderness in her look had to be love. She would refuse the thought… or fight it. He would wait. He let her take his hand as she stared out at the sea, a beautiful aquamarine in the morning sun, which was still gentle and had not yet seared the waves into glinting metal, and turned to look at it with her.

"When do you have to go back home?" he asked.

"I can stay for a couple of days. You?"

"I'll stay with you."

She smiled.

They went for a long walk on the edge of the water after breakfast. They moved easily together, she noticed, unobtrusively in sync, silent, content with the soothing repetition of the waves, which scuttled up to them and receded, washing away the sand that clung to their feet as they walked. She looked at their feet as they moved in concert, following the rhythm and pace Safdar let her set. She had always moved fast, eager, people said, not to miss anything.

The curving sweep of the beach, with its greyish Karachi sand, the intensifying glare of the sun, strong even in the milder temperatures of winter, gave a grandeur to the decision she had to make. She wondered when she would tell Safdar she was not going back, and why she had not. She thought about Khaled, urgent, passionate, driven—not so different from Safdar, after all—and how she would tell him.

"Be careful," she stepped around a blue bottle and pulled Safdar, interrupting his reverie along with her own.

"What are you thinking?"

"That perhaps sublimity and ordinary happiness can coexist," she said, waving at the sea and the sand and at the boys playing cricket ahead, realizing it was only partly an evasion.

"I thought you weren't a fan of the sublime," he grinned.

"I'm not, but..." she batted her eyelashes rapidly, "...I might come around. Or, being the good colonial I was raised to be: it's the Wordsworth talking."

"No daffodils here," he chuckled, "or," he caught the ball that had come flying at them and threw it back to the boys, "nun-like quietness."

"What about you?"

He paused as if trying to decide whether to speak, and then braced himself, "That I could get used to this and that I ought to stop myself but don't want to and won't."

"I don't know what to say."

"Then don't. Say it, whatever it is, when you do know."

"Okay."

It was time to stop pacing and write the letter to Khaled. It couldn't be avoided; it wasn't fair to him; she was being cruel—Andaleep attempted to motivate herself with self-accusation, rehearsing a familiar litany. It wasn't fair to Safdar either but she tried not to think of the two together, failing hopelessly, she thought, yet again.

She had been in a restless frenzy since she had returned from the hut three days ago, had practiced every evasion, glad that her parents were still away; read three books, awake all night, watched television, even made a long overdue visit to relatives, trying every form of avoidance she could imagine.

She *had* to acknowledge the truth, not just for Khaled and Safdar: she did not want to go back it was true; she had fallen for Safdar (also true) but the most difficult thing to admit or understand (she wasn't sure why) was that she was not leaving Khaled for Safdar. Somehow that would have been the easier reason, she had thought as she had paced and wandered and postponed.

As she walked to the study, Nadeem, one of the older servants, materialized suddenly, like a uniformed genie, professional, unobtrusive, aware of the absurdity of the servitude from which he was a little protected by a government job and pension. He inclined his head, silver grey with a distinction that always made her slightly uncomfortable when she gave him orders, as she asked for tea. He didn't like her in the kitchen she had told herself, so she couldn't just invade his domain and make it herself, worried she might be reaching for a comfortable lie. There were so many, she thought now, how did one confront them all? She shook her head, impatient, irritable. Every thought seemed to have been morbidly existential for the past couple of days; she really had to send that letter.

The study was her favourite room in the house. One wall was covered with antique bookcases with glass-panelled doors. A small two-seater sofa and an Ango-Indian plantation chair sat under the wall covered with paintings from her father's magnificent collection. A nineteenth-century desk, solid, lightly carved, Indo-Portuguese, stood at a right angle to a large window out of which she could see her favourite gulmohar tree, which was not yet in bloom. Reading or working at the desk, she turned the chair to look out of the window to look at the tree's blazing canopy, watching the sun light it as it set. The room was always in a playful dance with the tree as the sun's rays filtered through the fan-like branches with small leaves that almost seemed tessellated, casting filigrees of light and shade on different parts as the sun moved.

Nadeem came in and placed her tea on the desk behind her, leaving as quietly as he came, whether to escape attention or to test if they were capable of notice, she could never decide. She turned from the window and sat at the desk, pulling some paper and a photograph from the drawer, and placed the photograph against the carved raised ridge that ran around three sides of the desk. Khaled stood on the promenade in Beirut, eyes crinkled against the sun, thick black hair ruffled by the breeze, the Mediterranean behind him. A tall, confident man, with a trim moustache, finely turned out, elegance unmarred by the rosy glaze of the Polaroid shot.

She unscrewed the top of her favourite fountain pen, and began to write in a convent trained hand: "My dear Khaled," and paused. The pronoun seemed proprietary, hypocritical, asserting an intimacy the letter was intended to surrender, that she must seem *eager* to surrender. She crossed it out and then scrunched the paper into a ball and tossed it into a basket under the desk.

She began again:

Dear Khaled,

I hope this letter finds you well. You have waited for my answer, and my return, with patience and generosity. But I now realize that we both knew when I left that I would not be coming back. I should say that this is not yet another postponement but an end. I write this not to be cruel but because I do not want you to defer your own life. Vagueness would be dishonest at this stage.

With love and great sadness,
Andaleep

She reread the letter. *Note* was more accurate she thought guiltily, but the less she said, the less she would humiliate him with lies, or, she grimaced, the truth—whatever it was in this case. She loved Safdar but hadn't stopped loving Khaled and yet neither was responsible for her decision to stay. She stared at the photograph as if trying to look him in the eye, willing him across land and sea and pain to see the truth in hers and then, unable to hold the picture's gaze, twisted sideways to look out of the window. The late afternoon sunlight rippled through the leaves of the gulmohar. She smiled, remembering Safdar listing the names, earnest, impassioned, absurdly pedantic: Flame of the Forest, Royal Poinciana, Delonix Regia, Flamboyant Tree (with a grin at her), Peacock Flower; how it had probably arrived in the Subcontinent from Madagascar, how the Mughals had planted it along the roads to provide shade for travellers, guilty she thought of him now.

Every thought, every observation seemed so *entangled*, but she wasn't rejecting Khaled or choosing Safdar or even *this* tree in *this* changing light, she reflected. For a woman to surrender herself so completely, to move to a man's world—she winced at her own cruelty; Khaled's world was so little his own… But what if he was like all the others? It would be unbearable to leave everything just to be with him, only to find out that he was. She had not wanted to admit it to him, to herself, to Safdar but she could not do that. It was why she could not bring herself to give Safdar the answer he wanted either. The closest she had come to admitting the truth was in her antagonism with Tahira, she now realized. She folded the letter and opened the drawer to get an envelope. The box was empty. She would get some later.

She moved to the sofa and pulled her knees to her chin. The tea was too cold to drink and she didn't want to ask for another cup or leave the room. She sat looking out of the window as the afternoon gave way to dusk and the sky blazed a burnished crimson, making the tree seem to bloom. She stayed there, chin resting on knees, as the sky turned to azure and then a deep-hued cobalt and the night slowly made the tree invisible.

20

Safdar came home to find his father straining up and outwards in the little door inset in the gate, pushing his head into the Rangoon creeper twined above. He rushed onto the street, when he saw his son, and began to pace outside the gate, a few broken twigs of the vine tangled in his hair.

"Where have you been? We had no way of reaching you. Don't go in, yet." He grabbed Safdar, who had begun to rush in, crying, "Apa?"

"Listen to me before you go in. She's okay but I don't want you to disturb her more by asking her what happened. They came looking for you yesterday. One man, with a black cloth thrown across his face (the neighbour's son hid behind his balcony and watched) grabbed a branch of the laburnum to lever himself up over the gate, and then let the others in. They found your mother on her favourite perch, sewing a blouse. They held a gun to her forehead and asked where you were. She said she didn't know. There were three men. The one who seemed like the leader asked again, apparently more loudly. You know your mother. Can you imagine her answering a question like that, especially if someone was shouting it at her? She says she laughed. At which they hit her across the face and asked again. She told them she didn't know. The leader," Akbar paused and looked down, "The leader tore her blouse. By then the neighbours had been alerted by the little boy, and they arrived with knives and sticks and even the little lizard-hunting guns and scared them off. She wants to see you but she doesn't want to talk anymore."

Safdar covered his face with his hands, struggling to control himself and then kicked the gate. "I should have been here."

Akbar stroked his back, "Come, beta. It's not your fault. You couldn't have done anything. They would have hurt you more. I wish I had been at home. They might have been gentler with an old man." He shook his head, "Maybe not. If they couldn't be respectful to her… But we are both glad *you* weren't here."

Safdar stepped over the raised threshold of the door, on which his father had been standing. "I want to talk to her."

"Okay. But she doesn't really want to talk. You know what she's like."

"Yes, but I want to see her. We'll figure it out. Don't worry."

Mumtaz was sitting on the takht, reaching for her paan-daan, an intricate silver octagon with carefully stocked, immaculately maintained compartments. She looked up and smiled. He rushed to sit next to her, searching her face, concerned and a little fearful of what he would find.

"I'm okay."

"But…"

"It would have been harder to see them hurt you."

"You know that I can't say yes to that." He shook his head as if to rid himself of the thought. He took the paan-dan from her, "I'll roll your paan," and began to prepare it the way she liked,

"It's true."

"Not for me." He handed her the paan with a single cardamom and just the right pinch of tobacco, pierced with a clove.

"I suppose you are going to run around after me for days, anticipate my every desire, obey my every command?"

Akbar grinned at his wife's attempted evasion, waiting to see what his son would do.

"Of course. What else would I do?" Her son's tone became grimmer. "They might come back."

"I don't like people hovering," she said, irritable, a little querulous.

"Okay."

The men had uprooted many of the plants and torn books and stamped on them. The savaged plants were still lying in a corner, roots mangled and exposed to the sun, some severed and crushed, mixed with soil-stained, ripped books. Safdar got up to sift through them, identifying books and plants that could be saved, separating books that could be rescued, pots that could be reused and ones that needed to be discarded. He would give the boy across the street some money and ask him to tell Joseph Bhaiyya to come help him once he had organized things a little.

She realized he meant to stay just there and settled back against the bolster, not unhappy to have lost the battle.

~

Andaleep waited in the car as Waseem sprang out to ring Safdar's doorbell. A few minutes passed. Waseem turned to Andaleep, drumming her fingers on the side of the car. "It doesn't usually take this long. I'm sure he knew we'd be going together today."

"Yes. Be patient. Maybe something is going on. See… here he is." She smiled a warm, complicit smile as he materialized at the gate.

Safdar came out, face furrowed with guilt and worry. "I'm sorry. I can't come today."

Waseem stared; Safdar was exasperatingly scrupulous about his appointments. "What do you mean?"

Andaleep narrowed her eyes, searching his face, "Something has happened, right?"

"Some thugs—political, of course—came looking for me. I wasn't home, so they roughed up the house, for show, or because they were bored and frustrated, deprived of their target, who knows," he shrugged, "and since Apa was the only one at home, they tried to intimidate her."

Andaleep leapt out the car and Waseem began to rush inside.

"You know she loves you, but she doesn't want to see anyone. She's barely tolerating my presence." He had been in the little courtyard the night before and she had come out, unable to sleep and annoyed to be discovered in her insomniac agitation. His father could sleep through anything. She must have hoped no one would know. Safdar hadn't said anything, continuing to read by the light of the lamp he had rigged, using a power cord that extended into the kitchen. He sat there until dawn broke and she stood up to answer the call of the *Fajr azaan*, reading, and when he became too tired to do so, pretending that he was.

He said again, "I need to stay here today. I'm so sorry."

"Of course, you do, " Waseem said and Andaleep nodded vigorously. "Please give her my love," she said and, then, grinning and sighing at the same time. "We'll manage without you.... somehow."

"I'm sure you will." Safdar's eyes gleamed with laughter and a new familiarity.

Waseem caught the look and muttered "Oho" under his breath. The two did not notice, entangled in some exclusive memory. He spoke, reluctant to interrupt, "We really do have to go. We are late already and Haroon's friend will be waiting for us. Do you think we could stop by on our way back?"

"I'll prepare her. She won't stop me from having guests. Just don't be too solicitous. She'll get irascible in a way you've never seen. She doesn't say much, but she manages to transform the air around her. Even Abba runs for cover."

"And you?" Andaleep asked.

He grinned. "Me? I act like a stubborn teenager. Go," he said, and touched Andaleep's hands in a fleeting, tender gesture, wishing he could steal a kiss, but there were too many windows around.

"You be careful, okay?" she said.

"Yes, do," added Waseem. "I wish we could stay. I really don't want you to be alone if they return."

"They are everywhere," Safdar said. "Where do you go to hide? Who do you choose to protect?" He stood there as they drove away, missing her already, a little soothed she had come, a little sad she had had to leave. New love! He shook his head. Well… not *quite* new but love that seemed newly reciprocated even if she wouldn't admit it, making one obsessive and a little stupid, wonderful even in the midst of chaos.

In the car, Waseem turned to Andaleep. "Are you going to say anything?"

"I'm not sure what you want to hear."

"The two of you. I saw what I saw."

"I'm sure you did. We spent two nights at my parents hut by the sea."

"And I hear you took a job at the university."

"I did. But those two facts are not related."

"You didn't decide to stay and take the job because of him?"

"No. I decided to stay *despite* him." The car jerked. "Try not to have an accident."

"Try not to be enigmatic."

"You of all people should understand fear of captivity. And no," she raised her hand, silencing the murmur of protest, "It is not a stupid fear for a woman. It might, in fact, be the most rational one."

"Safdar is different *and* remarkably single-minded about you."

"Safdar, my dear, is a gorgeous man, a flirt, used to the attention of women. *I* am an ordinary looking woman with a *personality*. Part of my charm is my obsessive need for freedom. That charm comes with an in-built limit, with the conditions of its own demise written into it. And don't tell me our comrades are different. I've seen how women can be treated by revolutionaries—here, in Beirut, by Khaled's comrades. Anyway, I'm here. He knows that. It should be enough for now."

Waseem spoke without much conviction after a long pause, unable to argue with a future he couldn't disprove. "Yes. But he's so different with you."

"Okay."

They drove in companionable silence. After a while, mango orchards began to appear. The trees were beginning to show unseasonably early pale gold blossoms, the stems enveloped in the tiny flowers, covering the long leaves, ridged and curled like rams' horns.

"Funny, isn't it, how such a gorgeously sensuous fruit can be the result of such unglamorous flowers," she remarked.

He chuckled. "Maybe the tree needs to preserve all its energy for the fruit so it sacrifices the flower."

"Ugh. That sounds like some very virtuous theory of parenting.... You know I used to miss the mango season terribly when I was gone."

"I never really figured out how or why you stayed away so long. Your parents came back."

"I thought you knew. I enrolled in university in Beirut, got a B.A. in Political Science and then a Masters, and then went to England to get a second degree in History. I went back to Beirut to work on my Arabic. My parents had left by then but I had friends there. I stayed with a friend and her family and they found me a tutor—a Palestianian and a friend of Khaled's. That's how I met him."

"Hmm. I'm surprised Tahira didn't visit you in England. Shehzad goes frequently and she has gone with him a couple of times. She never told me. But then," he winced, "we hardly talk any more."

"I think the children were small. Besides, you are not the only one she avoids. You know that. And we avoid her too, to be completely fair."

"Yes," he grimaced, "and yes."

She picked up the thread. "But then I wanted to come back or, at least, not to have to stay there because of him, and I didn't want to be an exile, painful though that was to admit given his situation. Every choice seemed to be laden with irony and betrayal." She lowered the window further, breathing the air as it changed as they drove past farms and orchards, acquiring an elusive green fragrance, impossible in the city.

She was glad they had come even if the reason was appalling. Safiya and Haroon had asked them to help their friend, Saad—sympathetic to the ruling party but appalled by the excesses of the PM and some of the ministers—register for the election. The opposition and Party members perceived to be less than compliant were being intimidated and harassed. It had finally, she reflected, come home with the attack on Safdar's family.

"Safiya called to say she and Haroon might be late," Waseem said, "They are meeting another friend in the area."

"Okay. But let's hurry so we can get back and be with Safdar. I don't want them to be alone if those thugs come back."

Waseem pulled up by a shop, emblazoned with the name *Khuda Baksh Sweets* in Urdu and English. A lurid plate of green, brown, and orange sweets sat next to the legend.

"We are taking dessert?"

"Just checking directions." He pulled out a piece of paper. "It's close by."

He drove a little distance and pulled up in front of a small house.

A short, wiry young man, very tidily dressed in grey trousers, a maroon cotton sweater and collared shirt with small maroon and white checks came out, beaming, arms flung wide open. "Welcome! Thank you for coming. There's tea inside. We can go after we have had some. The office is close by. We can even walk and I'll point out some things of interest along the way."

Andaleep smiled, liking the way he masked his shyness with an expansiveness that verged on the comic. "Tea would be lovely. Although we are in a bit of a hurry."

Waseem told him what had happened at Safdar's.

"We should hurry then," he said grave and worried. "Of course, you shouldn't linger. But you should have some tea; it was a long drive. You can look over the papers while I get it." Then, a little wistfully, "What's happening to us?"

They walked inside. The living room was simple, furnished with a grey sofa, two armchairs and a coffee table. A fat bunch of crimson and mauve bougainvillea burst out of a blue ceramic vase on the table, a vivid splash in the sparse room. Saad saw Andaleep looking at the flowers. "I live with my mother. My father," he gestured toward a garlanded portrait on the wall, "died a few years ago. My mother loves flowers. She would have liked to meet you but her sister is ill.

"I'll get the tea quickly, I promise. The kettle's been on a while. It kept drying out and I kept filling it up." He gave a sheepish smile and rushed into an adjacent room. As he disappeared into the kitchen, Waseem and Andaleep heard the sound of approaching voices. In a moment, two men came in, guns in holsters hanging from diagonal belts slung around their hips, dark and heavy against the folds and flows of their brown kameezes and white shalwars; the brown shirts camouflaged the belts a little.

The taller one, sporting a large, waxed and twirled moustache that sat with an incongruous swagger on his very young face, turned to Waseem and said, "We have come to warn you, Saad."

"I'm not Saad."

"Warn?" Andaleep exclaimed.

"Where is he?" The other one, pudgy and clean-shaven, turned away from Andaleep with a contemptuous shrug, raising a dismissive hand when she began to speak. "I won't talk to you."

Waseem crossed his arms and said nothing, glaring.

Saad came out, crying cheerfully, "I thought I heard more than one man's voice. Are Safiya and..."

He came to an abrupt halt. The suddenness of the movement made the tea spill out of the overfull cups. "Who are you?"

The tall one spoke. "We came to warn you. Stop your activities, or else."

"Or else what? Get out."

Waseem turned to Saad, gesturing at the guns as the two men pulled the guns out of their holsters, as if parodying gunslingers in a Western, "Careful." He inched closer to Andaleep, trying to shield her. She came out from behind, reaching for a compliant, fake femininity, eyes slightly lowered, a scared, ingratiating smile on her face.

"Let's talk," she said. "We are all on the same side after all. What do you want? Perhaps we can come to an agreement."

"Shut up. Stop your activities. Don't think you can fool us." The tall one waved his gun at her, moustache bobbing up and down, terrifying and ridiculous at the same time.

Waseem pushed her back. "Please stop waving the guns. Someone might get hurt."

"SHUT UP." Both were agitated now, guns waving even more wildly.

The pudgy one approached Saad, moving surprisingly fast and hit him with the back of his gun.

Waseem and Andaleep rushed to his side, kneeling by him in a mess of tea, smashed china and scattered *Glaxo* biscuits, which were dissolving quickly in the milky brown puddle. Blood was beginning to ooze and swell like fat unstoppable tears out of a cut above his right eyebrow.

Andaleep stood up. "Let us get him to the kitchen."

The pudgy one pointed his gun at the floor. "Sit down, *Haraamzaadi*."

She wondered if he had practiced dialogue and mannerisms before he came; he was so young, the swagger so uncertain, a fat man-boy.

There was a sudden loud bang outside. Andaleep thought: gunshots and bursting tyres sound so similar.

She saw the man-boy jump, spooked by the sound, and press the trigger without intending to do so. She felt as if someone had rammed something into her heart, and fell before she could look at herself to see what had happened. Waseem leapt up. The tall one shouted, "What have you done? What have you done? We were just told to scare them not to kill anyone. Oh what have you done?" He began to cry.

Waseem knelt to feel the pulse in her neck. "No. Please. Not again. It's not possible." He saw the absence in her eyes and knew before he had touched her that she was gone. He dropped his head in his hands, trying to breathe, rocking slowly back and forth on his heels, and wondering, as if it were the only thing that mattered, what he would tell Safdar and Tahira.

The thugs began to fight among themselves, a blur of brown and white. Waseem wanted, suddenly, urgently, to know their names. How could he not know who had killed Andaleep? He needed to know dammit! He needed to know now. He began, implausibly, to ask but, before the words could form, he felt a sudden pain in his side and saw a large crimson patch appear and spread on his off-white kameez. The men ran out, shouting recriminations at each other as he fell next to Andaleep.

Saad stirred and groaned, regaining consciousness. He sat up, looking around, and saw Waseem lying on the floor, bleeding, whimpering slightly, an occasional spasm racking his body. Andaleep lay next to him, completely still, mauve and crimson petals and blue ceramic shards from the smashed vase scattered on and around her sprawled form. He stood up, leaning against the wall, knocking the garland off his father's portrait, and stumbled out of the door, calling: "Help. *Help!*" He saw Safiya and Haroon arrive at the gate, "Get an ambulance, please, Waseem Bhai and Andaleep Baji have been shot."

Inside the house, Waseem reached over to caress Andaleep's hair and whispered, "What a silly way to die, parrot. I don't even think they meant it," and died.

21

Tahira took the dupatta for the gharara Farida wanted to wear for a wedding in Faraz's family out of the bag. The work really was exquisite, she thought, the raised gold embroidery, fine and precise, its ornateness redeemed by its wondrous intricacy. Farida had been specific about the colours, off-white shot with gold, shocking pink border, gold embroidery. Tahira had bought the materials and given them to the tailors and the embroiderers, going back and forth to get them cut so they could be embroidered. She would take the gharara and shirt to the tailor for the final sewing once the karchob was complete.

Ever since that first visit to High Wycombe years ago, Farida had written and visited regularly when in Pakistan. Tahira had come, despite herself, to appreciate the generosity in the insistence on friendship, so at odds with the rest of Shehzad's family, and, in the absence of anything in common, responded as best she could by making sure Farida and her daughter were kept supplied with clothes, sending them with relatives, making sure there was a pile waiting when they came to Karachi.

But the clothes for this wedding weren't ready yet. The craftsman had stared with baffled contempt at her impatience, muttering as she left: "Strikes. Curfews. The city can burn but these begums must have their clothes on time!" He didn't understand, she wanted to say: if you didn't keep expecting things, then it really would be the end. She traced the embroidery, the metallic thread hard to the touch—the intricate pattern of arabesques was perfectly executed, the meticulously repeated pattern a marvel of centuries of transmission and craft.

The car pulled into the driveway. Shehzad was pacing, concerned, grim. He was never home at this time. "What is it? My parents?" Her voice rose, "The children?"

He took her arm.

"What is it? TELL me."

He sat her down on the sofa in the downstairs lounge. "There's been an accident."

Farah came down the stairs, slapping her cheeks. "Hai! Poor Bhabhi. Your best friend! Your brother!"

"Shut up, Farah," her brother snapped.

Tahira said, "Take me to the hospital."

"I can't. They are not there."

She stared at him and began to wail, a low keening sound without end.

The children, who had been playing upstairs, came running down the stairs. Saira tugged her father's arm. "Why is she crying? Why?"

Armaan tried to hug his mother. "Stop crying, Amma," and started crying himself, as she pushed him away.

Their father spoke. "Something has happened to Andaleep Khala and Waseem Mamu. We need to go to your Naana and Naani's house right now. He picked up Saira as she began to cry too. Tahira, eyes unfocused, continued to wail. He turned to Farah. "Call her mother and tell her to have a doctor waiting with tranquilizers."

He sat Saira next to Armaan, kissed each in succession,

and said, "Can you both stop crying to help me help your mother, please?"

Both stopped, staring intently at him.

Armaan spoke first, "Okay."

Saira said, "But what happened?"

"They were hurt," he said, waving at his mother and sister to be silent.

"But why is Amma making that noise?" Saira persisted, crying harder.

"Please Saira. Not now. Later. Okay? Don't cry, please."

She stopped crying. "But you when we get to Naana's you have to tell us. Okay?" She said again, eyes narrow, insistent, trying very hard not to cry, "Okay?"

"Yes." Shehzad turned to Armaan, "Tell the driver to get both cars ready, beta. We are going to need cars and drivers at your Naana's." Armaan ran to do as he was asked, followed closely by Saira. Shehzad half-carried, half-dragged Tahira to the car. He settled her in the front seat, reclining it slightly, and turned to the children who were trying to peer around him: "Get in the back and wait, please. I'll be right back."

They nodded solemnly, determined to be of help.

He went back in. "Farah, please give the bag with the childrens' things to the driver and tell him to keep them until he's asked for them. I don't know how long we'll be there. And there's going to be chaos.

"He will wait here for a while and bring you all when you are ready. Make sure the whole family comes, including Baba, yes, *including* Baba," he spoke over his mother's protest, "and make sure everyone behaves properly."

He went back out and climbed into the car. He drove as fast as he could, apologizing to the children as the car jerked over a pothole, steadying Tahira's sliding form with one hand. People were streaming through the open gates as they pulled up. He got out and shouted, "Please clear some space so we can park inside." People separated and rearranged themselves. Shehzad pulled in and parked. "Come on children. Help me. Armaan, put yourself under your mother's arm to help her stand when I get her out of the car."

One of Tahira's cousins came up to help, "Come with me, Saira, I'll take you to your Naani." Saira looked at Shehzad. He nodded, "Yes. Please go with your auntie, Saira."

He opened the door to pull Tahira out. They managed, lifting and pulling, to get her into the house. Mariam met them in the entryway, ashen-faced, but in control, trying to manage the arrangements and the dozens of family members who had arrived to help, each of whom seemed to need to cry with her individually. She wondered if they thought she had hidden an accountant's ledger somewhere, measuring and recording every tear, marking each ostentatious wail. "Doctor Mavalvala is waiting in her old room," she said.

"Where is it?"

"I know," Armaan said.

"Lead the way, then."

In the room, Shehzad sat her down on the bed. She lay down and folded herself into a tight ball and began to moan more loudly. Shehzad looked at the doctor, gesturing helplessly.

The squat, bespectacled man, who had been the family doctor for twenty years said, "I'll give her a tranquilizer. She always was highly strung. Just keep checking on her afterwards—every hour or so should do." Shehzad nodded, sent Armaan to be with his sister, and stood back as the man sat on the edge of the bed. He walked to the window as the doctor tried to talk to Tahira, saw a stack of canvases and began, absently, to flick through them, trying to compose his thoughts and prepare for the coming days, still struggling to overcome his disbelief. He had never liked Waseem and had been quite fond of Andaleep, yet both facts seemed equally unimportant. They were both gone. Forever. What would his wife do? How would their parents cope? What would he tell his children?

He came upon a portrait of himself. He looked handsome, he supposed, but also frightening, even a little sinister. He turned back to look at his wife as the doctor rolled up her sleeve to administer the injection. Is this what she thought of him? How could she, after all these years? Anger warred with pity as he looked at her listless form. Perhaps, he paused, he had himself to blame. Perhaps he should have been nicer to Waseem. Well! He could try to be nice now and make sure he was of use in the months to come.

He covered Tahira with a sheet, and walked downstairs with the doctor, said goodbye to him and began to look around to see what needed to be done. The children were with Seema, sitting on either side. She had her arms around them and was saying, "… they are in heaven."

"Both of them?" Armaan asked.

"Yes, both of them." She looked up apologetically as Shehzad approached. "I'm sorry I had to tell them. They were frantic, especially when they saw that even Abba was crying."

"Thank you," he said, relieved at being spared that duty. "Should I take them with me?"

"It's okay. I'll look after them and check in on Tahira Apa regularly. I think Amma and Abba need some younger, able-bodied men and someone who has authority within the family."

"I'll see what needs to be done." He walked towards Intizar who was sitting with Safdar, surrounded by relatives and Waseem's comrades.

The next day, Safdar washed Waseem's body with Intizar and Akbar, unable to look at the tears streaming down Intizar's face in a steady, uninterrupted fall, unimpeded by breath or movement or sound. As he helped clean the corpse, feeling its marble rigidity, searching for his friend in the body in his hands, he wondered, with a fury he didn't know how to direct, how this *thing* could have been a person. He was angry at everything, at his own invading fingers, at the terrible intrusion that allowed the living to clutch and turn and grope the dead, at the fact that this *thing* could not defend itself against the violation. He reached for the camphor and the body slid on the table. He saw Intizar's hands tremble and looked at his face to see the tears which continued to fall steadily, mingling with water and soap, anointing his son.

He tried not to think of Andaleep's body, washed by her mother and cousins, tried not to imagine its stiffness, which was a betrayal of the agility and laughter she had brought with her. You betrayed *me* he wanted to scream.

They dried the body and wrapped it in the gleaming white cotton with the help of two friends from university. Intizar added a few drops of attar, Akbar—who had been by Intizar's side throughout, unobtrusively propping him with a judicious hand under his elbow, on the small of his back, applying the gentlest pressure when needed—led him out. At the prayer, Safdar was grateful as he had been all day, that Akbar stood between Intizar and the people who descended upon him with a sympathy from which Intizar seemed to flinch and recoil, grateful today for his father's desire to connect with everyone and for the ability, not always visible to his son, that underlay the desire. Grateful also that Shehzad, whom Waseem had detested, had taken over the arrangements and the more social duties, which meant he had to stay away from Intizar, who was intimidated by him and preferred, visibly, not to have him too close.

Safdar helped carry the body with Waseem's friends and comrades. He called upon all his composure as they lowered the body into the ground and managed not to retch for Intizar's sake, helped by the need to focus on the task. After the burial they walked to the prayers for Andaleep. Akbar manouevred himself between Intizar and Safdar, slightly leaning toward him so he could provide any support his son might need.

Safdar moved, and prayed, and introduced himself as a friend of Andaleep's to her father, greeted a man with a trim moustache and an Arab accent, wondered why his eyes were so red, and walked behind the coffin, wanting to carry it himself, desperate to put some great distance between them, caught, he felt, in some somnambulant nightmare from which he would never awake. He watched them lower her body, wrapped in white cloth, so fragile and slender in its absurd swaddling, and wanted to destroy the earth itself as it swallowed her up.

22

Armaan was waiting outside when, ten days after the deaths, Tahira finally came out of her room. She had decided to be in her studio—there was nowhere else she *could* be. Armaan followed her, afraid he would be separated from her again if he didn't stay close to her. He had not been permitted in the room for more than a few minutes at a time for the past week and a half, put aside by grown-ups who came and went as if he weren't there. It would not happen again. He had never seen his mother like this, alien and wild-eyed, and so indifferent to him and Saira, even to his father. He wondered if this is what happened to everyone's family when they went to heaven. He wondered if the hush in his grandfather's house would ever lift. Even his beloved Naana would not take him to buy the milky sweets with cows on the wrappers any more. But now Armaan decided that even if he did ask him to, he would not go. He had to stay with his mother, to look after her, to make sure she didn't forget him completely.

She let him follow but shut the door when her mother tried to enter. In the studio, she toyed with her paintbrushes, leafed through her drawings, traced outlines with numb, searching fingers. This was the only place she could be. Near this. She knew that Armaan was with her, but did not know why. His body, so close to hers—he came closer and closer and she wanted to recede further away—was an imposition she would resent were she capable of recognizing any relation to him. She thought she ought to paint but didn't know why or how. A painting. Andaleep and Waseem would want that. She did not know why this mattered.

Armaan's body was too close. She pushed it away gently. His eyes filled with tears. She realized dimly, from some strange and remote place, that this was because of her but she couldn't understand why. As if he were beginning to sense that the only way he could stay with her was by effacing himself, Armaan retreated to a corner of the room, busying himself with some books, brave and proud as he set his jaw and blinked.

Several hours later, there was a knock on the door, and Mariam entered. "You must come out. Come and eat. For the children's sake at least."

"Go away," Tahira screamed. "*Get out*."

Armaan flinched and rose to go to his mother. He would make a wall with her against the world. Maybe then she would love him again. Then he remembered that she did not want him near her. He paused, then squared his shoulders and stood next to her, facing down his grandmother. This was not easy. He loved her too. A lot. But he had to regain his mother's love. Tahira sensed him next to her, ignored him and told her mother to leave the room again, "You must go," she spat the words. "*Now.*"

Mariam realized it was wiser to go. Evasive most of the time, Tahira could be immovably stubborn when she wanted. She knew that now was not the time to press but was stricken by Tahira's grief, which added to her own. One child, to whom she had not been inadequately responsive, dead; another, whom she had betrayed, first betrayed by circumstance itself, shattered. These two children who had provided such comfort and love to each other once both destroyed, while she had stood helplessly—and (this hurt most when she allowed herself to think about it) *unhelpfully*—by. After such knowledge how could an offer of solace not be colossal presumption? But she approached Tahira, hesitated, and then determined that she had to try again. She squared her shoulders and moved forward—unwittingly mirroring her grandson. She wanted to hold her daughter. She told herself it would be like holding Waseem; he would want this. She came close. Tahira flinched. But she clutched her shoulders and drew Tahira to herself. Tahira struggled violently and Armaan pushed himself between the two women. Stern and grim he looked up at his grandmother, "You are making my mother unhappy. Don't touch her."

Mariam stared at her grandson. How could this have happened to her family? Tears streaming down her face, she said, "Okay. But Armaan has to come down for meals. I'll send your food up later," and left the room. Armaan wanted to go to his mother, but was afraid that she would push him away again. Instead he returned to the books in the corner, and then decided to draw, trying to copy some of the figures of Impossible Animals from the *Namumkin Cheezon ki Bauhat Bari Kitaab jis ka naam The Big Book of Impossible Things bhi hai*. His uncle and mother had insisted the title had to be in English and Urdu. Drawing the figures made him feel closer to them both. Perhaps, he thought, if his mother realized he was here to protect her, she would come close to him and hug him and tell him a story. But for now he would be silent.

He evolved his own routine. Every morning, he went to his grandmother's room to dress. When he returned from school, he went straight up to the studio to check on his mother. Then he came down for lunch and then went back up to the studio to take a nap on the small bed that had been set up for him. He had asked for a little table to be placed there as well.

Here he did his homework every day, and every day he would take it downstairs to have Seema look it over. After dinner with his father, who came daily to see the children, and his grandparents and aunts, he returned upstairs. Tahira ignored him as he came and went. He wanted her to notice him, tried to get her attention in small ways, stumbling, pretending he had hurt himself, dropping things. He tried being very good, keeping his desk tidy, trying to fold the clothes she had taken to dropping by the takht on which she slept. He brought pillows and bolsters with shocking pink, burgundy and beige Swati covers from his grandmother's collection and arranged them on the takht and wondered why the colours didn't make her happy. Hadn't she told him herself that she *loved* bright colours? He picked the most vivid flowers he could find in the garden: "See Amma, aren't they bright?" and tried not to burst into tears when she simply ignored him as if he weren't there, as if no one had spoken. Nothing worked and he knew he was more sad every day, but he knew it was important that he remain there. So he did.

~

Shehzad was boiling some water for tea one day when Shireen came into the kitchen, "Beta, Dulhan is not accepting her brother's death in the proper manner. It's so unseemly this neglect of her family. You shouldn't have to make your own tea. It's a disgrace." She saw Shehzad's distaste but decided to persist. "You know that the children should be looked after. Is she doing that?"

"Her brother and best friend have died. She needs time. Her family is looking after Saira and Armaan; they make sure they go to school and look after them, and I go there everyday to have dinner with them."

He was *so* attached to the children; she persisted, playing her strongest card. "Yes, but the children will become distant from you. They will take them away. They are a terrible family." If only he would get another wife, one who would break the hold the children seemed to have over him, things might become all right again.

"They are staying," his answer sounded more final than he thought he was going to feel.

"You'll regret this."

That evening Shehzad took Saira and Armaan to Haidery for drinks and ice cream. "Do you children want to come home?"

Armaan was suspicious. "With Amma?"

"No. Without."

"*No.*" Armaan was emphatic.

Saira said, "But I like Seema Khala. I don't like Farah Phuppo and Daadi… I like Nilofer Khala too," she added, trying not to be unfair to the aunt she loved but who had been abroad and whom she knew less well. Then she burrowed her head in his neck so he would know she loved him.

For now Shehzad was satisfied.

In the studio, later that night, Armaan wanted to lie close to his mother, to ask her questions but dared not. She would push him away again. He wondered if it would be like this forever. He wondered how long 'forever' was. Saira was with with his aunts. He wondered whether he should go there, but decided he should look after his mother. He lay there making shadow puppets, and decided to fall asleep after the shadows on the wall resolved into an annoyingly predictable looking bird.

Downstairs, Mariam and Intizar lay in bed. Mariam wanted to speak to Intizar about Tahira but was overwhelmed by pity and by fear of his silence. He seemed to have barely spoken since Waseem's death. He seemed like a fruit that had suddenly, without warning, without any sign of external rot, collapsed inward. Could it have been a month already?

In the room they still shared, Seema and Nilofer were trying to make sure Saira was sheltered from the full effect of Tahira's collapse. Nilofer had returned the day of the burial and then taken an extended leave of absence from her university. Her sister turned to her and said, "I wish I knew what to do."

Nilofer nodded.

"Why won't Amma talk to anyone?" Saira asked Seema who was stroking her hair as she lay with her head in her aunt's lap. She had visited the studio a few times and then, baffled by her mother's silence, had stopped.

"Because she is upset about Waseem Mamu, beta. She loved him very much."

"Didn't you love him?" Saira sat up, suddenly intensely attentive. "Why are you crying?"

"I'm not," Seema rubbed away a tear. "I did, but your Amma was very close to him, just the way Nilofer Khala and I are with each other. Come I'll tell you a story."

Three months had passed and Tahira continued to refuse to go back to Shehzad's house. He had visited, and been uncharacteristically gentle, even remorseful about his treatment of Andaleep and Waseem. He felt a profound pity for his wife; and his faith told him, he told himself, to be kind to those who suffer. It helped that he was no fan of the PM. He had visited her but she said nothing, staring at him with blank insolence which he tolerated, he told himself, because he had decided to be kind, so he had taken to only seeing the children when he went. After all, they needed him more and someone had to be a parent.

Her response to Shehzad and to everyone else was to stare uncomprehending and resentful at their tedious demands. The sound of human voices fell on her like pins on a cushion stretched taut with human skin. Sometimes it felt like an assiduous, meddling hand was pushing them into her head, but she would not give anyone the satisfaction of witnessing her discomfort, so she stared blankly at those who came to console, or coax, or cajole.

All she thought was: I must paint. I must.

The canvas defeated her much as she did everyone else. It stared at her, mute and uncomprehending and insurmountably, terrifyingly blank.

Shireen approached Shehzad again. "What are you going to do about the children?"

"I'll talk to Tahira."

Shireen laughed mirthlessly. "Don't be a fool. I always thought she was unstable."

Shehzad, who had begun to wonder about this himself, was not ready to hear it from his mother. "I said, I'll talk to her."

"You need a second wife."

That evening he said to Tahira, "We need to talk about Saira and Armaan." Mariam had joined them, worried about the children, worried that Shehzad's patience might be wearing thin and that his mother might be able to persuade him to do something drastic, perhaps even get a second wife. "Yes, your husband is right. You have to go back. Armaan has become quieter and is visibly retreating."

Tahira stared at them blankly, as if trying to recognize them, "So?"

"So… will you come home? You have to come back some time. And I'm worried about Armaan. Your mother is right;

he's thinner and distracted. This is no way for a child of his age to live."

Tahira wondered why he insisted on talking to her, why everyone insisted on talking to her. What could she give them?

"I'm not going anywhere. I have to paint."

"You haven't done anything."

"But I must."

"What about your children?" he said.

"What about them?" Why was he trying to confuse her?

"I'll take them back with me."

"Okay."

But Shehzad could not make himself do this yet. He felt it was his duty to give Tahira more time. And he knew that Tahira's family would take better care of them than his own. So, he compromised. It was the right thing to do.

Mariam wondered how it would all end, wishing she could ask Intizar for advice, or comfort, or company.

One day Tahira heard that there had been a coup in the country. The Prime Minister had been arrested, and like so many other times a General had taken over the government. She knew this was wrong. It came to her in a sudden flash that Andaleep and Waseem would be incensed, and then came the dimmer, more elusive thought that so would she. She remembered that she had always thought that Generals were no solution to the political ills of the country. But the thought of the removal of the PM loosened in her a strange, half-forgotten ability to concentrate; and she thought that if he could be conquered perhaps so too could the canvas. She knew there was something wrong with this thought; bloodlust ought not propel her relation to the canvas that had defeated her for so long. But there it was.

She realized, surprised, that deep, jewel-like colours were

shimmering just inside the lids of her eyes. And, weird and surprising, they were not all the hues of blood. She didn't know why, but knew that this was important. She had over the past few months, she now realized, had repeated flashes of a crown of thorns, which came to her in a rush of images, a host of Veronica cloths with the suffering face of Christ, the patient face of the Virgin, a concentration of powerless suffering into a moment of complete and final loss. The patience haunted her. She had seen images of Apocalypse, of tortured and broken bodies contorted at the feet of an unforgiving God.

She had seen stylized women and men in postures of wistful yearning and great beauty, women with long and dark eyes staring out of carefully placed windows at the invisible sight of distant freedoms, the movement at a court of Mughal Kings. She remembered a romance in miniature of two lovers under an indigo sky, the fragility that pervaded the painting, the awareness that seemed to seep out of it that the world would soon rend their love and the private luminescence of the South Asian night, which appeared to give shelter to the boldness and rarity of the openness of their love.

She realized, astonished, that she was angry, deeply, insanely, bloodily enraged by this wistful capitulation to circumstance, to the defeat in the fetish of yearning and loss, as if wistfulness and yearning were themselves worth yearning for. And her rage began to give shape to a series of compositions. But before she could begin those paintings she had to do something else.

She waited for Armaan to come to the studio, and winced as she saw him cower when she walked towards him. "Don't be afraid, Maani. I'm better. I'm so sorry I've been mean to you. But I need to do something to get better. Will you help me?"

He nodded, a little fearful, a little happy and hopeful to

be spoken to again—"I missed you. Are you back?"—an unyielding, frighteningly thin plank, when she hugged him.

"You are all bone and muscle. We'll have to fix that." He recoiled from the heartiness, trying to pull away. She held him tight, appalled at her cruelty, and his loneliness and fear, relieved when he squealed and giggled, "You're crushing me," and that he didn't cry.

"I finally think I can paint and I'm going to be in here until I've done what I need to do and then I won't live in the studio again, I promise. Okay?"

"Okay."

She began. Slowly a portrait of Waseem took shape: his narrow, angular intense face, and eyes that seemed to pierce the distance, able to see a horizon invisible to others. There was sadness in the liquid resolution of his eyes, but also a tranquility that Tahira did not remember noticing when he was alive. The burnished glow of his skin and the dark of his eyes faded into the velvet of the indigo Karachi night Tahira had given him as his backdrop, so that the Karachi nights he loved so well would be the shimmering embrace that would embalm him forever. But he looked too solemn in this portrait; and she wanted to remember his laughter.

So she began another. This time she painted him against the Persian blue of the curtains in his room. She painted him in a chair by the window, a book in his lap, a stack of books piled with newspapers by his side, head turned toward someone unseen, eyes gleaming with vivid amusement. His hair was characteristically dishevelled, but his white kurta was starched and immaculate. His long graceful hands were suspended in emphasis. She painted his skin gleaming like lovingly seasoned mahogany against the sun-pierced blue of the curtains partially covering the window. Visible through the elaborate wrought-iron grille, she painted a pomegranate tree with scarlet flowers.

This portrait, like the first, had a classical ceremony of composition and Tahira's characteristic precision. They shimmered with an intensity and colour that was as luminous as the most concentrated Flemish painting. Tahira was pleased. If she were an anachronism, there was little to be done. We live, she thought, in anachronistic times. To pretend we have escaped them is not an act of liberation, but a refusal to understand, because of which we cannot be liberated. It occurred to her that she was thinking Waseem's words, and then was surprised that she was using any words at all. Complete thoughts that were not tentative or hesitant felt new and sudden. She decided that she would not fight them for now.

Seema and Nilofer came to the studio. She smiled at them for the first time. "But you can't stay," Tahira said gently.

They tried to peer inside.

"Not now," she said. "I'll let you see when they are all done."

Only Armaan and Saira were allowed to see the paintings as they progressed. When they came to visit, Armaan said, "It's good that you made Waseem Uncle laugh. I like it when he laughs."

Saira nodded solemnly. "He becomes big, like a happy sun."

Next, Tahira painted Andaleep. She started with a small portrait, concentrated and close. Caught between a dream and laughter, Andaleep's eyes stared straight at the viewer, inviting you in, Tahira thought, to smile, or think, or be. The background was a vivid, uncompromising dense, but elusively iridescent, marigold. She would have liked that, Tahira thought. The bottom of the portrait skimmed the top of a bright parrot-green dupatta, around her neck. Her skin glinted smooth and beige. The crookedness of her nose seemed itself an invitation to smile.

And then Tahira began another one of Andaleep. But she was not alone. She was speaking to a circle of people, which included Tahira and Waseem. Andaleep was the focal point of the composition. To her right was Safdar, who was looking at her with a teasing grin, which only slightly covered his adoration. Andaleep, like Waseem, in his larger portrait was in mid-action, speaking, vivid. They were sitting on the grass in front of the rockery Tahira had been drawing when Andaleep first catapulted over the wall. It was evening and the tall cactus in the background was laden with huge, white spiky flowers, like a defiantly ostentatious wedding dress. The crown-of-thorns bushes were scattered with crimson flowers. The thorniness of the rockery was a spiky contrast to the soft light of the Karachi evening and the evident, vivid happiness of all present. Saira sat in Andaleep's lap playing with her orange dupatta as she butted her head against her neck. She was wearing the disastrous watermelon-coloured dress Andaleep had made for Saira herself. You could feel and hear, and, you might be forgiven for thinking, touch their happiness.

When this was done, Tahira put down her brush and breathed. She cleaned her brushes and palette with slow, ritual care. And then she lay down on the floor, rubbed the cold marble with her cheek and cried for the first time since their deaths. She cried as if her body would tear apart as every atom of it tried to pull away from every other, as if being itself were a capitulation to the obscene injustice of their deaths. She cried until there were only hiccups and intermittent little whimpers and finally, late at night, fell into her first uninterrupted sleep since their deaths.

The next morning, Tahira went down to the lounge for the first time since the day Waseem and Andaleep had died, ignoring her mother's hungry, quickly arrested, move toward her. Saira came running—"You are downstairs. Hurrah!" She bent down to kiss her and smiled, "I am. I have to make a phone call. Will you give me some privacy, please?" She waved her hand in a vague gesture of inclusion. Mariam took the children and left the room, forcing herself not to ask if she were finally going to call her husband.

She called Shehzad. "I'll come back."

"Good."

"For the children."

"Good."

"But I want to move out of that house."

"It will be good for the children to move."

"And I want to spend all day in the studio. So I need to give up work."

"You already have."

"I mean I'm not going back to work for now."

"Fine."

23

In another age, Safdar thought as he woke sweating from yet another dream, he would have become a mendicant, a Sufi, a *bhikshu*, like the seekers and travelers in *Ag Ka Darya*, wandering across South and Central Asia, abandoning everything, following the rhythms of his grief, letting it guide him until he forgot himself and so his pain. Instead here he was, dreaming of that swaddled body being lowered into the gaping maw of the earth, the shroud unwinding, wanting to rush to cover the body, to protect her dignity, hoping it would unravel so he could see and touch her one last time.

But it's a thing, not her, the dream-self would speak: *That makes no sense. Don't call it her.*

There were variations. Sometimes he dreamt he was a wandering, wild-eyed beggar, singing and travelling, only resting if he found a gulmohar in bloom. Sometimes Waseem travelled with him singing and whirling, other times he stood by him at the edge of the grave, rushing to cover her body as the shroud unravelled. In yet others, Waseem's body was lowered with hers into a joint grave and his dream-self was—absurdly—jealous.

He dreaded the dreams and longed for them. Chores, responsibilities, the mundane did not save, he had learned.

The ordinary, unabsorbing task, the boredom, could not mask the pain; instead it rushed in and took over until he wanted to attack his own body to make it stop.

And then there was the world. Ever more of his friends and comrades were being rounded up since God's and America's anointed General had taken over, brandishing the mark on his forehead as divine authorization to kill and terrorize and destroy. Haroon was in jail; Safiya was beside herself. His parents were frightened. He wanted to place himself in greater proximity with dread, with death. They realized this and were all the more fearful.

"Leave the country," said his mother. His father concurred.

"And abandon you? No."

"You think it won't be an abandonment if those bastards torture you or lock you up in a dungeon or kill you? Go because we ask, not because they take you. Do that PhD you always wanted. We know you applied and got into London University and were only postponing the decision because of Andaleep. Go and then, if you can, arrange for us to follow you, if that's what it will take to make you stay away. *Go*."

More people disappeared. Friends called them, checking to see if Safdar had been rounded up.

Go they said again and again. Individually and in unison: "You are our only child. *Go*."

He paced and visited Joseph Bhaiyya and wrote. Finally, he brought a poem he had written to his mother, "Can it be an elegy if it's really about betrayal?"

She read it slowly, and was quiet for a long time. Then she looked up at him and said, "Yes."

He said, "I thought I had no faith to lose. I was wrong."

She said again, "Yes." And then, again, "Go, *please*."

So, finally, he went.

What Safdar wrote:

Abdications

I

In the pulpit of our discontent
We spoke about the purity of the other light
The perfection of that colour
There only to remind us of our own.
But slowly we forgot
And instead we learned
The qualities of grisaille
And wrote disquisitions on subtleties of grey.

We longed for orange,
And shuddered at our naiveté.
We coveted purple,
And retreated from the humid shimmer of our desire.
We yearned for indigo,
But no longer knew how to make our own ink.
We thought we were disrupting all forms,
In truth, we had no shapes to catch the memory of our colours.

We feared memory
So we crept into the caves under the shades
Where light would never pierce
The opalescent curve of our carapaces.

II

Nomads imprisoned in seasons,
Following the paths of birds,
And the trails of berries.
We returned to cold ashes.

III

She swore to return.
We tied silk threads to shrines.

IV

When the ship was sinking
We swore to plug the holes.
We jettisoned buckets,
And put our fingers through
Rotted, splintering wood.
Our fingers bloated, dark blood
Poured through lucid skin.
Logs drifted by
One by one we clutched and floated away.

24

They moved out with ease, much to Tahira's surprise. It was as if Shireen were relieved to be rid of them, exhausted perhaps by the impervious coldness Shehzad had turned on her. Tahira found this shift even more baffling but decided it was none of her business, simply glad to have left that place even if Shehzad's family were still in a house down the street.

She had taken on the task of moving and decorating her new home with ferocity and focus, determined not to be distracted from the larger aim, and so they settled quickly. She chose a beige and white sofa with turquoise accents and a turquoise and cream Irani carpet for the drawing room, lemon-yellow and apple-red and bright, parrot-green for the children's room, covered with pictures and filled with books and games. The bedroom was white with bright blue cushions and blue kilims. The house was light and bright and uncluttered. She could breathe and open her eyes without resentment and claustrophobia, without shuddering at a taste that felt all the more offensive for having so little to do with her. The thought surprised her and then she was pleased.

"So plain. No class at all," Shireen said, "Doesn't my son make enough money? Must you humiliate him?"

Tahira shrugged. "I like it."

Shireen tried again, practiced, ineffectual, compelled, it seemed, by habit, "It's my son's house. I knew bad days would come, but such disrespect."

"I like it," Shehzad said, obviously bored. Tahira realized, with a surprised glimmer of pity, that the tremor at the corner of Shireen's mouth might be an attempt to keep real tears from falling.

She spent every spare moment of the next few months in the studio. In the morning, she dressed the children in their uniforms, and drove with them and the driver to school. After having dropped them off, she went to her parents' house and sequestered herself in the studio. It was a disciplined, conscious withdrawal, broken punctually, and, because part of the routine, without reluctance, for lunch with the children. After they were put down for their naps, she returned to her studio. The children stayed with their grandparents and Seema—Nilofer had returned to England—playing and doing their homework, giving them something to do, helping them pretend to forget. Every day, Mariam's new cook made dinner for Tahira's family, which she took home with her, carefully packed in tiffin carriers and covered bowls, heated up and presented with the fresh rotis she made when she got home and Shehzad arrived from work.

The regimen was disciplined—it was a word she had come to use like a talisman—rigorous, brisk. She could pretend she didn't notice pain, her own, her parents', Seema's, Nilofer's—who wrote only to Seema—her children's baffled questions and cries of missing Andaleep Khala and Waseem Mamu; she could pretend she hadn't noticed *he* was having an affair again. The signs were there of course, the sudden, added lift in his step, the evenings at work, the daily variations in cologne, *Brut, Old Spice*, *Aramis*.

She did not allow herself to think of Shehzad's affair. One more, or less, pain made little difference in the alternations between a pain that suddenly, without warning, racked her body, catching her off-guard and making her want to double up and clutch herself and the numbness that had come to terrify her, so completely did it compound her already overwhelming guilt. She knew this dimly sometimes and, occasionally, with searing lucidity.

The routine kept things under control; the knowledge that she was doing this for Waseem and Andaleep made the rigidity of the discipline attractive, even a sort of ritual penance she thought sometimes, pleased at the thought. What she did not allow herself to think—or feel—was that she could not differentiate between the varieties of grief that assailed her, that the studio was the only space where the memory of pleasure was conceivable, if not yet ready fully to be retrieved.

Other habits and routines returned.

The first time Shehzad began to touch her at night, she found she did not need to hide her absence. She had dreaded this moment, not knowing if she had the capacity, the *concentration*, required to dissimulate. She had always been quiet, properly and, perhaps frustratingly for him, chaste and removed. But what had begun as shyness, and propriety, and she now recognized, a kind of terror at the inescapability of the future into which she had been entered, was replaced, without any need for recognition or noise, without *announcement*, by grief and stoicism and a different kind of terror in which the future seemed to unfold forever inhabited by two empty places where Andaleep and Waseem should have been. She imagined events with children and family and her own everyday chores as a reel of photographs, endlessly unspooling in her head, with empty silhouettes where Andaleep and Waseem would have stood and smiled and clapped and mocked.

She was glad that Shehzad had no way of recognizing this different absence. It occurred to her that he might not care and that perhaps she shouldn't either, but then was surprised that she thought so for she hadn't thought she cared at all. The reflection was fleeting and uninteresting and she let it pass largely unnoticed as she did so much else.

—~—

Shehzad screamed at her for the first time since the deaths. She looked at him, baffled. A tear made its way down her face. She didn't know why. She turned and began to walk away. "Don't turn your back on me, you bitch." Saira hurtled into the room, a small ball of fury: "Why are you shouting at *my* Amma?"

He breathed deeply. "I'm not."

"You *were*."

"It was nothing."

She shook a finger at him, eyes narrowed, all the more childlike in her outrage. "Don't do it again."

Tahira heard the exchange behind her, wondering why her daughter was so fierce, a little repelled by her strangeness.

—~—

She found a ripped piece of paper tucked in a collection of poems by Fehmida Riaz, trying to remember why she had placed it there, surprised she had thought like that:

A Memory of Myself in the Third Person:

As a bride she came to him beautiful and slender, impossibly slender, the entire weight of her personhood pushing through her hipbones, pressing against the petticoat of her sari, as if her person could never assert its presence in any other way. But she came to him beautiful, long-haired, almond-eyed, a cliché of North Indian beauty. She brought with her a willingness to be moulded, to be taught the person to be, to grow into him—until her person were an extension of his, the glow that that he would send into the world, by which his limbs, his fierce certainty could be delineated and softened. His hard lines would be outlined by her light from behind, the source always invisible because exactly aligned with him. And so she came to him, not knowing how to want more…

It seemed no less overwrought and self-aggrandizing for being, in some peculiar sense, true. She drew an unwavering, diagonal line through it.

She laughed for the first time.

God appeared to have decided to speak to the nation, constantly, in many forms. Through many media, on television, on radio, on billboards brandishing images of shrouded bodies with the legend, declaring terrifying and loud: "Say your prayers before your prayers are said for you." Through the General with the sinister eyebrows and ingratiating smile. She watched him on television one day, speaking through that smile that seemed to have floated off the face of a villain from a children's fairytale and suddenly imagined Andaleep saying, "Couldn't God have chosen a better dummy?" and laughed out loud.

"Why are you laughing, Amma?" Armaan asked.

"I'm thinking of Andaleep Khala. She thought ventriloquist's dummies were hilarious."

"I think they are scary."

Tahira laughed even more loudly.

The children were baffled but Saira decided she had to be part of the fun and laugh too.

Shehzad narrowed his eyes and wondered if Tahira was finally going mad.

That, however, was the world outside the studio. Inside, she read poetry, and novels, Ghalib and Hyder and T.S. Eliot and wondered about knowledge and forgiveness and history, about possibility and extinction. She studied books of painting and looked at the bodies in Varma and Tagore and Chughtai. She pored over the composition of large complex paintings, Van Eyck's *Adoration of the Mystic Lamb*, Botticelli's *Mystic Nativity*, Gauguin's *Where do we come from? What are we? Where are we going?* She composed and drafted and practiced, painting steadily, trying tempera and oil on wood, oil and acrylic on canvas, acrylic and gouache on paper, preparing for the large, grand painting that had taken shape in her imagination.

Safdar's mother began to visit her in the studio. They talked while Tahira painted. Tahira showed her the drawings, preparatory sketches and paintings. When Mumtaz exclaimed with pleasure and joy upon seeing the painting of Andaleep and Safdar. Tahira made a version for her.

One day Mumtaz said, "You have an astonishing eye for colour. It's quite wondrous."

"It feels like a failing these days. We use colour to cover our everyday brutality. I sometimes think I use beauty to submerge horror. Our weddings…" she trailed off. After a while she spoke again, "I argued with Andaleep, you know. I've been guilty of wanting weddings, wanting people walking in billows of lime and indigo and saffron silk, longing for the beauty of tradition, for memory and ritual stripped of meaning."

"Andaleep was hardly afraid of colour," Mumtaz chuckled, remembering the deliberate outrage of her clothes.

"She was when it was used to cover up chains."

The next time she came to visit Tahira, Mumtaz brought the poem Safdar had shown her before he left, "Our last conversation made me think of it again." Tahira read it and hesitated.

Mumtaz said, "I know it's not one of his best."

"It's not that." Tahira said. "It's silly to argue with a poem, but I think he's wrong. I don't think we fear memory. I think we fear the present."

"Perhaps we fear both."

Tahira talked with her as she did with no one else, as she wished she had spoken to Waseem. She told her so.

Mumtaz said, "Sometimes it's easier to speak to the dead than to the living."

"If I had told him I'd leave maybe we would not have drifted so far from each other. I feel sometimes as if I should leave to honour his memory. But now that both he and Andaleep are gone, I would have no support."

Mumtaz sighed. "We are an unforgiving people. You could live with your parents. Akbar and I would support you in anyway we can," she said without conviction. She had spent enough time with Intizar and Mariam since Waseem's death to realize how removed they were from their children. She wished Tahira would do it anyway but did not say so.

Tahira did not say that she had realized that to leave would be to give up any possibility of privacy, a surrender of all reserve. She could not live like that.

She said, "I don't think Shehzad would let the children go."

25

After months of reading and practice, of drawing and painting, months in which what had begun as conscious and determined discipline came to be lived as habit, Tahira began the triptych she had imagined almost a year ago. She acquired the wood on which she had finally decided she would paint, had the three panels hinged together by workmen, gathered the brushes and paints with, she recognized, characteristic ceremony and started. Three months later, she finally put down her brush and, without engaging in the daily ritual of cleaning and preparation for the next day of work, left the studio.

She stopped at the first landing, pausing to look at herself in the large mirror that hung on the wall facing the stairs. Her body had changed since the days when she had first stood in front of it, learning to tweeze her eyebrows. Now her hips were full and her waist had thickened. Two births, she thought, examining the changes. She leant in to see what other changes were visible, glad as she peered that not everything could be seen.

To the right of the stairs going down was a wall designed with a repeating pattern of almond shapes cut out of the concrete, making the back garden and neighbouring house visible through the intricate trellis and permitting the breeze and light to come into the interior, lighting up the landing. She had always loved its collapse of the distance between home and world.

She looked up at the top edge of the mirror; a bird had flown through and tucked a nest behind the mirror. Stray twigs and a few dried leaves dangled from the upper edge of the frame. Some had drifted to the floor. She knelt to pick them up and saw that a tiny nestling had fallen out and was lying on the ground, beady eyed and fragile, with transparent ochre skin that seemed not to have completed the transition from egg to bird. She picked it up, caressed its skin and the tiny belly through which the miniscule organs were still visible, and took it downstairs. It did not take much effort to bury it under the guava tree behind the kitchen, just a teaspoon-sized indentation in the soil, scooped out with a fingernail, the gentle placing of the nestling, and the earth brushed back over.

She walked to her parents' room. Saira, Armaan, and Mariam were playing on the bed. Tahira watched them for a moment, grouped around the Ludo board, which was primary and garish on the burgundy silk quilt made from one of Mariam's old saris. Mariam looked up, a little quizzical, completely silent.

Saira squealed. "Why are you here? You *never* come here when we play."

Tahira smiled, trying not to be hurt. "The painting is finished and I need a holiday. So we will spend the week together. We will shop and cook together and play—your holiday and my holiday too."

Armaan clapped.

Saira looked a little puzzled and then began to jump up and down on the bed, upending the board and sending the tokens and dice flying. "Can we go for ice cream *right now*?"

Mariam began to fold the board, smiling a small surreptitious smile.

~

A few days later, Shehzad walked in to the kitchen while she was letting Saira and Armaan help her make their favourite cake, "I left work early. I thought we would go to the beach and get some Chinese food on the way back."

"Yaaay! Chow mein *and* I can wear my new shorts," Saira yelled, already halfway to her room.

Armaan inched closer to his mother and looked up at her.

"That would be lovely." Tahira wished Armaan wouldn't turn every encounter with his father into a performance of loyalty. Shehzad narrowed his eyes but said nothing to Armaan.

"Okay."

At the beach, as the children ran ahead, he said, "What's happened? You are not usually home all day."

"I completed the large painting."

His head turned sharply towards her, eye a little wide, "Why didn't you say anything?"

She was surprised; he seemed hurt, "I don't know." She paused, angled her right foot and burrowed it into the wet sand, staring at the sunset, which had turned the sky into strips of fuchsia and gold. She ignored his irritated start, interrupting him as he began to say, "You are my wife. I should know what you are doing."

"No," she took a deep breath, summoning the will to speak more truthfully, "That's not it. I didn't know how I felt about it. What if it's not any good?"

She felt the tension leave his body, "I am sure it is. No one doubts your ability. You shouldn't either."

It was her turn to look at him, surprised, searching his

face. "Waseem," she stopped herself and then began again, forcing herself to go on, "Waseem used to say that."

"Then remember what he said."

She was not sure what she would find when she returned to the studio. She had needed distance from the work, needed, she now reflected, to step outside her own head, which was crowded with images and sounds and the anxiety of the years of desire for work, which persisted even as she worked and which was no less dramatic for being, in some not entirely comprehensible sense, trivial. She had wanted relief from the intensity, from the slow, steady throb of her thoughts and the quieter but never absent undertone of pain.

She hesitated at the door, wondering if the painting that awaited her was the one she had thought to paint. She thought of Shehzad's reassurance and of Waseem, took a deep breath and stepped in. The triptych was in the middle of the room, the two side panels folded in to cover the middle. Closed, it was four feet high and six feet across. On the outside, the panels were covered with abstract patterns, distantly derived from fabric and the swirl of weddings, a blaze of scarlet and saffron and emerald, deep hued, with a subtle iridiscence seeming to suffuse the painting from within. The abstracted shapes were sinuous, occasionally bulbous, fit into repeating asymmetrical patterns that seemed to burst out of their own lines and curves.

She walked around the closed triptych, twice, absorbing the pageantry, as if, she thought, she were at a banquet at which she did not want to eat. She walked to the front of the painting to open the panels, hands trembling a little. She opened them and stepped back. The world changed. The entire painting was in shades of white, with undertones of grey and green, ochre and sienna. In places, the surface suggested stone and sculpture and in places it shaded into brittle, bleached bone. With both panels open, the painting was twelve feet across. She had not been wrong. It was magnificent.

The scenes ran across the three panels, unfolding like a frieze. In the foreground in the right panel were an old man and woman sitting on a street with a bundle before them. The man's face seemed to droop into his long beard. The woman's mouth was rounded in shock and fear. In the front of the left panel, two young children sat on a pavement in the foreground, sharing half a mango, their heads—the girl's covered with matted, curly hair, the boy's shaved—slightly lowered, eyes gleaming with joy as they contemplated the fruit lying on a piece of dirty cloth between them. A little to their right in the central panel, an affluent looking man and woman sat at a table, sullen, estranged.

In the right background, two policemen were beating a man, cowering on the ground, curling himself against their sticks. Next to them was a scene of a man suspended by his arms, shirtless, face bleeding, another approaching with electrodes, a smile of leering anticipation on his face. In a corner in the background on the left panel, a man was running after a woman, belt raised, ready to whip. Not quite at the centre of the painting was the full, standing figure of a woman in a sari, partially in profile, staring into the distance, waiting. At her feet lay a broken kadamba bough.

Interrupting these arrangements of people were large textured empty spaces, occasionally marked with statues, or plants and flowers. Water fell over a rockery into a pool at the back of the central panel.

The signature was a small, sculptural calligraphic ball that seemed to flame and spin, composed of a couplets from the Ghalib ghazal she loved—"It's been a while since Ghalib died but he is still missed/ and so is that ability to wonder at every turn and corner what could have been"—rewritten with her name in place of his.

She pulled up the armchair and sat down, stroking the arms of the chair in a repetitive, rhythmic motion and stared at the painting for an hour. The next day, and the day after, she repeated the ritual, sitting in front of the triptych, mesmerized by its reluctant, haunted beauty. Occasionally, she flinched and got up and closed the panels and then, as if unable to bear the dazzle of colour, opened them, hurriedly, again. She wished she could show it to Waseem and Andaleep. They would have known what to do with it, what to say, would have ignored her demand for silence and reticence, she smiled, rueful and a little guilty.

Mumtaz was not around either. Akbar had decided they needed a vacation. "We honeymooned in Nainital you know," he had said to Tahira when she visited. "Time for a hill-station holiday, and the drive to Kaaghaan is too rough, so Nathiagali it is," he had grinned as Mumtaz shook her head and smiled.

Shehzad would have to do. So she finally invited him to come to the studio. He walked in, looking around, trying, she could tell, not to look too impressed. He went up to the closed triptych, circling it a few times, pausing occasionally to close his eyes as if he couldn't bear the intensity of the colours, or perhaps just to be able to see them anew each time. She opened up the triptych. He stepped back as if he'd been punched. He stood looking for a while, walking close to look at a detail and then stepping back several paces to get a more complete view. After a while, he turned to look at her. She wondered if it really could be a combination of awe and shame in his eyes. He shook his head slightly, as if trying to clear it. Then, as if pleased to have found something appropriate to say, he finally spoke, "Waseem would have been very pleased," and then again, as if he regretted saying anything, he walked closer to the painting to look at the couple at the table. He turned around to face Tahira, "What will you do with it now?"

"I don't know… It's a little frightening. I don't think Waseem and Andaleep knew what they were asking for."

He looked at her as if a stranger had wandered in, "I'm sure they did. It's magnificent."

She struggled to hide her contempt. He seemed not to understand anything. How could she say: they thought painting would save me? Do you know what that means? She said, "Thank you."

He looked at her as if trying to assess her tone. Seeming to have decided it was okay, he said, "What will you call it?"

"I wish I knew."

She returned to the studio the next day, a little gratified, a little irritated by Shehzad's response. She had seen him looking at her the night before with a kind of baffled respect. Then, as if to mask that, he had snapped about the food being cold. But his anger had seemed to lack conviction. It had subsided so quickly even Saira hadn't had time to speak. Tahira smiled a little and walked up to the open triptych: what *would* she call it? Why was it so difficult to decide? She wondered why she was reluctant to exhibit it.

It occurred to her one day to call it *The Waiting Woman*. She dismissed the thought. The title seemed narcissistic *and* lacking in ambition. She wondered how both could be true. She left the room. After a few weeks, weeks of staring at the painting and its varieties of loneliness, she thought: *The Love of an Absent God*. She paused and let it run through her and knew it was right and realized why she had not known what to do with the painting, why she had not wanted a precise, *truthful* title. She wondered what it would mean to confront that truth without destroying herself—or the painting. She shivered, relieved to realize she couldn't do that.

She walked to the table, creaking under the weight of books and wrote a note to Mumtaz:

I send this to you, to do with as you will. For now, I am reluctant to go where it will take me.

Yours,
Tahira

She folded the paper carefully and sealed it in a small blue envelope.

The next day the triptych was loaded on to a hired van. Muazzam Khan was to accompany it to Safdar's house. She gave him the envelope and asked him to give it to Mumtaz.

She went back inside the house to look for the children, who were worried by the signs of withdrawal in the sudden return of her distraction. "Come," she said to Saira and Armaan, "I'll bake you that cake you liked so much on my vacation."

She placed Saira on the counter, who squealed as a loosened strip of formica grazed the underside of her knee. Armaan sat down on a small chair by the table. Tahira cracked the eggs, separating the yolks, which gleamed primary and yellow in their shell, the albumen slid through her fingers, translucent, viscous. "Like mucous." Saira shuddered theatrically, body leaning in, obviously itching to reach over and play with it.

Tahira whisked the ingredients together and began to pour the mixture in the buttered cake pan.

Saira asked, emboldened by her mother's apparent calm, "Amma will you be okay now?"

Armaan put a finger to his lips, shaking his head, "Shhh."

"It's alright," Tahira said. "Let her ask."

Acknowledgements

Many years ago, when I was thinking about writing this book, the late Syed Mumtaz Saeed (Shamman Uncle), the late Obaidullah Baig, the late Syed Jamal Naqvi spoke to me about the history of the Pakistani left and about student mobilization in Karachi. My friend, Syed Yasir Husain facilitated some of these meetings. Accompanying my mother as she went to order clothes from, what I think was Noor Jahan Bilgrami's first block-printing workshop, fed an interest in craft that would grow over the years. Growing up, I learned a lot about South Asian painting and fabric from Naheed Azfar's collection.

Ali Altaf Mian helped me out with a research question regarding *Bahishti Zevar* at a crucial moment. Bilal Hashmi introduced me to the Faiz interview quoted in chapter fourteen. *The Heavenly Ornaments* quotations in chapters two and five, are my translations from Maulana Ashraf Ali Thanawi, *Bahishti Zevar* (Karachi: Darul Ashat, 1981). The Kierkegaard excerpt in chapter five is from *Either/Or* ed. and trans. Howard V. Hong and Edna H. Hong (Princeton: Princeton University Press, 1987 rpt. 2013). The Sahir Ludhianvi poem quoted in chapter fourteen is from *Ao ke koi kwab bunen* (Bombay: Alavi Book Depot,

1971). The ghazal in chapter fifteen is quoted from *Diwan-i-Ghalib* (Karachi: Ferozsons Ltd., 1989). In chapter sixteen, I refer to Zehra Nigah's poem, "Samjotha" ("Compromise"); Urdu and English versions can be found in *We Sinful Women: Contemporary Feminist Urdu Poetry*, translated and edited by Rukhsana Ahmed (London: Three Women's Press Ltd., 1991). A discussion of many of the painters from Pakistan mentioned in this novel can be found in Akbar Naqvi's *Image and Identity: Fifty Years of Painting and Sculpture in Pakistan* (Karachi: Oxford University Press; 1999, second edition, 2011). Throughout the text I refer to Qurratulain Hyder's *Ag ka Darya* and not *River of Fire*, simply because in the seventies she had not yet published her "transcreation," which is what she called her own English translation of her novel. At the same time, it's probably clear that I'm referring to the substantially changed English text she published as well as to the Urdu version. I thought about the inconsistency and decided to embrace it in the end. While the manuscript was going through the editorial process, I was thrilled to see Sibtain Naqvi's article about North Nazimabad being an intellectual hub from the 1950s to the 1970s: "History: the City of Lost Dreams." (*Dawn* Nov. 20, 2016. https://www.dawn.com/news/1297169/history-the-city-of-lost-dreams.)

Thank you to Nada Kittaneh and all the other students who insisted I complete the book…soon! Azra Apa (Azra Raza) and Raza Rumi read drafts of the novel. I was stunned and moved by the perceptiveness and rigour of Raza's reading at that long dinner. He made the manuscript new for me. Ruchira Gupta believed in the book and introduced me to Urvashi Butalia. I can't say how much Urvashi's wanting to publish the book continues to mean to me. I am very grateful for Anita Roy's careful reading and editing. The infelicities are my own.

Thanks also to my mother and my aunts: Khala (Mussarat Haidery) and Pai (Parveen Haidery); and my dear friends: Kamal, Sarita, Biju and Sangeeta.

R.A. Judy remains my closest, most thoughtful and most erudite reader. His erudition, which is vast, is exceeded only by his capacity for care.